THE QU

MARY VENSEL WHITE

The Qualities of Wood

authonomy
by HarperCollins*Publishers*

The Friday Project
An imprint of HarperCollins
77-85 Fulham Palace Road
Hammersmith, London W6 8JB

www.harpercollins.co.uk
www.authonomy.com

First published in 2012 by authonomy
This edition published by authonomy in 2014

ISBN: 9780007523580

For Jason, for everything

1

In the small, congested airport, Vivian didn't recognize her husband. Summertime. Outside, the sun beamed white on the runway and grassy fields. Inside, the terminal was stuffy and warm. Vivian passed a group of brightly-clothed summer travelers, this haze of blue, pink, yellow and green, and walked slowly along an eye-level, smudged window and into the crowded inlet beside the gate, all the while hunting for Nowell. Somehow, she walked right by.

She imagined the terminal was normally empty, the surrounding community being rural and unworldly. But it was the season of vacations: eastern hometowns, tropical beaches, exotic cities. Not everyone was headed to an abandoned house in the country, she thought. The travelers dispersed purposefully, trailing loved ones or heading solo toward the cars parked in rows at the front of the building. Vivian was pulled along with the crowd. Nowell was late. At first she felt irritated but quickly dismissed the feeling. It was a reunion, after all.

A large hand gripped her shoulder and she spun around.

'Where are you going?' Nowell's deep voice. His dark eyes.

'I couldn't see you,' she said. She reached for him, grasped his shoulders as though to pull herself up. 'I didn't see you.'

On the way to the house, she soaked him in: the shadowed gash of his cheekbone, his ruddy lips. Nowell kept his hand on her thigh. His touch felt curiously foreign after their four-week separation, but it ignited something too.

The drive wasn't long, the countryside a blur of sameness. Fields of indecisive green, hills falling short of remarkable. Here and there a white or brown-shingled house, some shadowed by barns. The predictable Midwest.

Nowell's hand left her leg to steer the truck onto a dirt driveway. 'What do you think?' he asked.

Vivian peered through the windshield. The small, white house was set back from the road and elevated slightly, like a judge on his bench. The sun lit the house from behind. White with dark green trim, there were wide strips of paint missing altogether; these sections of bare wood gave the impression of something bursting its seams. Two narrow windows gazed at the newcomers and beneath them, a bluish shadow stretched, tongue-like, down the front steps and onto the lawn.

'It looks stable,' Vivian said.

He chuckled. The truck made a strange revving sound after he removed the key. 'Just the timing,' he told her.

Vivian nodded. She knew the truck was like the house, old and in disrepair. Nowell had traded in their Honda when he left the city. They gave up the lease on their apartment and he moved first to arrange things. For a month, Vivian stayed at her parents' house, working at her job for a couple more paychecks. It was the longest they had ever been apart.

She hadn't been particularly attached to their Honda, a blue hatchback with gray seats, but the truck was big and awkward. The worn seat belt was loose over her lap, leaving almost enough room for another person. Vivian's feet grazed the floor. Like a child, she had only a limited view over the dash.

Nowell opened the passenger door and lifted her out of the truck. Vivian stood about five-four and her husband was over six feet. Everyone in her family seemed shorter than average, while his whole family was tall. At their wedding, the first few rows in church seemed like a tilted painting or a photograph enhanced for effect: his family on one side, hers on the other. Four years married, she thought. She would be twenty-eight this summer.

Late July heat lingered in the air and warmed the lawn, though the sun was beginning to fade. The air was fragrant with live things. In the shaded areas, cool grass poked through Vivian's sandals. She stood for a moment, studying her new home. Nowell's grandfather had built the house as a newlywed and when he died in a hunting accident, Nowell's grandmother stayed and finished raising their three children.

His grandmother was stubborn and tied to the place, Nowell said. She seldom took vacations or visited family. Vivian met Grandma Gardiner twice: at their wedding and when Nowell's brother Lonnie was injured in an accident. The old woman hadn't left much of an impression on her; she remembered spindly legs and gray hair pinned above one ear with a clip.

At one time, the house was probably fresh and welcoming but now showed its age. A wooden swing, dusty from neglect, hung unevenly from the porch rafters. Its chains were pocked with rust. Three small windows formed a triangle at the peak of the roof, under a section where the tiles had bubbled up. An attic, Vivian thought.

Nowell kicked up a cloud of dust. 'Lonnie left this morning,' he said. 'Sorry to miss you, but he wanted to get back.'

'Well, you had him for two weeks,' she said, picturing his burly brother. 'Did you get much done?'

'Definitely. I was glad for the help.' He rummaged through the bushes beside the porch, picking up twigs and scraps of paper with his long, elegant fingers.

'Do they still have that apartment?' Vivian asked.

'Yeah, but they want to move.'

'Why?'

3

'Too small. Only one bedroom.'

She looked at him. 'Ours had one bedroom.'

'And it was too small.' Nowell dumped the handful of garbage into a metal trash can and stared at the tall grass. It sprouted in clumps, trapping bits of rubbish next to the house.

'Is Lonnie working now?' Vivian asked.

'He'll look for something as soon as he gets back. They still have some of the money my grandma left.'

'That won't last forever.'

Nowell looked at her quickly. A warning. 'Dorothy has a job,' he said.

Vivian couldn't help but be skeptical where Lonnie was concerned. When Nowell had told her his brother was coming to help clean up the house, she figured he wanted something. And now there was a wife, too, whom Vivian hadn't met. She could only imagine a woman with the same lack of ambition if she'd been foolish enough to marry Lonnie. They'd been married for a few months now, had known each other only two weeks when they headed for city hall. Vivian's mother-in-law, Beverly, harped on and on about the elopement, a welcome change since she usually overlooked Lonnie's faults.

Vivian leaned on the banister enclosing the porch. 'When are we going to meet Dorothy?'

Nowell's face relaxed. 'He said they'll try to visit while we're here.'

'That's good,' she said, but her stomach tightened. She moved towards him. 'We might get lonely out here.'

He wiped his hands on his jeans and leaned down, setting his large hands on her hips. '*I've* been lonely.'

His touch still had an effect on her, a physical charge, and she'd missed it. 'Even though your brother was here?' she teased.

He smiled. 'Somehow it's not the same.'

The breeze picked up. It blew through Vivian's hair and brought goose bumps out on her arms. Nowell pulled her close then held her at arm's length. 'Let's look at the back before we go in.' His eyes fairly gleamed. He was proud of the house, she realized.

The grass was high in the front yard, higher still at the sides of the house. Nowell led Vivian by the hand, all the while talking enthusiastically. He showed her the well dug a short distance away. When they leaned over, the scent was damp and musty. Since Vivian left the rural airport, she had been intensely aware of the new sounds and smells around her.

'The chimney is unblocked,' Nowell said. 'And we cleared most of the leaves and large trash.' He shook his head. 'Three years of neglect. You wouldn't believe what was lying around.'

'Looks good,' she acknowledged.

'A road crew is paving the main road,' he added. 'They're about five miles away now, just outside of town. They should be past here by the end of the summer.'

'It'll be nice having a paved road,' she said.

'But that's why I bought the truck, for the bumpy dirt roads.'

Vivian pushed his arm. 'Poor Nowell. Your fantasies of country living.'

They turned at the back corner of the house and the open space hit her like a deep breath. The backyard was a large and unfenced expanse. Here, grass grew unchecked into a knee-high field, all of it shimmering in the gentle wind and crackling as they walked. About forty feet from the house, the land sloped downward. In the distance stood a line of trees, fairly thick against the sliver of orange that remained of the sun.

'We could barbecue out here if we cut the grass,' Nowell said. 'I found an old grill in that shed near the well. And look. This is the room where I've been working.'

Vivian was distracted by the fading sunlight, crisscrossing like lattice against the trees. As she stared at the pattern, she thought she saw a movement amid the dark trunks. She strained her eyes, but the light was too dim.

'Viv, did you hear me?'

5

'What?'

He stood near a wide window. 'This is the room where I've been writing.'

Vivian walked over and, cupping her hands around her eyes, pressed up against the glass. The room was mostly dark, but a streak of garish light from the kitchen divided the floor in half. She could make out the corner of a table or desk, the flowered pattern on the rug, and the keys of Nowell's computer keyboard.

'You left a light on,' she told him. 'How's the book going?'

'What?' Now he was distracted. She caught him gazing over her shoulder toward the line of trees.

'Your writing,' she said. 'How's it going?'

'Fine.'

'Is that your desk, there by the window?'

He nodded, bringing his attention back to her. 'An antique secretary. You know, one of those old desks with drawers and secret compartments.'

'You found secret compartments?'

'Not yet, but there has to be some.' He paused. 'I had to run a twelve-foot extension cord from the kitchen for my computer. No outlets. My grandfather added this back room much later. I guess he didn't want electricity in there. Or it was an oversight.'

Vivian looked again toward the trees. 'You have a good view of the forest from here.'

Nowell laughed and reached for her.

'What's funny?'

'I never thought of it as a forest.'

'What is it, then?'

Small wrinkles radiated from the corners of his eyes. He kissed her forehead, ran his fingers through her long brown hair. 'I guess you're right. I just think of forests as being vast, you know, near mountain ranges. Not a small parcel beside some meager hill in the flatlands.'

'I still don't see why it's so funny.'

'It sounded wild and dangerous the way you said it: the forest.'

Two quick whistles sounded behind the trees, startling them apart.

'What was that?' Vivian asked.

'Probably a bird.' He coaxed her toward him and held her back against his chest, his chin resting on top of her head as he leaned against the house. 'How was the office party?' he asked.

'The usual, only me this time. They had a cake and bought me a pair of overalls.'

'Overalls?'

'For living out here,' she said. 'A joke.' She relaxed a little more into him. 'I worked there seven years. I can't believe it.'

Nowell squeezed her waist. 'But you didn't care much for that job, did you? I mean, you weren't solving the world's problems or anything.'

'I won't miss it,' Vivian agreed. 'But who says water management isn't important?'

'You weren't managing the water, just the paperwork.'

'Right,' she said.

Nowell shifted his weight but she stayed against him. 'I think I'll get the book done out here,' he said. 'Do you think you can stand it for a year?'

'Of course,' she said.

The sun was completely gone now, the sky a darkening blue above the leaves and dotted with stars just blinking to life. In the cooling air, Vivian smelled the trees, like pine furniture polish but sweeter, and from somewhere, the faint scent of smoke. A small white light appeared amidst the trees.

'Someone's back there,' she said.

She followed Nowell's eyes as they picked up the white dot, which quickly turned into three more.

'Probably that sheriff,' he said.

'What sheriff?'

7

'From town. I thought they were finished when I left to pick you up. They're looking for something.'

'What?'

'He didn't say.'

'Isn't that part of your grandmother's land?'

'Yes. That's why he told me, I guess. I'm sure it's nothing. Maybe someone reported an injured deer or something.' Nowell broke away from her. 'Let's get your bag out of the truck.'

Vivian watched the lights a moment more. As Nowell tugged her toward the house, she glanced back over her shoulder beyond the high, swaying grass, which was quickly becoming invisible, still whispering in the wind and crackling again under her feet.

2

In the kitchen, Vivian opened and shut cupboards. Almost everything in the house had belonged to Nowell's grandmother. In one drawer, crocheted potholders, in another, faded telephone books. Here and there she saw something of theirs – a block of knives, Nowell's favorite coffee mug – and felt an odd kinship with the items. Their things stood out from the rest, their familiarity like a signal. Most of their belongings were in a storage place outside of the city.

'Where are the glasses?' she asked.

Nowell pointed to a pantry door near the entrance to the hallway.

Strange place to put glasses, she thought. She would rearrange things in the morning.

'You're having beer?' he asked.

Vivian had set two cans of beer on the table. Between them, steam rose from the bowl of pasta. Nowell went back to the oven for the bread.

'Yes,' she answered. 'Do you want one?'

He nodded without looking at her.

Vivian's chair cushion made a shhh sound when she sat. The backs of her thighs pinched as they stuck fast to the vinyl.

Nowell scooped noodles onto her plate. 'They have a great deli and bakery at the grocery store in town,' he said.

'Doesn't Lonnie like to cook anymore?'

'Sure. He cleaned that barbecue off and grilled steaks one night. He also made apple cobbler in a clay bowl. Right in the ground, on hot coals. We ate the whole thing.'

Vivian looked around the pale yellow kitchen. The curtains were a darker shade, embroidered with daisies. Mustard-colored specks in the countertop almost matched the dark yellow of the patterned tile. When she had peeked in from the back window, all of the yellow in the room seemed strange and overdone. Sitting inside gave a different impression; the warm hue was soothing.

'No dishwasher?' she asked.

'No, we've been roughing it.'

She remembered helping her mother with the dishes after a big, elaborate dinner, standing side to side, arms submerged in warm water. Vivian always rinsed. When she fell behind, her mother floated her hands in the soapy water and stared out the window until Vivian caught up. It felt good, like they were on the same team.

Nowell rose from the table and came back with a plastic tub of butter. She had a sip of beer and studied him. His hair had grown too long and he needed to shave the back of his neck. She thought maybe he'd gained a few pounds. The older women at the water management agency said once you get married, men have no reason to keep themselves in good shape. They warned Vivian about feeding him too much. But Nowell was tall and slender and had remained so, despite his sedentary job. Youth, the women told her. Just wait until you hit thirty.

'How are your parents?' he asked.

'They're fine. I think four weeks is beyond my threshold.'

'Pretty tough going back?'

'They haven't changed.'

10

'Did your mom have one of her formal dinners for you last night?' He smiled. 'I like the way she folds the napkins and puts place cards on the table.'

'You wouldn't like it so much if you grew up with that stuff. All the ceremony, and it was just the three of us this time.'

Nowell's lack of formality had attracted Vivian to him in the first place. They met in a large Geology class in college: a hundred students enclosed in a theater-like lecture hall. Nowell arrived late, ducking along the back row to avoid the professor's gaze. As he slid into his seat, he grinned at her and she noticed his brown eyes, the playful cocking of his eyebrows. Later, they were assigned to a laboratory group together. He was impossible to resist – handsome in the dark way she liked, smart, confident. Nowell told her later he found her funny and independent.

Even back then he knew he wanted to be a writer. He took Literature and History classes and published short stories in the undergraduate literary journal. Vivian didn't settle on the focus of her own studies until her third year, when Nowell helped her decide on a Business major. She took the job at the WMA while still in school and stayed on after graduation.

Nowell tore off a piece of bread with his teeth. 'Did you get the whole deposit back from the apartment?'

'Yes,' she said. 'I also have my last paycheck, with the vacation time I didn't use. And they'll forward my bonus.'

'Good. We'll need every bit. No paychecks for a whole year…'

'But we've planned for this,' she reminded him. 'There's the money from your first book.'

'That's not much.'

'And the money your grandmother left, and the savings. As long as nothing unexpected happens.'

Nowell looked up from his food. 'Did your parents drive you to the airport?'

She shook her head. 'Dad had an early class, so it was just my mom, harassing me all the way.'

11

'She thinks you should have kept your job since mine's so lucrative.'

'No. She still believes I've missed my calling in life, that I've overlooked some hidden talent.'

'She thinks I'm holding you back.'

'From what?'

'From something that isn't me,' Nowell said.

'I told her the move isn't just for you. If I can get this house cleaned up,' she motioned with her hand, 'and it looks like I've got my work cut out for me, then we can make a little for us when your mother sells it.'

'She sent some money,' Nowell said. 'My mom. She said to buy supplies, paint, cleaning stuff, whatever. Keep the receipts.'

'Do you really think the place will sell?'

'What do you mean?'

'It seems so out of the way.'

'Lots of people want to live in the country.' Underneath the table, he surrounded her feet with his larger ones. 'Besides, you haven't seen the town yet. It has modern conveniences.'

'Do they have a movie theater?'

'I think they do,' he said.

'It's probably a drive-in.' She rose and took her plate to the sink.

Nowell came up behind her. 'A drive-in might be fun.' He kissed her just behind the ear, dropped his hands to her waist. His breath was warm. 'We could take our new truck and break it in.'

'*Your* new truck,' she said. 'I don't think my feet will reach the pedals. I'll have to get those stilts that handicapped people use.'

He slid his hands upward from her stomach and she stepped back, forcing him to move away.

'Let me rinse these dishes,' she said, 'so there won't be ants or mice or whatever lives out here. I'll be there in a minute.'

'Deal.' He grabbed his beer from the table and leaned his head back, swallowing the last of it.

'Will you start unpacking my suitcase?' she asked.

He tossed the empty can into the trash and walked down the hallway.

Vivian hid a smile, imagining his reaction. She had purchased new lingerie, an emerald satin chemise and shorts, and packed it at the top of her bag for him to find. She hurried to clear the table.

Her attraction to Nowell was reliably strong, especially after a month's absence. There was something so comforting about the feel of his arms, something still so exciting about their legs entwined, her long hair spilling around them. She lost herself during their intimacies.

Afterwards, they turned down the quilt and lay on the bed backwards, looking out at the moon. The carved headboard blocked part of the window, which was wide and low like the one in Nowell's study. The moon, almost a full circle, sat in perfect view over the trees. There were so many more stars in the country, Vivian thought. The night was lit up by them.

The bedroom had been his grandmother's. It was small and exactly square, just wide enough for the bed and two wooden nightstands. Each table held a lamp shaped like a lighthouse, white with black details, the light beaming from the top. On the far wall hung an oil painting, a picture of a house and the surrounding field but the colors were strange: orange grass, green sky, a pink, tilted roof.

Nowell lay still, the sheet draped over his mid-section like a loincloth.

'You're quiet,' Vivian said.

He brought his arm around to rest heavily on her stomach. 'I guess you haven't changed your mind about things.'

'Why do you say that?'

'Because of what you said just now, at the end. And you're drinking beer.'

Vivian tensed. 'It's not even the right timing. Besides, you

13

promised you wouldn't bring this up for a while.' She swung her legs around and sat on the edge of the bed, then leaned over and picked up the green chemise.

'I know. Sorry. Come on, don't be mad.'

'You're always thinking about having a baby,' she said. 'Isn't it enough for now that I'm here?'

'I just don't see why, I mean, I thought we agreed to talk about it.'

'I'm not having this conversation again.' She found her shorts underneath the pillow at her feet and pulled them on. 'I've had a long day traveling. I want to wash my face and I might drink that last beer before I brush my teeth.' She added this last part to annoy him.

It worked. 'I have a lot on my mind too,' Nowell said. 'Just forget it.' He turned his back to her and pulled up the sheet. He left the blanket bunched at his feet. A ceiling fan whirred overhead, stirring the warm air into feathery layers of discontent.

Vivian walked down the hall and looked into the other rooms, flipping lights on and off. There were two bedrooms across the hall. In one, a small white dresser sat opposite a double bed. The other was filled with boxes.

In the kitchen, she opened another can of beer and took a long drink. A narrow, circular staircase jutted through the ceiling in the far corner of the room. An odd entry to the attic, the room with the triangular windows.

She had to step down when she walked into Nowell's study because it was built lower to accommodate the slope of the land. Feeling along the wall for a light switch, she remembered Nowell had said there was no electricity. She let her hand drop. Moonlight reflected from shiny surfaces and her eyes began to focus in the darkness. To her left, a narrow, cluttered bookshelf extended to the ceiling. To her right, a brown leather couch took up most of the wall. Against the window was the antique secretary. Vivian noticed the thick electrical cord that ran down the center of the room and into the kitchen. A metal floor lamp sat beside the desk, connected to the cord. She didn't turn it on.

14

She looked at the backyard, the expanse of grass stretching to the thick line of trees, now silver in the moonlight. She thought about the bouncing lights they'd seen and wondered how much of the land belonged to them, at least for a time.

The paper tray of Nowell's printer extended over the side of the desk. A stack of freshly printed sheets was in the wire holder. She picked up one page and squinted to read it in the dim light.

She was young and fast, a girl who knew too much and would soon understand why this was dangerous. She walked with purpose, swinging her lush hips and her long silky hair, as she glanced back over her shoulder at him, beckoning. He was unaffected at first, watching her this way, but his interest grew and he determined to see her. He waited, for days it seemed, always looking for her at the usual time, at the usual place, but for days and days she didn't come. He grew restless, angry. She was the kind of girl who didn't keep people waiting for long, and now here he was, waiting like a fool.

Vivian placed the paper back with the others in the tray. Nowell liked to give her portions of his writing in his own good time, like gifts meted out to an impatient child. His first book was a murder mystery and from the looks of it, this new one was too. That a sensitive, easy-going person like Nowell could write about deranged people and horrific events was strange but it was imagination, which could come up with just about anything, she supposed.

Why couldn't he be content with just her, at least until they got back to the city? Their life wasn't suited for a family right now, she thought. There was no room.

In the kitchen, she poured the last of the beer down the sink. With the yellow-patterned tile under her bare feet and only the thin layer of satin against her skin, she was getting cold. She turned off the light and felt her way along the wall to the bedroom. In the morning, she would take a better look around.

15

3

The sun rose at the front of the house and gleamed through the kitchen window, bright and overwhelming like a camera flash. Vivian liked the room's energy; the unrelenting yellow was a shock to her senses.

The place needed a lot of work. The house had stood abandoned for almost three years and every cupboard and closet was stuffed with clothing, books, papers, the assorted junk of a household. The boxes in the bedroom at the end of the hall needed unpacking, their contents dispersed between the Salvation Army and the dump. Vivian would have to go through everything.

The real work would begin after the sorting and clearing. The entire house needed a fresh coat of paint, inside and out. Many of the curtains and shades could be salvaged but needed washing or mending. A couple of the windows were rusted shut. Repair jobs ranged from a broken doorknob to the huge mildew stain on the ceiling in one of the bedrooms. The attic was its own unique challenge, as Vivian discovered after breakfast.

The stairs from the kitchen were steep and narrow, blocked at the top by a trap door. Vivian pushed and with a reluctant groan it swung open, landing with a bang on the floor above. She pulled herself up and looked around, surprised by the expansive size of the room. The rafters met in a point, like a triangle. The ceiling was high, even at the edges, so she could stand and most of the space was easily accessible. Cardboard boxes were stacked along each wall, as in the spare bedroom. She wondered if Nowell's grandmother had been planning to move and had begun to pack. Intricate patterns of spider webs decorated the corners of the attic and trailed between awnings like delicate suspension bridges. As Vivian walked, dust rose from the floor and fluttered back down.

The triangular windows let the morning sun through; the rays picked up these dust particles and held them in spirals and sheets. Underneath was a window seat. She cleaned it with a rag and sat down. The seat was hard and small, child-sized. Vivian swiveled and saw the red truck in the driveway. At a short distance, the road curved and disappeared over a hill. A few miles beyond that lay the town.

'Are you all right up there?' Nowell called, his voice muffled from below.

'This floor will look great after it's cleaned and polished,' she called back.

'I bet nobody's been up there for years,' he said. 'Be careful.'

In the far corner sat a large wooden bureau, its purplish color muted by a thick layer of dust. A black vinyl garment bag hung from the back. Vivian walked over and unzipped it. Inside, a garment of dark blue fabric was covered in plastic wrap. Next to that, three dress shirts in white and pale blue. More old clothes, she thought. A brass coat rack, tarnished and dented, stood in front of the bureau. Next to that was a small wire cage, a house for a bird but now choked with spider webs. Clearing the attic would be a big job, one that she resolved to leave for later.

The first days at the house passed quickly. Vivian conducted a survey of sorts, working her way from room to room, making lists. In the afternoons, she sometimes pulled a rusty lawn chair from the shed and took some sun in the front yard. She had first tried sitting in the back, where she could have a view of the trees, but the grass was too high; it scratched her between the canvas slats of the chair. Also, biting bugs swarmed, jumped, and hid in the tall grass. Nowell had promised to mow the lawn as soon as he reached a good stopping point in his work.

The world seemed to turn more slowly at the house. Lazy afternoons followed bright, sharp mornings filled with bird noises, clear sky, and country smells of warm grass and damp places. At mid-day the air became hazy and heavy and the birds quieted for a siesta. The house was shady then, a cool respite before the sun began its descent and beamed orange through the back windows. It was a lazy time. In the evenings, Vivian's energy level peaked again and her sense of hearing sharpened. She heard crickets under the house, and outside, the green, thick-veined leaves flapping, one against the other in the breeze. When a small branch snapped and fell, the other branches gently guided its descent.

In the week since her arrival she hadn't accomplished much with the house, but she didn't feel guilty. After all, she'd waived her annual vacation from the water management agency because Nowell had said the extra money would help. She deserved to take it easy after having worked straight through the last eight months.

So she was spending another afternoon relaxing. That morning, she had unpacked some boxes, mostly trash: used paperback romances, sewing things and scraps of fabric, an entire box of plastic silverware, plates and cups. She found it strange, going through someone's belongings, without knowing the person or their reasons for keeping things. She lay on her stomach in the front yard with her arms at her sides, feeling the sun bake her back. Eventually she sat up to look at a magazine. The heat felt good on her skin and caused a thin, sparkly layer of sweat to bead between her breasts.

She heard the low hum of a car approaching. The postman was early, she thought. It was just after one o'clock and he usually arrived closer to three. Vivian leaned back and closed her eyes, pushing the magazine underneath her leg. The car's engine grew louder until she heard dirt crunching under the tires. She looked up as a long, metallic-green car rolled up the driveway. The postman never came up the driveway, only stopped his little truck at the silver mailbox on the main road.

The driver's door opened and a woman got out. 'Hello,' she called cheerily. 'Don't get up, now. I'm nobody important.'

Vivian squinted up at her. She was tall, older than Vivian. Maybe almost forty. Over a pair of dark lavender pants hung a long blue T-shirt, decorated with a pattern of hearts and flowers. She walked up the driveway and stood blocking the sun.

'I'm Katherine Wilton,' she said. 'I knew Betty, uh, Mrs Gardiner.'

Vivian extended her hand. 'I'm Vivian Gardiner. Mrs Gardiner was my husband's grandmother.'

'Yes,' she said. 'I met your husband at the grocery store a couple weeks back.' Katherine Wilton's voice was pleasant and musical. 'I almost knocked a chicken out of his arms, wasn't paying attention to where I was going. I get distracted by the displays in the deli.'

'That deli is famous,' Vivian said. 'My husband and his brother couldn't say enough about it. I'll have to see it for myself soon.'

Katherine Wilton laughed again, crossing her arms over the flowers on her ample chest. 'The employees are all women with too much time on their hands, as far as I'm concerned. Anybody who has time to make a pie from scratch has got their priorities all messed up.' She dropped her key-ring into a tan leather handbag. 'Your husband told me you'd be here. I thought I'd see how you're getting on.'

'That's really nice of you,' Vivian said. 'I just got in a week ago. I haven't even left the house yet.'

'I see you're taking it easy. Good for you. City living gets hectic, I suppose.'

Vivian flushed, embarrassed at being caught doing nothing. 'Yes, I've been lazy.'

'Nonsense! You're spending quality time, as they say, rejuvenating mind and body.'

19

'That's a nice way of saying it. Would you like to come inside for something to drink, Mrs Wilton?'

'Only if you call me Katherine. "Mrs Wilton" always makes me think of my mother-in-law, and the less I think of her the better.'

Vivian laughed and stood up. The magazine stuck to the back of her thigh for a moment then fell to the ground between their feet.

Katherine scooped it up. 'That magazine's left an imprint on your leg,' she said.

'What, where?' She twisted her hips, trying to find the spot where the magazine had stuck.

'It's kind of weird, really, a little face right on your leg.' Katherine covered her grin with a ring-adorned hand. Brassy gold and multi-colored gemstones flashed in the sunlight. 'It looks like a tattoo, although I don't know why you'd want some supermodel's face on your thigh.'

Vivian could make out only a small patch of color, reddish with some black. She studied the magazine page: an ad for hair coloring. She wrapped a towel around her waist and picked up her glass.

Katherine leaned closer. 'I have a tattoo from my wilder days.'

'I always wanted one,' Vivian said. 'What's yours?'

'A black panther. Right here.' She pointed to a spot just above her pelvic bone. 'Nothing political intended. I just think big cats are so amazing. Believe it or not, I ran on the track team in high school. So that was it, speed and grace.' She smiled. 'Sounds stupid, but I never realized the implications of having a cat so close to … well, right there.'

Vivian inadvertently opened her mouth.

'Don't worry.' She rolled her eyes. 'My husband laughs about it all the time.'

They stepped onto the porch.

'What tattoo would you get?' Katherine asked.

Vivian paused. 'A rose, I think. On my ankle.'

'The ankle might not be a good choice. Too exposed, don't you think?'

'I'd never do it anyway. Nowell wouldn't like it.'

Katherine slowly nodded. 'It's the thought of something permanent. They like to think they invented you. Men, I mean.' She touched Vivian's arm. 'I don't know your husband well, of course. I was thinking more about an old boyfriend of mine.'

They lingered on the porch. Katherine had beautiful greenish eyes and clear skin. She's quite pretty, Vivian realized with surprise.

'Betty used to sit out here all the time,' Katherine said a little wistfully, 'working on her needlepoint or crocheting.'

'Really?'

'She used to throw bread to the birds, just like a regular old lady.' Katherine laughed and Vivian joined in, as though old age was something they'd never have to worry about. She already felt comfortable around Katherine. She was easy to be with.

The kitchen was cool and dark. Katherine sat at the table and Vivian poured lemonade into two of Grandma Gardiner's glasses.

'Betty was a sweet lady,' Katherine said. 'Always served me something. Just like you.'

'How did you meet her?'

'At a quilting class they had down at the high school. Max, my husband, thought it would be nice for me to have a hobby. I've never been one for sewing, but I thought it sounded all right.'

'I'm no good at things like that,' Vivian said.

'What kind of women are we?' She laughed. 'But quilts are nice, aren't they? I figured it might be fun to choose the pieces of fabric from things I had laying around the house, saving for God-knows-what. Like the dress I wore when I graduated from high school, or the kitchen curtains from our first apartment. When I started putting things together, pulling a shirt from here and an old sheet from there, it was real interesting.'

'Things you had forgotten you had,' Vivian ventured.

Katherine nodded, leaning back so the chair made a crackling sound. 'Going through those things was like looking through a photo album. Sometimes I'd sit with an old skirt or something,

21

just feeling the fabric and remembering the way it felt to wear it. Quilting brings up memories as much as anything.'

'I never thought of it that way,' Vivian said, 'and now I'm remembering all of the old clothes and things I probably have stored in boxes, tucked away and forgotten.'

'It's amazing what we keep lying around. The quilting class seemed like a good way to put some of it to use.'

'So Mrs Gardiner was in the same class?'

Katherine nodded. 'She was the sweetest woman. The first night, she brought a big box of fabric and we reminisced over it.'

Vivian thought guiltily about the box of sewing things and fabric swatches she had taken out to the trash that very morning. She wondered if it was still undamaged underneath the rest of the garbage. 'Did she use all of her fabrics in the quilt?'

Katherine laughed. 'Neither of us did. We both realized we liked sitting around shooting the breeze more than we liked the sewing, so we quit the class. Besides, working with those women was like being in the military. The first week, the woman who elected herself leader of the group gave us an outline of how each meeting should go. They didn't do any sewing the first three weeks, just sat around discussing the theme of the quilt, and looking over samples people brought in.'

'Sounds pretty boring.'

'I guess that's how you do it, but I swear, it just seemed like a lot of nonsense to sew a blanket. If I ever did a quilt I would want it to be just mine. I don't want to sew all my precious scraps together with strangers".'

'Did Mrs Gardiner like doing crafts and things?'

'Normally, yes. I was a bad influence on her as far as that class goes.' Katherine fluttered her fingers at Vivian. 'We kept talking about doing our own quilts, but when I came to visit we'd usually get to talking about other things.'

They sat quietly for a few moments while the shade enveloped them.

'Betty was a nice woman,' Katherine repeated. 'Didn't have many visitors, except her son every now and then. Before he passed, I mean.'

'Her son?'

'Yes, Sherman.'

Vivian shook her head. 'Nowell's father. I don't think he came out here much. He lived about four hours away.'

'From what Betty said, he came regular as rain, several times a year. She was real proud of him, always talked about how successful he was and those two tall sons of his.'

Nowell had told Vivian his grandmother was stubborn and difficult and they hadn't come to see her much. Even though he lived further away than the rest, Nowell felt guilty for not visiting, especially now that she was gone and had left them both money and the house. Between the insurance settlement, the grandfather's pension and Social Security, Grandma Gardiner had amassed quite an inheritance for her family. She divided the money equally between her three children: Nowell's father and his two sisters, neither of whom had any children. Which left Nowell's mother in charge of their third since Sherman was deceased.

'What's that for?' Katherine asked.

Vivian followed the direction of her gaze. She was looking at the thick sheet that Nowell had hung, curtain-like, to divide his study from the kitchen. 'My husband works on his writing in there.'

'Is he working now?'

'He works most of the day.'

'I think I'll just say hello.'

Before Vivian could stop her, Katherine jumped up from the table, crossed the tile floor and flung back the curtain with the zest of discovery. 'We meet again, Mr Gardiner!'

Nowell looked over from his position in front of the window. He appeared to be looking outside, taking a break from the computer. Vivian expected him to be annoyed, but he smiled. 'I thought I heard someone out there. Hello again.'

23

Katherine gestured and her bracelets clinked together. 'This sheet doesn't block much noise, I would imagine.'

'No, it doesn't,' he said, 'but it makes me feel sequestered.'

'It's all in appearances, isn't it, the things we let ourselves believe?'

Nowell made a move to join them, but Katherine waved him off. 'No, you get back to your work,' she said. 'I just wanted to say hello. I thought I might take your wife into town, if she's interested.'

'That's a good idea. I'm sure I'll see you again soon.'

Katherine took one look around the room, made a quick inventory, then let the curtain fall back. 'So, what about it? Want to ride into town with me?'

'I don't know,' Vivian gestured to her swimsuit. 'I've been outside sweating.'

'I'll wait while you shower. I don't mind.' Katherine took her glass to the sink and rinsed it, as comfortable in the kitchen as though she'd been there a thousand times. 'I thought I'd take you around and show you the hardware store, the crafts place. Your husband said you'd be working on the house. I swear, it's all I can do to keep my own place from falling into decay and ruin. A big job, keeping a house going. Poor Betty was a hard worker but her sight and energy were giving out. You should have seen how she kept this place before then. Neat as a pin, as they say.'

'You're sure you don't mind waiting?' Vivian asked.

'Not at all. I'll just sit out front for a while, see if those birds still come around.'

'It's very nice of you to take me. I've been avoiding driving that huge truck.'

Katherine looked down at Vivian and then through the screen door at the old red truck. She shook her head, eyes gleaming. 'Ain't that just the way with men?'

4

The color of Katherine's car made Vivian think of cool, green things: celery, lime sherbet, mint. Inside, the seats were plush and velvety and Vivian let her body sink in.

When Katherine started the engine, a deep voice crooned from the speakers. 'Do you like Placido Domingo?' she asked.

'I don't think I've ever heard him,' Vivian told her.

'That man's voice melts me, I swear.' She turned down the music and went through a series of preparations. She adjusted her seat belt strap and the rearview mirror, retrieved her sunglasses from a tortoise-shelled case, put them on and checked her reflection. Then she twisted in the seat, flinging her right arm across the seat back. Finally, she slowly reversed down the long driveway.

The scenery was just as it had been from the airport to the house, although they were headed in the opposite direction. Green rolling hills were broken up by plowed fields, the measured, parallel rows laid out as if by blueprint.

'Where do you live?' Vivian asked.

Katherine's eyes flickered toward her, then back to the road. 'West of town. There's a road that veers off this one; our place is set back about a mile.'

'Big house?'

Katherine shook her head. 'No, it's just me and Max. We've lived here all our lives, got married at the local chapel. Max owns one of the two dry-cleaning businesses in town. He used to have the only one until a few years ago. A family from out east moved here and opened one near the town center.'

'Did they take away much business?'

Katherine waved her hand and her thin gold bracelets clanked against each other. 'Oh, no. We've got loyal customers. Of course, there's always new people moving in. Mr Vega's store has a good location in the mini-mall and new equipment, but we've done fine, just fine.' She patted the steering wheel. 'Max bought me this new car a few years ago for our anniversary. Ten years then, thirteen now.'

'It's nice.'

Katherine glanced at Vivian's hand. 'How long have you been married?'

'Just over four years,' Vivian said.

'Newlyweds,' she said, a wry grin spreading across her face. Then she turned toward the window. 'Sometimes I think I could drive around all day, but there's not much to look at, just the fields and a cow here and there. It's peaceful, though. About forty miles outside of town, some scenic roads wind up into the steeper hills. I'll take you some day. We'll pack a picnic.'

Katherine was a good driver, cautious but not distractedly so, despite her preliminary procedures in the driveway. Her hands looked natural on the steering wheel and her back fit precisely to the seat. She wore huge, square sunglasses with gold ornamentation that matched the bracelets jangling on her arm.

Vivian leaned back against the seat. She was glad to get away. Being at the house was relaxing, but Nowell immersed himself in his writing and much of the time left her alone. Sometimes at night they watched television together, but there wasn't much to talk about. During the routine of her job in the city, Vivian had often daydreamed about coming to the house, about long walks in the country and the time to do whatever she wanted. Yet here she was, feeling lonely and a little stir-crazy after only a week. She decided to ask Katherine to show her some places in town, like the library and the movie theater. She needed to find things to keep busy, besides the work on the house.

She liked Katherine's easy manner. She reminded Vivian of her mother, the way she took charge of things, planning and deciding and leaving little for anyone else to worry about. Katherine was much younger than her mother, at an age where Vivian imagined herself carpooling children to soccer games and band practice, staying home to nurse sore throats. Yet here was Katherine, childless and seemingly unharmed by it.

'Your husband says you're staying for a year?'

Vivian looked over. 'Give or take. Nowell's writing his book and I've got the house to organize.'

She shook her head. 'Big job.'

'I'm starting to think so.'

'I'm happy to help out.'

'Oh, I couldn't ask you…'

'I'd be glad for the work and glad for the company,' Katherine interrupted.

They passed a road maintenance crew. A large truck pressed the newly laid asphalt like a rolling pin on dough while two workers in orange vests sat at the edge of the road, shouting to each other over the truck's clamor and eating their lunches from brown paper sacks. One of the men leaned back and laughed, slapping his thigh. A third man turned a hand-held stop sign around and waved Katherine through.

'I can't believe they're finally paving this,' she said. 'All of the roads out here are still dirt. There's a main interstate nearby, but it leaves off miles outside of town. Just swings right by us, never comes close. It's bizarre, I swear, like this town's been bypassed by the entire modern world.'

The scattered farmhouses along the road started to appear more frequently and form neighborhoods. Suddenly, they were in town.

They passed other buildings, a square gray post office, a blue-shuttered Sheriff Department. In a plaza surrounded by cobblestone and benches, a tall statue cast a narrow shadow over the road.

'Who's the guy on the horse?' Vivian asked.

'William Clement, the founder of the town.'

'Was he a soldier?'

'I don't think so. Why?'

'I thought with statues, they only put soldiers on horses. One foot of the horse is raised if the man died in battle, or something like that.'

'Really?' Katherine's eyebrows made two reddish-brown points above her sunglasses. 'I never heard of that. As far as I know, he wasn't a soldier. He thought he was pretty important, though. Huge ego. Named everything after himself and kept a pack of Indians as slaves, just about. Of course they were here in the Midwest before we came along. Lost everything.' She pursed her lips. 'Yet everyone wants to look up to Clement, make him a hero. Some people around here claim to be descendants, either on the white side or the Indian side, and they make a big deal out of it. Back in '82 when the new library was dedicated, there was a peaceful demonstration that ended not so peacefully. Made the national news.'

Vivian gazed out the window. 'People like to have heroes, I guess.'

'So do I, but I like mine realistic like people are, with good and bad parts but trying to do right. From what I've heard, Willie wouldn't have known right if it hit him upside the head. He did terrible things, and people line up to claim they're related.' She turned the car into a mini-mall parking lot. There were plenty of open spaces and she took one in front of Clement's Hardware. 'See what I mean?' She motioned toward the store sign and turned the engine off. 'Here's one of the famous descendants now.'

Inside, they bought cleaning supplies, wood stain and a small tool set. There was no one in the store except for the elderly man who took their money. As they left, Katherine grabbed Vivian's arm and turned her toward the far side of the mall where there was a donut shop and a dry-cleaners. 'The dreaded enemy,' she whispered.

'What? Is that the other dry-cleaners?'

The store had faded posters in the windows, photographs of models in outdated clothing. The sign read 'Kwik Kleaners' in cursive red letters.

'At least they're not Clements,' Vivian said.

Katherine chuckled. 'Oh, but they could be. On the Indian side somewhere, possibly migrated south and now they've returned for their rightful place. They're everywhere!' She pretended to choke herself and Vivian laughed.

They stopped at an ice-cream parlor for double scoops and ate them at a table outside. The ice-cream melted quickly in the afternoon sun and Vivian felt like a kid sneaking a snack close to dinner, something that was never allowed when she was growing up. She felt guilty and excited, as though Nowell would care.

'So what kind of books does your husband write?' Katherine asked. 'Betty only said that one of her grandsons was a writer and one worked construction.'

'She passed away before Nowell's first novel was published. He's written one book, a mystery, and is working on the second.'

'You're kidding! I love mysteries. I'd like to read it. Would he autograph a copy for me?'

'He'll be flattered you asked.'

'I'll pick up a copy in town this week. What's the title?'

Vivian wiped the corner of her mouth with a napkin. 'Actually, it's in limited release. You may have some trouble finding it. Besides, I'm sure Nowell would love to give you a copy. He has some at the house.'

'Great!' Katherine said. 'What's it about? Don't tell me too much, I hate that.'

Vivian bit her lower lip, contemplating what to say. 'It's a murder mystery about the deaths of two young men. Is that enough?'

Katherine nodded. 'If I know too much beforehand, the whole experience is ruined. That's the whole point of a mystery, isn't it? The *not knowing*.'

Vivian read Nowell's book for the first time just before it was ready for printing. He had gone to visit his mother and left the manuscript on the kitchen table at their apartment. He had tucked a note under the cover: *Couldn't have done it without you.* Two nights later, she finished it. She never read mysteries, although as a child, she loved hiding games and scary movies, the tight feeling of suspense and the release of discovery. Nowell's book, *Random Victim*, seemed well written and it held her interest although she had guessed the ending. She couldn't remember much about the story now.

They finished their ice-cream and started the drive back to the house. Katherine pointed out the library, a two-story brick building near the plaza with William Clement's statue, and the movie theater on the same street, between a clothing store and a diner. The current film was only about a month old; Vivian was encouraged by this. Maybe she wasn't out of touch with civilization after all.

'This was the first downtown street,' Katherine told her. 'Most of these buildings are very old.' She drove slowly down the street and like a tour guide, described the various businesses: who owned them, how good they were for shopping. They went by the Sheriff Department again and the Post Office. USPS was stenciled on the front in blue letters.

Then the cool-green car left the heated asphalt of the town's streets. They passed first the road crew, then the countless rows of grain, then the low, grassy hills.

'I volunteer down at the grammar school three mornings a week,' Katherine told her. 'Right now they're having summer school. I read stories to the kids, help corral them outside. And I work at our store every now and then, but the rest of the time I'm pretty free.' An upbeat number played on the stereo; she tapped her fingers on the steering wheel. 'It'll be nice having you around for a while. Most women in town are older, or tied down with a pack of kids.

And I'd be glad to help you out with the house, any time.'

Vivian shook her head. 'Sounds like you're pretty busy.'

'When you're redoing someone else's, it's more fun. Picking out curtains, painting – oh, remind me to give you the number of Max's friend with the carpet business. He'll give you a good deal.'

'That's probably something we'll do last, after everything is moved out, including us.'

'Keep it in mind, anyway.' Katherine looked over, her eyes shaded by the huge lenses. 'I never asked, what did you do in the city?'

After a moment, Vivian realized what she meant. Her job. 'I just worked in an office.' Down the road a short distance, she recognized the long driveway that led to Grandma Gardiner's house. She reached down to get her purse.

'What's Sheriff Townsend doing out here?' Katherine said.

Vivian looked up. A police car was parked in the driveway.

Katherine pulled behind the red truck, next to the cruiser. As they walked to the porch, they heard voices in the backyard. They turned and followed the sound. In the high grass behind the house, three men stood in a straight line like the trees behind them. Two wore the ill-fitting beige uniforms of law enforcement. One was taller and broader and wore a hat. He gazed at the tree line as the other one, a shorter and younger man with wispy blond hair, spoke to Nowell.

The women waded through the tall grass. Nowell noticed them and waved, and the two policemen looked over.

'Hello,' Vivian said.

'Hi, Viv.' Nowell looked pale, even in the orange late-day sunlight, and he shielded his eyes. Vivian hadn't seen him outside since the night she arrived.

'Are you the welcoming committee, Sheriff Townsend?' Katherine asked.

The taller, older man cleared his throat and said, 'Mrs Wilton.'

Katherine turned to the younger man. 'Don't you two look solemn. What is it, Bud?'

Bud, the shorter and younger man, glanced at the sheriff, who was gazing into the trees again.

Nowell spoke first. 'They found a dead girl back there.'

Katherine's hand moved quickly to her mouth, her rings shooting yellow and orange sparks.

'Back in the trees,' he added.

Vivian shuddered. 'A little girl? Where?'

Sheriff Townsend motioned with his hand. 'Seventeen years old. Just 'bout a half-mile, northwest towards Stokes's land.'

They all stood looking beyond the trees. After a moment, Katherine asked, 'Who was it, Sheriff?'

'Chanelle Brodie.'

She gasped loudly and closed her eyes. 'Her poor mother,' she said. 'Her poor mother.'

Vivian glanced from the sheriff, who was staring at Katherine with his hard, gray eyes, to Bud, whose eyes were lowered, to Nowell, who was watching her reaction. All of them were eerily illuminated by the liquid-orange sunlight behind them. 'What happened to her?' she asked.

The sheriff's forehead creased into deep lines.

Bud said, 'Hard to say. We found her face-down on a rock with her head split open.'

Sheriff Townsend's eyes shot him a warning and Bud quickly corrected himself. 'Severe head trauma, looks like.'

Katherine was incredulous. 'Someone killed her?'

'Now, Mrs Wilton,' the sheriff said. 'We don't know anything yet. We just found the girl this morning. So far, it looks like an accident.'

'Oh my God.' She shook her head.

'Is that what you were looking for last week?' Vivian asked.

The sheriff nodded.

'Mrs Brodie reported Chanelle missing,' Bud said, 'so we conducted a preliminary search of the area.' He glanced at Nowell. 'The Brodies live on the other side of your land.' He pointed towards town. 'After a few days went by, we decided to give it another look-through.'

'Probably didn't look too hard the first time,' Katherine said, 'since that girl was running off every few weeks. Not the easiest child to keep track of, I would think. That poor woman!'

'We're just about finished here,' Sheriff Townsend said. 'I was asking your husband whether he'd seen or heard anything, Mrs Gardiner. He told me you just arrived last Thursday.'

'Yes.'

'And you both saw lights back there that evening?'

She nodded. 'Nowell said it was probably the sheriff, well, you, looking around.'

'Have you seen or heard anything since then?'

'No.'

He nodded slowly then turned abruptly to Bud. 'Let's get going, Deputy.'

'Wait.' Vivian touched Nowell's arm and he flinched. 'Is she…?'

'The coroner's been and gone,' Bud said.

The men turned again to leave. Vivian was looking at the trees, trying to imagine what was beyond them when a lone figure emerged from the woods and advanced slowly but steadily up the incline and through the high grass, the tall trees at his back like a house he'd just left through the front door. 'Look,' she said.

The sheriff's hand went to his holster; Nowell and Katherine took a collective step backwards.

The grass crunched under the feet of the stranger, closer and closer until Vivian could make out a plaid shirt, blue jeans, black-and-silver hair. Something about his stride was familiar, the loose-jointed smoothness of his gait, like her father's. This man was much younger, his face more angular, she thought.

Sheriff Townsend called, 'Evening, Mr Stokes.'

They sighed, leaned back on their heels, and began to stir again.

Flushed slightly from his walk and his eyes shiny with moisture, the man looked around at each one of them. 'Evening, all,' he said.

5

When Vivian was nine, she and her parents spent a summer in the east, in a cabin surrounded by trees. Her mother was participating in a seminar for writers, having been invited to give two workshops on non-fiction. Backed by a well-known writing school, the seminar ran for six weeks and drew fledgling writers from all over the country. Her mother directed a general course titled Writing about History and another on Finding the Story within the Story. Vivian remembered these details from the brochure that arrived several weeks before the trip. She'd been intrigued by the picture of her mother inside, a grainy, indistinct photograph, black print on brownish paper. Held at a distance, it looked like her mother, but held closer, it was only a pattern of tiny dots, uneven splotches of ink.

A genuine log cabin was their home for the month-and-a-half, gratis for her mother's efforts with the struggling writers-in-residence. Her mother, Dr Shatlee to her students at the university and simply Margery to the workshop participants, dreaded the time with the amateur writers. But she was excited by the prospects of a real vacation for Vivian.

'You always teach summer courses,' she said to Vivian's father, who was also Dr Shatlee to his students but Drew to his fellow teachers, 'and the past two summers I was busy with the Tiwi book. It'll be good for us to get away.'

The Tiwis were a group of Aboriginals in Australia. Her mother had written a book about the construction of a hospital in a remote Tiwi village. She spent over a month in Australia interviewing people and sifting through records. Overall, she worked on the book for almost three years. By focusing on a small group of villagers, she made it a personal tale but she wove historical information throughout the narrative. This was the general method for each of her five books. Her most successful one, about the sinking of a cruise ship, came later, when Vivian was thirteen. By far the best-selling of her books (most of which appealed only to specialized groups), *Down Goes the Ambassador* had a title like an action movie and chronicled the sinking of an Alaskan cruise ship. The Tiwis, with their wide-set facial features and caramel-colored skin, were too strange and distant for a popular audience, but the cruise ship seemed to be peopled with one's family, neighbors and co-workers. The tragedy was imaginable.

'It'll be nice to spend time as a family,' her mother said. 'You and your father can explore the woods while I'm suffering through readings, and I'll be free in the afternoons.'

'It's a great opportunity,' her father agreed. 'What do you think, Vivie?'

Vivian shrugged. She had been looking forward to swimming at her friend's house during the warm weather, but now she'd be cloistered away with her parents in the middle of nowhere for half the summer. It wasn't fair.

Upon their arrival, she immediately liked the log-stacked cabin, which was nestled between fir trees and set a good distance from the cabins on either side. Beginning in the clearing that served as a parking area, a narrow path branched and formed trails between the cabins. Rustic and comfortable, their cabin was equipped with fresh linens, firewood, and all the necessities for cooking. Above the kitchen was a loft where Vivian would sleep.

'Careful up there. Don't come near the edge,' her mother instructed. 'I don't know if she should be up there, Drew.'

'It's fine,' he answered. 'She's smart enough not to jump. Right, Vivie?'

'Yes,' she called down. When her mother went back to the car, Vivian kneeled and peeked over. Her father was putting food away in the kitchen. He turned around, saw her, and pointed his finger in silent warning. She grinned and crouched out of sight.

Her mother was the disciplinarian, while her father was a protector and ally. He had certain limits though, and his disapproval was heavier to bear than her mother's, which was more easily and often provoked.

In the mornings while her mother was teaching, Vivian and her father cooked strange, inventive breakfasts: pancakes with raisins and brown sugar or omelets with green olives and cheese. For lunch, they packed cold chicken or sandwiches into backpacks and took long walks through the woods. Her father told Vivian things about the plants and the dangerous wildlife they hoped to see. Mostly, they encountered birds and small creatures, squirrels eating with their miniature arms and twice, lean brown rabbits. Her father didn't know much about nature. His specialty was ancient cultures, Greek mostly, although he did know a fair amount of other things. At least, it seemed so to Vivian, who liked to hear him talk.

In the afternoon, her mother would return, usually tired and cranky. Her patience with her students dwindled as the days went on, and she never wanted to do much in the afternoons but linger about the cabin. Vivian made friends with a small group of kids. They played chasing games or swam at a roped-off, shallow area in the lake.

Her parents seemed closer than they had for some time. At night, they sat outside, laughing and reading aloud to each other from their books. Her mother talked about the workshop classes, lowering her voice if she thought Vivian was still awake. But Vivian knew how she talked about the novice writers, about their unsophisticated methods and childish themes. It was a struggle for her mother, Vivian knew, to circulate in less intelligent crowds.

During the third week of their stay, Vivian got lost in the woods. It was a turning point and in many ways, the end of the vacation. Nothing was the same after that. The day started in the usual way. They had gone for their lunchtime walk, and when they reached a spot Vivian thought she recognized from her trips to the lake with the other children, she suggested they have their picnic there. Busy spreading the blanket on the ground, her father didn't notice when she slipped away behind the thick trees.

She noticed the spot where they had gathered pinecones, she and the garrulous blond girl in the cabin four down. Just beyond a shallow ditch and over the spot where they'd found a fallen bird's nest. After a short time, Vivian realized she truly had no idea where she was, nest or pinecones or not, and that maybe things had gotten out of her control. She didn't panic right away. She walked and walked, staring at the sky beyond the green clouds of trees. She called out but heard nothing in return.

The sun began to abandon its position. Vivian sat down on a rock. The two pieces of gum she found in her backpack made her even hungrier. The day was getting cooler, shadowy, and she didn't have a watch or a jacket. When she began to walk again, her chest was tighter, her breaths short. Eventually, she found a house. She walked up the stone path and knocked on the door. A man opened the door and looked down at her. A marbled-wood pipe hung from the side of his mouth.

She clenched her jaw and said, 'I'm lost.'

'Yes, you are.' He opened the screen door.

The house was dimly lit but smelled clean. Vivian walked in and looked around. Wood paneling covered the walls and a clock ticked loudly from the hallway. On a short table next to a brown reclining chair were two pictures of school-age children, a boy and a girl. This made her feel better.

The man motioned to the couch and Vivian sat on the edge. He brought her a glass of water, tepid but clear, and she gulped it down. He made a bologna and cheese sandwich on dry wheat bread and served it to her on a paper napkin. Then she heard him talking in the kitchen, his voice too loud as though he didn't use the telephone often. 'Yes, sir... yes, she's here now... All right then, I'll keep her here.'

Vivian walked to the kitchen with the crumpled napkin and the empty glass. The man jumped a little when he turned and saw her. 'You were hungry,' he said.

She nodded. 'Can I use your bathroom?'

He pointed down the hall.

When Vivian returned to the living room, the man was leaning back in the recliner, holding a glass of water on the paunch of his stomach. She sat on the couch again.

'They're coming for you directly,' he said.

'Okay.'

The man was nice looking. He had friendly eyes and black wavy hair with gray patches in front of his ears. 'What's your name?' he asked.

'Vivian.'

'That's a nice name.'

They both looked absently around the room, mostly toward the television as though willing it to go on. Then they spoke at the same time.

'What's your name?' Vivian said, just as the man said, 'I have a daughter.'

He smiled. 'Joe Toliver, but you can call me Joe. I was saying that I have a daughter about your age. Here's her picture, and her brother too. He's older than her.'

Vivian walked over to the table and looked at the pictures. Then she returned to her seat, this time relaxing against the couch. 'Where are they?' she asked.

'With their mother, but they come here in the summer.'

'Why don't you live together?'

He thought about this for a moment. 'We are better separated than we are together.'

A blanket was draped over the armrest of the couch, and Vivian pulled it over her legs. 'What do your kids do when they're here?'

'Same as you, I expect. Run around and swim.'

'Where do they swim?'

'At the lake down there.'

Vivian figured it must be a different lake, perhaps a different town. She was sure she'd walked miles. 'Do you ever take them on vacations?'

'Sure. We used to come here and camp out in a tent when they were real little.'

After that, Vivian didn't remember much but the hum of Joe Toliver's voice, deep-pitched and certain. She felt comfortable and warm underneath the blanket. She fell asleep. Then she was lifted from the couch, her face against Joe's soft checkered shirt. Her father tumbled from a car and took her into his arms. The whole proceeding was somber and serious and she felt very important. Her parents had been so worried that in the end, she wasn't punished. Instead, her mother blamed her father and made the rest of the vacation unbearable. Vivian thought it was brave of Joe Toliver to live alone, considering.

Perhaps it was the wooded backdrop or his dramatic entrance that made Vivian think of Joe Toliver when Mr Stokes stood before them in the high grass of the backyard, the day the sheriff found the dead girl. Maybe it was his plaid flannel shirt or the light-and-dark combination of his hair. Or the way he talked, with one side of his mouth lower than the other, or maybe it was the time of day, that same pre-dusk time when she had leaned against the scratchy brown couch and slept.

For any one of these reasons, Mr Stokes evoked the image of Vivian's kind savior from that summer afternoon when she was nine, and as the sheriff recounted the day's events for him, she relived her initial feelings of panic and fear at the news of the dead girl and felt again for a moment, lost. When Mr Stokes finally spoke, his calm voice had the soothing effect the memory of Joe inspired, even now, and Vivian forgot her panic for the second time that day.

'It's a tragedy to lose a young one,' Mr Stokes said when he heard what had happened. 'I run into Mrs Brodie on occasion and I've seen her girl now and then.' He scratched the side of his jaw. His deep-set eyes and unwrinkled brow gave the impression of practiced patience.

'I'd like to ask you a few questions,' Sheriff Townsend said. 'Do you have the time?'

He nodded. 'Why don't you come up to the house now? We can talk on the way back.'

Sheriff Townsend explained to Vivian and Nowell that Mr Stokes owned much of the land directly behind the Gardiner acreage. His house was about a half-mile to the west, deep in the trees.

'These are Mrs Gardiner's relatives, Mr and Mrs Gardiner,' the sheriff said.

Vivian watched as Mr Stokes greeted Nowell, then she shook his rough, warm hand. He wasn't much older than them, maybe Katherine's age, but there was a maturity about him that made Vivian feel childish in his presence.

'I'll drive you around to your side road,' the sheriff said. 'Let's leave these people to their dinner.'

'Yes, Max will be wondering about me,' Katherine said.

As a group, they all started to move.

Nowell touched Vivian's elbow to lead her but she turned instead toward the sheriff. 'You'll let us know what you find out?'

He nodded.

'Especially,' she continued, 'if you think there's any danger...'

'Come on, Viv.' Nowell pulled on her arm.

She looked up at him irritably. 'What?'

Sheriff Townsend cleared his throat. 'Mrs Gardiner, I'll keep you apprised.'

Katherine fidgeted with her purse.

Mr Stokes watched Vivian intently and she began to get the impression she was making everyone uncomfortable but didn't know why.

'Thank you,' she mumbled. 'Thanks, Katherine, for the tour.' She turned and walked toward the house, looking back once to see Nowell raise his hand in silent farewell to their visitors. Vivian took his gesture as an act of sympathy between them, between the men, as though apologizing for her outspokenness. She strode angrily to the house, not waiting for him to catch up and not looking back again.

6

Vivian was standing at the refrigerator opening a beer when Nowell came in.

He walked toward her and she moved abruptly away.

'What's your problem?' he asked, glowering over her.

She swallowed a gulp of beer. 'You didn't have to act like I was some crazy person for asking a few questions.'

'Listen,' he said. 'I didn't mean to cut you off with the sheriff. I'd already been talking to him for a while, and I figured he probably wanted to get out of here. Besides, I can take care of things.'

'What do you mean?'

'The sheriff. I can take care of it.' He turned to leave.

'You didn't ask him when he would call us,' she said.

Nowell spun around. 'That girl was practically in our backyard. You can be sure he'll let us know.'

'I didn't realize you were such an expert in the protocol of police investigations.' She grinned, but now he looked angry.

'You just have to know everything right away,' he said. 'But there's nothing to know yet. You threatened the sheriff…'

'Threatened him, by asking questions? I was just concerned. Aren't you worried about our safety?'

'Not until I have a reason to worry.'

They stood several feet apart. An impasse. Outside, tree branches slapped against the north side of the house and leaves blew across the porch. She had noticed, in some peripheral zone of her brain, storm clouds forming. 'I wonder what happened to her,' she said.

'I don't know,' Nowell said. 'I really don't.' He shook his head, looking down at the weathered yellow floor. Vivian realized he was more affected by the sheriff's visit than she had thought.

'It's going to rain,' she said. 'My elbow hurts.'

'We should close the windows,' Nowell said. He walked down the hallway.

She went to the back door, rubbing her elbow and watching the flurry of weather outside. The night had come alive; the sky was brooding and thickly dark. A strong wind pushed the trees crazily into each other and lifted leaves and papers into tiny, racing cyclones. Vivian thought about the girl they had found and tried to picture her splayed across a wide, flat rock. The sheriff said she was seventeen years old. Vivian wondered how long she was there before the sheriff came, what she'd been wearing. She thought about their neighbor, Mr Stokes, marching over the land like he owned it. The way he looked at her had been questioning, judgmental.

Nowell returned to the kitchen, rubbing his hands together. 'They're all closed now,' he said. 'It's really something out there.'

On cue, a crack of thunder echoed through the yellow kitchen. They both jumped.

Nowell asked, 'Do you need ice for your elbow?' He nestled behind her, wrapped his arm across her collarbone.

She felt a familiar tingle. 'So you did hear me,' she said.

When the weather was wet and cool, the joints in Vivian's knees and elbows were prone to soreness. An ingrown barometer, they alerted her with more accuracy than the weather forecast in the newspaper. When she was young, her mother called it growing pains and was uncharacteristically patient with her when it

43

happened. Now that Vivian was an adult, she wasn't sure what caused it. Surely, she was finished growing.

That poor woman, Katherine had called the dead girl's mother. Vivian remembered being seventeen; she and her own mother had rarely seen eye-to-eye. High school changed Vivian, gave her a flavor of independence. By her third year, she was staying out every weekend, often missing her curfew or disregarding it altogether. She argued with her mother constantly, even threatened to move away.

Nowell had gone into the living room, a small, blue-carpeted area next to the kitchen. Seldom used, the room was cramped with furniture and dimly lit. A brick fireplace took up most of one wall and on its mantle sat a porcelain owl with wide, black eyes. As Vivian entered, lightning brightened the room, throwing stark shadows against the walls. A clap of thunder followed, echoing in the chimney. Rain pelted the windows; fat drops slid down the glass. She sat next to Nowell on the sofa, pulling her knees up to her chest. He was watching a nature program. On the screen, two female tigers squared off against each other, their backs and ears raised. She thought about Katherine's tattoo and suppressed a grin.

'Let's go into town tomorrow morning,' she said.

'Why?'

'I want to sign up for the newspaper. Maybe we could have breakfast while we're down there.'

'Why don't you just call the newspaper office?'

'I want to buy one for tomorrow, see if there's anything on that girl. We could see a movie afterwards, and...'

'I can't,' Nowell said. 'I'm not at a good stopping point.'

She sighed. 'I'll go by myself then. I guess I have to drive that truck sometime.'

The tigers were in a group of five now. Two of them had young to look after. The cubs rolled around on the dirt, smacking each other with their large paws.

'How's the book coming?' she asked.

'Good,' he said.

'How far have you gotten?'

'What do you mean?'

'How many chapters?'

'About nine I guess.'

On the television screen, the cubs frolicked in the grass. 'Is it going to be like the other book?' she asked.

'I hope not.'

'I mean, the same kind. A mystery.'

'Yes.'

She put her legs down and leaned over, pressing her hand on Nowell's chest. 'Come on, tell me something about it.'

'You know I don't like to. It's not complete, not even the idea of it. Right now, it's all stored in my mind, in some sort of inexplicable order.'

'I don't get it.'

'You don't have to get it.'

She sat upright. 'I guess that's just one more thing we can't talk about tonight. Can't talk about the sheriff, can't talk about your book.'

A vulture watched the group of cubs as they dove in and out of the tall meadow grass.

'I talked to my mom today,' Nowell said. 'They're trying to reduce her pension.'

'Who?' Vivian asked.

'My dad's old company. They're saying something about a time limit or something. She's really upset.'

'I thought pensions were forever.'

'There's a new tax law. She told me all about it, but I couldn't follow the rules and regulations. That place has turned very corporate since Dad died. I can't believe his old partner would do this to her.'

'What's she going to do?'

Nowell shrugged. 'She's worried about losing that money. She's never had a real job.'

'How much is it?'

'Not much, but she depends on it.'

'She has savings and the house, the money from your grandma...'

Nowell leaned forward. 'But it's regular income and she's entitled to it. She got a lawyer, an old friend of my dad's.'

Nowell kept in very close contact with his mother, which took some time for Vivian to get used to. Communication between herself and her own parents was more sporadic and less involved. She spoke to her mother every other week, about mundane things – jobs, illnesses, the weather. And her mother talked about her work. She taught Sociology courses at the university and was usually working on another book.

Vivian's father didn't like the telephone. Normally, all she could get out of him was a general statement about what he was doing before he passed the receiver on. In person, he could be quite animated about his work. He was a good listener and never gave advice.

But Beverly Gardiner unburdened all of her problems onto her sons. Nowell helped her decide on appliances, insurance and doctors, and he worried about every problem with her house or car. At first, Vivian thought him kind and responsible for assuming some of his father's responsibilities but recently, she'd witnessed the unnecessary worry Beverly caused. The pension issue, like many others, would probably end up being nothing.

After a long commercial break, the vulture carried off a tiger cub that had fallen sick and died.

'That's disgusting,' Vivian said. 'Is he going to eat it?'

Nowell chuckled, pulling her next to him with his long arm. 'It's the way of nature.' Then he coaxed her onto his lap so that they faced each other.

After a moment he asked, 'What's all that stuff out in the garbage?'

'Assorted junk. A whole box of plastic silverware and plates, sewing stuff, stacks of paperbacks.'

'You could take the books to a used book store.'

'They're romance novels,' she said, leaning in. 'I figured you'd think the world is better off without them.'

Nowell gripped her hips. 'Because of poverty, I've had to reconsider my high ideals.'

'We're not in poverty.'

'Okay. Without means.'

'You're right, I could have traded them for something to read.' She shrugged. 'They're all wet now.'

'What else have you uncovered?' he asked.

'Nothing exciting. Mostly clothes, junk. I really haven't gotten much done yet.'

'There's no rush. You deserve a break.'

'So do you, so how about that movie tomorrow?'

He shook his head. 'I told you. I can't.'

'It's only one day.' She moved back to her spot next to him on the couch.

'Viv, please. I'm trying to do something here, for both of us. I have a hard enough time staying focused. *Random Victim* did pretty well, but I've got to produce something else. Besides, Dani wants me to start doing some promotion in the fall for *Random Victim*, getting ready for the new book.'

Dani was Nowell's agent. She had a husky voice and like a used car salesman, was overly and suspiciously friendly.

The rain had let up; occasional drops splashed against the windows and the wind was calmer.

'Let's plan a day off soon,' she said, 'you and me. We'll pack a picnic lunch and go for a long walk.'

'Maybe next week,' he said.

The remaining tigers were enjoying the spring sunshine. They were leaner now, learning to hunt. In the high grass, they crouched and chased each other around.

Maybe the girl was taking a walk when it happened, Vivian suddenly thought. Sometimes it's nice to be alone, only your thoughts for company and no one telling you what you should be doing. Maybe someone saw her, someone with bad motives and a sudden opportunity. But the sheriff had said it looked like an accident. Maybe someone was with her and the other person ran off afterwards. But people don't normally run away from accidents, she thought, unless they're guilty in some way. She squeezed her elbow, trying to rub away the insistent throb.

'I'll get you that ice,' Nowell said, and he went out to the kitchen.

7

The storm had pushed soggy leaves against the house and left a puddle directly below the porch steps. Broken branches lay scattered about, their leaves still green and beneath the bark, clean white fiber gleamed. Vivian kicked off her shoes, the damp grass cool between her toes as she gathered the debris. In the shed next to the well, amidst rusty gardening tools and bags of old potting soil, she found a straw broom. She swept the porch and gathered everything into a black garbage bag. By mid-morning, the grass dried into scented vapors and the dirt driveway lightened, strip by strip, as the sun moved higher over the trees.

Nowell was in his airless study, hidden behind the curtain like a sick ward. Vivian's mind had started to believe that the divider was solid and soundproof; it gave the illusion of complete separation. Nowell's touch on the keyboard was light. She seldom heard any sounds from the room. If she strained, sometimes she could make out a soft, steady tapping, like raindrops on a distant roof. Most of the time, she forgot he was in the house.

She telephoned her parents but reached their answering machine, her mother's staid, succinct recording. Then she went to the study.

'Nowell? Can I come in?'

'Hey, Viv,' he called back.

She pulled aside the curtain, an old sheet with delicate baby blue stripes, and stepped down. 'It's so stuffy in here,' she said without thinking.

This was a continual disagreement between them, at their apartment and now here, at Grandma Gardiner's house. Nowell kept windows sealed; Vivian liked to air things out, even in the winter.

'It's cold in the morning,' Nowell said. 'There's no sun back here. I wish you'd leave the windows alone.'

'I opened them in the afternoon, when it was warm.'

He raised his eyebrows.

'All right,' she said. 'It's your room.' She perched on the edge of his desk. 'I'm going to head into town now. I'm going to the newspaper office and having lunch with Katherine. She called earlier.'

He moved some papers to the side. 'Are you sure you're comfortable driving the truck?'

'I think so.'

The night before, he adjusted the seat and brought a pillow from the house for her to sit on. It seemed demeaning to her, like a booster seat for a child, but she was determined to drive the thing.

She climbed into the cabin as effortlessly as possible given its height, started the truck, and backed it slowly down the driveway. As she turned onto the road, she glanced up at the house, looking for Nowell in the windows. She felt sure he was watching, to see how she'd do.

Vivian had no trouble driving to town and finding the newspaper office. The Sentinel was tucked between two squat office buildings, its white-painted brick façade standing stubbornly between the modern structures. She walked through the double doors at the front and a bell tied to the doorknob jangled, reminding her of Christmas. The woman at the desk looked up and smiled. Above her, a wooden placard that said 'Customer

Service' hung from the ceiling under two thick cables. The woman had a double chin that protruded underneath her first chin. Bulbous and jiggling, it extended down in a rounded curve to the opening of her shirt. 'Hello there,' she said.

Vivian tried to focus instead on her eyes, which were dull green but friendly. 'My husband and I just moved here,' she said, 'and we'd like to receive the newspaper.'

'Surely.' She took a sheet of paper from a plastic tray at the side of the counter. 'Just fill out this form.'

Vivian set her purse on the counter. 'I'm sorry,' she said, 'but could I borrow a pen?'

'Surely. Take mine and I'll fetch another one.' The woman made slow movements to disembark her chair, which was a high, backless stool pushed up close to the counter. She turned to the side and scooted forward a little, then straightened her torso so that her rear slid over the edge of the seat. Finally, she landed with a grunt on the floor, her neck shaking up and down.

'There are three different kinds of subscriptions,' she explained when she came back with the pen. 'There's every day service, which includes every day of the week except Tuesday and Thursday. We don't print those days. So the 'every day' title really means every day we print. Then there's Monday, Friday and Sunday service. Basically that excludes Wednesday and Saturday. Then there's Sunday only service.'

'I'll take the second one.' As the woman checked the paperwork, Vivian looked around the office. Behind the counter, two desks sat side by side, each cluttered with papers. A doorway at the back of the reception area opened to a larger room. Two people were working in that section. A man leaned on the corner of a desk, talking to a woman and smoking.

'I see you're out on the main road,' the woman said.

Vivian looked back to her milky green eyes and nodded.

She lowered her voice. 'Did you hear about the girl they found out there?'

Vivian answered in her normal speaking voice. 'Yes. She was found near our house.'

The woman's eyes widened and as she lowered her head, her neck creased into white and pink bands. 'Right near your place, you say?'

'Practically our backyard.'

'Goodness! How terrifying for you!'

Vivian didn't like her conspiratorial tone or the way she had lowered her voice.

'You poor thing,' the woman continued. 'Your husband's out there with you?'

'Well, yes. Why?'

She looked at Vivian curiously. 'For protection.'

'The sheriff seems to think it was an accident.'

'That's not what I heard.' At once, the woman changed her posture, straightening her back. She looked over her shoulder. 'I can't—'

Vivian leaned forward. 'What did you hear?'

The woman contemplated for a moment then squinted, her eyes catlike. 'I heard it's not a foregone conclusion.'

'What do you mean?'

'They say the girl fell, right?'

Vivian nodded.

'And hit her head on the rock?'

'Yes.'

The woman paused, puckering her lips. 'Say you're running and you trip on something and fall. Where would your hands be?'

'My hands?'

'You're running and your feet hit something and you fall forward.'

'I don't know.'

The woman shook her head irritably, then glanced over her shoulder again. 'Your hands would be up, near your chest or your face, depending how far they got.' She demonstrated. 'You would try to break the fall, by instinct. That's why kids on roller-skates are supposed to wear those wrist things, because they break their wrists more than anything else.'

'So?'

'Chanelle Brodie's hands were at her side, like this.'

Vivian peered over the counter to see the woman's arms, pressed to her sides like a soldier at attention.

'Weird, isn't it?' the woman said.

'I guess.'

'Like an execution,' she almost hissed.

They concluded their business and Vivian thanked the woman. Outside, the morning brightness was a shock. She locked the truck and started down the street toward the restaurant Katherine had suggested, thinking about the conversation with the woman at the newspaper office. What she had said about instinct seemed reasonable. Small children often fell on their faces, cutting their lips open or bruising their cheeks, but after a certain age, injuries happened more to limbs. Older children scraped their knees and elbows, broke arms and fingers. It seemed logical that if a seventeen-year-old girl had fallen in the woods, her hands would have gone up to break her fall.

Vivian passed a toy store and a women's clothing boutique. The streets were quiet for mid-morning, most businesses still closed. She lowered her sunglasses to read the sign on the door of a flower shop: Open weekdays at eleven. Most of the places were the same. She was meeting Katherine at eleven-thirty, and still had an hour to kill. She reached the plaza with the statue of William Clement, sat on a red-painted bench, and opened her complimentary copy of *The Sentinel*.

There were two articles about Chanelle Brodie, the first one on the front page: LOCAL GIRL, 17, FOUND DEAD. The article was short, just covering the most basic facts; the body was found face down, on a large rock, and that the death was believed to be an accident. More information would follow after an autopsy, it said.

53

The other article, buried on page six, talked about an impromptu memorial service to take place at Chanelle's high school. The entire fence surrounding the football field was threaded with flowers. The formal services would be held in a few days.

Vivian wondered again what Chanelle had been doing in the woods behind their property. She remembered a small box she buried in the backyard when she was young. The box contained mementos: notes she had received from a boy, a plastic multi-colored bracelet, a picture of her mother as a teenager. Between the gnarled roots of an old, dried-up tree, she dug a hole and covered the box with a thin layer of dirt. She thought: Maybe Chanelle had a hiding place in the woods; that would explain why she went there alone. Then again, maybe she did most things by herself. Being an only child, Vivian could relate to that.

'Hey there!'

She opened her eyes. The sun glared through her sunglasses.

Katherine moved over, blocking the light. 'I thought that was you. I drove by a minute ago.'

'None of the stores were open,' Vivian said. 'I thought I'd read the paper and enjoy the sun a little.'

'I keep telling Max that we should open later like everyone else, but some people like to drop off their cleaning on the way to work.' She looked up at the sky. 'Feels like another hot one, doesn't it? July is going out with a bang, I swear.'

They walked across the plaza, over the jagged shadow of William Clement and horse.

Katherine said, 'This place has a great salad bar, and it should be pretty fresh since we'll get there before the lunch crowd.'

Vivian looked up and down the street, which was clear but beginning to show a few sporadic signs of life. She couldn't imagine any type of crowd anywhere on this street, lunchtime or otherwise. There was a pregnant stillness, like a suspenseful movie. Any moment, a mad gunman would burst from the bank or someone would scream and fall from the top of a building.

'Those kids were a handful today,' Katherine said.

'What grade?'

'Third. Eight and nine years old. They're hard to handle during the summer. It's like the heat gets to their little brains.' She laughed, pleased with herself. 'What did you think of that storm?'

'Windy, wasn't it? I filled a trash bag with leaves and branches.'

Katherine grabbed Vivian's upper arm. 'I still can't believe it. One of the teachers at the school heard Chanelle had been missing for almost three weeks. She has a friend who knows Kitty.'

'Kitty?'

'Mrs Brodie, Chanelle's mother. Her name is Katlyn but she's always gone by Kitty.' She made a clicking sound with her tongue. 'She had a hard time raising that child alone. Chanelle was a magnet for trouble.'

'More trouble than most teenagers?' Vivian asked.

'That's a good question. It's been so long since I was one myself.'

They were seated at a table on the restaurant's patio, and when they were comfortable with iced teas, Katherine resumed the conversation. 'Chanelle was a very pretty girl and arrogant about it. I think it's a special time and a dangerous one, when a young girl discovers her sex appeal. Don't you?'

Vivian flushed slightly. 'I guess.'

'She had a way about her. Arrogant, but sad. She wasn't going to let anybody tell her anything.'

'Did she have brothers or sisters?'

Katherine shook her head as she sipped from her straw. 'Kitty had her real young, in high school.' She set her glass down. 'You should know that in a small town, everybody goes to the same school and knows everybody's business. I swear, it's almost intimidating sometimes, knowing you can never get away from yourself. You can never change, not really. People are always reminding you who you are.'

Vivian hadn't lived in her hometown since she moved away to college. She hadn't ever thought of it in those terms, but she did like the anonymity of the city. 'Were you and Kitty friends in high school?' she asked.

'No. She was a year back and hung around a different crowd.'

Vivian smiled. 'Let me guess. She was a cheerleader and you were a diligent student.'

Katherine chuckled. 'Something like that. She never was a cheerleader, but boy, she wanted to be. She pestered the in-crowd until they had to let her in. She was very pretty. Still is.'

'Was Chanelle pretty?

Katherine nodded, but something passed over her face. Vivian thought that maybe it hurt her feelings, remembering how she and Kitty differed in high school.

'I see the kids around here,' Katherine said. 'They have no fear. I've seen Chanelle riding around at night, six or seven of them in the back of a truck. Cruising up and down the main street, trying to make something happen.'

'The street with the statue of William Clement?'

'Yeah.' Katherine paused. 'I can't explain it, but they act like they own the town. I was never completely fearless, even at my worst.'

Vivian envisioned the circular plaza surrounding the statue of Clement. 'That's probably the turn-around point,' she said, 'where the statue is.'

'You sound like someone who's done some cruising yourself.'

She shrugged. 'Maybe once or twice.'

'There's something else.' Katherine lowered her voice. 'About a year ago, Chanelle and two local boys got arrested for stealing a car from the mini-mall parking lot. They were raging drunk too. Lucky for them, Sheriff Townsend is an old friend of Kitty's father. They all got bailed out and the charges were eventually dropped. I think they got some kind of probation.'

'What about the owner of the car?'

'She used to work for the sheriff when he owned his construction company.' She winked. 'Everything worked out.'

Their salads arrived and for a few moments, they ate in silence.

Katherine sighed. 'I think Chanelle had a lot of boyfriends, that sort of thing. Like her mother. But she was still in school. She could have done something with her life, especially with that stubborn streak. Life takes perseverance, doesn't it? It's a real shame.'

Vivian set her fork down. 'I saw the story in *The Sentinel*.'

'You know,' Katherine said. 'It doesn't give the exact location. People won't know it was near your place.'

'Do you think they'll want to leave flowers at the site or something?'

'No, I just thought you wouldn't want people bothering you.'

'People? What people?'

'I don't know.'

'They can come over and look if they want to,' Vivian said. 'Why? Do people think we know something, do they…'

Katherine waved her hand, bracelets sounding an alarm. 'Oh, no, no, no. There are all types, that's all. The curious, the downright nosy.'

Vivian hadn't once imagined the possible implications of the girl being found on their property. She'd been thinking only of their safety.

'The man who owns this little café is so nice,' Katherine told her. 'His father designed the fire station, and the county office addition…' As she talked, Vivian stayed alone in her thoughts, which weren't about office additions or salads but instead were vivid contemplations about Chanelle Brodie and the nature of her final moments.

8

When Vivian came in, Nowell was on the telephone, speaking patiently into the receiver propped between his shoulder and ear. 'I can't tell you anything until I speak to him. What's his name again?' He paced the room, very intent on the conversation, pausing only to give her a brief nod. 'Richards or Richardson? I've got it. And his number?'

The curtain divider to Nowell's study had been pulled back. Through the window, the back lawn was a vivid, monochrome green. Vivian noticed an empty plate and a fork on the end table near the couch. She stepped down into the room to get them.

'I'll call him today or maybe first thing tomorrow. What are you doing? No, not you. Viv, what are you doing?'

She turned with the plate in her hands to show him.

'Mom, they can't do that. No, I will call Richards, or is it Richardson? I'll call him. You just wait to hear from me. I'll let you know what I find out.'

Vivian set the plate and fork in the sink then walked down the hallway toward their bedroom.

Nowell came in as she was adjusting the straps of her bikini. 'You're going outside?' he asked.

'Yeah.'

'My mom said she'd call to talk to you later this week. She's too upset today.'

'Why, what happened?'

He sat on the edge of the bed. 'The pension thing. She's all worked up about it and wants me to call that lawyer. She doesn't trust him.'

'What are you supposed to do?'

He shrugged. 'She needs someone to look out for her, and Lonnie's no good in these situations. I may have to drive over there and meet with this guy.'

She looked up. 'What?'

'I don't know what else to do. I've got her calling me in hysterics. I can't do anything from here. I'll stay overnight so I can meet with him during office hours.'

Vivian wrapped a beach towel, a bright print her parents bought on vacation, around her waist. She leaned against the doorframe. 'I just don't see why it has to be you. You're trying to finish your book.'

'There's no use arguing about it. I have to go.' He crossed his arms over his chest, looked at hers in the bikini top. 'If you don't feel comfortable staying here alone, you can come with me.'

She shrugged, watched his gaze and waited.

'I've got to get back to work,' he said. He left the room and after a few moments, she followed him, suddenly angry. She poked her head into the makeshift office. 'Am I allowed in here?' she asked.

'What do you mean?'

'You act like you want me to stay out.'

'I like my privacy. Is that such a big deal?'

'No, Nowell. Nothing's a big deal. You don't leave this room for days at a time, but you can take two days off to bail your mother out of some imaginary problem. No big deal.'

'You think I want to do this?' He sprung from his chair and was suddenly towering over her. 'Drive all the way there, talk to some lawyer about something I know nothing about, knowing my mother is depending on me? A little support would be nice, Viv.'

59

He ran his hands through his dark hair and looked, in that moment, vulnerable.

She reached for him. 'I'm sorry but...'

'I have work to do.'

'Okay,' she said, and went to the kitchen. She knew he needed time to cool off.

They hadn't fought much during the first years of their marriage, although it was a tense time. Nowell had just graduated from college and Vivian had a year left. He took a low-paying job at a bookstore while she worked part-time at the water management agency. Money was limited and anxieties were high. The rent on their apartment went up twice in one year. Everywhere, real estate prices were skyrocketing and rents were keeping pace. The boom of the 90s, people were calling it. Even with the money difficulties, they were happy.

They married after two years of dating. Although Vivian spent quite a bit of time in Nowell's studio apartment, she shared a dorm room on campus with three other girls until a few weeks before the wedding. Nowell's mother sprung for a resort honeymoon, and her parents paid for the small ceremony at his family's church. After the wedding, they rented the one-bedroom apartment and combined their things.

In the beginning, they were both very busy. With Nowell's encouragement, Vivian finally decided on a Business major. She had been wavering between Art History and Business, taking low-level courses in both. She imagined herself working in a museum, perhaps owning her own art gallery one day.

During her freshman year, she stumbled into an Art History class after not getting into an overcrowded introductory literature course. She had been focusing on Business then, but still needed a few liberal arts classes. The professor of the art course was young and hip, enthusiastic and funny. Vivian had a crush on him, with his silver earring and long black ponytail, his tawny skin and brown suede coat. And when Dr Lightfoot showed slides of sculptures and paintings, museums and cathedrals, and talked about the creativity and methods that formed them, it was the ultimate escape. Vivian was hooked.

Nowell said that Art History was a major like English, designed for those who wanted to teach and she'd need a doctorate degree if she followed that course. The Business major was more broadly applicable, he said, non-limiting. She could have Art History as a minor; Business would guarantee her a job.

When Vivian announced her plans to her parents over dinner one night, their reactions were restrained. Her mother gazed at her over her reading glasses. 'I thought you were really interested in art,' she said.

'I am,' Vivian said, 'but I think the Business degree would open up more avenues, that's all.'

'Why do you need other avenues, if art is what you enjoy?' Her mother stared at her plate, slicing her prime rib with the efficiency of a surgeon.

'I'll still have a minor in Art,' she said. 'It's hard to find a job with a Bachelors degree in Art.'

Her mother only raised her eyebrows but her father lifted his wineglass to Vivian. 'I think it's a fine decision, Vivie,' he said.

She knew they wanted her to follow them into academia, but she lacked their self-discipline, their ability to narrow focus. She didn't have their attention spans; her mother had said so herself on many occasions when Vivian put down a book to watch television, when she abandoned a project before it was finished.

Vivian kept her office job after graduation and was promoted within a year to Administrative Assistant. Nowell moved from the bookstore to a short stint at a bakery, to his last job at the magazine, editing and proofreading. In the evenings and during weekends, he worked on his book. Between her job, housework and keeping up with friends, Vivian's life seemed just as full as when she attended classes and studied for finals.

They settled into steady jobs and a stable routine, but started to fight more for some reason. Nowell was incredibly tense throughout the writing of his book. Frustrated by the long hours at the magazine, he stayed in and wrote most weekends, often from Friday evening until Monday morning. In the cramped apartment, his tension was infectious. They bickered over small matters. Vivian tried to get out of the way during these times. She'd spend a day at the mall with a friend or drive around the city, doing errands. She didn't mind doing things alone. Being an only child had given her a certain self-reliance. Like her mother, she could content herself with her own tasks and ruminations.

After the book was finished, Nowell relaxed into his old self and became easier to live with again. When his grandmother died and he presented the idea for an extended working vacation, Vivian had been unwilling at first to leave her job, where she had seniority, three weeks of vacation and a decent salary. But in the end, quitting had yielded no regret, only a slight wistfulness for leaving a part of her life behind. She was ready for something to change.

In the fragrant grass in front of the old, white house, Vivian reclined on the fold-out chair and thought about Dr Lightfoot, the way he paced back and forth in front of the chalkboard, the cable to the slide projector trailing after him like a microphone cord. When he wanted to explain something more clearly, he asked the girl in the last row to flip on the lights then he'd look into the students' eyes or write on the board in furious scratches of chalk. He showed slides in every class, excitedly pointing out notable features of the art. His hands were delicate over the screen, seemed to curve around the edges of the sculpture or brush the surface of a painting with soft, tenuous fingers. He had a deep respect for art, even the mere projected image of it.

'Viv!'

Her eyes opened. The lawn chair was mostly covered by shade; only her feet and the bottom half of her legs were still in the sun.

The screen door squeaked as Nowell poked his head outside. 'Your mother's on the phone.'

Vivian walked gingerly over the still-damp ground, groggy and disoriented.

Her mother was working on a new book; she'd been distracted and unable to talk about much else. Her research would take her to the site where a volcano erupted fifty years ago. She planned on taking a sabbatical and going in the fall for at least a month. Vivian asked about her father.

'He's at school,' her mother said. 'That summer course.'

'Tell him I said hello.'

'I will. How's Nowell's book coming along?'

'He's been working non-stop since I arrived. It's so quiet out here. I think it's been very good for him.' Vivian shifted her weight on the chair, which was cold and sticky against her bare legs.

'Has he established a regular schedule?'

'For his writing?'

'Yes.'

'He works most of the day,' Vivian said. 'He starts early, before I get up.'

'And how is your work on the house going?'

'It's going to be a big job, that's for sure.'

Her mother shifted the phone. 'Worse shape than you'd imagined?'

'There's a lot of junk around,' Vivian acknowledged, 'and the entire thing needs painting.'

'That should keep you busy.' Her voice sounded doubtful.

'So far I've been taking it pretty easy.'

Neither spoke for a few moments. The silence over the phone line was vapid, like air. Vivian had the impression of pressing her ear against a hole in a wall. On the other side, openness and space. 'Mom?'

'Yes?'

'Do you remember that vacation, the summer when you taught the writing workshop?'

Her mother answered quickly, without thought, 'Of course.'

'I did it on purpose, you know.'

'I don't know what you're talking about.'

'When I got lost,' Vivian said, pushing the receiver to her ear. 'It wasn't Dad.'

There was a pause; emptiness again like the line was dead.

'You were eight years old.'

'Nine.' Vivian stared through the screen door. On the lawn chair, the beach towel rose in ripples with the afternoon breeze, its corners flipping wildly back and forth. She spoke more hesitantly, her voice losing strength. 'It was my fault.'

'You wandered off, that's all.'

'Then why…'

'Hold on Vivian.' Her mother set the telephone on a hard surface. Vivian could hear her definitive steps fading then after a short time, growing louder again. When she came back on the line, she changed the subject.

'What have you been reading, Vivian?' Her mother believed everyone should constantly be reading something, preferably something of substance.

'Fashion magazines and the TV guide,' Vivian answered to irritate her.

Another silence like an empty room, like the inside of a bubble.

They talked about the weather for a while and when this most generic and easy of topics was exhausted, they said goodbye.

Vivian replaced the receiver in its cradle and walked over to the curtain that divided the kitchen from the study. There was always the faint taste of misunderstanding where her mother was concerned. As much as they went through the motions, neither ever felt entirely comfortable with the other.

She wondered if Nowell was still angry or if he would, as they had both learned to do, drop the argument before they reached the unsolvable issues at its center. 'Knock, knock,' she said loudly.

The faint clicking sound ceased and she waited while he took a moment, only a brief moment, before his voice called out in answer to hers, 'Come in.'

9

The funeral for Chanelle Brodie was small and uneventful. *The Sentinel* printed a short obituary and a news article that summarized and in effect, closed the case of her death. The coroner ruled it an accident. The photograph printed with the obituary looked like a school portrait, grainy and white-framed. Chanelle had a round, heart-shaped face, full lips and straight, dark hair. She looked like an average teenager, but Vivian saw something in her eyes, a spark of defiance. Fearlessness, Katherine had called it.

Work on the house proceeded. Twice, Vivian drove into town to deliver clothing and other small household goods to the Salvation Army. There was an old hand-held blender, a metal juicer, a set of hot hair rollers. Boxes of towels and sheets, bags of knick-knacks: candleholders, glass figurines, homey plaques. Things she didn't think anyone wanted, but Vivian felt a twinge with each item. She couldn't help but imagine someone going through her own things after she was gone. The personal items were harder, a drawer of nail polishes and files, a small box of costume jewelry, a gold, silk-trimmed bathrobe. Things that meant nothing to others but probably quite a bit to Grandma Gardiner.

The larger items, the newer things and everything else would be saved for a yard sale. Vivian was getting used to driving the truck. On a third trip into town, she and Nowell saw a matinee and did some grocery shopping. He was in high spirits that day, having just finished a major segment of his book. In the empty theater, they ate popcorn and joked through the entire movie, a mediocre comedy about a man with supernatural powers. Then they went home and lounged in bed until dinnertime. It was a glimmer of their old life.

The crew working on the road was progressing rapidly. In the afternoons when Vivian walked to the mailbox, she could see them at a distance, their trucks and orange flags moving closer until they were over the small hill and finally, nearing the house.

One morning, someone knocked on the door while Nowell was still in the shower. Groggy and squinting in the yellow kitchen, Vivian opened the door in her robe.

'Morning, ma'am.' Five feet from the screen stood a man in an orange vest. 'I'm with the county. We're paving the road out there.' White teeth gleaming from his tanned face, he said this like a question.

She nodded, smoothing her hair back.

'We're set to start in front of your house. You need to get out?'

'I hadn't planned on going anywhere today,' she said.

He leaned back onto his heels. 'We're mostly smoothing and clearing today. Tomorrow we lay the asphalt.'

'So we can get out today?'

He nodded, taking in her legs under the short robe. 'We'll try to get it down early tomorrow. Should take most of the day to set. You'll have to stay put then.'

Vivian noticed his attention and adjusted the robe around her neck. He had broad shoulders, rugged, dirty hands and rough skin. 'Well, thanks for letting me know,' she said.

He nodded, staring.

She closed the door, her face flushed.

Nowell poked his head around the corner. 'Who was that?'

'Someone from that road crew,' she told him. 'They're working out front today and tomorrow, so if we need to go anywhere we should go today.'

'That was fast. I thought it would take them longer.' He walked back into the bathroom, a towel wrapped around his waist.

She thought maybe the road was to be finished in time for the reunion Katherine told her about. It was for the descendants of the town's founder, William Clement, and would be held at the end of the summer. The ballroom at the local Best Western had been rented out and hundreds of people were expected.

The newspaper had run a few stories about the reunion. In a biographical piece about William Clement, Vivian learned he came from old money, much of which he invested in the town. Most of the older downtown section was built under his direction; he financed the construction of the Sheriff Department, the Post Office, and the office building for town officials, which now served as a community center. He populated the buildings with relatives and friends, even appointed his oldest son as the town's first sheriff. He opened a bank and began to help people build homes, run farms and start businesses. Various real estate developments were handled from a corner office with windows that looked out over the plaza where he was now immortalized in bronze.

The newspaper story named a few singular descendants, those who had risen to some level of greatness. One of Clement's sons had served three terms in the state senate, and a granddaughter had a short-lived career on Broadway. Katherine claimed William Clement had sired another batch of descendants with several Native American women who worked for him, but this lesser-respected line was not identified in the article. When Vivian mentioned this to Katherine, she merely laughed and said, 'Who do you think owns the newspaper?'

Her thoughts returned to the construction worker, his bold stare. Why is it always like that, she wondered. You always have to be on guard. And yet a part of her was flattered and excited, and she couldn't help but pull back the kitchen curtains to catch a glimpse of the crew where they worked further down the road.

In high school, a boy had taken Vivian to a party then abandoned her near a cavernous overpass, a concrete structure lined with yellow lights, when she wouldn't do what he wanted. He was a popular boy, one whom everyone liked and admired, and up until his fit of anger, Vivian had been feeling quite special. As he drove off, she pulled her jacket around her throat and watched the receding taillights. Then she walked to a convenience store and called home. Her mother was up late reading.

Once Vivian was inside the family Buick, her mother stared at her. 'Are you all right?' she finally asked.

'Yes,' Vivian said.

'You smell like a brewery.'

Vivian didn't answer. Being in the car, drunk, with her mother, was surreal. Outside, things looked strange and desolate and lonely. The sole cashier in the mini-mart watched them over the stacks of newspapers.

Her mother turned the car onto the empty road. 'So what happened?'

'I told you,' she said, 'I couldn't get a ride home.'

'I thought that boy who picked you up would be bringing you back.'

'So did I.'

'If he drank as much as you, I hope he's not driving.'

She shrugged.

'Listen, Vivian, I'm relieved that you called me.' She ran her hand through her curly reddish hair.

From the side angle, Vivian could see smudges on her oval glasses, places where her fingers had been.

'I even understand this rebellion to some extent,' her mother said in a practical tone. A lecture tone. 'It's very natural, I suppose. I don't want to make a big deal out of it.'

'Good,' she said, thinking: here it comes.

'What I am concerned about, however, is your general lack of purpose. You're not getting the kind of grades that'll get you into a good college.'

Vivian groaned.

'That's what I mean. You'd cut off your nose to spite me. Why? If I told you not to go to college, would it make you want to go?'

'I don't know.' She leaned her head against the seat and closed her eyes.

'I suppose you don't know much of anything right now, do you? In your present condition...' Her voice droned on and on and in a weak moment Vivian wished she could tell her about Scott Ridling, about the smooth ride in his Camaro and the way his blue eyes glinted when he laughed. About the awed expressions on the faces of her friends that day he crossed the concrete court-yard and asked her to the party, and about the way her skirt swished lightly over her thighs when they danced together. But her mother's world was too matter-of-fact for such things. She would say Vivian didn't need Scott or his approval, which Vivian, in her rational mind, already knew very well. But that wasn't the point. He had made her feel small and she needed rebuilding. And she realized that once again, she'd have to do it herself. Her mother didn't have the tools.

In the afternoon, Vivian went out to retrieve the mail. She had just showered, and her wet hair slapped against her back as she walked. The dirt road in front of the house was smooth and packed, and the crew was working some distance away, about a hundred yards toward town. One man drove the roller truck over the thick asphalt, another marched ahead directing him, and a third leaned against a hand-held stop sign. The man with the sign looked over and held up his hand. It was the one she had spoken to earlier. She raised her hand and turned abruptly, careful to pace herself up the driveway, feeling his gaze on her back. At the side of the house, she glanced over her shoulder and caught him watching her through the scattered trees.

She wasn't ready to go inside. She dropped the mail on the

porch and proceeded toward the backyard. She stopped at the well Nowell showed her the day she arrived. Behind the brush and beyond the small shed, the well blended into its surroundings, its brick like the reddish parts of the earth, its chain and bucket like the drooping, leaf-heavy branches of the trees. Leaning over the side, she smelled mildew and metal. She picked up a small stone, dropped it inside, and waited for the small plunging sound. She listened to the sound of her name echoed down the cold tunnel, felt a chill on her face as it faded then disappeared.

In the backyard, the sun beamed hot over the trees. She turned to see if Nowell was watching her through the window of his study, but the curtains were closed. She walked down the slope toward the line of trees that stood unyielding, their backs turned. They were closer than she had thought. She kept walking until she was immersed; their wide scaly trunks smelled old and sharp and their shiny leaves were a fluttering palette of greens. Vivian kicked earth up as she walked. A chirping sound came from her left and over-head, something scampered through a tree, the weight of its body rustling the leaves. She walked for some time, careful to look back once and again to keep track of how to get back. Through the density of trees, a rust-colored object caught her eye, appearing then disappearing among the wide trunks. Vivian watched for a moment. A sudden cracking sound echoed through the woods. She strained her eyes and made out a shirt, a flash of face. Must be that Mr Stokes, she thought. He's cutting wood. She turned around and began to retrace her steps. A snapping sound rever-berated as another log splintered, but this time the noise was followed by a long wail. Vivian perked her ears.

'Ohhhhh.'

She realized that the wailing was coming from the opposite direction. She was disoriented, looking one way then the other.

'Oh, my poor baby.'

Vivian ran toward the edge of the trees. It seemed to take a long time but finally, the grassy field of their backyard appeared in glimpses through the trunks. She stopped. Three figures stood in the high grass at the peak of the gradual slope. The one in the middle, a woman, leaned on the arm of the tall man next to her. By his hat and bearing, Vivian recognized him as Sheriff Townsend. The three began to descend towards the woods.

Behind her, she heard a branch snap.

'Of course I'm sure,' the woman said loudly, 'I've got to see where my baby, I've got to, ohhh.' Her voice faded and then, she gasped.

Vivian had emerged from the trees.

The sheriff, the woman, and the third person, whom Vivian now saw to be his deputy, stopped. They stared at her across the high grass.

'Who's that?' Sheriff Townsend called.

'Vivian Gardiner,' she called back.

'Oh, Mrs Gardiner.'

She kept walking and when she had almost reached them, Bud stepped to the side, looked over her shoulder, and said incredulously, 'Now who could that be?'

As they followed his gaze, a rust-colored figure emerged from the trees, walking purposely toward them into the light.

Vivian heard a whooshing sound, like air pressed out of a cushion, and she turned back in time to see the sheriff reach across and catch the woman as she swooned, her knees buckling underneath her.

10

Sheriff Townsend steadied the woman, who shook her head and pressed a palm to her cheek. Vivian, the deputy and Mr Stokes stood a short distance away, watching her.

Vivian turned to Mr Stokes and whispered, 'You scared me back there.'

His eyebrows raised but he didn't answer.

The woman said, 'I'm sorry. I don't feel well.'

'You had a fright when Mrs Gardiner came out of the woods,' the sheriff told her. 'This is Mrs Brodie,' he explained. 'She's here to see where we found Chanelle.'

'I'm so sorry about what happened,' Vivian said, realizing as she spoke that it wasn't quite the right thing to say.

Mr Stokes shifted on his feet. 'Mrs Brodie,' he said.

The haziness melted from Mrs Brodie's face as the full realization of where she was and why she was there came back to her. Vivian wondered if she woke each day like that, forgetting for a few peaceful moments about her daughter's death, only to suddenly and painfully remember. At Grandma Gardiner's house, in the sleepy, early mornings, Vivian stared at the vague outlines of the furniture before they sharpened and took shape, smelling the unfamiliar scents of the house, the old wood of the doors and the starchy sheets, until she remembered where she was. Perhaps it was like that for Mrs Brodie, she thought, the slow focusing of perception.

Vivian pictured a teenage girl with a round, childish face sprawled awkwardly over a large boulder. Her long hair was dark like Vivian's, her face expressionless. The defiance of the obituary photo was gone; only a crumbled form, a spent energy. The girl's arms were down at her sides.

Mrs Brodie regained her footing and the sheriff let go.

'Like I mentioned,' he told her, 'Mrs Gardiner and her husband are staying in Betty Gardiner's place for a while.'

Mrs Brodie smoothed her sweater. 'It's nice to meet you.' Tears flooded her eyes. Her eyelashes left brushstrokes of mascara on her skin.

Mr Stokes pulled a handkerchief from his back pocket and stepped across the short distance to hand it to her.

The policemen took Mrs Brodie to the edge of the trees. In their tan uniforms, they blended immediately into the background; only Mrs Brodie's vibrant sweater, an unnatural green, was visible as they weaved in and out of the tree trunks.

Soon, Vivian and Mr Stokes could see nothing. 'How far back did they find her?' she asked him.

'Not too far. About halfway between the end of my property and where you were a minute ago.'

'I don't know where the property lines are,' she said.

'Don't you though?' Mr Stokes's eyes seemed to taunt her, like the evening they met.

She felt defensive. 'No, I really don't. How far would you say it is?'

He opened his mouth then closed it. She realized she may have misjudged him. He had no reason to accuse her of anything.

Mr Stokes rubbed his chin. His rust-colored shirt was tucked into a loose-fitting pair of jeans. The sleeves were rolled up to his elbows and the top button was undone. Perspiration dotted his

73

brow and moistened the chest hairs that poked through the shirt. He appeared to be about forty-five, older than she had originally thought. He had a well-used, tanned face with deep wrinkles at the corners of his eyes and creases in his forehead. The day was hot, but Vivian couldn't imagine that he ever wore shorts or short-sleeved shirts. He was just one of those types of men, old-fashioned and modest.

'Listen,' she said, 'I'm sorry if I barked at you. I was flustered when I saw you in the woods.'

He nodded. 'Maybe you shouldn't walk around back there by yourself.'

'I don't see any reason why not,' she said.

He shook his head. 'Not just 'cause of the Brodie girl. It's easy to get lost when you're not used to the area. All those trees start to look the same. Maybe it's not someplace you'd get lost for days, but you sure could spend most of an afternoon wandering around in there. We're the biggest animals around here, but there are raccoons and good-sized squirrels that might scare you.'

'I've seen squirrels before,' Vivian said. 'They don't scare me.'

Mr Stokes grinned, revealing hidden laugh lines and straight, clean teeth. 'No, I don't suppose they do. I didn't mean to tell you your business. That other fella at your place didn't like me telling him what to do either.'

'What other fellow?'

'A few weeks ago. Tall, strapping guy?'

'Oh, Lonnie.'

'I saw him back there a couple of times, walking around. One night there was smoke coming up through the trees, so I came over to make sure everything was all right. He was cooking a pie or something, down in the ground.'

'Apple cobbler,' she said.

'A real outdoorsman,' Mr Stokes said, and Vivian couldn't tell how he meant it.

Lonnie had a rough, natural quality; at least to her, he seemed more at home outside. His career choice in construction attested to this, as did his hobbies: hunting, fishing, camping. How the two brothers grew up so differently was difficult to say. Vivian wasn't much for nature, either. After eloping, Lonnie and his wife pitched a tent in the mountains for a week, which wasn't her idea of a honeymoon at all. Grandma Gardiner's house, surrounded by trees, tall grass and birdsong, was as close to nature as she ever wanted to get.

'Nice fella,' Mr Stokes added. The sun highlighted the silver amidst his dark hair.

'What did you tell him?' she asked.

'When?'

'You said that he didn't like it when you told him what to do.'

'Oh.' He chuckled. 'I did my Smokey the Bear impression, about starting fires in the woods.'

Vivian laughed.

'Mrs Gardiner,' he said, meeting her eyes. 'Do you suppose you could do me a favor?'

Vivian felt a churning in her stomach, a slight warning. 'Oh, sure.'

'Just call me Abe, that's all. Everyone in this town calls me Mr and it makes me feel awful old.' He looked down, kicked at the dirt almost shyly. 'I think it's because my father insisted on it for himself. But I'm not my father.'

She smiled, relieved. 'Only if you'll call me Vivian.'

Mrs Brodie returned, the sheriff leading her by the elbow. Her face was pale, but she held herself erect and walked with recovered confidence, a comfortable awareness of her body that Vivian envied.

Mr Stokes said goodbye and headed home beyond the tree line. Vivian walked Mrs Brodie and the police to the driveway.

'Damn car is covered with dust from that road work,' the sheriff said. 'But it's about time we got some civilization around here. You'd think we're in the backwoods, the way the county doles out money.'

Mrs Brodie reached out and clasped Vivian's hand. 'Thanks for letting us on your land.'

'It's not my...' Vivian started, but stopped. 'You're welcome,' she said, and that seemed wrong too.

'We'll meet again, when this is, well, at a better time,' Mrs Brodie said. Daintily, she reached for Sheriff Townsend's arm.

The police car drove slowly over the packed dirt of the road and headed toward town. Vivian picked up the mail from the porch and looked through it. An assortment of advertisements, an electricity bill, a letter from Nowell's agent. The road crew's machinery was abandoned on the embankment. The dirt road was even and smooth, ready for asphalt in the morning.

Nowell was standing in the kitchen when she got to the door. 'Where were you?' he called through the screen. 'Did you see the sheriff?'

'Yeah. And the deputy, and that girl's mother.'

'What happened?' He pushed the door open.

She walked under his outstretched arm into the kitchen. 'Nothing, really. Mrs Brodie almost passed out when she saw me coming out of the woods.'

'The woods? What were you doing back there?'

'I went for a walk.'

'I don't know if you should be back there, Viv.'

'Why not?' She spun around. 'Doesn't anyone read the newspaper around here? What happened to that girl was an accident.'

'You don't know your way around.'

'It's not the forest,' she said, 'and I'm not a child.'

'All right, all right.' Nowell put his hands up in surrender. 'What happened with the sheriff?'

'Mrs Brodie wanted to see the spot where they found her. I talked to Mr Stokes while they went back.'

'Mr Stokes?'

'You remember, our neighbor?'

Nowell nodded. 'Did he say anything?'

'Who?'

'The sheriff.'

'About what?' she asked.

'I don't know, whether they'd be coming back. I thought that was important to you, his future contacts.'

'I think it's over now,' she said.

Nowell took a drink from a bottle of juice and it dribbled down the side of his mouth. He cursed and swiped his hand across his face, then pushed past her into his study. Sometimes, he just seemed to shut down, to leave the conversation without any notice. His moods fluctuated without warning. An artistic temperament, she told herself.

She thought about what Mr Stokes said about Lonnie, about him being an outdoorsman. Nowell and Lonnie were almost the same height and both had the wide brown eyes of their mother. Certain parts of their faces were similar: the curve of the jawbone, the high square forehead, and they had the same shade of dark brown hair. With beards, they looked less alike. Nowell's had a reddish hue while Lonnie's matched his hair exactly, dark and thick. And Lonnie was heavier than Nowell, more muscular from physical work and fleshier because of his appetites.

Vivian often felt sorry for Lonnie. He couldn't seem to get anything right in his life and he continually spurned the efforts of the one person who had always tried to protect him, Nowell. Lonnie called his brother 'Number One', because Nowell was born first, but also to imply that he was favored in the family. Sometimes Nowell wouldn't hear from Lonnie for months at a time. He faded in and out of their lives.

When Nowell was born, his father Sherman went to a bar and drank until he passed out. The bar was full of people whose loved ones were in the hospital, and Sherman's news was rare and joyous. They plied him with scotch-and-sodas until his forehead hit the oak table. Sherman's father-in-law came and took him home, and his hangover lasted until two days later, when he drove his wife and the squalling baby home. Nowell's mother said despite how lousy he felt, Sherman passed around cigars and toasted with seltzer water. She could put a favorable light on anything related to her husband or sons. Nowell would always say he couldn't picture his dad getting drunk like that, and Beverly would explain that he'd been too polite to refuse the drinks everyone sent over. She liked telling the story of Nowell's birth. She and Sherman were in their mid-thirties when they started a family. After Nowell, Lonnie followed, thirteen months later. The story of Lonnie's birth was mostly a litany of complaints about how late he was in coming, and how much Beverly had been suffering through the surprise pregnancy with her swollen ankles, sore back and a heavy toddler.

Sherman spent the early years of their marriage building his appliance repair business. He started out with a truck and a tool set and finished with a partner, twelve employees and a fleet of six vans. Nowell said his father didn't care that neither of his sons wanted to be involved with the business. Vivian suspected that from Nowell, Sherman expected greater things, and he didn't think Lonnie capable. Because Sherman died suddenly of a heart attack earlier in the same year that she met Nowell, Vivian never met him.

Lonnie had a certain wariness, like something freed from a trap. But he could also be reckless, with no regard for authority. The first time Vivian met him, he was unemployed and living with his mother again after a few years out on his own. She didn't know then that these ups and downs were the normal circumstance of his life. In the past six years, Lonnie had moved back home twice, changed jobs at least six or seven times, and more recently, married on impulse. The last time they saw him was at Beverly's house, over a year ago.

They were having a weekend visit. Lonnie arrived unexpectedly at six a.m. He threw open the door to the guest room and woke them up, threatening to cannonball onto the bed between them.

'Don't do it,' Nowell warned.

'All right, but get up already. Me and Ma have been awake for hours.'

'When did you get here?'

'Around three.' Lonnie stood in the doorway, filling it almost, his face spread into a wide, expectant grin.

Nowell rubbed his eyes. 'Why aren't you sleeping?'

'Come on, you know it's not my nature to be tired.'

Nowell laughed. 'Yeah, right.'

'Hey, Number One, I think your wife is dead. Vivian? How can you sleep like that, so straight? You look like a corpse.'

'Very easily when people aren't yelling,' she told him.

'Right.' He put his finger over his lips and backed up. Nowell threw his pillow, barely missing Lonnie as he closed the door.

They played Hearts that day, the two brothers against Vivian and Beverly. Vivian and Nowell had a policy not to play cards as a team if they could help it. They each had different reasons: Nowell because he thought her playing inferior and Vivian because she didn't want him bullying her. They both said it was to prevent arguments, which was, generally speaking, the truth. In the afternoon, the brothers went out for a while and Vivian and Beverly watched a movie on television then started making dinner.

Lonnie and Nowell returned after six-thirty, high-spirited and smelling of liquor.

'Hitting the bars so early?' Beverly asked.

Nowell smiled. 'They're open all day.'

'Looks like you both could use some dinner.' She pointed to the table and said, 'Sit.'

As they ate, Vivian and Beverly couldn't help being influenced by their good humor. Nowell told a story about the skinny kid who broke Lonnie's collarbone when he was twelve. The crux of the story was amazement such a small boy could have done injury to the mighty Lonnie, who was stocky and tall even then. Nowell described the boy to them as mere skin and bones, a wiry nine-year-old who collided with Lonnie during a game of street baseball. 'He rounded second and ran smack into him at shortstop.' He turned to Lonnie. 'He got a home run off your team, didn't he?'

'How would I know?'

'You know, you just don't want to remember.'

They laughed for some time at Lonnie's unease, expecting a reciprocal story from him, an attempt to embarrass Nowell. But he just grinned. It wasn't until Nowell fell asleep early and Beverly turned in as well that Lonnie's mood began to darken. He said he was going to visit an old friend. Vivian suspected he returned to the bar. When he got back, she was watching television in the darkened living room.

Lonnie sat on the couch and kicked his shoes onto the floor. 'What are you watching?'

'Some old movie. How was your friend?'

'Fine, everything's fine.' His eyes were watery in the greenish light of the television, his face blurred in the dimness.

'That's good.'

'Nowell's a good guy,' Lonnie said.

'What?' She glanced at him, noticed his intent look.

'He's smart and talented, Dad always said.'

'Hey, Lonnie, I was going to make some coffee. Do you want some?' She got up from her armchair and started to walk past him, but he grabbed her arm and pulled her onto the couch.

'You know that, don't you Vivian? He's got everything, always has.' His face was close to hers, his breath heavy with liquor.

'Lonnie, let go.' She tried to pull her arm away and stand up, but he grabbed her around the waist with his other hand.

'You know what he doesn't have? Honesty. He's dishonest to himself. He doesn't see things that are right in front of his eyes. I'm not like that and I don't think you are either.'

'Let me go,' she said again, and her voice was menacing enough that he released her.

'You've dealt with guys like me before, right Vivian? Look, I didn't mean to scare you. I'm just trying to tell you, he needs help.'

'Nowell needs help?' She stepped away from him. Such a waste, she thought, his continual running and running and never getting anywhere. Her legs shook but before she left the room, she managed to say in a steady voice: 'Take another look, Lonnie.'

In that way, maybe the brothers were alike. Mood shifts, inexplicable moments of barely constrained something. It was something she had to live with, but she didn't have to acknowledge it. She picked up the letter from Nowell's agent and stepped down into his study.

11

Nowell was quiet as he read the letter from his agent.

'What does Dani have to say?' Vivian asked.

'Nothing much. She sent me a copy of the magazine ad.' He dropped a paper onto the kitchen table.

'For your book? Let me see.' Vivian looked at the advertisement, which was less than two inches square and printed along the side of a page. The title, *Random Victim*, arched across the top in vivid, wavering letters, like a scream.

Nowell hadn't been allowed much input on the cover. Dani had chosen an impressionistic drawing of a dark, menacing figure with large, shadowed eyes. Swirling black clouds hovered over his head. The image was made up of thousands of tiny dots, like the photo of her mother in the writing workshop brochure.

Vivian sat on Nowell's lap. 'It's a great ad,' she said. 'I'm glad she got them to put some more effort into marketing it.'

'I'm not sure it'll matter,' he said. 'It's been out for quite a while.'

'Did you get any work done today?' Vivian asked.

'Some. The phone kept ringing while you were out. I have to tell you something and I don't think you're going to like it.'

She leaned back to see him more clearly. 'What?'

'I have to drive over to my mom's. I'm meeting with her lawyer the day after tomorrow.'

'Okay.'

He raised his eyebrows. 'That's it?'

She shrugged. 'I know you have to go.'

'I'll leave tomorrow,' he said. 'I should be back the day after by seven or eight o'clock.'

'At night?'

He nodded. 'Are you sure you don't want to go with me?'

Vivian stood up. 'No, I've got plenty to do around here. How about sandwiches for dinner tonight?'

'Sounds good to me.'

In the refrigerator she found a loaf of the deli bread and a package of sliced ham. They also had some leftover potato salad and peach pie for dessert.

Nowell came into the kitchen. 'Are you sure you don't mind staying out here alone? I hadn't thought about the fact you won't have a car. It's a long drive, but I don't think we should spend money on airfare.'

'I'll be fine. I can call Katherine if I need anything.'

'My mom's not going to be around much while I'm there. She's gotten herself involved with another function at the church, a summer barbecue or something. My dad used to say she lets people bully her into doing all the work. I think he was right. Don't you remember that situation with that woman, what was her name?'

'Nona.'

'Yes, Nona. My mom met her at some card club and the next thing you know, she's moving into Lonnie's old room with her kid.'

'Your mother likes to help people.'

'Helping and being taken advantage of are two different things.'

The woman, Nona, told Beverly she needed a place to stay for a month while she got back on her feet. She had a little boy, three years old, who was completely undisciplined, almost wild. Nona was slovenly, lacked motivation to do anything but watch soap operas and late at night, her estranged boyfriend would climb through her window.

Nowell grabbed a slice of ham from the counter and chewed it loudly. 'One time my mom gave away my dad's golf clubs for a charity auction. I don't think he talked to her for a week. I never saw him golf, not once. My mom called him selfish.'

Vivian brought the food to the table. 'Your dad had a strong personality, didn't he?'

'What do you mean?'

'I don't know, controlling?'

'No,' Nowell said. 'He was opinionated. I remember eating out at restaurants and being embarrassed sometimes by the way he talked to people. That's all. He was strong and he worked hard. He always encouraged me, told me I could do anything I wanted.'

They were quiet for a few moments as they ate. Outside, the sound of the asphalt truck droned. Remembering what Katherine had said, Vivian asked, 'Did your dad come out here much to visit your grandmother?'

'No. My mom and grandma didn't exactly get along, and Dad was always so busy. After he entered into partnership with Mr Ward, he started doing some traveling for the company. He kept himself pretty busy.'

'How often do you think he visited her?'

Nowell set down his sandwich. 'Why?'

'Katherine thought he came out pretty often, a couple of times a year.'

He shook his head. 'He hardly ever took a vacation or a sick day.'

'But you said he always took care of your grandma.'

'My grandfather died when he was only fifteen – the hunting accident – and he became the man of the family. My aunts were older, one in college already. For a while it was just my dad and grandma out here. He stayed until he was almost twenty-two.'

'Why didn't he go to college?'

'Felt like he had to work, I guess. My mom says my grandma had a strong hold on him. She says when he finally left, he moved four hours away to put some distance between them.'

Vivian thought it sounded similar to Nowell's relationship with his mother. She said, 'It's strange he wouldn't visit more, after they'd been so close.'

'He still took care of her,' Nowell said, an edge creeping into his voice. 'He called her and helped her with things.'

'Didn't you ever come out here when you were little?'

'A few times. Lonnie loved it. He'd spend hours in the woods. He had a Davy Crockett hat back then, raccoon skin with a tail. One time, he got lost back there and when he came in, he wouldn't admit to it. I thought my dad was going to beat the hell out of him. I think he was scared, my dad. I never realized that until later.'

Vivian thought about the family photograph that Beverly still kept on the mantle of her fireplace. The two brothers, Nowell and Lonnie, were tall and gangly teenagers, with large Adam's apples and protruding collarbones. Lonnie looked robust in a plaid shirt with silver snaps and embroidered pockets, while the deep blue of Nowell's velour sweater made his complexion seem sallow. They stood on either side of their father, surrounding their mother, who sat with her legs primly crossed on a high-backed, ornate chair. Sherman looked into the camera lens with an intense expression. He had broad shoulders and thick gray eyebrows that almost met in the center. Both of his large hands gripped the back of his wife's chair, and each of the brothers had one hand on the chair, on the engraved mahogany finials with their bulbous ends. Lonnie grinned affably, but Nowell's expression was forced, his close-mouthed smile threatening to turn into a frown. Beverly's grin was the brightest and most genuine, her lips curving up to tiny red points that dug into her heavily rouged cheeks, her gums showing pink above her teeth. But Sherman was the centerpiece of the photo. He was a striking man.

Nowell packed a few things for his trip and telephoned his mother to let her know he was coming. Vivian decided to work in the attic. When she had safely climbed the narrow stairs, she stood and surveyed her previous work, a feeble effort to form three large stacks: things to discard, things to keep, things to ask Nowell about. These stacks spilled and crowded into each other and she had to concentrate for a moment to remember which was which.

She found a box of board games, many of which she recognized from her own childhood: Life, Risk, Sorry. She put the box in the pile with the other things to ask Nowell about. In the top drawer of a short dresser, she was surprised to find folded clothing, a man's white undershirts. She held one up, noticing its size, extra-extra large. Behind the shirts was a stack of boxer shorts. She opened a garbage bag and scooped the underclothes from the drawer. The second drawer held stale-smelling linens – Grandma Gardiner never threw away a cloth napkin, Vivian thought – and she threw those in as well. The third drawer was empty. The bottom drawer held a few scarves and a variety of boxes. One was a series of boxes, one nested into another. She thought of her mother, who also saved any jewelry box she was ever given. One leather-covered box held a tarnished watch, another a set of cuff links. She set those aside to show Nowell. And when she had cleared out the boxes and slammed the drawer, she heard something clatter and had to go back through, opening and closing drawers until she found what was making the noise: a gun. Carefully, she picked it up. Like the other items, it was old. Probably doesn't even work, Vivian thought. Nevertheless, she was careful to keep it pointed away from her body. She set it on top of the dresser. She wondered if it had been Grandpa Gardiner's. Lonnie would probably want it, she thought. She'd have to ask Nowell what to do with it. Hanging from the back of the bureau was a bag, which held the blue suit she had seen before, two pairs of blue jeans, a pair of olive green dress slacks, all men's, and three shirts that were similar to each other, short-sleeved with collars. Everything was pressed nicely, hanging in thin plastic bags.

The clothing was too modern to have belonged to Nowell's grandfather. Were they Sherman's? Vivian wondered. And why are these clothes here? If, as Katherine had claimed, Sherman visited often enough to warrant use of a dresser, why didn't Nowell know about these visits? Was the gun Sherman's?

She decided to take a board game downstairs and finish the attic later. Maybe Nowell would play Life with her. Diane, her best friend in grammar school, had a Life game and whenever Vivian stayed for a sleepover, they played. Vivian seldom had anyone to play games with; her parents usually suggested she read a book instead.

In Life, she always hoped to land on the square awarding graduation from medical school, because being the doctor paid the most money. After obtaining a profession, she and Diane moved the plastic cars around the board, filling them with little pegs when they landed on the squares for children. This was the most elaborate part of the game, because they'd name their pretend children with first, middle and last names, and keep them all in order, often going around an extra time and filling a second car with progeny.

Vivian thought about Nowell's desire to have a child. He hadn't brought up the subject again since her first night at the house and she was glad. She didn't comprehend her position enough to defend it. She imagined having a family in the future, in an abstract manner much like putting little blue and pink pegs into the plastic Life cars. She didn't think she was ready, but she couldn't really understand or explain why. Nowell, on the other hand, presented having a child as the next logical step in the order of their lives, and she couldn't compete with him, couldn't argue her way out of it. At best she could stall him while she figured out what it was, exactly, she wanted to say.

She decided to take Sorry downstairs instead. Nowell was sitting in the living room, watching television. 'All packed?' she asked.

'Yeah. What do you have there?'

'Sorry. Wanna play?'

'Maybe later.'

She put the game on the coffee table and sat next to him on the couch.

Nowell said, 'I want to give you some pages from the new book to read while I'm gone. The first two chapters. I'm trying something a little different this time, and I want to see what you think of it.'

'It's another mystery, right?'

He nodded. 'Mostly, I'm experimenting with point of view. I mean, with who tells the story, whose insights and thoughts you get.'

'I think I know what point of view is. First person, third person, right?'

'Exactly. I don't want to tell you too much about what I'm doing because the readers will have to make certain discoveries as they go along. For instance, you may not know who is speaking at first, but I want to make sure it's not too evasive or confusing.'

'The last novel was from the detective's point of view?'

'Pretty much. It was third person, but the emphasis was on the detective. You got mostly his thoughts, but some insight into others. I thought it would be interesting to limit perspective even more, to really get a look inside what's going on with one person. Anyway, read it and let me know what you think.'

'Okay,' she said. It seemed to her that all you could ever truly get was one person's perspective, your own. But she'd read it and hopefully, see what Nowell meant.

He asked her to wait until he was gone, but after he went to bed that evening, Vivian read the first chapter in the yellow glare of the kitchen. The writing had the same doomed tone as the piece she'd found on the printer, the short paragraphs describing a young girl walking with purpose, beckoning, and the restless man who watched her. These pages told a similar story, but the circumstances had been altered.

Each day as she walked over the hill toward the house, she hoped that the man would be waiting. Some days he was there, pacing through the empty rooms and others, he wasn't. But she could feel him on the days she couldn't see him, watching her as she moved her hips from side to side and swished her hair over her back, bare under the thin straps of her blouse, concave between the shoulder blades.

Each day she grew bolder, coming closer and closer to the picture windows until finally one day she was peering through them, her hands pressed against the cool glass and her slim nose leaving the slightest smudge mark. She wondered what she would do if he came out, if he answered the unspoken challenge of the past few weeks.

She started to think about going in. It wouldn't take much, just a screwdriver applied to a rusty lock or pressed into the crack of a window. It infuriated her that he watched her as she watched him. After several days of thinking along these lines, she knew it had to end.

The chapter included fragments of the girl's troubled childhood, the mistreatment by her parents and her virtual abandonment at the age of fourteen. As Nowell had feared, Vivian was confused by the perspective. The girl's voice was unsettled and seemed to have too much insight. She was glad she'd have some time to decide what to tell him. She hid the pages in a kitchen cupboard and went to bed.

The next morning, Nowell went into his study for a few hours before he left. Vivian was sitting with her coffee when someone knocked on the door.

The road crew worker was there, looking at her boldly. 'We're all set to lay asphalt. I wanted to let you know. I noticed you didn't go anywhere yesterday, so if you need to get out today, we'll leave a narrow path you can use. Your truck should handle it fine.' He motioned toward the red truck. Emphasized against his tanned face, his teeth were bright white.

Vivian's eyes adjusted to the morning sun; she noticed the direction of his gaze. 'When do you think you'll finish the road?'

'We still got a ways to go. The end of summer, I guess.' He pointed with his hat toward the south side of the house. 'Would it be all right if we used your faucet out here for water? Gonna be hot as hell today.'

Vivian remembered the hook-up under the kitchen window. 'No problem.'

'Thanks.' He looked again at her legs then paused on the bottom step of the porch. 'Will you be going out then?'

'My husband may leave for a while,' she said, 'but he'll be back.' The man's bold look disconcerted her. The way he'd monitored her actions yesterday, his notice of the truck and the faucet. It all seemed intrusive.

'See you around.' His eye teeth caught sunlight like mirrors as he gave her one last thorough look.

Vivian irritably shut the door. She poured the rest of her coffee down the sink, her face burning hot from the encounter.

Katherine had invited her to dinner when she'd heard Nowell would be gone. Vivian thought Nowell might have called her. 'I'll come and pick you up,' Katherine had said. 'You don't have to worry about a thing.'

After lunch and a sweaty session in the back bedroom, Nowell left. As promised, the men working on the road stopped to direct him out of the driveway. Vivian watched from the kitchen window as the brake lights of the truck flickered then extinguished; the tires kicked up a haze of dust.

She stayed in most of the afternoon. In Nowell's study, she ran the vacuum cleaner, something she hadn't been able to do since her arrival. He had left everything orderly and neat. On the corner of the desk, clean white paper was stacked next to the computer monitor, but there was nothing on the printer tray.

The antique secretary didn't allow much space to work. Four small drawers with keyholes and little ivory handles were set above the desktop; two of these were partially obscured by the computer monitor. Vivian touched the smooth handles. They were all locked. The drawer beneath the desktop was locked as well. She could hear its contents shift as she pulled on it. She realized Nowell must have the key.

There were things that Vivian didn't understand about her husband, like his craving for privacy and his occasional secrecy. Sometimes his periods of withdrawal were followed by an outpouring of confidence that dazed her. One winter evening, early in their relationship, he had talked to her about his father's death and cried. It was the first time she had felt that they might have a future together. He told her about his fear that he had disappointed his father, and she felt an overwhelming urge to comfort him. At other times, he left a distance between them that howled like wind, an empty chasm she was often too stubborn or too preoccupied to cross. She consoled herself with excuses like sometimes people have to work things out alone.

Besides, she had her own secrets. Whenever she began resenting Nowell's guardedness, she thought about how it comforted her to think of her own private self, buffeted and protected and perhaps mostly unknown even to herself. If Nowell told her everything about himself, what would that leave to discover, to talk about?

One weekend he showed up at her dorm room at seven in the morning, and they drove most of the day to a small town in the mountains, to the site of a wine festival he'd heard about on the radio. They washed their feet and jumped into the big vats; fleshy grapes pressed between their toes, staining their feet purple to the ankles. There were baked goods and ham cooked over an open fire, and the fruity wine sticky in their throats. Nowell was the type of person everyone in a group strained to hear speak. Only with Vivian was he quiet. The more time they spent alone, the more she missed the public side of him, the engaging person he could be in social settings.

She went out to get the mail. The men were working past the house now, but directly in front of the driveway, the road was finished. The fresh asphalt glittered in the afternoon sun, smelling like oil and sweat. Vivian was determined to let the man know he hadn't bothered her that morning. He was assigned to sign duty again and when he saw Vivian's wave, he raised his hard hat. She got the mail and turned back, feeling his eyes over the tall, wild grass, over the waves of heat rising from the new black road. But she had made her point.

The day was a scorcher, as he had predicted. Vivian decided to clean herself up before Katherine arrived. In the midst of her shower, the water suddenly turned scalding hot, and she hopped around until she could turn it off. As she reached for a towel, she heard the squeaky sound of a faucet and remembered telling the man that he could use their water. He had ruined her shower.

12

The road crew had quit for the day. The hot smell of the new asphalt infiltrated the car, but the road was dry and usable. Katherine wore a bright yellow blouse trimmed with white lace. Her house, also yellow, had brick accents and stood at the crest of a circular driveway. Rose bushes framed the cement steps leading to the front door.

'Max planted those,' Katherine said when she saw Vivian linger. 'I don't have much of a green thumb.'

In the sunny living room, Max greeted them. Slightly shorter than his wife, he grasped Vivian's hand in both of his, grinning widely. 'So nice to finally meet you,' he said.

'Thanks for inviting me,' Vivian replied.

His reddish hair was starting to recede and he had the slight paunch of middle age, but Vivian could envision his younger self in his clear blue eyes and the firm muscles of his arms.

'Sit down, please,' he said. 'You too, honey.'

'Let me show Vivian around the place first,' Katherine said.

There were three bedrooms, each neat and modestly decorated. At the back of the house, the kitchen was large and airy. The rear door led to a screened patio cluttered with greenery. Tall plants in clay pots stood in each corner, and against the house, smaller plants in painted ceramic containers lined two long shelves. Many of the plants were flowering; blooms of purple, pink and white stood out against the buttercup-yellow paint of the wall.

'It's like a greenhouse,' Vivian said.

'This is Max's area. My only contributions are some of those pottery pieces.' She motioned to the shelves. 'Before that quilting class I told you about, I learned how to make pottery down at the arts and crafts store. I bought my own wheel and a small kiln, but I haven't used them much lately.'

'You made these? They look professional.'

Katherine waved her hand in modesty. 'Thanks.'

'That's something I've always wanted to do,' Vivian said.

'It's fun but very tedious. Each step takes a long time. Even the painting – you have to put layer after layer to get it to look right. You think you have enough but when it dries, it looks completely different.' Katherine straightened a green metal chair, pushing it into place under the glass table.

'You must spend a lot of time out here,' Vivian said. 'So cool and shady.'

'We like to have our meals outside during the warmer months. Max always wants to barbecue, like most men. I thought we'd eat out here tonight, if you don't mind.'

'Not at all. I like it out here.'

Max brought out a platter of seasoned chicken and three cold beers, which he placed on blue, fish-shaped coasters. Katherine went into the kitchen, promising to be gone only a few moments.

'This is a great patio,' Vivian told Max.

He opened the valve on the beige tank underneath the gas barbecue grill and adjusted two knobs. 'We spend a lot of time out here.' He closed the lid on the grill. 'We'll just let that heat up.'

She sat at the table. 'I guess Katherine told you my husband is helping his mother with a legal situation.'

Max took a drink of beer; the moisture from the outside of the

94

bottle ran down his forearm in a narrow rivulet. 'I hope it's nothing serious.'

'Not really. His father's gone, so he helps her out now and then.'

'He's a good son.'

Vivian nodded. 'We'll have to return the favor one night, have you and Katherine out to the house for dinner.'

'That would be nice,' Max said. 'She really liked Mrs Gardiner, tried to visit her every couple of weeks.'

'I didn't know her well,' Vivian said.

Katherine brought plates, silverware and folded linen napkins and set them on the table. Vivian thought about her mother's insistence on cloth napkins, never paper, even on weeknights. Sometimes, formal rituals were nice; her mother just overdid it.

'I'll get these, honey,' Max told her.

'Thanks,' Katherine said. 'I've just got a few more minutes on the potatoes, then I'll bring everything else out. Are you going to cook that chicken today or what?'

'Yes, dear.' Max tried to pinch her with the long-handled barbecue tongs, and she laughed and jumped out of the way. He placed the chicken on the grill and poured the juices from the platter over each piece. The meat sizzled and dripped. 'Katherine sure was shook up over the Brodie girl,' he said, 'that night she ran into the sheriff at your place.'

'It was terrible,' Vivian said. 'Mrs Brodie came out the other day to look at the place where they found her.'

'She did?'

She nodded. 'She was very upset, almost fainted.'

'Kitty's an emotional woman by nature, but this time she has every right.'

Vivian took a long drink; the beer glided down her throat, slick as oil. 'Did you go to school with her too?'

'For one year, but mostly I know her from the store. She's very talkative.'

'Have you seen her since the accident?'

'Only once. She brought in some stuff this week.' Max held the tongs aloft like a pointer. 'Strange, isn't it?'

'What?'

'Just the type of accident it was. So senseless.'

She nodded.

He flipped the chicken over, one piece at a time, then sat back down at the table. 'How are you enjoying it out here otherwise?'

'It's very relaxing. I don't know if Katherine told you. I've been working on the house, trying to clean it up.'

'You're going to sell it after a while, right?'

'With any luck,' she said.

'You shouldn't have a problem. The population's been growing for some time. With the improvements to the road, there's bound to be even more people moving in. Better access to the bigger towns. Things will be changing around here, that's for sure. We've already had some developers looking around. A guy stopped in my shop a few months ago, talking about an apartment complex or a mini-mall. I told him my place wasn't for sale presently. But between you and me, I have my price, if he comes back.'

Vivian laughed.

He leaned back in his chair. 'We've always wanted to do some traveling. We stick around here because we know it, and because of family. But I could see myself breaking away some day.' He looked over Vivian's shoulder. 'We always thought we'd take family trips.'

Katherine came through the door with a bowl of salad and a plate of baked potatoes. 'Is the chicken ready?' She asked. 'I just have to grab the bread.'

'All done,' Max answered.

She brought out a loaf of French bread and two more beers.

'Sit down, Katherine,' Vivian said. 'You're making me feel guilty.'

'I'm done. Don't you worry. I'll make you help with the dishes.'

Max brought the chicken to the table. 'She'll work you to death, if you don't watch it. A real tyrant.'

'I shouldn't have opened my mouth,' Vivian teased.

'Max, you know the rules about company.'

Vivian smiled, watching their playful looks and the way their movements coordinated.

'Guess who we ran into at the grocery store last night?' Katherine asked.

'Who?'

'Abraham Stokes.'

'Oh, my neighbor?' Vivian didn't know why, but she was compelled to add: 'Is that his first name, Abraham?' As if she didn't know.

Katherine sliced a baked potato in half, right through the aluminum foil. 'Most everybody I know calls him Mr Stokes. Do you know anyone who calls him different, Max?'

'Mr Garrison calls him Abe. I saw him in there one day when I was buying something for the house.'

'Mr Garrison is the man who waited on us that day at Clement's Hardware,' Katherine explained to Vivian. 'He owns the store. His mother was a Clement, but do you think he would call his store Garrison's Hardware? No way!'

'People have a right to be proud of their heritage,' Max said in a patient tone, as though they'd had the conversation before.

'What about his heritage on his daddy's side? Didn't the Garrisons ever do anything worthwhile? I guess they didn't own a town.'

'Do people still care about that stuff?' Vivian asked.

'You bet they do,' Katherine said. 'Max thinks it's ridiculous too, but he likes to give me a hard time about it.'

'You take it so personally.' Max's blue eyes twinkled. 'You're too passionate, that's your problem. You and your Latino lover music.' He turned to Vivian. 'I can hear it when she pulls up the driveway.'

Katherine rolled her eyes.

'Sometimes I think you wish you'd married a Clement,' he said.

'Sometimes I think you wish that,' Katherine said.

'Not a chance.'

They were quiet for a few moments as they passed dishes.

'This is great,' Vivian said.

'Max is a wizard with the barbecue,' Katherine said. 'He's got most of the domestic talents around here.'

'That's not true,' he said. 'You don't like to cook, so you pretend you're not any good at it.'

Vivian laughed. 'Maybe that's what I do.'

'More bread?' Max asked.

She shook her head.

'She eats like a bird,' Katherine said.

'I do not!'

'It's nothing to be ashamed of. That's why you're so slim. Wouldn't hurt me to learn by your example. She looks great, doesn't she, Max?'

He nodded. 'You must work out.'

'Not really. Most of it is lucky genes. My mother is very thin, always has been.'

'Both of Vivian's parents are professors at a university,' Katherine told him.

'What do they teach?' he asked.

'My father teaches History, and my mother Sociology and some-times, writing classes. She teaches less than he does, because she's also a writer.'

'You're just surrounded by creative types, aren't you?' Katherine said.

Vivian shrugged. 'I guess I am.'

'It must be so interesting having parents like that,' Max said. 'My pop never had much to talk about after a day of dry-cleaning, except stories about the customers.'

'Max learned the business from his dad,' Katherine explained. 'They ran it together until he retired.' She winked at Vivian. 'Don't you want to hear what Mr Stokes said about you?'

She looked up from her plate.

'The poor man was in line at the deli, buying cold cuts and prepared casseroles. People must think you're a bachelor too,' she said to Max, 'the amount of things we buy there.'

'What did he say?' Vivian asked.

'Just that he ran into you that very day, and you were snooping around in the woods.'

'He said that?'

'Not in so many words.'

'Not in any words,' Max interjected. 'He never said snooping.'

'He implied it. He said he was chopping some wood when he saw you, and he gave you quite a scare.'

'That's true,' Vivian admitted. 'I guess the whole thing with that poor girl had me jittery. For God's sake, he had an ax.'

They all laughed.

'He's a strange man, that's for sure,' Katherine said. 'A loner.'

Vivian wiped the corners of her eyes with her napkin. She had laughed a little too hard; she felt loose and warm from the beer.

'He's been on his own a long time,' Max said. 'I feel sorry for him.'

'What about his family?'

'He's lived in that house his whole life,' Katherine told her. 'His parents are both gone now and he was an only child. Never married, although he came close once.'

'You don't know if that story's true,' he objected.

'It's true.'

'Well, what's true is that something happened with him and Ronella Oates. I just don't know if it happened the way people say.'

Vivian leaned forward in her chair. 'What?'

'Mr Stokes is in his early forties now,' Katherine said, 'although he seems older. Not a bad looking man, is he?'

'I guess not,' she said.

'So he was in his early thirties and Ronella was a bit younger than him, maybe late twenties, when things started up. His father,

Jesper Stokes, was still alive then. People say he had no good feelings whatsoever for Ronella.'

'Why?'

She leaned in, her green eyes bright. 'Max and I went to school with her and she was a normal kind of girl. She had gotten married and divorced young, worked down at the bank as a teller. I don't know why the old man didn't like her; maybe he just didn't want his son taken away. If you think the current Mr Stokes is a hermit, you should have seen his father.' She shook her head. 'He never came out of his house, except for long hunting trips. They have some distant relatives over the state line and he'd go for weeks at a time during hunting season. People didn't see young Abe Stokes much either, except when his father was out of town. Then he'd turn up at the tavern, or hang around the hardware store.'

Max got up from the table. 'Do you need another beer, Vivian?'

'No, thanks, but I'll take a glass of water.' She turned to Katherine. 'So what happened with the woman?'

'I've heard it different ways. Some say there was an awful scene one night, when Jesper Stokes came home after a trip and found her there. Others say nothing happened at all. About the ending, everyone agrees. Ronella moved away one day and didn't tell anybody.'

'Where did she go?'

'No one knows. It's a mystery. Her parents still live around here, and two brothers. Nobody's ever heard from her again.'

'Even now?'

'Nope.'

Max handed Vivian a glass of water. 'I thought she called from back east once.'

'I never heard that,' Katherine said.

'One rumor's as good as another.'

She gave him a hard look and turned back to Vivian. 'Then the story changes again. Some people say Mr Stokes went off looking for her, some say he just holed up in that house. He's definitely gotten stranger. His father died a few years later and since then, nobody sees much of him.'

'I've only been here a few weeks and I've seen him twice,' Vivian said.

'That's true,' Katherine said. 'But you're neighbors.'

Max said, 'Vivian says Mrs Brodie went out there.'

'What for?'

'She wanted to see the place they found Chanelle,' Vivian said.

Katherine frowned. 'Now there's a woman who would've driven old Jesper Stokes crazy. Too bad she and Abe Stokes never hit it off. And to think, they've been neighbors all this time and she's never cast her magical spell over him.'

'Now, Katherine,' Max said, 'the woman just lost her only child.'

'I know, but it doesn't change the past. If I didn't trust you so much, I'd worry about her bringing her clothes in for cleaning.' She gave Vivian a strange look, as if she just realized something, then just as quickly, she looked away.

As they sat on the patio, night spread over the land like a thick, black blanket. After they had coffee, Katherine and Max both came along for the drive to Grandma Gardiner's house. The old white house looked dark and abandoned from the road, with the truck gone and only the porch light on. Katherine walked Vivian inside and waited while she turned on lights and checked around.

'Thanks again,' Vivian said. 'It was fun. Max is a great guy.'

Katherine looked around. 'Are you sure you're going to be all right here?'

'Of course.' They walked out onto the porch. Vivian waved to Max in the car then went in and closed the door. Katherine called from outside: 'Lock it.'

Just like a mother, Vivian thought as she locked the deadbolt.

She turned off all the lights except for one lighthouse lamp in the bedroom. The bluish glow extended down the hallway. She followed it to the kitchen, where she poured a glass of water. Through the window in the study she saw a small, bouncing light

101

in the trees, like the flashlights they saw the night she arrived. This time there was only one light, fading rapidly back into the woods as she watched. In a moment it was gone, and she began to doubt whether she'd seen it at all. She listened to the whisper of the trees as they flowed with the night breeze and she strained her eyes, searching over the waves of tall grass and back through the tangled mass of trees in the direction of Abe Stokes's house.

13

Vivian dreamed she was in a room filled with books. On each side, wooden shelves extended from floor to ceiling, stacked with multi-colored spines. A stepladder rolled soundlessly on a narrow track and from the top rung, her father threw books down. They dropped like bombs. Leaping this way and that, she called to him but he ignored her. The books made a loud, slapping sound when they hit the floor.

Like soft fingers tapping against her brow, the sharp, steady impacts echoed in the room that Vivian slowly recognized as Grandma Gardiner's. There was the faint smell of waxy, aged wood and the steam-ironed starchiness of the sheets. There was the oddly colored painting with the green sky and there was the worn armchair in the corner. The thuds continued, becoming more distinct. Slowly, she realized they were coming from outside. Someone was chopping wood, she thought, and in the same instant her mind raced ahead: Abe Stokes.

In a few moments, she was striding through the tall grass of the backyard, the cool blades tickling her ankles, brushing against her calves. She had tucked the T-shirt she wore to bed into denim shorts and slipped on a pair of sandals. The morning sun was low and liquid, spilling over the ground in high contrasts and soft tinges of red and yellow. When she reached the edge of the trees, she looked back and saw her reflection in the window to Nowell's study. From that considerable distance, it was only a flash of color and her long, dark banner of hair. She turned and plunged in. She kept her course straight, first following the chopping sounds then directing herself toward a bluish figure amidst the trees, Vivian soon reached the source of both. She called out: 'Hello!'

Mr Stokes propped the long-handled ax against his shoulder like a baseball bat. 'Mrs Gardiner?'

She entered the small clearing. A log lay across a wide tree trunk that served as a chopping block. Next to the trunk was a small stack of kindling, the wood clean and recently cut. The blue she had noticed through the trees was Abe Stokes's denim shirt. He also wore blue jeans, and his face was flushed from exertion.

He swung the ax and set it down. 'Is something wrong?'

She shook her head, suddenly embarrassed. Why had she come? 'Did the noise wake you?'

Vivian glanced at her wrinkled T-shirt, a souvenir from one of her parents' vacations, and reached up to smooth her hair. 'Not really,' she said. 'I needed to get up anyway.'

'Sometimes I forget that other people are around.' He motioned for her to sit on a smaller log. 'Before Mrs Brodie got that job at the nursing home, she'd come over now and again to complain, but I thought I was in the clear now.'

'And then your new, bothersome neighbors moved in,' Vivian said.

'No,' he grinned. 'I forgot how easily sound travels in the morning. It's one of the reasons I like to get up early. Peaceful.'

'I've been too lazy to notice until now,' Vivian said.

'You don't strike me as the lazy type.'

'Don't I?' She pulled her feet onto the trunk and hugged her knees. 'Maybe it's giving up my job, I don't know. I've been restless lately.'

'What did you do before?'

'My job?'

He nodded.

'I worked in an office, a water management agency.'

'Managing water?' he asked.

She smiled. It sounded misguided, even unnecessary, the way he said it.

He poured coffee from a thermos and gave her the plastic cup-shaped lid. It reminded her of the thermos her father took on their picnics back east, the same one she used at school for several years.

'Where's Mrs Brodie's house from here?' she asked.

He pointed to his right. 'A good distance that way.'

'Do you know her well?'

'We've been neighbors a long time. Almost fifteen years now, ever since old Mrs Duncan died.'

Vivian sipped her coffee. It was strong and tasted of walnut. Abe Stokes cleaned the edge of his ax with a ragged yellow cloth that looked like it used to be part of a curtain then continued to chop wood.

'Why are you cutting so much firewood in the summer?' she asked during one of his pauses.

'It wouldn't do to try and cut it in a snowstorm. Haven't you ever seen squirrels collecting nuts for the winter?'

'The other day you said I might be afraid of squirrels.'

He smiled his lopsided grin. 'If you quit running from them long enough, you'd notice they store things. Didn't you ever have a hamster as a kid?'

'My mother wouldn't allow pets.' She watched as he drove the ax through the log. 'How much wood does one person need?'

'I usually burn a couple of logs a night in the winter months.'

'I guess that adds up,' she said. 'Don't you worry about depleting your supply of trees?'

Mr Stokes put one foot on the trunk and leaned on his knee. His face was serious. 'No, I don't. I only use what I need and I get kindling from what's laying around or from trees that are already dead.'

A few awkward moments passed. She stood up. 'I guess I should get going. I didn't mean...'

'Wait,' Mr Stokes said.

She turned toward him.

His ran his hand through his hair. 'Listen, I know you didn't mean any harm. I'm not so great with people, with conversation.'

'Mr Stokes, don't worry about it. I'm sure you're very responsible with your land.'

The muscles underneath his shirt clenched and released as he gripped the ax. Vivian thought about the story Katherine told her, the woman who abandoned him without warning. 'We all have things that we're sensitive about,' she said.

The glint returned to his clear eyes. 'I thought we agreed you'd call me Abe. Why did you come out here, other than to tell me to stop making such a racket?'

'Actually, I came to give you a hard time about what you said to Katherine and Max Wilton. About my snooping the other day.'

'I didn't...'

'Because if that's what you think, you're wrong. I was just enjoying nature, like you this morning.' She crossed her arms and looked up at him through her eyelashes.

'That's it, is it?'

'Yes,' she said. 'That's all.'

Abe Stokes took an awkward drink from the narrow opening of the thermos then wiped his lips with his sleeve. Vivian thought about the way her father dabbed the corners of his mouth with a napkin, first one side and then the other. She heard a rustle in the trees.

'Good thing for squirrels,' Mr Stokes said. 'They help spread around more trees.'

'What?' Vivian said.

The sunlight cast geometric shapes on his chest and shoulders as he lifted a log onto the chopping block. 'Savers and burrowers drop things now and again in their rush. All of these squirrels running around collecting nuts makes for a pretty good planting system. So you don't have to worry about the tree supply.'

'I bet you know a lot about nature,' Vivian said.

'I'm no expert,' he said. 'I just try to get along out here, but sometimes I wonder...' He looked away.

'What?'

'What you said about my chopping wood.'

'I didn't mean anything,' she objected.

'I know. But sometimes I wonder if we should cut trees or not.'

'What do you mean?'

'Evolution.' He brought the ax down with a crack. 'Survival of the fittest and all that. Aren't we the fittest? Maybe it's our duty to take over the land and build on it.'

'Then some people would question what we use the wood for,' she said, 'whether the things we build are necessary for survival or not.'

'What does it matter, if we're the fittest? Animals don't kill just for meat. They have their own ways of showing strength.'

'But shouldn't we worry about the future? About trees?'

Mr Stokes raised his eyebrows. 'And water?'

'Yes,' she laughed, 'and water. We're arrogant, aren't we, to think that we can have a big effect on this planet, and we're naive if we don't?'

He took another swing at the log. 'It has to matter. It's morality, really. I have to believe that it matters.'

'Morality?'

'Whether our actions matter or not,' he said. 'Morality.'

Vivian noticed the narrow rivulets at the corners of his eyes, like a tangle of thin branches. 'That's a complicated issue for so early in the morning, isn't it?' She stood and wiped the dirt from her shorts. 'Thanks for the coffee and the conversation. You've given me something to think about today.'

'Sorry again for the noise.'

'Don't worry about it.' Vivian started to walk back the way she came, but turned abruptly and caught him watching her leave. Quickly, he began straightening the pile of kindling at his feet.

'We're going to have the Wiltons over for a barbecue one night,' she said. 'You should come too.'

He slid his right hand into the front pocket of his jeans. 'Thank you. I can bring something for the grill.'

'Okay,' she said.

Vivian walked back through the trees, confident of her direction now. Back at the house, she made scrambled eggs and toast. She was hungrier than she'd been in the morning for some time. As she ate, she heard the rumble of the road crew's truck outside and realized it was just about the time she got up most mornings. The whole incident with Abe Stokes could have been a dream; it might never have happened. As the birds raised their voices in competition with the drone of the truck and the occasional shouts of the men who were now working some distance from the house, she thought about Abe Stokes, about his confident movements and the vulnerability in his eyes. He was a man with a story waiting to be unraveled and for the first time since she had arrived at the house, Vivian felt truly interested in something.

She took a quick shower then sat down to write a grocery list. She wanted to plan the barbecue for the following weekend. Earlier than expected, she heard the old truck rumble up the driveway.

When she went outside to greet him, Nowell pulled her down from the porch. Her legs dangled above the ground as she clung to his neck. 'How's your mother?' she asked.

'I didn't see her much.'

'How did things go with the lawyer?'

'He seemed to have everything under control. I don't know why my mom is so worked up.'

What a surprise, Vivian thought.

In the kitchen, Nowell set his bag on the table. 'I have some great news,' he said.

'What?'

'Lonnie showed up this morning to introduce Dorothy to my mom. I invited them to come out and stay with us for a couple of weeks.'

'Oh?'

'He got a new construction job, but it doesn't start until the fall. They've got some time to help out.'

Vivian followed him as he took his bag to the bedroom. 'So you met Dorothy?'

'Yes.'

'What was she like?'

'Nice. They seem to get along great.' Nowell motioned to one of the spare bedrooms. 'Do we have sheets for the extra bed?'

'I think so. There are linens in one of these hall closets.'

'I'll help you get the room ready today. We'll just move those boxes into the other one.'

'We don't have to do it today,' she said. 'You had a long drive.'

'They'll be here tonight.'

'Tonight?' She felt the grip of something, like a cool breeze across her skin.

'I know it's short notice, Viv, but we don't have much going on. Everything doesn't have to be perfect. They know we're in the process of cleaning this place up.'

'But we don't have much food in the house...'

Nowell pulled her against his chest. 'Poor Viv. Spontaneity isn't your thing, is it?'

'What do you mean? I don't mind last-minute planning, I just like to have certain things ready.'

'Then it's not last-minute, is it?'

'I'm always up for adventure,' she said weakly.

'You've never seemed that way to me.'

'You're Mr Schedule, Mr Routine. What time do you get up every morning?'

His brow wrinkled. 'Seven o'clock, why?'

109

'Never seven-fifteen, seven-thirty?'

'Sleeping in makes someone adventurous?' he asked.

Vivian broke away from him and stretched out on the bed. 'It can.'

'Sleeping in or staying in bed late?' He joined her on the bed. When he leaned down to unbuckle her sandals, he said, 'Your shoes are muddy.'

'That area out front isn't dry from the storm yet.'

'And there's grass and look, a pine needle stuck in the side of your shoe.'

She thought about her morning visit with Abe Stokes. 'I was outside yesterday,' she said, 'taking things to the garbage in back.'

'Looks like you've been through a jungle.'

Nowell was slow in his lovemaking and for once, Vivian wished he would speed it along. Her mind was on other things, like evolution and the Midwestern tree supply, and Mr Stokes's lonely existence in the woods. An hour later, Nowell stood humming in the shower while Vivian called her parents from the kitchen. She felt a need to hear about their normal lives, the subjects they were studying. After four rings, her father picked up. His voice sounded old and tired.

'Don't you have a class today?' she asked.

'No, but I've been reading student papers most of the day.'

'You could always take a summer off.'

'Then what would I do?'

'Mom would say you could take a vacation.'

He laughed. 'Yes, well, your mother's the traveler in this family.'

She thought: I like to travel.

'What have you been doing out there, Vivie?'

'Taking it easy mostly.'

'How's Nowell's work coming?'

'Fine, I think.' Vivian suddenly realized she'd forgotten to read the other chapter from the book. She'd have to finish it after Nowell went to bed that night. 'It's very peaceful here,' she said.

'I can imagine. Listen, Vivie, your mother's not home right now. She ran over to the library to do some research.'

She tried to think of something to ask him.

'Wish Nowell good luck with his writing,' he said. 'When are you coming to visit?'

'I don't know. Lonnie and his wife are coming for a couple of weeks.'

'I'll tell your mother that you called.'

'Okay, Dad.' Vivian hung up. Outside, the mailman maneuvered his shiny white truck over the embankment then back onto the asphalt after he deposited their mail. What do you think about evolution, she imagined herself saying to her father. She could ask him: Why do you suppose a girl, a young woman really, would fall forward but be unable to break her fall? She recalled the open-ended but leading style of the questions on many college exams: *What does this suggest about gravity,* she would ask, about human behavior and reflexes?

She noticed the mud caked around her toenails and the green grass stains on her heels. It reminded her of being young, of skinning a knee or stubbing a toe, and the way children smelled after a day of playing outdoors. She walked down the hallway toward the sound of Nowell's humming. Maybe he was finished with his shower so she could wash her feet in the tub.

14

Vivian discovered at an early age that behind closed doors, her parents had intellectual conversations. Their house was a single-level with four small bedrooms, one of which was a study. There was a wooden table for a desk, shelves of books and two tall file cabinets. Her father kept his books in the study but usually spread his things over the dining room table when he worked. The clutter rattled her mother's nerves but she never complained, because this reserved the study for herself. Many nights, Vivian was comforted by the soft glow of the reading light across the hall.

In Vivian's presence, her parents talked about day-to-day things – a student who handed in a paper two weeks late, the unreasonable demands of a dean, the long line at the grocery store – but they stayed away from the topics that motivated their research, writing and teaching. While growing up Vivian hardly noticed this, but now she regretted knowing little about the subjects that fueled their intellects. They saved the passionate subjects for after she'd gone to bed.

They met in graduate school, that much Vivian knew. They did things in a proper order: first graduation, then marriage and teaching appointments. Then Vivian. They had wanted two or three children, but her mother was unable to have more. Her mother named her after the Spanish verb, *vivir*. Vivian always wished that she'd been named something more modern, and from a less odd source.

As a girl, Vivian was shy around adults and older kids. She had a few playmates in the neighborhood. Her mother gave her a boundary for her outdoor roaming, and it widened as she got older. By the time she was eleven or twelve, she could canvas the entire neighborhood on her bicycle, eight blocks of houses just like hers, painted in varying colors. She spent time alone, losing herself in private games and daydreams or working on secret projects. Her mother took her to get a library card when she started kindergarten and they made regular trips for books. There was one author in particular she loved, a woman who wrote stories about real-life adventures for children. In one book, two friends were trapped in a museum after hours and in another, a brother and sister were separated from their parents during a cross-country train ride. The children in these books were forced to rely on their own ingenuity, and Vivian always dreaded the endings, when they returned home to normal life.

During the summer, Vivian occasionally stayed at her grandmother's when her parents were away. Grandma Shatlee, her father's mother, was a serious but lenient woman with long, graceful limbs. Although she was unaffectionate in a physical way, Grandma Shatlee was trustworthy and kept Vivian's confidences. Her only inflexible rule was that Vivian join her and Grandpa Shatlee for each meal: breakfast at eight o'clock, lunch at noon, and dinner promptly at five. As the taillights of her parents' car receded, Vivian watched, still as a soldier, refusing to wave. The car grew smaller and smaller and Vivian felt the same way, as if she was shrinking into herself, folding up like a summer lawn chair.

They took a few family trips, but her father was right: her mother was the traveler in the family. She made the plans and coerced her father into taking the time away from the university.

Of the occasions they went without her, Vivian thought they wanted to be alone or didn't think she'd be interested in going. Her mother also left for research sometimes, collecting information for one of her books.

Vivian would never forget the way her mother ruined their vacation at the cabin. After the day she got lost, she dragged Vivian to the writing workshop each day. Vivian sat sullenly in the back, looking through books and writing bitter letters to her friends back home. Her father distanced himself, angry that her mother was angry. Many times when Vivian and her mother returned to the cabin, he was gone. He started taking long drives through the countryside. For three days in a row, he didn't come back until after dinner.

Vivian was confined to the area directly in front of the cabin, and none of her former playmates were willing to stick around to keep her company. She spent long hours staring down the path toward the makeshift parking lot, straining her eyes and ears for the old Ford Pinto they owned then. For the remaining two weeks of the vacation, Vivian sulked around, and neither of her parents seemed to notice. They were too absorbed in their latest battle of wills, a contest that inevitably, her mother would always win because of the lengths she was willing to go. Neither Vivian nor her father was a match for her; they needed her more than she needed them.

Nowell finished his shower and started moving boxes from one of the spare rooms to the other, preparing for his brother's visit. In the hall closet, Vivian found a set of sheets and threw them into the washing machine.

The spare room seemed larger after the floor was cleared, brighter with the faded gauzy curtains pulled back from the window. Vivian dusted off the dresser and swept the hardwood floor while Nowell moved back and forth between the rooms.

'So your mother was busy?' she asked.

A box had left a strip of dust across his thighs. He slapped at the dirt, causing tiny clouds to disperse into the air. 'She was down at the church until almost ten o'clock last night. We talked for a while when she got in.'

'Was she glad to see Lonnie this morning?'

'I think so. It was unexpected, but that's Lonnie. They showed up early.'

'You wouldn't recognize him if he arrived at a decent hour.'

'True.' Nowell reached for a box in the closet and it tipped over, spilling its contents over his head.

Vivian couldn't reach the box, which tilted precariously against his shoulder, but she picked up the shoebox and square-heeled leather shoes that had fallen out. Nowell bounced the larger box onto the bed.

'Whose are these?' she asked.

'I don't know. They look pretty old.'

'I'm starting to get the impression that your grandmother never threw anything away.'

'Sometimes people are like that,' he said. 'Sentimental. Maybe once we have a big house we'll feel differently about throwing everything away. Hard to use space you don't have.'

She followed him into the other room, carrying the shoebox. 'I found some clothing in the attic, all folded and put into a dresser drawer like someone had used it recently.'

'I don't think she went up to the attic much,' Nowell said, 'but maybe she kept some of her things up there.'

'No, it was men's clothing. Reminded me of the type of things your dad wore, I mean, from the photos I've seen. And there was a gun,' she added, watching his face.

Nowell looked up. 'A hunting gun? My grandfather used to hunt.'

'I don't think so,' Vivian said. 'A hand gun.'

'What did you do with it?' Nowell asked.

'It's on a dresser in the attic.'

'I'll go up later and make sure it's not loaded.'

Vivian lowered her voice. 'But why is it here? Whose is it?'

Nowell rolled his eyes. 'My grandma lived out here alone for many years, Viv, and this isn't the city. Everyone out here probably owns a gun.' He turned to leave. 'And the clothes, you can get rid of them.'

Seven years earlier, Nowell's father died suddenly of a massive stroke during the hottest part of a hot summer. He was fifty-seven years old, so active and healthy, Nowell said, that it had been hard to imagine anything happening to him. Beverly found Sherman on the kitchen floor and woke Nowell. Together, they moved him to a more dignified position before she called the paramedics. Nowell was home from college that summer, helping his father with the repair business to earn spending money. Lonnie was away on a fishing trip. Everything was over within two weeks: the funeral, the packing of Sherman's things, the selling of the family's share of the repair business. In three weeks, Nowell was back at school. He said later that he couldn't believe how quickly his whole life changed.

'Dorothy can help you out with the house while they're here,' Nowell said.

Vivian looked at him. 'Are you sure she's coming here to work?'

'They'll benefit from the sale of the house too,' Nowell said. 'Lonnie knows that.'

'My mom always says that one kitchen is too small for two women,' Vivian said.

'That's not very progressive of her,' he remarked.

Vivian heard the sound of gravel crunching under tires. She pulled back the curtain and saw a faded black jeep with an open top. Lonnie jumped from the driver's seat and a blond woman turned and pulled a duffel bag from the back seat.

'They're here already,' she said.

Nowell galloped to the kitchen entrance and stood with a fixed grin, hands on his hips and head tilted to one side, like a dog listening to a rustle in the grass.

Lonnie's bulky form eclipsed the sunlight as he stood in the doorframe.

Nowell had moved to the far end of the kitchen, at the square entry to his study. The dark support beams of the ceiling tapered off like bars behind his head. 'So you made it in one piece,' he said.

'Number One, what's new?' Lonnie stepped onto the yellow-patterned tile. 'Hey, Vivian.'

Their hug was brief and awkward; Vivian turned her head and Lonnie's collarbone pressed into her cheek through his scratchy plaid shirt.

A small woman moved around him and grinned. 'Hello.' She looked at Nowell. 'Hello again.'

'Hi,' Vivian replied. 'You must be Dorothy.'

'The one and only,' Lonnie said.

Greenish eyes squinted above Dorothy's small, amber-freckled nose. Her hair was blond with flashes of red and ended in a gentle wave at her shoulders.

Vivian extended her hand. 'It's great to meet you at last.'

'Don't shake her hand!' Lonnie roared. 'She's family, isn't she?'

Vivian hugged her. Dorothy smelled faintly of vanilla.

Nowell came forward and embraced both of them. They all stood in the center of the kitchen.

Lonnie looked well. His skin was ruddy, his cheeks like two round apples. His dark hair was very short, like a military haircut.

He noticed her looking. 'How do you like the hair? Wanna touch it?'

'Get your own wife to touch it.' Nowell pulled Vivian against him.

Lonnie punched his brother lightly in the arm, then Nowell reached for him quickly, unaware that his elbow collided with Vivian's arm. As the two men struggled into a wrestling hold, she rubbed the sore part of her arm and stole a glance at Lonnie's new wife.

Dorothy's face held the bemused look of a mother watching her toddler. With her pale skin and hair, and her soft, pliant expression, she reminded Vivian of a painting of the Madonna and child they studied in Art class. It was Fra Filippo Lippi, she believed, and his rendition stood out from countless others because of the humanistic way he painted. Dr Lightfoot spoke at length about the use of shading and line, but what Vivian remembered most was the animated, loving expression of the young mother; the way the painting came alive. She gazed at Dorothy and as Nowell and Lonnie grunted and pushed against each other, Dorothy turned and rolled her eyes.

'Enough already,' Vivian said to the men. 'You're going to break something.'

Lonnie backed Nowell against the table. 'Give,' he ordered.

Nowell laughed. 'Okay, okay. When did you get bigger than me?'

Lonnie peeled the checkered shirt from his body and hung it on a hook next to the door. Underneath he wore a plain white T-shirt. 'Got anything to drink? Heating up out there.'

Dorothy touched Vivian's arm. 'Where should we put our things? And please, call me Dot.'

Vivian thought that she and Dot were opposites in some ways. Vivian was small and dark, with dark brown, almost black eyes and olive skin. Dot, while similar in size and proportion, had light, strawberry-blond hair and fair, freckle-prone skin. At times Vivian had wished to be taller, but she prided herself on her narrow waist, her silky hair and her vein-free hands. People used to tell her that she should be a hand model, selling fingernail polish or jewelry, but her mother said that models had to be tall, no matter what kind they were.

Vivian showed her the spare bedroom. Dot walked directly to the window and peered outside. 'I feel so gritty from the drive,' she said. 'Lonnie wanted to ride with the top down the whole way. He's like a kid, happy with the smallest things.' Her eyes glistened.

'He's simple in the nicest ways. Uncomplicated, you know?'

Vivian smiled.

'So you've been married a long time,' Dot said.

'Four years, but I remember what it's like to be a newlywed.'

Dot unzipped the duffel bag then straightened up, her hair falling into her eyes. 'What's it like?'

She shrugged. 'Exciting, new. You can hardly stand to be apart.'

'And all that changes?'

She chuckled. 'No, not all of it. The parts that stay come back really strong at times. They surprise you.' She met Dot's gaze. 'At least that's how it is for me. By the way, congratulations.'

'Thanks. I wish we could've had a different kind of wedding, you know, with family and friends. But Lonnie was stubborn about that. It was all pretty sudden.' Dot looked again through the window. 'It's nice out here.'

'I've had a hard time getting motivated,' Vivian said.

'Lonnie says you're fixing up the house?'

'Trying to. It's not very exciting work.'

Dot started lifting things out of the bag and shoving them into the dresser. 'I understand. I still haven't unpacked most of the boxes since we got married and moved. It seems like we've been all over since then, and I don't know how long we'll be there, you know? I mean our little apartment. Lonnie wants something with more space, and to me, it doesn't matter. So the boxes sit in our living room. Seems pointless to unpack them just to pack them again.' She shut the dresser drawer. 'I'll be glad to help you with the house.'

'You don't have to…'

'What am I supposed to do, watch you work while I lounge in the sun?'

'I've been doing some lounging around myself.'

'Then we'll do that together too.'

'I'll be glad for the company,' Vivian admitted. 'Nowell writes every day so I'm pretty much left to myself.'

119

Dot's eyes narrowed. 'Do you have any sisters?'

The question surprised her. 'Sisters? No.'

'You seem like you do.' She set a purple cosmetic bag on the dresser. 'Lonnie says that the little town is just a few miles up the road.'

'Yes. We'll have to drive in for lunch or a movie sometime while you're here.'

'That would be great.'

Lonnie and Dot insisted on buying some groceries. They went into town and brought several bags back. After a while, the men decided to drive back for beer, after determining that the supply in the refrigerator was insufficient. Dot took a nap while Vivian spent some time in the front yard, flipping through magazines. When she heard Dot rummaging around in the kitchen, she went inside.

'Good nap?' Vivian asked.

Dot had a reddish crease on her cheek that almost matched the hue of her freckles. 'Yes. Lonnie had me up at five o'clock this morning.' She pulled some ground beef from the refrigerator.

'What can I do?' Vivian asked.

'Just sit there and take it easy.' She stood for a minute, scanning the kitchen. 'I need a skillet, which I'm sure is in this cupboard here. Yes, here it is. You've put everything just where I would have.'

'At least let me make a salad,' Vivian said.

'All right,' Dot said, 'but that's it.'

They both heard a car in the driveway. Vivian said, 'That was fast.' A few moments later, the screen door rattled as someone knocked on it. 'No one's home!' she called.

'Excuse me,' a deep voice said.

She spun around and saw Sheriff Townsend peering in, the bill of his hat pressed against the screen door.

'Oh, hello, Sheriff,' Vivian said. 'We thought you were someone else.'

When she opened the door, he took off his hat and stepped

inside. 'Sorry to disturb you at the dinner hour.' He nodded at Dot. 'I noticed the out-of-state license plates on that jeep outside. I wanted to make sure everything was in order.'

'That's my jeep.' Dot came forward, wiping her hands on the front of her shorts. 'Mine and my husband's.'

'Sheriff Townsend, this is my sister-in-law, Dot Gardiner,' Vivian explained. 'She and my brother-in-law just arrived this afternoon for a short visit.'

'I see.' He looked again at Vivian, his face slightly flushed. 'I really don't mean to bother you. It's just that you and your husband are here to take care of things for the late Mrs Gardiner, who was a member of our community for some time. I guess what I'm saying is, I figured you'd had enough trouble since you've been here, and I've made it my job to keep an extra eye out for you.'

'I understand,' she said. 'And we appreciate it, really.'

The sheriff looked at the hamburgers sizzling on the stove. 'I should let you get back to your cooking. Something sure smells good in here.' He looked at the opening to Nowell's study and the curtain that hung bunched at the side.

'Dot's made herself quite at home in the kitchen,' Vivian said. 'I'm afraid I'll get spoiled if she keeps cooking like this.' She winked at the sheriff. She had never been a winker, hadn't even thought of it until she saw Katherine do it.

'You don't have to worry about that,' Dot said. 'Cooking isn't exactly a talent of mine.'

Sheriff Townsend lingered in the doorway. 'Will you come down for the festivities in town at the end of summer? It's not too far off now.'

'You're not talking about the reunion for the Clements, are you?'

'I was talking more about the town anniversary festival the following weekend. They'll have music, carnival rides and such. All to celebrate the founding of the town.'

'You're a relation of William Clement, aren't you?' Vivian asked.

'Yes, ma'am. He was my great-great-great-grandfather.'

'How many Clements will be there?'

He laughed. 'Hundreds, I would guess. I expect many will stay through the week. Should be a real boost for local business. Along with the road finally going in.'

'Sounds fun,' Vivian said.

He twirled his hat around in his hands. 'I'll leave you to your cooking.' He turned to Dot. 'Nice meeting you.'

'Likewise,' Dot said.

Sheriff Townsend stepped outside and put on his hat. Vivian watched as he slowly descended the steps of the porch then walked to his car, the shiny white cruiser with tan and black stripes. He looked around as he went, taking in every detail of their yard.

'Talk about a hard-working police force,' Dot said.

Vivian walked over to the counter and continued slicing a tomato. 'They certainly are.'

'What was that about? I mean, the part about the trouble you've had?'

Vivian looked at her. 'Didn't Nowell mention anything to Lonnie about what happened?'

Dot's forehead wrinkled. 'I don't think so.'

'It was the day Lonnie left, the same day I arrived.'

'What was?'

'They found a dead body,' Vivian said, pointing with the knife towards the woods. 'Practically in our yard.'

Dot inhaled quickly.

'A young girl who lived nearby. Seventeen years old.'

'What happened to her?'

'It was an accident. They did an autopsy and didn't find anything suspicious. She died from head trauma. She tripped on something and hit her head on a rock.'

'How terrible.'

Vivian dropped the core of the tomato into the sink. 'A woman I met here says she was a wild girl, always in trouble.' She shook

122

her head. 'I don't know why I said that. It's only gossip.'

'Her family?' Dot asked.

'Just her mother. She was here the other day, the mother.'

'Why?'

'The sheriff brought her. She wanted to see where they found her.'

Dot groaned.

Vivian nodded. 'It was awful.'

'That must've been pretty big news for a small town like this,' she said.

'Not really. They ran a couple of stories in the paper, and an obituary, of course. But once they reported that it was an accident, there wasn't much else to say. Bad things happen everywhere. There was an automobile crash just last weekend, some kids from a neighboring town. They were out partying and one of them, the driver, didn't make it.'

Dot took the plate of steaming hamburgers to the table. 'I guess we think of the country as an escape from all that. Crime, violence, you know.'

'But there are reckless kids everywhere. I'm sure they have their share of domestic problems here, drugs, everything.'

'It was nice of him to stop by,' Dot said, something implied by her raised eyebrows.

'What?' Vivian asked.

They heard the truck rumble up the driveway.

'They're back,' Dot said. 'Perfect timing. I'm famished.'

15

Lonnie leaned back in the chair, his hand circling a near-empty bottle of beer. 'There are people who have physical proof of their abduction,' he said. 'Coded messages scratched into their arms, burn marks on their temples, blackouts. Some of them wake up in places and don't know how they got there.'

'Maybe they're sleepwalkers,' Nowell said.

Dot's eyes sparkled in the light. 'You should see this documentary, that's all we're saying. There are too many coincidences between these stories. People who don't even know each other, living in separate parts of the country.' Her cheeks were blazing and her blondish-red hair was molded against the sides of her face. They were all a little drunk, sitting on the porch after a long dinner.

'Yeah,' Lonnie said. 'How could they have the same experiences? Being put on a lab table and having samples taken, or being watched through a monitor in a small room with no windows.'

'Maybe it's because they've all seen the same movies as you,' Nowell said.

'What movies?' His eyes widened. 'There's proof. Haven't you ever seen pictures of those big craters where the crafts have landed, or heard from the people who say it happened to them? What proof do you have that there's no other life out there?'

'You're asking me to prove a negative thing, which is impossible.'

'Then what's there to argue about?'

Nowell laughed. 'I'm arguing that it's extremely unlikely that any of these desperate people on your video were abducted from their trailers by aliens and tested. Don't you think that intelligent life would choose a more diverse and accomplished cross-section of humanity? Scientists, artists, political leaders?'

'Maybe they take what they can get. It would be hard to snatch someone in a big city.'

'Now we're really getting into mere conjecture.'

As the yellow porch light softened around her like melting wax, Vivian worked on her fourth beer.

Dot spoke softly, and everyone turned toward her. 'I just think it would be nice, wouldn't it? To know we're not alone in the universe, that other types of life are out there.'

Nowell took a long drink. 'How would it change anything?'

Lonnie said, 'For one thing, we could travel there, set up space stations.'

'You've never left the United States,' Vivian said. 'What makes you think you'd go to Mars?'

He smiled at her, nodding his head. 'You're right. Maybe you should go first.'

Dot got up and stood behind Lonnie's chair. 'Maybe it wouldn't make any real difference in our lives,' she said, 'but it would show us another way of living, a new perspective.'

Nowell crossed his arms over his chest. 'There are millions of people on Earth, all with varying perspectives.'

'But people are the same more than they're different,' she said.

'I don't think that's true,' Vivian objected.

'You know how they talk about separating people by race,' Dot said, 'that it really doesn't mean anything, at least not nearly as much as we make of it? Because when you get down to people's genes, you know, there's such a small amount of difference…'

'…that it's inconsequential,' Nowell finished.

She nodded. 'So when you think about human nature, about our feelings and what makes us tick, maybe there's not much difference there either, you know, when you look at the whole range.'

Nowell slapped his leg. 'So a greedy child who, say, won't share his candy is basically the same as some tyrannical ruler who wipes out an entire population to feed his ego?'

Dot's eyes blazed. 'Okay, yes. Greed, fear, happiness. What if there's a system that's different, you know? A completely different type of life.'

'That's too philosophical for me after so much beer,' Vivian said. She looked up at Dot, who remained standing behind Lonnie, her small hands on his shoulders. 'Let's hear about your whirlwind romance instead.'

'There's not much to tell,' Dot said. 'Lonnie came into the store where I was working.'

'I was visiting Sal Brewer. Remember him, Nowell?'

'The guy you worked with at Build Rite?'

'Yea. Sal moved out west a few years ago and invited me to come hang out for a while, check out the coast.'

'They came in to buy beer,' Dot said, 'and I was having a really bad day.'

Lonnie peered up at her. 'She had just moved up there, and she hated her job.'

'A convenience store, all I'd been able to get.'

'So I started teasing her a little. She told me off. Later, I came back and we got to talking. She finally agreed to go out with me.'

'And I quit my job and we went up to the mountains, lived like real naturalists, you know?'

'You should have seen it up there,' Lonnie said. 'The trees, the sky at night. We camped near a little creek filled with fish. It's like you have the whole world to yourself.'

'It was beautiful,' Dot agreed.

'I asked her to marry me,' Lonnie said. 'I told her I wanted to live around here, though.'

'And I didn't mind. There wasn't anything keeping me there.'

'We're glad to have you in the family,' Nowell said. 'I was afraid nobody would ever marry Lonnie.'

'Very funny, Number One.'

'I've been bailing him out of trouble my whole life.'

'Now...' Lonnie started.

'Remember that time you and your friends had to go back down Birch Street, apologizing to everyone on the block?'

'Why?' Dot asked.

'They drove down the street and knocked over all the mailboxes with a baseball bat,' Vivian explained. 'Didn't you have to try to put them back up?'

'We tried,' Lonnie said. A wide grin pushed his cheeks into two round masses. 'But some of the poles were busted, just splintered like firewood.'

'I can't imagine you and your rough friends knocking on all those doors and telling people you broke their mailboxes.' Nowell shook his head.

'Why would you do something like that?' Dot asked.

Lonnie looked up at her. 'We were just blowing off steam.'

'But why knock down mailboxes? Did you have something against the Post Office?'

'It was just for fun,' Vivian said. 'Weren't you ever reckless, out of control?'

Dot looked from Lonnie to Vivian. 'How is being out of control fun?'

'Oh, forget it, honey,' Lonnie said. 'We were just kids.'

Vivian carried some dishes inside and Dot followed. Dot sat down at the table. 'I'm completely exhausted, even with the nap.'

'Long day,' Vivian said. 'You were at Beverly's pretty early this morning. Is this the first time you met her?'

'Yes. She was very nice. Surprised to see us so early, you know, but Lonnie told me she wouldn't mind.'

Vivian stretched her neck, yawning. 'I think we're all used to Lonnie's habits by now.'

'I guess you must be.' Dot stood up. 'I think I'll take a hot shower and go to bed. Any big plans for tomorrow?'

'Not really. I need to drive into town for a few things, if you'd like to come along.'

'What time?'

'Not early. Whenever we get up and around.'

'Yes, I want to go.' She went to the screen door. 'Lonnie, I'm turning in.'

'Be there soon,' he told her.

Dot paused in the hall. She looked small in the dark space. 'Thanks, Vivian,' she said. 'For everything.'

Vivian opened the screen door and went outside. Lonnie reclined in the swing, one leg propped up on the bench and the other extended out. Nowell sat on the banister opposite him, leaning against the narrow column.

The breeze, cool now, spread over Vivian's skin like balm.

Nowell was saying, 'So this Mr McDermott, the lawyer, told me the claim is unsubstantiated. Mom's protected by the first document.'

'That's good,' Lonnie said. 'These big businesses, these firms, they've always got people looking for loopholes to make them money. So what if it's a widow, right? Anything for a buck.'

'At first, I was angry with Dad's former partner,' Nowell said, 'but talking to the lawyer, I realized it's more complicated. There's a board of directors now, and Mr Ward is actually trying to get everything settled.'

'Sure he is. He waits until Dad dies then he settles things. Just takes everything he can.'

'It's not so simple. There isn't always a bad guy or an easy solution.'

'I don't see why not. Give Mom the money; that's an easy solution. Dad's the one who built that company from the ground, not Mr Ward. He's been benefiting from Dad's hard work for years.'

Nowell sighed. 'Sometimes talking to you about things is as bad as talking to Mom. You can't be rational.'

'And maybe you're too rational.' Lonnie sat up. 'Doesn't this whole thing piss you off?'

'Being pissed off doesn't solve anything. It never has.'

'I thought everything was settled,' Vivian said.

Nowell nodded. 'Mom's lawyer is meeting with the company's lawyer early next week and he's going to take care of it.'

The headlights of a lone car appeared over the hill towards town. As it passed on the empty road, they listened to the rising then falling hum of the engine and the faint melody of music from the car's radio.

'Oh, Viv,' Nowell said. 'Lonnie and I are going fishing tomorrow, with a few of those guys from the road crew.'

'The road crew?' she said.

'I met them when I was here before,' Lonnie said, 'and we ran into them at the store. Four-thirty, Number One.'

'Don't remind me,' Nowell groaned.

'You're going to take a day off?' she asked.

'Just the morning. We should be back by two o'clock.'

'You must be at a good stopping point.'

He ignored the tinge of sarcasm in her voice. 'Almost.'

'I think I'll go to bed too,' Vivian said. 'Suddenly, I'm very tired.'

'Okay, Viv. I'll be in soon.'

'Dot's going with me into town,' Vivian told Lonnie.

'I'll give her some cash,' Lonnie said. 'Remember, we're paying for half of everything while we're here.'

'You don't have to—' Nowell started.

'Oh, come on,' Lonnie interrupted. 'You're not exactly rolling in it. We're not normal guests, we're family.'

Vivian went into the living room and grabbed the pages Nowell

129

had given her to read while he was gone. Her face was burning. Weeks of shutting himself in that room, practically ignoring her, she thought. His baby brother arrives and now it's a big party. She washed her face and brushed her teeth and by the time she had crawled into bed with the pages from his book, she had talked herself out of being angry. Nowell had been busy working very hard. He deserved a break, she knew. She shut their bedroom door and skimmed through the first chapter, which she had already read. The second began:

> He was a young man, older than her but inexperienced still in many ways. And she was much older than her years in ways that mattered. For her, life was an easy thing, no grand design, no complications, no detours. She worked during the day at a regular job, cooked sometimes in the evenings and sometimes went out with friends.
>
> There were things that she had forgotten, either by effort or by chance, and these dark moments of longing from the past cropped up then sunk again into the oblivion of memory and time. Seeing the man caused one of these moments, a memory or re-memory taking shape but distorted and uncertain, leaving her only with a feeling of controlled anger.

Vivian yawned and pushed herself to a more upright position. She scanned the remaining paragraphs. The story was beginning to form, despite these distracting sections, and it centered around the girl, the man who had sparked her memory, and the girl's roommate, a friendly middle-aged woman who mothered her. Vivian's eyelids were heavy, and the room began to contract around her. At her side, the glare from the lighthouse lamp softened and dimmed.

Suddenly, the door opened with a popping sound, and Vivian opened her eyes.

'What do you have there?' Nowell asked.

She began to gather the pages into a pile. 'I was looking over the writing you gave me. I wanted to read it again before I said anything.'

'So?'

'It's great,' she said. 'I can't wait to read the rest.'

'You didn't think it was difficult to follow, the way I told the story from her point of view?'

Vivian spoke cautiously. 'I had questions as I went along, but it seemed like they would be answered as she discovered things.'

Nowell unfastened his shorts. 'But didn't you think her world was a confusing vantage point? Her thinking is so subjective, so pointed.'

'I would think readers can be objective.'

'That's what I thought.' He nodded slowly a few times, contemplating.

She asked, 'Did you and Lonnie finish your argument?'

'It wasn't really an argument. He starts with his conspiracy theories and his aliens and makes all these generalized, ridiculous statements that add up to nothing. Sometimes it's all I can do not to reach over and shake him.'

'A lot of people believe in alien abductions.'

Nowell climbed into bed. 'I don't want to know about it.'

Vivian gave him the extra pillow. 'You were right. Dot is very sweet.'

'Yeah, I like her. I hope Lonnie doesn't screw it up.'

'That's not nice.'

'You don't know him like I do, Viv. He sabotages his life on purpose, especially good things that come along. Like when we were in school. His grades were average mostly, but then he'd get a good grade on a project or a report, something that interested him. Almost like it was an accident. Then before you knew it, he'd be in trouble or getting kicked out of class again for goofing off. By the time he reached high school, I think he'd finally fallen behind.'

131

'He always talks about school like it wasn't very important to him.'

'What about that great job he had a couple of years ago? Was that important? He got fired for not showing up. All he had to do was make a simple phone call. What about that apartment that my aunt cosigned for him to get, in the building her friend owned? Remember?'

She nodded.

'He had the money for the rent, Viv, I know he did. Like I said, he's always shooting himself in the foot. I just don't understand him.'

'Maybe he's grown up since then.'

'I hope so.' He reached over and turned off the lamp on his nightstand.

They lay for a few moments in the dark, then Nowell shifted his position and soon after that, Vivian listened as his breathing slowed.

Silently, she got out of bed, pulled on her shorts and stepped into the hallway. The door to the spare room was closed and no light came from underneath. She followed the glow from the kitchen, running her fingers along the wall. When she turned the corner, she was startled to see Lonnie sitting at the kitchen table.

'You're still up?' she said.

He looked at her. 'What? Oh, yeah.'

'I just need some water.' She went to get a glass from the cupboard.

'Dot likes you,' Lonnie said.

Vivian shut the water off and turned around. 'I like her too.'

'That's good. The women in a family should get along, don't you think?'

'I guess so.'

'Dot's a great girl. I want things to be easier for her now.'

'We're really happy for you, Lonnie. Really.'

He leaned back in his chair, folding his hands over his stomach.

'This is a great house. We never came here much when my grandma was alive. I don't know why.'

'It's a long drive.'

'No, it's not. My dad didn't want to come. I never understood it.'

It was cold in the kitchen, and Vivian crossed her arms. 'He kept busy with work, didn't he?'

'She was our grandma and we hardly knew her.'

'Are you sure he didn't visit much?'

Lonnie shook his head. 'I remember being here maybe three times. Once he yelled at me after I stayed out all day. There was a boy who lived around here, or he was visiting his grandparents or something. We didn't realize how long we were gone until the sun started to go down.'

'Did you get lost?'

'No. Who told you that?'

'I'm just asking. I've been back there a couple of times. You wouldn't think you could get lost so easily, but once you're beyond the trees it gets confusing.'

'Not for me.'

Vivian wondered which story was true, Lonnie's or Nowell's.

Lonnie finished his beer, tilted it upright and let the last foamy drops fall into his mouth. He brought the bottle towards Vivian, waited while she opened the cabinet underneath the sink, and then he dropped it into the plastic trash container underneath. When he stood up, he stayed close to her. 'Listen, Vivian, I haven't seen you since that weekend at my mom's.'

'Lonnie, it's not…'

'And I know you were mad at me then.' Vivian could smell him, the leathery saltiness of his skin, the beer on his breath.

'But I'm not anymore. Forget it, Lonnie, really.' She stepped around him.

He chuckled. 'I don't really remember what happened.'

Of course you don't, she thought. 'It was nothing,' she said. 'I'm going back to bed. Nowell's probably wondering where I am.' She closed the front door, locked the dead bolt.

'Vivian?'

'What?'

He ran his hand over his short, stubbly hair, and it made a scratchy sound. 'I always thought you were great, I just wanted to tell you that.'

'Thanks,' she said, her face flushing. 'Goodnight, Lonnie.' As she walked down the dark hallway, Vivian realized that having Lonnie around could get very irritating, especially if he drank every night. She didn't like the edge in his voice, his directness, his lack of respect for personal space.

As quietly as she could, she opened the door to their bedroom and exhaled with relief when Nowell remained motionless on the bed. She let her shorts fall around her ankles and slowly got into bed.

16

In the morning, Vivian woke with a headache and an uneasy feeling. She wondered if it would be awkward to see Lonnie after their exchange. Then she remembered that Nowell and Lonnie had left early for fishing. From a corner of her mind, a hazy image surfaced, Nowell leaning over to kiss her forehead.

She got up and padded on bare feet to the kitchen. The house was already warm, the sun bright in the golden room. The screen door suddenly opened and Dot came in. Her hair was more red than blond in the morning light, and she had pulled it back into a ponytail that teased the nape of her neck.

'That truck is huge!' she said. 'I was curious, you know, so I borrowed your key and climbed inside. How in the world do you drive it?'

'With a cushion,' Vivian said.

Dot laughed. 'It's like that movie where the woman shrunk and everything was huge, a ten-foot toothbrush and spoon.'

Vivian walked to the sink and set down her glass from the night before. 'Once I'm in, I like being up so high.'

'There are some things men shouldn't shop for alone, you know?'

'Furniture,' Vivian said.

'Clothes,' Dot added.

'Groceries,' she said. 'Before I got here, Nowell bought everything from the deli. No regard for a budget.'

Dot hung the truck keys on the hook by the door. 'Lonnie does most of our shopping and cooking.'

'Really?'

She nodded. 'He likes to cook. Does it by instinct, without recipes. I can cook anything with clear instructions on the box, but Lonnie, he's the pinch-of-this, drop-of-this type. It's a luxury for men, you know? They never feel like they have to cook. More of a hobby. I guarantee you, if Lonnie knew he had to make dinner every night, he'd get tired of it real soon.'

'Nowell told me about a pie that he made.'

'Fruit cobbler, in a clay cooking bowl. It's really good.'

'Well,' Vivian said, stretching, 'he can cook every night while you're here if he wants to.'

Dot waved her finger. 'Be careful what you ask for.'

Vivian thought Dot looked pretty. Her skin was smooth and creamy, her green eyes glossy and bright. What she saw in Lonnie was a mystery.

Dot leaned against the sink. 'My mother used to say that every man has a desire to spread his seed around, and a wife's job is to stick close to him, you know, trying to catch most of it.'

Vivian blinked. It was as if she had read her thoughts about Lonnie. 'What?'

'Oh, yeah,' she said. 'My mom has many wise sayings. About the place for women, you know, what they should or shouldn't do. For a long time, I thought there were meetings to discuss the rules, like witches at night, gathering to go over all their potions. Then I realized her ways of teaching were quieter.'

'Have you ever felt that you're turning into your mother?' Vivian asked. 'I mean, in small ways?'

Dot nodded emphatically. 'My mom used to say "hold your horses," and "get the lead out," and I say both of those all the time.'

'Mine makes faces,' Vivian said, 'to show her approval or disapproval. She'll lift her eyebrows, or move her mouth to the side, like this.'

'I've seen you do that,' Dot laughed. 'I think you were better off than me. I could've ignored my mother if she was only making faces. I moved in with a roommate after high school and we had a huge fight. I think she just didn't want me to go, but she gave me all kinds of crazy reasons, you know? She told me having two grown women in a household wasn't natural, that it would never work out.'

'I've heard that,' Vivian said.

'It's sad, isn't it? We're raised to be suspicious of each other. I asked her why and she said something about only one hen ruling the roost. She didn't trust other women, you know? I guess she figured they were running around too, trying to catch her man's seed. I told her that she and I had been living together for years, so what was the difference? She said, "I said grown women." I was only eighteen, you know.'

'Does she still live in the same house?'

'Yes.' Dot looked away. 'She's very sick, so I don't know how much longer she'll be able to stay there.'

'I'm sorry.' Vivian wanted to say something else but Dot had moved to the door and was peering outside. 'Was she happy about Lonnie?' she asked instead.

'Oh, sure,' she said. 'That's all she ever wanted for me.'

'Mine didn't want me to get married,' Vivian said. 'She's waiting for me to find my calling in life. My parents are both professors at a university, so education is a big deal with them.'

'Not with my mom,' Dot said. 'She never mentioned college, not once. All I could think about was turning eighteen so I could get the hell out of there.'

'It's so important then, the freedom?'

'Still is to me.'

'You're right,' Vivian said. 'It is. I remember that every time I speak to my mother and feel like I'm twelve again.'

'Want something to eat?' Dot asked.

Vivian made a face and waved her hand.

She put the kettle on the stove and lit the burner.

'You grew up with just your mother, then?' Vivian asked.

'Pretty much. I had a father but he left when I was ten, found another woman or got sick of us, I don't know. At different times, my mom would give different reasons why he was gone.'

'You never saw him again?'

'Nope.'

'I'm sorry,' Vivian said.

'Don't be, really. I remember him a little, but we never spent time together or anything, you know? In my mind, he's a lump on the sofa, grunting every now and then, or a door slammed late at night.'

Vivian couldn't help but wonder if Dot had made a good choice. Lonnie was nearing thirty – they all were – but it seemed he'd never grow up.

'I have a confession to make,' Dot said.

Vivian looked up, a dull throb behind her eyes. Dot wore a red tank top and denim overalls cut into shorts. Although she had matched Vivian beer for beer the night before, her face was bright and rested. Vivian wished that she could look good as effortlessly as Dot seemed to. 'What?' she asked.

Dot sighed. 'I hate that wallpaper in the hallway, really hate it. I know I just got here and it's none of my business, but were you planning on keeping it?'

Vivian glanced toward the hall. 'I'm not sure I ever noticed it.' She got up and they both walked to the hallway. After a few moments of looking, Vivian said, 'It's hideous.'

The wallpaper had a cream-colored background, with wide gold stripes. Every fifth stripe was actually an ornate carousel horse on a pole, suspended at varying levels along the length of both walls. The horses had leering facial expressions and the overall effect, when standing at the end of the hall and looking down, was of driving at high speed past some sort of demented carnival.

Vivian's head was pulsing now; her throat was dry. 'Let's tear it down,' she said. 'First, I need an aspirin.'

'I'll make you my favorite hangover fix – Brains and Sugar,' Dot said.

'That doesn't sound good,' Vivian said.

They went back to the kitchen and Vivian laid her head on the table, her face against the cool surface. Dot rummaged around. She opened the fridge; she ran the blender. Soon, she placed a glass of something orange in front of Vivian.

'It looks okay,' she said. She noticed that Dot had one too.

'Bottoms up,' Dot said.

'I need an aspirin.'

'It's in there!' she said with great cheer.

It was cold and thick and very, very sweet. Vivian finished in two long gulps.

'Now I'll tell you how to make it,' Dot said. 'Orange juice, one aspirin, one egg – that's the brains – a quarter cup of sugar…'

'A quarter cup!'

'…one tablespoon of pancake mix. You know, to bind it.' Dot paused and drank hers all at once.

Vivian's stomach felt warm and settled.

'Oh,' Dot said. 'I forgot the most important ingredient. Quarter cup of vodka.'

That would explain the warmth, Vivian thought. But she actually felt better. 'Hey, I want to show you something,' she said. 'Wait here.' She climbed up to the attic, brought down the black garment bag and spread it over the table. 'It's a suit.'

'Whose is it?' Dot asked.

'Good question.' She unzipped the back and pulled the garment out. Pressed and clean, the suit was navy blue with pinstripes.

'Nice,' Dot said.

'Nowell says his grandmother never went up into the attic, but I found clothing in a dresser up there, clean and folded like someone just used it. And now this suit. Their grandfather's been dead since Sherman was a teenager, so it's definitely not his. It's too modern.'

'Maybe Grandma Gardiner had a late-life romance,' Dot said. 'She was out here by herself all those years, you know?'

'I never thought of that.'

'Did you ever meet her?' Dot asked.

'Twice,' Vivian said.

'What was she like?'

'Like any old woman.' Vivian searched through the suit, poking her fingers into the pockets. 'She was quiet. My friend Katherine knew her.' In the breast pocket, she felt something square and thin. 'I guess I won't have to ask Katherine about Grandma Gardiner's secret lovers,' she said after a moment.

'Why, what's that?'

She held out the small stack of business cards and Dot leaned over to see. The name of Nowell's father's repair business was embossed across the top in bold green letters and in the lower right corner: Sherman Gardiner, Partner.

'So it was Lonnie's dad's suit. I wonder why he'd leave it here?'

Vivian felt the fabric. 'I don't know.'

'It's been here a long time,' Dot said. 'How long ago did he die?'

'Over six years.'

They were both still leaning over the suit, staring at the business cards, fingering the smooth texture of the jacket, when a soft knock on the door startled them both. Vivian dropped the jacket and it slid onto the floor. Dot cursed and then immediately covered her mouth with her hand.

A few feet back from the screen stood a woman in a bright orange outfit, with a yellow scarf tied around her neck. Vivian quickly recognized Mrs Brodie. She looked much better than the last time Vivian had seen her. Her golden hair was perfectly styled and green, glittery eye shadow radiated above her eyes. Her lips were two stripes of moistened pink.

'Mrs Brodie,' Vivian said. 'Please come in.'

'Thank you.' Her hand was already on the lever of the screen door. She stepped in and closed the door quietly. Her perfume was sharp and fruity. 'Thank you, Mrs Gardiner.'

'Please, call me Vivian.' Remembering Katherine's joke, she added, 'Mrs Gardiner makes me think of my mother-in-law.'

Mrs Brodie smiled tightly. 'It reminds me of Betty Gardiner.'

'This is my sister-in-law,' Vivian said. 'Dot.'

Her eyes widened and her hand went up to her yellow scarf. 'Lonnie's wife?' she asked.

Dot stepped forward. 'Well, yes. You must be Katherine,' Dot said.

'This is Mrs Brodie,' Vivian said. 'She's thinking of Katherine Wilton,' she explained. 'They haven't met yet.'

'Oh yes, Katherine.' Mrs Brodie exhaled loudly. 'Please, call me Kitty, both of you.'

'Would you like a glass of tea?'

'No, thank you.' She shifted her purse, a square-shaped bag with tortoise-shell handles, to her other hand. 'I really just wanted to stop by and apologize for the other day.'

'That's not—' Vivian started to say, but Mrs Brodie waved her off.

'I was very upset, but you didn't need a hysterical woman passing out in your yard.'

Vivian remembered her moans, my poor baby, and the way she crumbled when she saw Vivian come out of the woods.

'I don't know what to say, Mrs, uh, Kitty. It's certainly understandable. I'm so sorry, we're all so sorry for your loss.'

Mrs Brodie's hands gripped then released the handles of her purse. 'The thing is,' she said, 'the thing is, you looked like her, like my Chanelle. And when I saw you come out of the trees, it spooked me. I thought for sure it was her, I really did, for a minute. I've been a little crazy lately, not sleeping well, and I guess my imagination took over. For a split second, that first second when

141

I thought you were my Chanelle, I thought everything was a big, horrible mistake. But then it came back, the memory, and it all happened so quickly, in that split second.' Her eyes were watery.

Vivian pulled a tissue from a box on the counter and handed it to her.

'Thank you.' She pressed the tissue to the edges of her eyes, careful not to smear her makeup. 'You have hair like hers, long and dark. Beautiful hair. Chanelle's father was part Indian, but I never told her. I didn't know how she'd feel about it. I keep remembering lots of things like that, things I didn't tell her.'

'If there's anything we can do...'

Mrs Brodie nodded. 'Thank you. I don't know what you've heard, but she was a good girl, my Chanelle. All kids run around a little, don't they? I know I did, and there's nothing wrong with having some fun. But she was smart and so pretty. I had dreams for her, hopes and plans.'

Dot looked steadily at Mrs Brodie. 'You must miss her very much.'

'Yes, I do. We were very close.' Mrs Brodie dabbed at her nose with the tissue. 'She depended on me, asked my advice on clothes and things. It was more of a friendship, really, than a mother-daughter relationship.' Mrs Brodie opened her purse, dropped the wadded tissue inside then closed it with a decisive snap. 'That's all I wanted to say. I'll leave you alone now.'

'Are you sure you won't stay?' Vivian asked. 'Have some tea?'

'No, thank you. I have to be somewhere.' She rubbed her lips together, freshening her lipstick. 'It's nice to have some young neighbors. Not that I had anything against Mrs Gardiner, you understand. I never saw her much. But sometimes it feels lonely out here. Everybody keeps to themselves.'

'You know Mr Stokes, don't you?'

'I don't see him much either.' Her keys jangled in her hand. 'I'm sorry again for the trouble the other day.'

'It wasn't any trouble,' Vivian said.

As Mrs Brodie turned toward the door, her gaze fell on the blue suit where it lay on the floor. She walked over and picked it up, her hands lingering as she draped it over the garment bag. 'Goodbye for now.'

The fruity smell trailed after her, persisted in the yellow kitchen until it turned acrid in the warm air. They watched as she walked down the driveway to her car. Her clothing, almost the same bright orange as the vests worn by the road crew, seemed even more vivid in the sunlight.

Vivian had just finished telling Dot everything she knew about Mrs Brodie when they heard another car pull up the driveway. 'I can't believe it. No one comes to visit us for weeks, and now that you're here, everyone comes.'

Dot peered around her shoulder. 'Who is it?'

'It's Katherine.' Vivian met her on the porch. 'What are you doing out here?'

Katherine carried a Tupperware container and her bracelets bounced loudly against it as she walked. 'Just came to bring you some cookies. You know me, Little Miss Homemaker.'

'They're homemade?'

'Sure they are. Some of the mothers brought them for a little show the kids had at the school. There were so many left over and I sure don't want them at my house. Being around you has made me decide to finally go on a diet. Believe me, it's long overdue.'

They stepped into the kitchen and Vivian introduced Dot.

'I was just telling Vivian that her tiny figure has depressed me and here you are, just as thin as her!'

'Great to meet you,' Dot said.

'I wanted to see if I could take you both into town for lunch.'

'Guess who was just here?' Vivian said.

'Who?'

'Mrs Brodie.'

'That's not what I thought you'd say.' Katherine's eyes gleamed.

'Do you know her, Katherine?' Dot asked.

'Didn't Vivian tell you? All of us in this town went to the same high school.' She laughed. 'Lots of people knew Kitty. She was very popular.'

'She said she was sorry for coming over the other day,' Vivian said. 'She thought she made a scene.'

'Did she?'

Vivian looked at Katherine, surprised by her sharp tone. 'It's understandable, don't you think?'

She nodded half-heartedly.

'You don't like her much, do you?' Vivian asked.

'No. But I should be more considerate of her during this time. Sorry.'

'Did Mrs Gardiner ever say anything about her?' Vivian asked. 'Mrs Brodie said she hardly saw her.'

'Not that I remember.'

'Did she have many friends in the community? Mrs Gardiner, I mean.'

'I think so,' Katherine said. 'She attended the Methodist church in town, and she knew some families down there. I think she knew Jesper Stokes, before he died of course.'

'She did?' Vivian said.

'They were neighbors a long time. Way back when, Abe Stokes's grandfather, Manus—'

'Manus?' Dot said.

Katherine nodded. 'Manus used to hunt with Betty's husband. So Betty knew Jesper Stokes when he was young, and the current Mr Stokes too.' She looked over. 'Vivian's friend.'

Vivian tilted her head in warning. 'Didn't Mrs Gardiner tell you that Sherman used to visit often?'

'At least three or four times a year,' Katherine said. 'Sometimes more in the summer.'

'He left some clothing here,' Vivian said. 'That suit was his.'

Katherine peered over, raising her eyebrows. 'Nice.'

'Where would he wear it around here?' Vivian asked.

144

'Plenty of places,' she said. 'To church, for one. There are two very good restaurants, Cecil Clement's Italian place and a steak and seafood over in the next town. And they put on formal dances at the community center. Last fall, Max and I finally went to one. It had the feel of a high school reunion, but we had a good time. You wouldn't know by looking at him, but Max can really dance.'

Vivian laughed. 'Nowell tries hard, but he always hunches over, like tall people do sometimes.'

'Lonnie doesn't,' Dot said. 'He sticks his head right in the air and looks everyone over. He loves being in the middle of everything, you know. He wouldn't like it so much if he were my size and felt like everyone was going to squash you.'

'It wasn't very crowded at the community center,' Katherine said, 'so we didn't have to worry about that.'

'Do they have a dance every fall?' Vivian asked.

'A couple of times a year. Usually it's put on by churches or different clubs.'

'Did Mrs Gardiner ever go to one of the dances?'

'Goodness, no! I can't imagine.'

'But you think Sherman went?'

Katherine held up her hand in protest, her bracelets clinking together. 'I didn't say that. I said that someone could dress up to go to one of those things. Why are you asking me all these questions about Sherman?'

'I don't know,' Vivian said. 'I guess when you're going through people's things, you get curious. You know, I never got to meet him.'

Katherine crossed her arms. 'You should've asked Kitty Brodie about Sherman.'

'What do you mean?' Vivian asked.

'I heard Sherman helped Kitty out with things around her house now and then, repairs and what-not, her being on her own and everything.'

'Really?'

'Just being neighborly, I guess. Lord knows she couldn't ask that Mr Stokes for anything. He's got a high horse, that one, and I don't think he cares much for Kitty.'

Vivian wondered why Mrs Brodie had said she hardly knew Betty Gardiner. Did Mrs Gardiner exaggerate or had Sherman hidden the frequency of his visits for some reason? Maybe Sherman was embarrassed by the way his mother needed him, she thought, much like Nowell's mother continued to ask so much of him. Maybe he disguised his visits as business trips, keeping them from his wife and family in order to appease everyone involved. Or maybe it was more complicated; perhaps Sherman had more to hide than a strong attachment to his mother. Vivian felt sure there was something else.

17

'I've got two containers of casserole getting cold in the car,' Katherine said.

Vivian leaned against the kitchen table. 'What for?'

'Oh, I help take food to people who are feeling poorly or can't get out much anymore. Today, I'm headed to Mrs Grossmont's – she's out here by you – then I've got another run further up in the hills to Mr Miller's.' She moved toward the door. 'How about I stop back by after I'm finished and we'll see if you two are up for lunch?'

Vivian followed her gaze, down to the wrinkled T-shirt she had worn to bed. Her hair must be a mess. 'Thanks, Katherine. That would be great.'

'We'll be ready,' Dot added.

They watched Katherine's green car turn onto the main road. Dot turned to her with wide eyes. 'We need tools,' she said.

'I don't think we have time,' Vivian said. 'She's coming back...'

'Let's just start. We need a scraper thing.'

The warm feeling from Dot's hangover remedy still coursed through Vivian. She remembered Nowell's directives, to finish sorting things before they started doing anything about the painting or décor. 'I'll go out to the shed and look.'

The shed was a bountiful source. Vivian found hammers, rusty screwdrivers, a mallet with a cracked wood handle, a dust-choked electric sander, a box-cutter, even a scraper. When she brought the items to the kitchen and set them down, Dot handed her a tall green thermos.

'What's this?'

'More motivation.' Dot's eyes were gleaming, and she reached over and picked up another thermos, maroon and black.

'Where did you get these?' Vivian asked, lifting the thermos. It was plastic, with an airtight lid that Dot had removed. Inside, orange liquid swirled within the metallic lining.

'The cupboards,' Dot said. 'I had to dig through all the tea cups. How many tea cups can an old lady use, anyway?'

Vivian sputtered orange liquid at this, then wiped her mouth and laughed some more. As far as she could tell, the concoction was orange juice and vodka only.

'We have our manly thermoses and our manly tools,' Dot said. 'Let's go.'

At first they had no system. Vivian tried cutting the wallpaper with the box-cutter, which left long ridges in the wall. Dot hacked away with a flat screwdriver and the mallet, which left gouges but sometimes provided a corner that they could tear. They set their thermoses on the ground and returned to them often, and they thought of ways to describe the horses.

'This one has gas,' Dot said. 'He's so uncomfortable.'

'There's a gray one here,' Vivian said. 'He looks lost, can't find his family. He's going to cry any minute.'

They laughed and drank and worked on the wallpaper until they had developed a system. Vivian used the screwdriver to pry away the paper in the corners, then Dot followed up with the scraper. They had to lean over each other at times, which also led to laughter and once, to Vivian falling onto the carpet.

'This one is evil,' Dot said between gulps of air. 'Look at him.'

Vivian crawled over to see the horse, which was low on a pole halfway down the hall. On the way, she knocked over her thermos, which had been recently emptied.

The horse was brown with a jewel-encrusted headband. His eyes were small, black and decidedly evil. The two girls rolled around on the floor, clutching their stomachs in a giggling fit. Every time they would stop and look again at the horse, they'd start again. Eventually, the laughter subsided.

'We're doing a good job,' Dot said, sitting up. 'I'm going to make another drink.'

'Good idea,' Vivian said. She stood up and surveyed their work. They had done quite a bit, almost half of the hallway on one side. The wallpaper came off more easily than she had imagined it would. Here and there, they had missed little sections, so she took the scraper and went to finish up.

She thought about the house and its small rooms, and the trees brushing against each other with their soothing sound, and the smell of damp grass and wood. Maybe we could live here, she thought. We could paint the walls and get our things out of storage. Nowell would have his own room for writing, and I could get a job in town like Katherine. She shook her head as she peeled a small square of paper from the wall. I would feel trapped, she reminded herself. And as she stood there, the scrap of wallpaper hanging from her hand as the horses pulsated in front of her eyes, she realized that the house had grown very quiet. What's happened to Dot? she wondered.

Slowly, she walked to the end of the hall. The fresh air in the kitchen hit her face like a cool breeze. The orange juice container, now empty, was on the counter, as was the vodka bottle. The thermoses had been filled, but Dot was missing. Vivian would have seen her if she had headed to the bathroom. She checked in the living room and Nowell's study. She climbed the steps to the attic and peered inside. Finally, she opened the screen door and stepped onto the patio.

Suddenly, a blast of cold water hit her in the chest and trailed down her legs. She crouched down and when she looked up, Dot was laughing hysterically at the side of the house, holding the green garden hose.

Vivian hurried into the house, opening cupboards until she found something: a pitcher they used to make iced tea. She filled it at the sink. Water bubbling over the edges, she carried it onto the patio, went down the steps, around the side of the house, looking for Dot. A streak of red from the backyard, the flapping of bare feet, and Vivian managed to get most of the water onto Dot as she flew by. Then she grabbed the hose and soaked her more, as Dot tried to make it back to the house. Their squeals echoed through the open space and the world became a blurred, frenetic place. Dot filled the pitcher and doused Vivian again; neither of them was really trying to avoid each other. They ended up at the back of the house, each tugging at the extended hose, screaming and laughing, with a spout of water drenching them both. They were having so much fun that they didn't hear the green car, didn't hear the soft music of the bracelets, didn't hear the footsteps.

'Girls!'

They both froze at the spot, the water gurgling out and over their hands.

'What in the world is going on?' Katherine stood at the threshold to the backyard, hands on her hips.

Vivian chuckled and pulled the hose away from Dot. She walked over and shut it off. Dot walked with her, head down, a stifled smile on her face.

'There's water all over the patio, like a flood,' Katherine said. 'Water in the kitchen. Somebody's gonna break their leg.'

Vivian shrugged. 'We were just having some fun.'

Katherine grinned, looking from one to the other as they stood shoulder-to-shoulder before her. 'Well, my, my. Are you girls drunk?'

Dot snickered, then covered her mouth. 'No, of course not.'

Katherine shook her head, her hair sending reddish sparkles in the sunlight. 'It's eleven o'clock in the morning, girls.' She turned. 'Let's get you cleaned up.'

In the kitchen, Vivian explained their morning's project. They showed Katherine their handiwork and explained how they just couldn't stand the demented horses for one more day.

'They're awful,' Vivian said. 'How anyone could pick that out...'

'Maybe a circus clown, the kind with the sad face!' Dot laughed again then noticed Katherine's expression.

'Everybody's got their own tastes,' she said. She leaned down and started picking up the scraps of wallpaper they'd left on the floor, her bracelets clinking as she gathered them.

'We were going to pick that up,' Vivian said. 'We weren't finished.'

'Oh, I'm happy to help out,' Katherine said, looking up to smile. 'Why don't you girls get dressed and you can drive with me to Mr Miller's? I didn't make it out there yet because Mrs Grossmont had lots to tell me this morning. Poor lady, all by herself out there.'

Dot and Vivian exchanged a glance then went to their respective bedrooms to change. Soon, they were sitting in the car, with their hair brushed and dry clothes. Dot sat in the front with Katherine.

'Where are your men, anyway?' Katherine asked.

'They went fishing,' Vivian said. 'Lonnie met some of the men who've been paving the road. I guess they have a boat at some river.'

She nodded. 'There's a great fishing river past town, up in the hills. Remember I told you we should take a picnic up there one day? It's very scenic, lots of greenery and rock formations. The roads are curvy and lined with trees. Max and I go up there sometimes.'

Dot turned in her seat and flung her arm over the back. Vivian could see the shiny, amber hairs in the soft hollow of her armpit. Her own hairs were coarse and dark and seemed to grow quickly and conspiratorially, sprouting up like tiny tracking missiles in areas she had momentarily neglected. Vivian considered the

151

constant regeneration of hair one of the great injustices of life.

They drove with the windows down and the air, although rather warm, had a sobering effect. In about thirty minutes, they pulled into a driveway much like the one at Grandma Gardiner's. A small brown house with a tin roof, a black and white dog thumping his tail on the porch.

'Why don't you come up with me,' Katherine said. She opened the trunk of her car and pulled out a foil-covered dish. Vivian and Dot followed obediently to the door.

They spent about an hour at Mr Miller's house, talking about the weather and Mr Miller's rheumatoid arthritis and his grand-children and eventually, sharing part of the casserole Katherine had brought for him. As they sat around his table on ancient wooden chairs, passing the sliced bread he had brought from his cupboard, Vivian felt something spread over her. A peace. A sense of being in the presence of something good, something right. Her appreciation for Katherine deepened and she felt ashamed for her own lack of motivation.

On the way back, Katherine took what she called a 'scenic detour', and they passed through areas that were different from the plains and stripes of muted green closer to the house. Here, the land jutted upwards in crags and clumps of reddened earth. The trees remained, stubbornly reaching from the uncertain levels, crowding together at times and sometimes, going it alone. The road was a series of languid turns, slow climbs and gentle descents. Vivian leaned her head against the car window and looked up to the scattering of puffy clouds. She thought about possibilities, about appearances. The sky was three-dimensional, a vivid, jaw-dropping blue with the depth of stained glass and the luminescence of candlelight. It was a sky that seemed, at first, impossible to replicate on a flat surface. Soon, she began to recognize patterns: swirls and ridges, curves and textures, in the consistent blueness of that sky, a blue expanse that was impenetrable at first glance. Vivian remembered staring at her desktop in grammar school, during rainy-day, heads-down games or boring lessons, and noticing the variety within the wood, the scant pencil remains from the students before her, the distinct markings of the grain. Like a fingerprint, each section unique to itself and to the seer. Eyes can become discerning, she thought, if you look long enough. The sky, the qualities of wood. She wondered who invented the microscope, what made them think there was anything to see. Dr Lightfoot said that the motivation driving the scientist and the artist was the same: to create. Vivian thought about pictures she had seen of early autopsies, fifteenth-century artists monitoring dissections in order to paint the body more faithfully. She thought about Da Vinci's notebooks, the embryo in the womb and his precise sketches. If you look long enough, close enough. Is that what artists do? The sky, the qualities of wood. Dr Lightfoot was wrong. Scientists seek to improve, while artists merely represent, reflect, interpret. Vivian stared through the smudged glass of the car window, wondering how she would describe or paint the sky. She leaned back in the seat, breeze ruffling her long dark hair and, for a moment, felt perfectly content.

In time, they sailed over the newly asphalted hill before the descent to the house.

'What's that?' Katherine pointed out the window, her bracelets clanking like an alarm.

Over the fields of high grass dotted with pastel late-summer blooms, dark smoke curdled in a narrow cyclone toward the sky. Vivian scooted over and peered at the smoke, trying to estimate its source. Dot leaned over as well, and as the car slowed in front of the driveway, they all swiveled to look through the windshield.

Beside the white house in the dirt clearing next to the driveway, several figures circled a large, black object. From its center, huge flames blazed up and whipped at the air. Katherine parked behind a dusty blue-and-white van that was behind Lonnie's jeep. As they got out of the car, Vivian heard a reverberating crack, which she

153

immediately recognized as the sound of an ax on wood. They walked around the van and approached the jeep. Lonnie and another man took turns chopping at a wide tree several yards back.

The men around the fire, one of whom was Nowell, talked loudly, each holding a can of beer. They all looked sunburned and jovial.

'I think it's a tribal feast,' Katherine said in a low voice. 'Like on National Geographic.'

Dot snickered. 'You don't see a wild boar roasting on a stick anywhere, do you?'

'Hello!' Vivian called.

The men looked over. The fire was issuing from an old barbecue grill; the domed lid sat on the ground. Vivian recognized one of the county road workers, a tall, thin, copper-haired man with a friendly smile. The man next to him was unfamiliar, and next to him was Nowell. The fourth man turned around and it was Mr Stokes.

'Hello, Mrs Gardiner,' he said. 'Mrs Wilton.'

I thought we had agreed on first names, Vivian thought.

Dot had walked toward the two working on the tree, and when Lonnie saw her he called out. 'Stand back, honey! This tree's coming down!' The other man was the road crew worker who had come to the house. Lonnie had said that his name was Jerry.

'Where were you?' Nowell leaned over and kissed Vivian's cheek, his face hot and smoky from the fire.

'We went with Katherine on an errand.'

'Hello,' he said to her.

Dot rejoined them, walking gingerly around the fire.

'This is Tom, and Eduardo,' Nowell said. 'They both work with the county. They're here paving the road.'

'It looks like you're getting ready to do some serious cooking,' Katherine said. 'I'd love to stick around and see if it survives that fire, but I'm late picking Max up.'

'Thanks for taking us,' Vivian said.

154

Katherine winked at her. 'You betcha. I'll talk to you this week.' She turned and went to her car. When she reached the road, she honked twice and waved.

Dot asked Nowell: 'Why are they cutting that tree down?'

'Mr Stokes said it was dead. It's rotted out in the middle and it could fall over onto our vehicles.'

'God forbid,' Vivian snickered.

'It doesn't look dead,' Dot said.

Vivian wondered if she were one of those people who got all worked up about trees.

'Well, it is,' Mr Stokes said. The flames reflected from his wet teeth as he smiled; his eyes were bloodshot and squinty.

'You really think it would have fallen over?' Vivian glanced at the beer in his hand and wondered how many he'd had.

He cocked his head to the side, grinning strangely. 'It could've stayed standing for another twenty years,' he said. 'But that doesn't mean it was alive.'

The flames died down and Nowell began scraping the bars of the grill with a long metal brush. 'Lonnie wants to chop the whole thing up and sell it as firewood,' he said. 'Make us a little money. This is the time of year people start stocking up, because the wood is dry.'

Vivian glanced at Mr Stokes. 'Is that right?'

'I hope they know what they're doing,' Tom said. 'There's a certain way to cut a tree, so it falls in the right direction.'

'I'll be right back,' Nowell said. 'Anybody need anything from the house?'

'Food!' somebody yelled.

'Coming right up. Viv, give me a hand?'

She ducked underneath the cloud of black smoke and followed Nowell to the house. When they entered the kitchen she asked: 'Did you catch any fish?'

'Lonnie caught two and I caught three. One of mine was huge. Hey, where is this thing plugged in?'

155

Vivian saw that he had the radio from the counter under his arm and was impatiently pulling on the cord.

'Oh, here, I got it,' he said. 'Do we have batteries?'

'There's some in there.'

'By the way,' he said, touching her arm. 'What happened in the hallway?'

Vivian shrugged, looking away. He had told her not to do any redecorating until the clutter was cleared. 'We just started taking that wallpaper down.'

Nowell patted her back. 'Can't say I'll miss it,' he said. 'I always thought those horses were creepy.'

Reaching around his waist, Vivian pressed her face into his chest. He leaned down and she felt his chin on her head. All at once, a memory surfaced: on the day of her graduation from college, Nowell filled their apartment with flowers. Roses, her favorite, in all imaginable colors, overflowing from glass vases placed on every open surface. The graduation ceremony had been in the afternoon, an impossibly sunny day, rows of white fold-out chairs on the school's grassy field. Afterwards, they had dinner at La Grange, a French restaurant they couldn't really afford, just the two of them because her parents had to get back home early for their classes the next day. And it was almost as if Nowell had anticipated the letdown she would feel. She wouldn't forget the sight, their small apartment transformed into a magical place, awash in color, the air fragrant and sweet, and the look on Nowell's face as he waited to see her reaction.

18

Nowell took the radio outside and in a moment Vivian heard music on the porch, a soft rock number turned up rather loud. He rushed through the screen door again, grabbed the platter of meat from her hands, and took it outside. She decided to make more iced tea. The pitcher was washed and dried and had been placed next to the sink by Katherine, who had also mopped the kitchen and cleaned up while they got dressed that morning. Vivian dragged a chair over to the pantry. As she reached for the box of tea bags on the highest shelf, she heard a deep voice: 'Need any help with that?' and suddenly, she was aware of the brevity of her shorts and the angle of vision that her elevated position gave the person at the door.

'No thanks.' She quickly stepped down from the chair, the box pressed against her chest. She saw that it was Mr Stokes. 'Please, come in.'

'My shoes are a little muddy,' he said through the screen. 'It was damp up there, and we had to walk a good ways back to the river.'

'It's okay,' Vivian said. 'Come on in.'

'Thanks. I wouldn't mind getting out of the heat for a while.' He opened the door and stepped inside. His work boots and rough, nicked hands seemed out of place in the delicately colored kitchen, with its hues of yellow and its cheery, lace-trimmed curtains. He looked out of place indoors, under artificial lighting. His presence saturated the room like steam, the briny smokiness of him, the suntanned ruggedness of his face. 'Do you have a glass of cold water?' he asked.

'Sure,' Vivian said. 'Why don't you sit down for a minute?'

'I really feel my age on a day like today. Can't seem to keep up with those young ones.'

'Right now they're running on pure alcohol,' Vivian said. 'Nowell will be exhausted tomorrow.'

'Will he? Yeah, we were up before the sun. My favorite time of day, the morning, but then you know that already.'

Vivian handed him a glass of water, removed the tea bags from their paper holders and draped them one by one over the wide mouth of the pitcher. 'I had no idea you were going fishing with them,' she said.

'I ran into your brother-in-law last night and he asked me to come along.'

'Last night?'

He nodded as he gulped the water. 'I was smoking some beef outside. I like to make jerky for the winter. He said he could smell it all the way over here.'

'Hm,' she said. 'Excuse me for one minute while I set this out in the sun.' Vivian had to walk to the side of the house for sunlight because the shade had stretched almost the entire length of the driveway. Dot was sitting in the open, back doorway of the blue-and-white van with one of the road crew. Nowell was engaged in a deep discussion with the other man; something about a new gun law, and Lonnie and Jerry had taken a break from the tree and were standing near the barbecue, eyeing the meat. She went back into the house.

'I hope you don't mind, I helped myself to another glass of your tap water,' Mr Stokes said.

'Of course not.'

'I guess this isn't the barbecue you had in mind,' he said.

'We'll just have to have two. Katherine couldn't stay this time, and Max wasn't here. We'll invite you back some other time.'

Mr Stokes held his water glass with both hands. 'Tomorrow I'm going out of town for a few days.'

'Where are you going?' Vivian asked, quickly adding: 'I don't mean to be nosy.'

He swirled his finger around the rim of his glass. 'I have some relatives up north. I try to visit once or twice a year. They're elderly and really enjoy the company.'

'You'll drive?'

He nodded. 'I have a beat-up truck that won't quit working. I'd like a new one, but can't seem to let go of it.'

'Sentimental value?'

'No. Just practical, I guess.'

Vivian pulled her hair over her shoulder, ran her fingers through it and flipped it back.

'That meat sure smells good,' he said. 'I think I'd better fight for position out there.'

'Mr Stokes?' she said. 'Um, Abe?'

'Yeah?'

'Do you think it would be inappropriate, I mean, would it be insensitive or strange to invite Mrs Brodie to the barbecue?'

His brow wrinkled into deep crevices and his eyes turned hard and dull. The mention of her had pained him in some way. 'I didn't know you knew her.'

'I don't, really. I saw her that day, when we both saw her. And she came over today.'

'Today?'

'Just stopped by. She's still torn up about the, about her daughter. She said they were very close.'

He looked away.

'What?'

He brought his gaze back to her. 'I just wondered why the girl kept running off if they were so close. I've heard that woman screaming for her through the woods, hollering her head off like somebody had…'

'…died,' Vivian finished.

He looked down, embarrassed.

'Teenagers fight with their parents,' she said. 'I know I did.'

'I suppose Mrs Brodie doesn't want to remember it that way,' he said.

Vivian leaned against the counter. 'Maybe that's not the important part,' she said. The air in the kitchen was stagnant and warm. She sat at the table, and Mr Stokes seemed to flinch when she did. 'Did you ever meet Mrs Gardiner's son, Sherman?' she asked.

He lifted his glass and set it down gently, then lifted it, then set it down. The glass made low thuds like fingertips drumming. 'I did, once or twice,' he finally said.

'He used to help Mrs Brodie out with repairs, things around her house?'

'I wouldn't know.'

She remembered Katherine had said Mrs Brodie's father and Sheriff Townsend were old friends. 'Does Mrs Brodie have relatives or friends nearby?'

Mr Stokes left the glass in the center of the table and wiped his palms on his thighs. 'Not anymore.'

'That's too bad,' she said. First Katherine's behavior, she thought, and now this. Why did everyone act so uncomfortable when she brought up Nowell's father? Or Mrs Brodie, for that matter?

'Your brother-in-law has quite a temper,' Mr Stokes said.

Vivian shook herself from her thoughts. 'What?'

'That Lonnie. He's got a bad temper.'

'Why do you say that?'

'They were having a competition all day, who could catch the most fish. That Lonnie was behind, and when everyone was packing up, he started yelling.'

'Yelling?'

'He didn't want us to leave. He threw his pole into the water.'

'I'm afraid Lonnie drinks a little too much sometimes,' she said, 'and if you were out in the sun all day...'

'It wasn't liquor,' Mr Stokes said. 'Something else.'

'He competes with Nowell,' Vivian said quietly.

'He apologized, made a joke out of the whole thing.'

She looked into his eyes. 'Why are you telling me this?'

Outside, someone yelled: 'There it goes!'

They heard the snapping and creaking as the tree began its descent to the earth, and they reached the patio in time to see it rest, pushing up flurries of dust and sending birds fluttering through the standing trees.

'Are you happy now?' Dot called.

Lonnie made celebratory whooping noises: 'Yes, I sure am!'

Nowell called from the yard. 'Viv, bring the buns, would you? And some napkins, and the ketchup. Oh, forget it, I'll come in.'

'Soup's on,' Mr Stokes said, and he lumbered towards the door.

The hamburgers were thick and tasted of smoke. The men remained around the fire eating. Vivian went to the shaded porch and set her plate on the banister. The men stood in two small groups, one near the jeep and the other next to the barbecue grill.

Dot brought her hot dog towards the house. 'Got room up there for one more?'

'Sure,' Vivian said. 'Didn't you get anything else?'

She settled into the peeling porch swing. 'I didn't want anything. I had a lot of that casserole.'

'I don't know why I'm so hungry,' Vivian said.

'Don't worry,' Dot said. 'You're thin.'

'I wasn't always,' she said.

The men erupted into laughter, deep tones like thunder. Vivian peered around the porch column. Jerry was talking, gesturing emphatically with his hands. She noticed again his broad shoulders and narrow waist, the rough quality of his skin. Suddenly expressive,

161

his face was sunburned across his forehead and cheekbones, but still white around his eyes. She remembered the sunglasses he'd worn the day he waved at her from the road. The oval, mirrored lenses reflected the world as a tiny microcosm of shrunken, distorted forms. She had glanced at them as they picked up the fleshy hue and sloping curve of her bare legs.

'So that's the Mr Stokes you mentioned?' Dot asked.

'Yes. He lives behind us, back past the trees.'

'He seems nice. Sort of quiet, you know?'

'I've only talked to him a few times,' Vivian said, 'but he's interesting. He looks at me like he already knows what I'm going to say.'

'Sometimes we click with certain people,' Dot said. 'There's a chemistry. You meet someone and know right away you want to be around him. Maybe it's a sense of smell, you know, because they say it's the most important of our senses for things like memory and longing. Goes back to our animal natures, tracking by scent. Or maybe it's something else, some hidden instinct.'

'I don't think it's anything animal,' Vivian laughed. 'He's just a neighbor.'

'Oh, I know.' She crossed her legs on the swing. 'But aren't you drawn to him in a way? If there were twenty people in a crowded room, you'd probably approach him first.'

'You're making it sound like a sociology experiment. I only said I found him interesting.'

'Sorry. I guess I was thinking about Lonnie, because that's how I felt about him when we met. There was an immediate connection, you know, like two planets being pulled together.'

Vivian shook her head. 'Maybe I'm intrigued by some gossip Katherine told me about him. Or maybe I've got too much time to sit around and imagine things.'

'What gossip?' Dot asked.

'A story about his lost love.'

'A lost love? That does sound interesting.'

Vivian smiled and took the last watered-down drink of her tea. The ice cubes had melted and the small lemon wedge lay limp and stringy at the bottom of the glass.

Suddenly, Mr Stokes stood at the base of the porch steps, a stack of used paper plates in one hand and the greasy tongs that Nowell had used to turn the meat in the other. 'Which one of you has a long lost love?' His mouth stretched into a crooked smile.

'Doesn't everyone?' Dot asked.

Vivian looked away, noticing the stubborn weeds that had cropped up next to the house, tangled together in the crevice where grass met wood

Mr Stokes looked at Vivian. 'I'm heading home. Thanks for the meal.'

'You're welcome,' she said. 'Nice to see you again.'

His eyes met hers briefly. 'It was real kind of Lonnie to ask me along.'

'That's Lonnie,' Dot said. 'Glad to meet you, Mr Stokes.'

He nodded at her. 'I'm not used to having such friendly neighbors. This house has been empty for so long.'

Vivian wondered again about the strained relationship between him and Mrs Brodie. Although Katherine said that over the years, the rest of the town seldom saw him, Mr Stokes suddenly seemed quite sociable.

He made his way towards the rest of the men. They were still standing near the barbecue, which was now mostly embers and a few crackling briquettes.

'Have a good trip,' Vivian called.

He nodded then continued to the group of men. After goodbyes, he headed towards the woods that led to his house.

'So what do you think your special talent is?' Dot asked.

Vivian lowered her hamburger. 'What?'

'You said your mother was hoping that you had a hidden talent, some calling.'

'I don't know,' Vivian said.

She leaned forward. 'Something you're really good at.'

'What's yours?'

Dot shrugged. 'Well, I can play the piano a little. A girlfriend of mine was rich and I spent a lot of time at her house, you know? She took lessons and taught me. Actually, I wasn't very good.' She paused, looking up at the withered porch awning. 'I'm a good friend, I think. I'm loyal and I try to be honest. Oh, I can make great paper airplanes. I had a book once on how to do it.'

Vivian laughed.

'I guess I haven't found one great talent, not yet. I hope I'm not disappointed when I find out what it is.'

'Don't you think it's possible to be good at many things,' Vivian said, 'but not great at any one thing? Your average person. Average talent, average ability.'

'No,' Dot said. 'I like the idea of a special talent. It doesn't have to be something artistic, you know, or something impressive. Some people are great mothers, that's their talent. Some people are intuitive, they can read people. Then you have your pianists, your painters.'

'Scholars, writers,' Vivian added.

'Exactly.' She tilted her head so that her hair waved back and forth.

'Have you always had long hair?' Vivian asked. 'I have.'

'Pretty much,' Dot said. 'I'm too lazy to change it.'

'In the fourth grade, I had a perm,' Vivian said.

'Oh, no.'

'My mom's idea.'

Dot smiled. 'How was it?'

'Horrible, of course. At the time I thought it was great, but perms weren't very advanced back then. It was dried-out and kinky and I had to use a pick.'

'Whoever invented them is very rich today,' Dot said, 'especially the ones you can do at home. Women's vanity is always a good investment, you know? Just look at all the cosmetics we have, all the different kinds of shampoo, hair color, nail polish. It seems like everyone I know has had a perm at one time or another.'

'Me, too,' Vivian said.

'I used to want to invent things,' Dot said. 'As a kid, I would spend hours and hours sitting around, trying to think of inventions. I thought a lot about being a scientist. There was a chemistry set I wanted so badly one year.'

'I didn't know any girls who thought about being scientists.'

'Neither did I.' She swung her legs from the swing. 'I worked at it, though. I mixed up secret ingredients, collected spare parts, things I found in the street. Once I thought I could invent something to bring things back to life.'

'Like what?'

'Eventually people, I thought. It was a potion. It had Still Grow in it, you know, that plant food for bigger tomatoes, and I used eggs, since I had recently found out that they were actually unborn chickens.'

'Brains,' Vivian said, grinning. 'How old were you?'

'Ten or eleven. I don't remember what the other ingredients were but there was a simple kind of logic to all of them, you know? The main thing was the Still Grow, I remember that. I had a parakeet that died and I kept it hidden under my bed for almost three weeks. Every morning and every night I'd put the secret potion down its throat with a medicine dropper.'

Vivian handed Dot a towel. 'For three weeks?'

She nodded. 'It started to smell of course, but I really wanted the bird back. I'd only had it for a few months. My dad gave it to me. By the time it died, my father was already gone.' She reached over and picked up some silverware to dry.

'What finally happened?' Vivian asked.

'To the bird?'

She nodded.

'It shriveled up, got smaller and smaller. At first I pretended it

165

was transforming into another life form. Even then, I'd seen too many science-fiction shows. It was strange, you know, the way it shrunk. Like it was collapsing into itself. Sometimes I think about that on days when I feel like being alone, you know, when you want to stay in bed all day. I think about collapsing into myself, like that bird. Maybe that's how death feels.' She shook her head slightly. 'Anyway, I had this whole method for giving the bird the secret potion. I'd tie a bandanna around my face because of the smell. I kept it in a shoebox. Oh, and I wore gloves, you know, the kind for washing dishes. So all of this stuff was under my bed and my mom found it.'

'She could smell it?'

'No. She went on a rampage one day, clearing all of my dad's things out of the house.'

'Oh.'

'Normally she wouldn't have come into my room.'

'Was she mad?' Vivian asked.

'Not really. When I came home from school she told me she'd thrown my bird away, and I went out to the garbage can and there was everything – the gloves, the box, the bandanna laid over the top. There were stacks and boxes of things next to the trash, all of my dad's belongings. His clothes, his old record player. The shoebox was on top of his collection of *Playboys*.'

'Didn't your mom think it was strange that you'd kept a dead bird?'

Dot shrugged. 'I was always doing weird things. Only child, you know?'

Vivian dried the last piece of silverware and set it in the drawer. 'My friend Diane's father kept *Playboys* in his nightstand,' she said. 'She was my best friend from the second to the fifth grade. We used to sneak in and look at them.'

'Really?'

'It was one of the most exciting things about going to her house. We'd pick favorites and pretend to be models.'

166

Dot shrugged. 'I saw them all around my house, so it wasn't a big deal with me, you know?'

'I always thought it was strange that my dad didn't have any,' Vivian said. 'I looked all over, but never found anything except history books and news magazines.'

'Maybe you just never found them.'

'No. He didn't have any. I'm sure he didn't.'

The sun was descending, leaving a twilight of smoky air and quiet. The trees, a natural frame to the scene, had grown silent since the felling of their tall, seasoned brother; the air was unnaturally motionless, the moon a chalky impression on the sky. As the day drained away, the men's voices grew louder and then quiet again. Vivian went into the house and heard the traveling remnants of conversation as the party broke up, then the grinding of dirt and metal as someone put the domed lid back on the barbecue and wheeled it into the shed.

19

Vivian's mother once spent a month interviewing descendants of coal mine strikers and researching black lung. She was gone the entire month of August that year; Vivian was sixteen.

Vivian and her father had always gotten along in a quiet, comfortable way. They talked about worldly things such as baseball or foreign affairs, or local things: their cranky next-door neighbor, what to have for dinner, the items her class was including in their time capsule. Or they were quiet together, watching television or sitting with their books or magazines, sharing tidbits from their reading now and then as she imagined he and her mother did. Her father was an equalizing force to her mother's high-strung ways, a ground to absorb the shocks of her irregularities. Vivian relied on his steadiness. Because her mother often had evening classes or was working on a book, they became fast-food connoisseurs, sometimes eating out every night of the week.

As a young man, her father had been straight and lean, with a full head of dark hair and muscular legs. Vivian saw a high school picture. Since then, his hair had thinned on top, but he still combed it straight back. The points over his temples receded further each year, making his face larger. At the time her mother left for the book on black lung, he had recently quit walking the two miles to the university as had been his custom in the warmer months. The lack of exercise and unhealthy diet had taken their toll; at forty, her father seemed in some ways like a much older man.

That summer she was sixteen, Vivian enjoyed the great freedoms her mother's trip afforded. Her father was teaching a summer class three afternoons a week, and her curfew had recently been adjusted by one hour. She half-heartedly looked for a summer job. She had one interview at a convenience store, but her mother wouldn't allow her to work past nine o'clock.

Vivian's best girlfriend at the time didn't have a job either. Linda lived in a large, two-story house with a tennis court and pool in the back. Vivian spent most of her days there, watching television or sunbathing, hoping to catch a glimpse of the two good-looking brothers who lived next door. She and Linda played tennis some-times, but Linda was bored with the sport. And there were parties on the weekends, and hanging out at the mall. Linda had her driver's license and a brand new convertible. They drove every-where, showing off around town.

At home, Vivian and her father passed each other like two lodgers in a hotel. She often stayed for dinner at Linda's and sometimes, she'd notice his failed attempts at cooking dumped into the trashcan, or the cardboard and paper remnants from whatever place he had stopped for a burger or burrito. A few times they went to their old favorite restaurants, but they brought their meals home. Vivian suddenly felt awkward eating in public with her father. Besides, she didn't want to miss any calls.

When she was home, she spent most of her time in her bedroom, talking on the telephone or listening to the radio. Her father sometimes checked on her before he went to bed, and Vivian would let him know if she'd be home for dinner the next day, or whether she'd be sleeping over at Linda's.

After a couple of weeks of this schedule, her father knocked on her door one night.

She was talking on the telephone as usual.

He opened the door slowly and peered in. 'Can you hang up? I want to ask you something.'

Vivian's eyes rolled back in her head, almost before she could stop them, but she ended the call. Her father stepped inside, leaving his hand on the doorknob. He cleared his throat. 'Would you like to go to a movie on Saturday, a matinee? They're showing that new one, about the alien.'

'Linda said that movie was stupid,' she said.

'Or another movie. Your choice.'

'What time?'

'In the afternoon. I told your grandparents that we'd come over for dinner afterwards.'

'This Saturday?'

'Yes, this Saturday.'

She pushed herself up. 'I can't. I already have plans to spend the night at Linda's.'

She watched the transformation in his face. The corner of his mouth twitched and his jaw went rigid.

'You'll have to change your plans,' he said. 'I've already told them, and we're going.'

'But…'

'Listen, Vivie. You've had your run of the place these two weeks. You know as well as I do that your mother wouldn't let you spend every weekend at your friend's house.'

'Yes, she would.'

'Well, I won't,' he said. 'I've asked you for one day.'

'But we're doing something special that night.'

His tone was flat. 'Reschedule your plans for the following weekend.'

'I can't.'

'You have to.'

When Vivian realized he wouldn't budge, she got angry. There was a big party Saturday night, and she wasn't going to miss it. 'I'll try, Dad, but I don't know if Linda can find someone else…'

'Vivie,' he interrupted. 'You will be here all day Saturday and you will have dinner at your grandparents' and stay here that night. I don't want to hear another word.' He turned his back and walked out.

Vivian furiously dialed Linda's number, and what they planned was this: Vivian would go along with the movie and dinner at her grandparents'. Grandma and Grandpa Shatlee would start settling into their armchairs around seven, and her father would be ready to come home. She'd tell him she was tired and go to bed. Linda took advantage of the situation to break her own parents' rules. She'd tell them she'd decided to stay home and would go to bed early like Vivian. Then, both of them could sneak out, attend the party, and stay out as long as they liked.

The plan was doomed from the start, although they were foiled in a way neither of them had considered: Linda's older sister.

The party was one of those crazy, grand events of youth to be recalled countless times later, almost mythologized. Among the monumental things that happened were Linda skinning her knees in the middle of the street after leaving a message in lipstick on someone's truck and Vivian dancing on top of the covered Jacuzzi in the backyard until the wooden cover splintered, cutting her ankle. They had no idea older kids would be there. By the time Linda's sister reported to her parents (who immediately phoned Vivian's father), Vivian and Linda were intoxicated, injured, and generally, having a great time.

When they brought Vivian home, her father was waiting for her. There was a quiet chill in the air, like before a storm. He opened the screen door and she walked under his outstretched arm into the house as he exchanged a few words with Linda's parents. He didn't yell at her, only asked if she needed any help, then he followed her to her room and lingered in the doorway. His face drooped in soft folds. 'Who do you think you are, treating me like this?' he asked.

She sat on the bed and looked up at him. She'd never heard his voice so sad.

'Vivie, I thought we had an understanding, a trust.' Slowly, he turned and walked away.

He never told her mother about the incident and they never spoke of it again. Later, Vivian bragged to her friends that she'd suffered no ill consequences, unlike Linda, who lost her driving privileges for one month. But something had changed; a transition that started quite naturally in her relationship with her father had gone off course somehow, and Vivian felt the gap with every low-lidded look from him, with every strained silence. Who was she, to treat him like that? In those brief moments, the question surfaced and she pushed it out of her mind. Who was she becoming? He'd never given her any reason to lie.

The memory of sneaking out for the great party came to her unexpectedly, during the late afternoon of the day following the impromptu barbecue, when she pulled back the curtain divider and found Nowell's study empty. A thought came quickly: Has he snuck out?

They were alone in the house. Lonnie had taken Dot to the spot where he fished with the other men. Vivian glanced at the clock that morning when she heard the smooth hum of Lonnie's jeep: 7 a.m. After the evening of drinking, even Nowell ignored his regimented schedule and slept until after nine, but as always, Lonnie proved himself impervious to lack of sleep.

Vivian had spent most of the morning out in the yard, clearing the debris that seemed to accumulate daily and poking around in the shed, taking inventory. Aside from the tools they had used the day before, there was a push mower, two rakes, some sort of canvas sack, five metal stakes, a proliferation of spiders. Perhaps an entire colony, she thought. Having the house and the land to look after was proving to be a bigger burden than she'd anticipated. She wanted to have a yard sale soon, so she'd been trying to keep the grounds presentable. She didn't want anyone thinking they were low-class squatters, Mrs Gardiner's ignorant relations from the city.

After she had lunch, she unraveled the hose at the side of the house, hooked it up to the faucet under the kitchen window and filled a large pot with soapy water. Under the bright sun, she carefully washed the old red truck. She worked hard, without pause, until her sandals were soaked through and traces of soap and water darkened her T-shirt. A tattered towel made four uneven rags, and she blackened them scrubbing the hubcaps and underside of the truck. After she had hosed the soap from every surface, she stood back and surveyed her work. The red paint looked sleek and new with the coating of water; the chrome glared in the sunlight. As the water evaporated, Vivian noticed streaks of light-colored dirt. She washed these sections once more, rinsing again with water from the hose. After a few trips back to touch up areas, she decided that the job was good enough. She dried the still-wet surfaces then gathered the soggy towels into her arms.

The muscles in her shoulders and the backs of her thighs were sore, but she found the physical labor invigorating. It was a completely different type of work than, for instance, her job at the water management agency. Sitting at a desk gave her aches and pains, but they were of a stiff, fatiguing variety. After a day of work on the house, sorting and clearing things, cleaning and reaching into corners and high up to shelves, her body felt warm and pliant. The blood raced through her limbs.

Vivian glanced at the kitchen clock, a round-faced model with a picture of a rooster, as she took the towels to the washer and drier. Her focused attention to the yard and the truck had taken most of the afternoon and dinnertime was nearing.

She took a quick shower and put on a clean pair of shorts and a T-shirt from one of her parents' vacations. The house was quiet. She could hear the whooshing sound of the breeze through the trees and the soft hum of the refrigerator. Nowell had gone into his study after his late breakfast and she hadn't seen him since.

173

She knew he must be hungry; there weren't any dishes in the kitchen to indicate that he'd eaten. She stood at the divider to his room, called his name several times, and slowly pulled back the curtain.

The room looked the same as always, neat and shady. On the computer screen, the word processing program was open; at the top of an otherwise blank page, two words were centered: Chapter Thirteen. The curtain billowed with the breeze, and a stack of blank paper next to the printer ruffled and settled. She pulled back the curtain and saw that the window was open about six inches. There was an opening in the screen, where someone could push two fingers through.

A flash of red caught her eye like a stop sign. Someone was moving behind the trees. Had Nowell worn a red shirt that morning? Where could he have gone? She let the curtain fall. If he had left through the front door while she was washing the truck, she would have seen him. Should she check the other rooms? Did he climb out the window?

A car pulled into the driveway; tires crunched on the dirt. Vivian peeked behind the curtain again. It was Nowell, out in the woods. He had cleared the line of trees and strode rapidly towards the house. Out front, a car door slammed. She turned quickly and knocked two books onto the floor. The deep tones of Lonnie's laugh echoed on the porch; his keys jingled. Quickly replacing the books on the desk, she bolted across the room. As the screen door creaked, she raced down the hall. Lonnie's voice reverberated in the kitchen as she leaped into her bedroom. 'Hello!'

'I'll be right out,' she called. She draped a towel around her shoulders. Her wet hair had left a v-shaped damp spot between her shoulder blades. She walked toward the window, listening for sounds from the study. She couldn't hear anything.

When she entered the kitchen, Dot was unpacking the cooler they had taken, and Lonnie was washing his hands at the sink. 'How was your drive?' she asked.

Dot looked up, her face brightening. 'Great. Can you tell I got some sun?'

'Looks good,' Vivian said. 'You'd better put some aloe on your shoulders, though.'

Dot pressed a finger into the flesh of her shoulder, and watched as the white impression faded quickly to pinkish-red. 'You're right,' she said.

Lonnie's rough hands strangled a dish towel then left it in a clump on the counter. 'Where's Number One?'

'Still working, I guess.' Vivian glanced towards the study and watched as Dot took two beer cans from the cooler and carried them to the refrigerator. 'I guess you weren't too thirsty for beer after last night,' she said.

Dot wrinkled her nose. 'I couldn't even finish one. You know, I think I had five or six at the barbecue. And that was after our morning festivities.'

'How do you feel today?' Vivian asked.

'A little tired.'

'You didn't seem tired to me.' Lonnie winked one of his red-rimmed eyes.

'Oh, please.' Dot pushed his chest.

He staggered back. 'I feel great.'

'Not even a little tired, Lonnie?' Vivian asked.

'Who's tired?' They all turned as Nowell emerged from behind the curtain divider.

'Vivian was saying you were,' Lonnie said.

'No way.' He pounded his chest with his fists.

Dot lifted the cooler and took it outside to dump the ice.

Nowell asked: 'Did you show Dot that place where the road curves, past those rocks?'

Lonnie nodded. 'We drove about forty miles past the fishing spot, past the state line. We had fried fish for lunch at a shack down by the river, some old-timer with his own little place. Unbelievable.'

'How did your writing go today?' Vivian asked Nowell. Her blood was pumping; she felt like her chest was expanding.

'I finished a chapter and started a new one.' His face was lined with perspiration.

'Great,' she said.

Lonnie pushed Nowell as he walked by and Nowell lunged toward him.

Dot came back into the kitchen, her arms damp after hosing off the cooler. 'No wrestling in the house,' she said. 'You animals take it outside.'

Vivian looked at Nowell, wondering where he'd been. Had he really climbed out the window? Was there any other explanation? For weeks he had claimed to be working in his private room, separated from her and all outside activity by a ridiculous make-shift wall, and now she had to wonder what he'd really been doing. Was he trying to get away from her? Where did he go?

She shut the cupboard loudly. If Nowell could sneak around, so could she. Mr Stokes had said he'd be gone for a few days, so there was no chance of running into him back there. There had to be some reason why Nowell had gone into the woods. Mr Stokes had seen Lonnie in the woods, two nights before, when he invited him on the fishing trip. She wondered if Lonnie and Nowell had some special place, some clearing where they cooked-out before she arrived. Maybe she could find it, figure out what drew them there.

She knew everyone was tired, whether they wanted to admit it or not, and while she had felt sluggish earlier, she was now strangely rejuvenated by her plans, excited in the same way as when she and Linda secretly plotted to attend that party. She waited anxiously for them to sleep.

20

Everyone retired early. Once Nowell was asleep, Vivian eased herself out of bed and picked up her jeans from the floor. The bedroom was lit by the greenish tint of the half-moon outside, but in the hallway it was darker. Feeling her way with her fingertips, she paused briefly at Dot and Lonnie's door. It was quiet everywhere, just after eleven o'clock.

In the kitchen she pulled on her jeans and slipped into the sandals she'd left by the door. In a drawer near the pantry, she found the flashlight that had recently been replenished with new batteries.

She didn't fully understand why she was going into the woods. The idea struck her that afternoon, when she discovered Nowell was missing. She couldn't get over what a strange thing it was for him to do. Maybe he wanted to take a break but didn't want to spend it with her, didn't want to have to explain why he wanted to be alone. There were other, half-formed reasons. Both Nowell and Mr Stokes had warned her against venturing beyond the trees alone, and she wanted to prove her independence, if only to herself. But it was even more than that. Lonnie had been seen twice in the woods by Mr Stokes; once before she arrived, the night he was cooking his cobbler, and again two nights ago. And, Mr Stokes had been popping up quite a bit, despite Katherine's description of him as a veritable hermit. And now Nowell. What was everybody doing back there? Chanelle Brodie, Nowell, Lonnie, Mr Stokes. Vivian didn't know exactly what she would look for: perhaps some sign of their clandestine wanderings, some trace left behind. What she did know is that she would head in the general direction of Mr Stokes's house.

She kept thinking about their quiet neighbor. At the mention of Nowell's father, Mr Stokes had acted strangely and he seemed to harden each time she brought up Mrs Brodie. *That Lonnie. He's got a bad temper.* When he told her about Lonnie throwing the fishing pole, it seemed like he was trying to get some point across, to warn her about something. Vivian was no stranger to Lonnie's drinking and the tense moods that followed. But who was Mr Stokes to make a remark like that? He didn't know Lonnie, or any of them. Why did he look at her with a sense of knowing that felt alternately comforting and disturbing? Why was he suddenly in their lives, starting with the day they found the Brodie girl? Who was he to them?

She quietly closed the door and crossed the porch. The wind rustled the grass, making a great hushing sound. As she walked around the side of the house, a droning noise started up, and she turned in time to see the headlights of a car rising over the hill. As the car passed, she put her back against the wall of the house, holding the flashlight near her side, pointed to the ground. You're acting like a television detective, she chastised herself as the taillights shrunk. Crickets chuckled at her from their vantage point under the house.

The grass, which was still uncut, crackled and broke under her feet. The tallest blades sparkled in the ivory glow of the half-moon. Hanging slightly above the treetops and surrounded in the velvety blue-black of night, this moon reminded her of a smile, a lopsided, toothy one not unlike Mr Stokes's. She walked by its radiance until she reached the line of trees, which seemed denser and taller at night, and then she turned on the flashlight and waved the beam in a half-circle in front of her feet.

She walked slowly, straining her ears and scanning the area, side to side with the beam of the flashlight. The woods were pungent with sun-baked earth, grass and blooming things; the piney fragrance of the trees enveloped her in the darkness. After a short time, her pace quickened involuntarily and she reminded herself to be alert and slow down. Estimating she had walked about half the distance to Mr Stokes's house, Vivian kept on at a steady pace. When something glinted in the flashlight's glow, she diverted her course and walked towards the object. Soon, she stood directly over it: an empty beer can. Lonnie drank a variety of brands, but she had only seen this one in the store. She kicked it with the toe of her sandal.

She continued in the direction of Mr Stokes's house. Overhead, a branch cracked loudly and she paused, watching the treetops. The branch splintered again then fell, its leaves rustling when it landed. The noise startled her and as she quickened her steps, she suddenly tripped. She stumbled for a few more steps, juggling the flashlight and finally, she steadied herself inches from a flattened, slate-gray boulder that had risen suddenly from the ground, blocking her path.

Moving the flashlight slowly from top to bottom, she examined the surface of the large rock. Under the corner near her feet was a thin yellow piece of paper, partially hidden from view under the bulky stone. Vivian reached down and picked it up, noticing the bold, black letters on its plastic-like surface. Police tape. She looked at the rock, realizing at once that it was the same place, the rock where Chanelle Brodie died.

She dropped the flashlight; the ray of light danced crazily then bounced against the trees when it hit the ground.

Calm down, she told herself. Get it together. She took a deep breath and retrieved the flashlight. Scanning with its stark beam, she checked out her surroundings.

Aside from the small bit of yellow tape, the area looked pristine, unspoiled. The rock was roughly oval-shaped, about three feet wide and five feet long. Its surface was clean, white in the moonlight that fought its way through the mesh of high branches. The side of the rock closest to Vivian's feet protruded just above the ground, but the other end was thicker and raised about three feet, so that the great stone angled from the ground upwards, sloping like a horseshoe might after being thrown. She imagined Chanelle Brodie sprawled over the rock, her arms pinned underneath her body. *Your hands would be up here. You would try to break the fall, by instinct.* Sometimes Vivian liked to sleep like that, on her stomach with her arms at her sides. Chanelle's hair, thick and dark like her father's, like Vivian's, would have been fanned around her head.

Footsteps dotted the dirt in places and near the rock; the ground was pocked with tiny gouges. About two yards to the left, a wide-trunked tree, its roots bent above the ground like a spider's legs, sprouted to the sky. Beneath the overhang of the higher section of the large rock, a cluster of small bushes crowded furtively together in what must be a shaded area during the hot part of the day. Shaking the dirt from her sandals, Vivian backed away from the scene.

It seemed like a very long time since she had left the old white house. The air was cool deep in the woods; the soft earth crept into her sandals and left her feet chilled. Pushing her way through the undergrowth, she found what appeared to be a path, an area where the foliage was trampled into a narrow groove. She followed it and soon found herself in the place where Mr Stokes chopped wood. She breathed a sigh of relief. The wide trunk he used for a worktable jutted from the center of the clearing. A few pieces of kindling were scattered nearby. Shining the flashlight in wide arcs, Vivian picked up a glare from what appeared to be a window. Mr Stokes's house, she thought. She headed toward it.

As she neared the dark house, the voice of caution spoke and she shook off its message. *What are you doing? Where do you think you're going?* She avoided the wheelbarrow at the edge of the yard and stepped over a row of flowering bushes. A quick scan with the flashlight revealed tiny red blooms and leaves that were fat and round like tongues. She thought: Why am I suddenly suspicious of him?

The house was dark save an amber-tinted porch light buzzing with insects. The light seemed harsh and discriminating, leaving deep, dark shadows under the concrete steps leading to the door. The landing glowed like a pool of water. Like a Rembrandt painting, a dark canvas lit in parts from some external source. Dr Lightfoot had talked about Rembrandt's fascination with light and the way objects could appear entirely different at various times of the day. Many times, a single beam or sheet of yellow light cut across a painting, illuminating only certain things. Another way for a painter to be subjective, he said, to decide how much light and what it would reveal.

Vivian walked to a set of windows and peered inside, using the flashlight to see. The kitchen had dark cupboards and softly gleaming countertops and in the next room, a small wooden table was pushed against the wall, surrounded by three chairs. In a moment she spotted the fourth chair, set apart against an adjoining wall. She walked to the next window and looked into the living room. There was one leather armchair, a table with a lamp, and a couch. Everything in the room seemed dark: the polished wood of the square table, the upholstery of the furniture. She was reminded of the house where she had taken refuge after getting lost, the uncluttered tidiness of Joe Toliver's living room. A bachelor's home.

She walked back to the door, an informal rear entrance, and watched the bugs bang against the cylindrical porch light. No one is home, she thought. Should I? The doorknob was cold to her fingertips and acquiescent when, on impulse, she turned it. The door opened soundlessly, like some well-oiled machine. Vivian stood for a moment on the landing as the voice of reason and caution fired missives in a rapid, confusing sequence – *what are you, this is not your, against the law, you don't know, what if you get* – then she looked over her shoulder and went inside.

The house was still and airless. She walked through the kitchen and maneuvered around the dining table into the living room. Her eyes adjusted quickly to the dark. Copies of *Reader's Digest* and *Newsweek* were stacked on the small table she had seen from the window. In the seat of the armchair was a thick book titled *Wildlife on the Plains*. Over the couch, a framed picture of a black Labrador hung next to an antique candle lamp.

She found Mr Stokes's bedroom at the end of the short hallway. She paused in the doorway, shining the flashlight around. A roughed-up pair of work boots stood to attention next to a small bookshelf, and the closet door was open, revealing a neat row of shirts and pants. On a long dresser, several pictures were arranged on a wooden tray. Vivian imagined that the young couple in the wedding photo were his parents; the boy with the fire engine Mr Stokes as a boy. One yellowing picture was a group photo of six young men, all outfitted in camouflage suits; two had rifles propped against their shoulders. Vivian searched for a youthful Mr Stokes, but didn't recognize him in any of the faces.

On the floor next to the bed was a small stack of newspapers. As Vivian directed the flashlight over this area, something familiar made her stop and walk closer for a better look. The paper on the top of the pile was almost a month old. The headline was the first one about Chanelle Brodie: LOCAL GIRL, 17, FOUND DEAD. A shiver ran through her.

She hurried down the hallway. What am I doing? What if I got caught? A grown woman! She banged her thigh into the shallow table at the end of the hall. She sucked air through her teeth. The painful spot was like fire on her skin. The other door in the hallway was closed, but she'd had enough. She wanted to leave.

Her breaths were coming fast; her heart beat like a throbbing wound in her chest. As she reached the dining room table, her eyesight started to blur and a wave passed through her. She groped around, finding a chair.

She sat down, put her head between her knees and took several deep breaths. It was a trick she learned in high school from the gym teacher, Miss Alston. Vivian was always on diets then, prone to dizzy spells and periods of faintness. During her sophomore year, she was on a liquid diet and she had Miss Alston's class in the afternoons. She almost passed out three or four times that year, each episode provoking a private chat from Miss Alston, who was concerned that she may have diabetes or anemia. Vivian confiscated the notes sent home for her parents and told Miss Alston that the doctor had prescribed vitamins.

She opened her eyes. Underneath the chair was a set of binoculars. She sat up and looked through them. From the vantage point of the low window, the view was direct east, toward the clearing where Mr Stokes chopped wood and further on, Grandma Gardiner's house. But the woods were black with night; she could make out only brief glimpses of shadows and light where the moon infiltrated the dense trees. She replaced the binoculars underneath the chair and stood up.

Closing the door quietly, she stepped back into the night and quickly reached the small clearing. She turned for one last glimpse of the house, perhaps to make sure that she'd left it looking undisturbed, and as she watched, a light flickered behind the second window, in what she now knew to be Mr Stokes's living room. She thought at first it was the faint hall light that had been on all along, but then realized that it seemed brighter. She turned and walked quickly, dirt and small plants crunching under her feet.

Her mind racing, she dodged trees and shrubs, reaching further and further ahead with the long arc of the flashlight beam. Through the trees she could barely see Mr Stokes's house now, but it seemed that the light in the dining room was off again. Your imagination, she told herself, but her heart pounded almost painfully nonetheless. She was almost running, her face burning as she kicked branches out of her path and thought again of Chanelle Brodie, wondering what her last moments were like. Miraculously, she went back exactly as she had come. She walked purposefully, anticipating her route with the flashlight. Despite her fright, she refused to look back again. She had become resolute, driven. There was the outstretched rock and a few minutes later, the line of tree sentinels directing her home.

When Vivian pushed from the tree line, panting and sweating from her labor, she greeted the sight of the house at the peak of the slow-rising incline with gratitude. Thank you, she whispered over and over under her breath, thank you.

In the kitchen, the two skinny arms of the rooster clock were past the upright position. After one o'clock, she thought. I must be crazy. She took her sandals off and left them again near the door, then quietly slipped out of her jeans. As she passed Lonnie and Dot's room, she heard a soft buzzing, almost like a cat purring. Lonnie was snoring. Across the hall, she carefully opened the door, dropped her jeans next to the bed and slid under the covers. Nowell stirred slightly.

Looking at the digital clock on her nightstand, Vivian felt the accusation of the three angry red stripes: 1:11. She waited for her heart to return to normal. I must have imagined the light in the house, she thought. She had found nothing in the woods to explain everyone's wanderings, even her own. Now safe in the starchy comfort of the sheets, her adventure began to seem more like a dream. She thought about the copy of *The Sentinel* next to Mr Stokes's bed and the binoculars under the chair. She pictured his face, the deep lines radiating from his eyes and the smug tilt of his smile. Why had he made it a point to tell her that he was leaving for a few days?

She recalled the story of Ronella Oates. Something like that could leave a person very bitter. Maybe subconsciously, Mr Stokes blamed all women. He didn't seem to care for Mrs Brodie or

Katherine. Maybe she was kidding herself to think they'd struck up a pleasant friendship. He warned her about walking through the woods and teased her about being afraid. And he made a disparaging remark about Lonnie. He seemed to crop up everywhere: the day they found Chanelle, the afternoon that Mrs Brodie came by, the fishing trip and the barbecue afterwards. Almost as though he was keeping an eye on them. Even the morning she went over to his house, it was because he was causing a disturbance outside.

She drifted off to sleep thinking of Mr Stokes, the way his powerful shoulders drove the ax into the pliant wood, his awkwardness in speaking to her, his rough hands and beaten-up boots. And she dreamed a surreal dream of the woods between their two houses, as if the night's events were repeating themselves in a distorted, confused form. The dream began in the daytime, with Vivian and her father walking leisurely through the woods, but it ended in the pitch-black of night, with Vivian alone and running from someone.

She twirled around in a circle, searching for her father. The canopy of leaves swirled and dipped above her; the sky turned dark and violent. She was standing on a large, flat boulder, and she jumped down and began to run. Trees began to fall around her, crashing to the ground with an awful clamor. Up ahead, she could see the edge of the woods, the portal to safety. The cracking of an ax echoed through the woods. 'Number One!' a deep voice called behind her.

She reached the tree line and burst onto the long grass. Falling to her knees, she began to crawl up the small hill, the ache in her throat preventing her from crying out. When she reached the top, she saw her mother through the window to Nowell's study. Her mother was sitting at the desk with her reading glasses on. Vivian tried to call out but it came as a whisper. Her mother's hands moved quickly over the keyboard.

'Mom!' Vivian squeaked.

Suddenly, something struck her in the back. Framed by the grayish moon, Lonnie juggled empty beer cans, laughing as they fell like bullets against her arms, her upturned face.

The cracking sound, loud as thunder now, rumbled through the air, vibrated through her body. Lonnie's supply of cans never ran out; his juggling became more frenetic as she scrambled away from the shower of aluminum. As she reached the side of the house, a pair of dark, shabby boots stepped around the corner. One boot pressed down on her hand and she struggled to pull it free.

She shook herself awake. It was just after five-thirty. Her limbs were stiff from tension, the back of her neck damp and warm. It took a few moments before she remembered where she was, before she recognized the old furniture and cramped space of Grandma Gardiner's bedroom. She was incredibly thirsty.

For the second time that night, Vivian got out of bed and walked gingerly through the house. In the kitchen, she took a glass from the cupboard and plodded across the cold floor. Her eyes were barely open. The water went down easily, filling her stomach. As she set the glass in the sink, she heard a noise outside, the grinding sound of footsteps. Motionless, she strained her ears, then, as she turned to go back to bed, a heavy footstep sounded on the porch. She jerked her head toward the door as it opened and Lonnie's hulking form blocked the light from the porch. They both jumped.

'Jesus, Vivian,' he hissed.

'You scared me,' she whispered back. 'What's wrong? What are you doing?'

'Nothing.' He sat on a chair near the table and bent to untie his shoes.

'Where were you?' she persisted.

'What time is it?'

'Almost six.' She rubbed her hands across her arms, suddenly aware of her thin nightshirt.

'What are you doing up?' he asked.

Vivian noticed now the disorder of his hair and clothing, the mud flaking from his shoes onto the floor. His eyes were small and the skin underneath brownish and puffy.

'I was thirsty,' she answered. 'What about you? You don't look like you've been to bed at all.'

'I fell asleep in the woods.'

'What?'

Lonnie scratched his head, ran his hand across the stubble on his chin. Vivian saw the dirt caked underneath his short, jagged fingernails. For a moment, in the pained expression he gave when he had to repeat himself, the hard scowl that changed his face, she saw the resemblance between him and Nowell. There was something in the lines of the mouth, the slight flare of the nostrils, the broad plane of his forehead.

'I said I fell asleep outside.'

'Where?' she asked.

'Just outside.'

'I thought you went to bed with Dot. What were you doing out there?'

'I couldn't sleep,' he said. 'It was so warm, I decided to go for a walk.'

'In the middle of the night?'

'What's so strange about that?' He glared at her.

'You don't think it's strange?' she asked. 'Were you drinking?'

'Who are you, the police?' For the first time since he'd walked through the door, his face relaxed into a grin.

'You just scared me, that's all.'

'Listen,' he said. 'I'm beat.' He raised himself slowly from the chair. His knee cracked loudly when he put his weight on it.

'I can imagine,' she said, making a point to look over his rumpled clothing before she turned and walked to the hallway.

As he followed her, Lonnie seemed groggy, unsteady on his feet. He was so much taller than she was; Vivian knew she wouldn't be able to stop him if he fell.

21

Is everyone in this house sneaking around? Vivian wondered. She had a difficult time falling back to sleep. When she finally drifted into a restless doze, Nowell's alarm clock buzzed, promptly at seven o'clock. He went into the bathroom and she heard the water running. The aroma of coffee drifted into the room when he opened the door to the hallway. She heard voices in the kitchen.

She couldn't sleep anymore. She pushed back the covers and stretched her legs. Today, I will clear up some things, she thought with resolution. I will stop letting my imagination get the best of me. After a hot shower, she went into the kitchen.

'Good morning!' Dot said cheerfully, and for some reason, she crossed the room and gave Vivian a hug. She had a clean vanilla-and-soap scent, her usual fresh face and something searching about her eyes.

Vivian released her and headed to the coffeepot.

'Long night,' Dot said.

Vivian's hand paused for a moment, then she continued pouring the coffee.

'You know,' Dot continued, 'I think the weather's turning. I tossed and turned, one minute chilled, the other sweating.'

188

Vivian faced her with the steaming cup. 'Well you don't look tired. You never do.'

Nowell entered the kitchen with his coffee cup. He leaned down and nuzzled Vivian's hair before getting a refill. 'Where's Lonnie?' he asked.

'Still sleeping,' Dot answered. 'He barely moved when I got up this morning. Dead to the world.'

'That's strange,' he said. 'Viv, the truck looks great. I didn't know you washed it.'

'I think I'll drive it through the automatic one in town next time,' she said. 'It was a lot of work.'

'Thanks for doing it,' he said, and something about his tone made Vivian look up. He was staring at her, his brown eyes glossy. 'I just want you to know, Viv, that I notice what you do, and I know you're working hard here and well, I appreciate it, that's all. And I love you.'

Dot shifted at the table; Vivian felt heat in her face.

'Thanks, baby.' She moved towards him, found her position under his arm and leaned in.

Dot sniffed loudly. 'You're going to make me cry, really, you two. This is just so, so... *precious.*'

Nowell released Vivian and laughed. He made a move as though he would smack Dot playfully on his way to the study, and she ducked.

'Nowell?' she said.

He paused at the entrance, looked back.

'You know, we're looking forward to reading your book,' Dot said. 'I keep asking Lonnie to get a copy. You don't have one here, do you?'

'Actually, I do. I have some spare copies in the room there. I'll get one for you.'

'You're kidding?' She stood up and Vivian could see the outline of her bra, red or dark pink in color, underneath the sheer fabric of her shirt. On the second toe of her left foot, a gold ring encircled the flesh between the two joints. Her toenails were painted a glittery peach. When did she do that? Vivian wondered.

Nowell brought a copy of *Random Victim* from the study and gave it to her. From across the kitchen, Vivian could see the black, brooding eyes of the man on the cover, the storm cloud like danger over his head.

Nowell went back to work. Dot announced that she was going for a walk, and Vivian declined the offer to join her. When Dot left, she called to Nowell through the fabric divider.

'Come in,' he answered.

She pushed through the curtain and immediately lost all of her former resolve to remain civil when she encountered the dingy grayness of the room. Why does he sit in the dark? The curtains over the wide window were closed and the air was stagnant and stale. 'Why won't you open a window in here?' she asked, thinking: You opened it yesterday to sneak out. Anger overwhelmed reasonableness. Something about his room, this place where he spent so much time without her, incensed her.

'Obviously, I like them closed. We've had this discussion before, haven't we?' He put his elbow on the antique desk and looked at her, waiting.

'It's just so musty in here,' she said. 'You're not getting any fresh air.'

He watched her, tapping his foot against the ornate claw at the bottom of the desk.

She walked further into the room, passing his line of sight until she perched on the arm of the leather couch.

He was forced to swivel in his chair to face her. 'What is it? You never come to visit me.'

'That's not true,' she said. 'In the first place, I didn't think you liked to have visitors while you're working.'

'Normally I don't, but there are exceptions.'

'In the second place, I came to visit you yesterday and you weren't here.'

The smile faded from his lips. He straightened up in his chair. 'When?'

'Yesterday afternoon, just before Lonnie and Dot got back.'

'You came in here?'

'Listen, I'm not accusing you of anything.'

Nowell leaned back in his chair, drumming his fingers against the desktop. 'It's nothing exciting, Viv. I just went for a walk. Some fresh air, like you're always telling me.'

She tilted her head as though speaking to a small child. 'Why didn't you ask me? I would have gone with you. We haven't had much time together, with your writing and with Lonnie and Dot here.'

'Do I have to be with you every second I'm not doing something else?'

'Well, no…'

'I went for a walk by myself. That's all. You never used to scrutinize me so closely.'

'I never had to. Maybe I found it strange that you would climb through a window to go for your casual walk.'

'Who said that I…'

'I saw the window, Nowell. Is this a regular thing with you? Is it me, something I did?'

He rose from the chair and sat next to her on the couch.

From her position on the arm, she looked down at him. 'I saw you coming out of the woods. What's back there?'

'Nothing.' Nowell patted her knee. 'Trees and birds and rocks. Nothing.'

'Were you thinking about Chanelle Brodie?' she asked. 'Were you thinking about what happened to her?'

His head snapped up, a dark look spreading like ink over his face. 'Are you still dwelling on that? For God's sake, Viv, read a book or something. You've never been one to create drama like this.'

'Create drama? A death in our backyard isn't dramatic enough for you? You're the creative one…'

'Wait. This is getting off course.'

Vivian tucked her hands underneath her thighs.

'Give me a minute to tell you everything.' He paused. 'I'll tell you everything.' Faint lines crisscrossed his temples and his skin had an unhealthy pallor. 'I walked over to Mr Stokes's property,' he said. 'That's where I was, looking around his place.'

Vivian opened her mouth.

'Wait, let me finish.' He took a deep breath. 'I don't know what I was looking for or why I did it. The other day, Mr Stokes said he was going to visit relatives. That's when I started to think about it. Not in a specific way, but just some vague idea of how I would show him.'

Vivian wondered if Nowell went into the house, whether he saw the binoculars or the newspaper in the bedroom. Despite his outward nonchalance about Chanelle Brodie's death, he must have been worried about it all along and suspicious of Mr Stokes.

'That's all it was,' he continued, 'my twisted idea of revenge or something. There was nothing productive or sensible about it.'

She looked at him. 'Revenge? What do you mean?'

'There's more. The other day when we were fishing, Tom told me something.'

'Tom?'

'One of the construction guys,' Nowell said. 'He didn't mean to tell me, really, it just slipped out. Besides, he thought we already knew.'

Vivian shifted on her seat. It wasn't making sense. 'Knew what?'

'You know that my Grandpa Gardiner died when my dad was fifteen, in a hunting accident, around here somewhere?'

She nodded.

'At lunch time we docked the boat,' Nowell said. 'Jerry and Mr Stokes walked back to the van to get the sandwiches, and Lonnie went behind some trees to pee. When they were gone, Tom leaned over and told me how surprised he was that we invited Mr Stokes. Because of what happened with his father and my grandfather.'

He leaned forward, his dark eyes sparkling. 'Because it was Mr Stokes's father who shot him. He killed my grandfather.'

'Jesper Stokes?' Vivian said. 'Wait. How can that be? It was so long ago, and Mr Stokes is only about forty, so his father...'

'His father was a kid at the time, a teenager I think. He'd gone along with the men, including his father, Mr Stokes's grandfather.'

'Manus Stokes,' Vivian said.

'How do you...' Nowell started.

'Katherine,' she said. For a moment, she let the information sink in. Jesper Stokes shot Nowell's grandfather, when he was a teenager, before Abe Stokes was born.

'So you already knew?'

'No,' she said.

'Tom felt terrible for bringing it up.' Nowell ran his fingers through his hair. 'I made him tell me everything he knew.'

'What else did he say?' she asked.

'That maybe it wasn't an accident.'

'What? You said yourself Jesper Stokes was just a kid.'

'There are rumors. People say he was never the same afterwards, that he kept to himself and acted strangely.'

'That's a tough thing to live with,' she said. 'Even if it was an accident.'

'They say that something was going on between Mr Stokes's grandmother and my grandfather.'

Her eyes widened. 'You mean, an affair or something?'

'I don't know, yes.'

She shook her head. 'So this young kid, this teenager, shot your grandfather for messing around with his mother?'

'That's the story.'

'That's a rumor,' she said.

Nowell shrugged. 'Tom says it's common knowledge around here. He says the relations between the families were always strained after the accident, that my grandma had property lines drawn up immediately afterwards.' Nowell pointed towards the desk. 'She kept a file on everything. I found a copy of those papers; they were dated a year after my grandfather's death.'

Vivian thought for a moment. 'Maybe someone advised her to have those papers done, because she'd recently been widowed.'

'Maybe,' he said. 'But there has to be some basis to this story.'

'No, there doesn't.' She stood up. 'Wouldn't Mr Stokes's grandmother have been much older than your grandfather, like Mr Stokes is older than us?'

'Not necessarily. My parents had me and Lonnie in their thirties, and if Mr Stokes was born when his father was younger…'

'It doesn't matter. It's crazy to believe some fifty-year-old story. How would this Tom know anyway? I thought those road workers were shipped in from somewhere else. Don't they work for the county?'

'Tom grew up around here.'

They heard water running in the back corner of the house, an indication that Lonnie was finally awake. Nowell said, 'He slept late today.'

Vivian nodded and didn't mention that Lonnie had spent most of the night in the woods. 'I still don't understand why you went to his house,' she said. 'Even if that story is true, it happened a long, long time ago. It was an accident. I'm sure Jesper Stokes had to live with this his entire life. And Abe Stokes too.'

'They should have to. What if it wasn't an accident? What if it's true?'

How could he have gotten away with something like that? It wasn't possible, she thought.

Nowell looked around the room. 'I didn't even know him, only from pictures and the few things my dad said. Hell, he didn't even get to know him very well, his own father. My grandfather built this house. Don't you think that's amazing?'

Vivian looked up at the dark wood supports that ran the distance of the room, standing out from the white paint like bars.

194

'I've always envied Lonnie for working in construction,' he continued, 'that he could do something like that, actually make something, something that would last.'

'Books last,' Vivian said.

He shrugged.

She remembered when Dr Lightfoot had taught a class on linear perspective. He said it was an architect who rescued the lost theories of perspective, changing the art world forever. It was an architect who pointed out the relationship between reality and representation, between actual and imagined space. Without these practices, paintings would have remained flat, lifeless.

Nowell sighed. 'When Tom told me it was Mr Stokes's father who fired that rifle, it made me angry because Mr Stokes never mentioned anything to me. Nobody told us.'

'What was he supposed to say?' she asked. 'Hello, Mr Gardiner, welcome to our neighborhood and by the way, my father accidentally shot your grandfather?'

'You'd think he would have said something,' Nowell said.

'You want him to apologize.'

He looked at her, considering this. 'He got to have his father.'

'But he wasn't even born when this happened.'

'He should have said something.'

Lonnie plodded down the hallway; his heavy footsteps echoed through the rooms. 'Hello?'

'We're in here,' Nowell called.

The footsteps halted in the kitchen. 'Where's Dot?'

Vivian couldn't see Lonnie through the curtain divider but she could picture him, standing in the middle of the kitchen like a child who's lost his favorite toy, his arms hanging dejectedly at his sides. 'She went for a walk,' she called. 'There's sausage in the refrigerator.'

'We'll finish talking about this later,' Nowell said in a low voice.

'No.' She leaned forward, catching his arm as he tried to rise from the couch. 'I want to hear what you did at Mr Stokes's house.'

'There's nothing to tell,' he said. 'I walked around his property like a stalker, looked through the windows and broke into his tool shed. I don't know why I did it, I really don't. He kept this secret, and maybe my trespassing somehow made up for it. One secret for another, one indiscretion.'

'He doesn't seem like a very exciting subject.'

'No, nothing scintillating at his place. Just some guy's house.'

'I wonder if your father knew him,' she said.

'I don't know. He would've been much younger than my dad.'

Vivian had been thinking about more recent years, about the unacknowledged visits made by Sherman to his mother's house. Maybe Mr Stokes's reaction when she mentioned Sherman sprang from the legacy of the hunting incident. It wasn't his fault that his father had been part of the horrible accident, but guilt naturally filtered down in a family, creating an atmosphere of mistrust and guardedness in which children grow wary and defensive. Maybe there were other reasons why Mr Stokes didn't like Sherman, and maybe there were none at all.

'I didn't mean to alarm you, Viv.' Nowell squeezed her shoulder, pulling her against his side.

In the kitchen, Lonnie slammed cupboards and foraged through the refrigerator.

22

Several days went by and the inhabitants of the house fell into a routine. Nowell wrote and Lonnie tinkered around outside, and both helped whenever something heavy needed moving. Lonnie ran the errands and reported back from town. Vivian and Dot went through the rooms, clearing and organizing, and one afternoon, they finished removing the wallpaper in the hallway, without the help of alcohol. And they finally attacked the kitchen, the cupboards full of Grandma Gardiner's supplies. They kept a small amount of things for their own cooking and serving, but there were extra items that could be boxed and labeled for the yard sale Vivian was planning. There was a waffle iron, canning jars, a Dutch oven, a bread maker and as Dot had noticed, an overabundance of tea cups. The non-essential items were in boxes lined up in the den, already labeled with prices. In fact, most of the house had been gone through, but in the attic a good quantity of unsorted boxes remained, as well as some furniture: the short dresser in which Vivian had found the men's clothing and the gun, a dilapidated trunk with rusty hinges, the wooden headboard of a child's bed. Vivian planned to bring the larger items down a few days before the sale, which she had tentatively planned for the weekend of the Clement reunion, just under two weeks away.

Since their discussion about Mr Stokes, Nowell had thrown himself into his work with a new dedication. Almost a week had gone by and Vivian saw him only during brief dinner breaks or not at all if he took his plate back into the study. At night he worked late and he got up in the mornings before her. An aura of concentration hovered about him; a deep horizontal groove became a permanent feature of his face, separating his forehead into two near-equal halves.

Vivian and Dot often divided tasks and sometimes worked together, but conversation stayed at a minimum. There was no unpleasantness, just a shared dedication to the work that needed to be done. Vivian felt limber and productive and slept well each night.

One warm morning, Vivian went up to the attic. She shoved a straw-ended broom into the corners near the ceiling, breaking up the spider webs. She imagined how her footsteps might sound to Nowell, typing quietly below in his study. Treading softly on the dusty wooden floor, Vivian swept in rows toward the dustpan, which lay beside the hatch door that opened to the staircase below. Leaving the dirt and debris in a small pile, she went to the dresser. She took the bag with the nicer clothing – the blue jeans and olive green slacks, the suit and dress shirts – and set it aside. She had already cleared the dresser and gotten rid of the underclothes that had been inside. Those items didn't seem appropriate to sell. Nowell had forgotten about the gun; it still sat on the dresser.

It was cool and heavy in Vivian's hands. She held it up and looked through the sight, then took it over to the window and tried to aim at the mailbox.

Sitting on the little seat and pressing her forehead against the window, Vivian looked for Dot, who was lying on a lawn chair in front of the house. The angle was too sharp; she could make out only the end of the chair, the plastic slats that extended beyond Dot's feet. She turned around in the narrow seat and leaned back, the gun resting on her lap, its long barrel reaching across her thighs.

Vivian had a birthday coming up, only five days away. She would be twenty-eight, the same age as Nowell for six months, until he had his birthday again. She usually looked forward to birthdays, but this year was different. Since they had moved into the house, it felt as if they had taken a hiatus from their regular lives. At the old, white house, they lived according to their own calendars. Similar days succeeded each other and Vivian was responsible only for the maintenance of her mind and body, and for cleaning up the house on her own schedule. The days of the weeks lost meaning, any Saturday being just like a Tuesday. It seemed unofficial to celebrate a birthday, a passage in normal time. In the same way, Vivian had insisted on having their wedding in a church, even though she had never regularly attended one.

There was something else. This birthday, Vivian's twenty-eighth, brought a vague, gnawing pang that felt suspiciously like regret. For the most part, she had put it out of her mind to such a degree that she had been genuinely surprised when a box arrived that morning from her parents and she opened it to find a smaller package inside, wrapped in bright paper. Her mother was always punctual, often early.

Outside, Lonnie's jeep barreled up the driveway and Vivian turned in the window seat as he pulled into the space behind the red truck. Dot appeared in the sunlight, wearing a green-and-white checkered bikini. Her hair was loose on her shoulders, golden-red in the mid-day sun. Leaping up, she wrapped her arms around Lonnie's neck and he picked her up easily, sliding his hands underneath her buttocks. Like a child, she wrapped her legs around him, nuzzled her face into his neck. They shared a few words and kissed. Lonnie laughed and Vivian could hear the deep timbre faintly, like sound through a tunnel. She noticed the movement of his hands as they gripped and released and the rotation of Dot's hips against them. Vivian looked away. What if someone sees them?

She and Nowell used to have spontaneous moments. He'd pick her up at her dorm room and sometimes they couldn't make it the few miles to his apartment. They'd park in abandoned parking lots or at the side of the road if it was dark. Sporadically, remnants of this early passion surfaced, surprising them both, but Vivian had found that married life was a series of phases.

Before they left the city, their lives ran a smooth course. Vivian had her job and friends and Nowell had his writing. They usually spent weekends together, unless Nowell was busy working. When they could afford it, they'd try new restaurants or catch a second-run movie at the renovated theater down the street. In the few times of emotional crisis they'd encountered, Nowell had been steady, sensitive and practical.

Two months before Vivian and Nowell's wedding, Lonnie flipped a motorcycle over an embankment on a country road and tore much of the skin off his back. He broke two ribs and a leg. Beverly called, frantic, in the middle of the night, and Nowell left before sunrise. Lonnie was flown to Beverly's house, where he would convalesce. Nowell was expected to stay and help. When the second weekend came, Vivian drove over to bring Nowell home.

Her mother-in-law's house had the dimness and antiseptic aroma of a sickroom. Lonnie had commandeered the entire living room. His crutches and wheelchair were propped against the wall in the entry and a bed sheet was draped over the long couch, on which he half-reclined with his broken leg elevated on a pillow. Vivian was shocked by his appearance. Stitches closed a gash over his left eye and the skin surrounding it was colored in varying shades of purple and yellow. His entire torso was bandaged with thick strips of tape that crisscrossed under his armpits, across his chest, and around the top of his belly.

Nowell was patient with him and Beverly didn't seem to notice Lonnie's complaints or general crankiness. He was on heavy pain medication.

Every morning and every evening, Nowell brought Lonnie two chalky pills with his meal, and every afternoon he helped his mother change the bandages that grew sticky and dark on his brother's back. When Vivian arrived, things seemed to have fallen into an organized routine, but Nowell assured her that the earlier days had been worse. She looked at the dark patches under his eyes and noticed the way Nowell's shirt hung, askew and loose, from his broad shoulders. She wondered if it was possible to lose weight in ten days. She was glad he was coming back to the city.

On the Sunday they were to leave, Grandma Gardiner made a brusque and informal entrance. Her visit was unexpected. She knocked solidly on the door and refused Nowell's offer to carry her bag. She explained that a friend of hers was coming into town to visit friends, and she decided to take the free ride and the opportunity to spend two days with her daughter-in-law, helping to care for her grandson. Nowell and Lonnie hadn't seen her for several years.

Beverly fixed sandwiches and tossed salad for lunch. The four of them – Nowell, Beverly, Grandma Gardiner and Vivian – gathered around the polished maple dining room table normally used only for holidays, because Beverly didn't want Lonnie to feel that he was eating in the living room alone.

Grandma Gardiner picked at her salad, separated the radishes and the red cabbage from the rest and made a small red pile on her napkin. Beverly reached over and handed her another napkin, and in her halting, self-conscious movements, Vivian envisioned the newlywed daughter-in-law she must have been, nervous and anxious for the older woman's approval.

She couldn't remember much of what was said during that lunch, only the general, tense mood of the occasion. Beverly was extremely tired and Vivian would catch her staring at the side of a chair or at the deep folds in the tablecloth, a glaze coming over her eyes. Nowell was the same. She remembered that Grandma Gardiner wore a large round medallion on a tarnished gold chain. She remembered skinny legs, mottled with brown spots, and the golden clip in her hair. Grandma Gardiner was nondescript, especially to the mind of Vivian, who had a tired fiancé to think about and only two more months to plan for her wedding.

Vivian heard Lonnie and Dot conversing on the porch. When she pushed herself up from the child-sized window seat, something fell from her lap, making a loud bang on the wooden floor. The gun had just missed the top of her foot and now lay pointing toward her. She listened, but no one called up to her. Everyone was accustomed to the noises she made while working around the house. She picked the gun up, careful to point the barrel away from her body, and placed it in a box near the window, which held a set of iron candleholders and plated bookends shaped like buildings. Metal things, her organizing self thought.

She needed to get back to work. A brass coat rack dominated one corner of the room and Vivian struggled with it until she had moved it aside. Bending her knees, she lifted a box that had been sitting behind the rack, blocking the lowest drawer of the tall mahogany bureau. She carried it over to the dresser, and when she dropped it on top, dust ascended in a great cloud, covering her face.

'Vivian?' Dot called from the kitchen.

She spit dust particles from her lips. 'Yeah?'

'Would you like some iced tea?'

'Sure.' Shortly, Vivian heard the squeak of the staircase before Dot's head poked through the opening on the floor. 'You didn't have to bring it up,' she said, coming forward to take the moist glass.

'I wanted to see how things were going up here.' Dot put her hands on her hips and looked around. She wore a pair of khaki shorts and her bikini top.

'Now you know my secret,' Vivian said.

'What do you mean?'

'I haven't done much. Every time I'm up here, I get distracted. Maybe it's because there seems to be so much, um, stuff. If I shift it around a little, I feel as though I've accomplished something.'

'You've got some sort of organization happening here.' Dot

202

motioned to the boxes lined up against the wall. 'What are these?'

'Those were already here. I need to go through them.'

'We'll have to get one of those price guns, you know? We can probably make some real cash. You'd be surprised how much money people make at these things.'

Vivian was beginning to wonder if Lonnie and Dot had any plans to leave. Initially, Nowell told her that their visit would be two weeks long and they were past that now. Vivian didn't care, not really. Aside from the two times she encountered Lonnie drunk, their stay had been uneventful. Having them around had even been fun. She enjoyed talking to Dot, and Lonnie could be really funny, when he wasn't being obnoxious.

Maybe some part of her resented their presence. Nowell took more time off to do things with Lonnie than he did to spend time with her. Since the one afternoon they went into town for a movie, she hadn't been away from the house with him. They slept together, but because they were developing disparate sleep schedules, that time was beginning to count for less and less.

Dot looked around the attic. 'What can I do, anything?'

Vivian pointed at the purplish bureau. 'I haven't looked in those drawers yet. Could you see what's in there, also in that small box sitting on top?'

Turning back toward the dusty box on the dresser, Vivian opened the top slats and pulled them back. Inside were baby items: a delicate crocheted blanket in white, lime and yellow, a scuffed pair of leather boots in a box, a plastic bag filled with outfits.

'Look at this,' she said. 'Baby clothes.'

'There's a whole drawer full of pictures and papers over here,' Dot said. She walked over to touch the baby items.

There was a tiny sailor outfit, complete with a rounded navy blue hat and knickers made of a coarse material. Dot held up a tiny pair of socks. 'Is there anything written on the box?'

'It looks like boy clothes,' Vivian said. 'And they're old, so probably Sherman's?'

Dot fingered the tiny socks. 'You can keep it all if you want. I just thought, you know, that Lonnie might like to have some of them.'

'You keep them,' Vivian said.

'No. We should split everything. There are two blankets, you know, these can still be used.'

'Really, Dot. I don't want any of it.' Vivian picked up the box and set it away from the others, near the exit. 'Let's take this down when we're done and you can show Lonnie.'

The purplish bureau had two empty drawers and one drawer full of more men's clothes. Shirts and shorts on one side, a brown and yellow flannel shirt and a gray sweatshirt on the other. Vivian handed Dot an empty box to put them in. The bottom drawer was full of photographs. They sat on the floor and sifted through them. Most were older, black-and-white shots. Grandma Gardiner had pasted many family pictures into photo albums that were downstairs in Nowell's study. These pictures were taken much earlier. Some were labeled, although neither of them could identify most of the names written carefully on the back. In the pictures that she appeared in, Grandma Gardiner had written simply 'Me', rather than Elizabeth or Betty. After a while, Dot and Vivian surmised that the photographs consisted mostly of her parents, brothers, sisters and assorted other family members during her childhood. Vivian set aside one photograph of the young Elizabeth on a bicycle, her plain dark dress bunched up around her knees and a look of pure abandon lighting up her normally sedate face. She thought that Nowell might like to remember his grandmother this way. She and Dot sat side-by-side, leaning across each other now and then to view a photograph one of them had found. Dot hadn't showered after lying in the sun; she smelled briny and damp over the sugary scent of the bubble gum that she popped and blew into pasty, pink globes. Vivian's neck began to feel stiff and her feet grew numb from her cross-legged position. 'I think I've had enough,' she said. 'I'm getting uncomfortable here on the floor.'

'Me too,' Dot agreed. 'I need to get rid of this gum. I've had it for hours.' She stood up quickly and extended her hand.

Vivian groaned as she pulled her up; their hands were warm and moist and they both laughed afterwards, rubbing their palms against their clothing.

Dot positioned herself mid-way down the staircase, and Vivian passed the box of baby things to her through the opening. 'Let's bring down that box of men's clothes too,' she said. 'We can sell those.'

The screen door slammed and Lonnie said, 'What are you doing?'

'We're bringing down some stuff from the attic,' Dot told him. 'Getting ready for the yard sale, you know?' She whispered something that Vivian couldn't hear.

'Let me bring down those boxes for you, Vivian,' he called up.

'Just one more,' she said, leaning over the staircase. 'You're taller though. Why don't you just catch it?'

Dot was standing on one of the bottom steps and Lonnie's arm reached through the railing, stroking her knee.

'Ready,' Lonnie said.

Vivian sat at the edge of the opening and lowered the box between her legs. She felt a slight pressure and suddenly, she was left holding the empty cardboard container. The box had burst open on the bottom, spilling its contents over the stairs and onto the kitchen floor below.

Lonnie laughed and pulled the empty box from her hands. Vivian stepped down the ladder, closing the hatch door over her head. As she reached the kitchen floor, Lonnie picked up one of the short-sleeved, collared shirts that had fallen from the box. 'Where did you get this?' he asked.

Vivian looked over. 'In the attic.'

Dot came down the hallway and opened her mouth when she saw the clothing scattered over the stairs and the floor.

'Where in the attic?'

'Why?'

'What's going on?' Dot asked.

'Look, honey.' Lonnie held the shirt toward her. 'This was my dad's.' There was something tense and uncontrollable about his voice.

She took the shirt. 'It's nice.'

'Of course it's nice,' Lonnie said, rising to his feet. 'His Number One son bought it for him.' He grabbed it from her. 'Hey, Nowell.'

Dot looked over and Vivian shrugged. They began to pick up the spilled clothing.

'Nowell?' Lonnie called again, watching the curtain divider.

'What?'

He pulled back the curtain and walked in. 'Do you remember this shirt?'

Nowell squinted up at his brother like a mole surprised in his tunnel. The room was dark as always, lit only by the small desk lamp at his side. 'You said it was Dad's?'

'Yeah. Do you remember it?'

He reached up and touched the shirt, which Lonnie held out, gripped in his fist. 'Not really. It looks familiar, I guess.'

'Father's Day,' Lonnie said. 'A couple of years before he died. I was living at home, just before I moved into that house out by the cannery. I was really broke, between jobs and I still owed bills from the last apartment. You were away at school, remember?'

Nowell shook his head.

'And I called you and asked if we could split the cost of a present for Father's Day. I said that I would pay you back later since I was so strapped.'

'None of this sounds…'

'And you said don't worry about it, that you weren't going to buy a present because you'd only been working that part-time job at school. You said that you didn't have any money either, that he'd understand.'

Nowell's face was guarded.

'And then you came home that weekend and brought him this lousy shirt, and he thought it was the greatest one he'd ever seen. And there I was, looking like a jerk. His Number One son brought him a gift all the way from college and me, a loser with no place of his own, showed up with a card.'

'I have no idea what you're talking about,' Nowell said. 'And stop waving it in front of my face.'

Lonnie let out a forced laugh and flung the shirt over his shoulder. 'You know what, Number One? I believe you. I'm sure you don't remember anything about it. Another day of normal operations for you.'

'If that happened, and I really doubt it, then I'm sure it was a misunderstanding. Maybe I meant the shirt to be from both of us.'

'You acted like I never called you. You said that you thought we'd agreed to do our own thing.'

Nowell leaned back in his chair, his eyes flashing fire. 'So you're accusing me of what? Of making you look cheap? Of buying a shirt behind your back?'

'It was always that way with you. I don't think you knew it yourself, the things you did to me.'

'Give it a rest, Lonnie. Maybe I don't remember that particular Father's Day, but why are your memories always different from everybody else's? Every holiday or family function another time when you were the victim, everybody out to get you. Like most of your memories, you've changed this one.'

'I remember everything.'

Nowell crossed his arms. 'You remember things in your own way. Maybe there was some sort of mix-up over Dad's gift, but you remember it as some scheme to discredit you. I'm sure I had other things on my mind back then, like studying for exams and writing papers.'

'I had other things on my mind, too,' Lonnie said. 'But I

remember that when I first called, I suggested a shirt or a tie. He'd been traveling more for the business, do you remember that?'

'Lonnie, just drop it.'

'He bought a couple of suits and I figured he could use some ties, but you said Dad didn't need clothes.'

'How would I know what he wanted? I never told you that.'

'I thought you didn't remember.'

Nowell turned back toward his computer. 'I have work to do,' he said evenly.

Vivian and Dot had finished packing the box and had carried it between them into the spare room. Afterwards, they listened to the argument from the hallway. When Lonnie pulled the curtain divider back into place, they emerged.

'Hey, Dot, what's to eat around here?' Lonnie's face was flushed and glowing. He seemed jubilant, almost happy.

'Can't you wait for dinner?' she asked. 'We thought we'd order pizza tonight, maybe in an hour or so.'

Nowell came into the kitchen. His face was drawn and pale. 'Might as well order it now. I'm not going to get any more work done.'

Vivian couldn't remember the last time they'd all stood in the kitchen at the same time, especially the two men, whose tall, rugged bodies made it seem crowded and airless.

'Well, ladies,' Lonnie said. 'The king has spoken.'

Nowell whirled around to face Lonnie. 'What's your problem?'

'I know you remember that shirt, that's all.'

'I thought that conversation was over.'

Lonnie reached for the baseball cap hanging on the hook near the door and plopped it on his head. His eyes had a wild, watery look. From another hook, he took his car keys. 'Maybe I'll go for a drive while you think about it,' he said. 'After all this time, you still haven't figured things out.'

'What things? Things according to Lonnie? You're right, I'll never figure that out.'

208

'It was different with us and you know it. You had your special place and you made sure I never came close.'

'I don't know what you're…'

'Goddammit, yes you do!' Lonnie's voice resonated through the yellow kitchen, echoing over the smooth surfaces and drowning out the ticking of the rooster clock.

'All right, Lonnie,' Dot said softly.

'I can't believe after all this time, you're still living in your little fantasy world,' he shouted. 'Sure, he thought about you early on. Such an achiever, always bringing home good news, with your Little League championship and your science award.'

'That was in the fourth grade!' Nowell's voice was incredulous.

'But then he wasn't thinking about anyone, was he? You, off at college, pretending things were still the same. The great father–son relationship. You made it all up. Don't you see that now? You made it up, and while you were away living your dream life, things at home were falling apart. Mom lost all that weight and you never noticed.'

Vivian and Dot lingered nervously at the edge of the kitchen, exchanging helpless glances.

'At least he could depend on me not to screw up,' Nowell said. 'You have no idea what it was like, going to bat against him for you, for you! You can't manage the simplest thing, can't keep your life together for one month without one of us having to bail you out. And it was usually me, wasn't it? Why was that, Lonnie? If you and Mom were so close – she still calls you her baby – if you're so close, then why was it always me?'

'Who asked you?' Lonnie bellowed and before their astonished eyes, the keys flew out of his hand toward Nowell's head. Barely missing, they crashed into the wall next to the window and slid into the sink.

By the time they looked back, Lonnie was gone. The screen door jerked back and forth as it slowly closed.

'He's lucky he missed that window,' Nowell barked. He took his own keys from the counter and strode through the door. In a moment, they heard the truck's engine, the tires slipping then taking hold on the dirt driveway.

They went to the door to watch Nowell leave. Vivian looked over and noticed that Dot was near crying. Teardrops crowded her eyes, threatening to spill. 'Sit down,' she told her.

Dot pulled a chair from underneath the table and sat down. When she reached up to wipe her eyes, her hands were shaky. 'His temper is so sudden, you know? I never know when it's coming, or what causes it.'

'I think that's how tempers work.' Vivian sat down across from her and handed her a tissue.

She dabbed at the corners of her green eyes, which seemed paler, more yellowish than usual. 'I used to think it was just another aspect of passion,' she said. 'You know, deep feelings. We've only had a few really horrible fights, but they always end with Lonnie losing his temper, throwing or breaking something.'

Vivian looked at her with concern.

'Oh, he's never touched me,' she said. 'And I don't believe he ever would.'

'But he threw those keys right at Nowell.'

She wiped her eyes again, leaving a smear of mascara underneath one eye. 'I don't think he meant to, you know? He loves Nowell and he loves me, and when he gets angry like that, it's not the person he's mad at, it's the situation and his own feelings. All that rage at himself and there's nowhere to direct it.'

'I'm glad he missed,' Vivian said.

Dot reached over and grabbed her wrist. 'He feels awful about it, I know he does.' Tears flowed freely now down her cheeks, ending at the corners of her mouth. 'Please don't be angry with him, Vivian.'

Vivian covered Dot's hand with her own.

'I'm starting to think that it's weakness more than passion, you know, his temper. I have to admit something to you and it might sound strange.' She peered into Vivian's face. 'The first couple of times he lost his temper, I found it, I don't know, exciting. Sure, I was angry and one time he broke our television remote and I was mad about that. But it was passion, you know? Here he was, big and crazed, crashing around our apartment and at the same time I was frightened, I was excited by it.'

'But it's so childish.'

She shrugged. 'There's no restraint and in a way, it's refreshing. Haven't you ever tried to make Nowell mad, maybe during a time when he hasn't been paying enough attention? Haven't you ever said something to pick a fight? Maybe you don't know at the time that you're doing it, but you make him angry so you can see his feelings.'

'I don't know,' Vivian said.

'There are things about Lonnie I didn't know when I married him. I'm not ashamed to admit it. There's a whole other person, the hidden, small one that only comes out during moments like that. I keep discovering new things about him.' After a moment, she asked: 'Do you know what Lonnie's real name is?'

'Leonard.'

'He hates it.'

'I always wanted to be a Lisa, or Michelle,' Vivian said. 'One of those names everybody has.'

Dot shook her head. 'No, Lonnie really hates his name. He made me swear never to call him by it, even as a joke.'

'That's silly.'

'We might think so, but this is what I'm telling you.' Dot's voice was emphatic. 'For some reason, he's very disturbed by it, you know? The mention of it makes him feel foolish, or small, or helpless. Knowing these things about another person makes them very special to you.'

'Or very irritating,' Vivian said, removing her hand from Dot's. 'Aren't there more important things to worry about?'

'Maybe. I don't accept everything without question. There are things I don't like, things that make me uncomfortable.'

The kitchen had grown shady as the sun moved over the house, and Vivian had a hard time focusing her eyes. The air was still and cool.

Dot cleared her throat. 'Lonnie told me once that he and his friends used to shoot at cats with their BB guns. He said that a couple of times, they actually killed one and dragged it around on their bicycles.'

'Boys do that kind of stuff all the time,' Vivian said, although the thought actually appalled her.

'But I can't help wondering how someone could do that. It's one thing to hear stories about boys who are cruel to animals, but to imagine the details, you know? Tying the poor thing with string, making sure it's tight. How could someone do that? How could someone walk away from something like that? Wouldn't it make them hard, at least some part of them?'

'I don't know,' Vivian said.

Dot's cheeks were soaked with fresh tears. Vivian reached over and pulled Dot's shoulder and she came quickly, resting her head on Vivian's shoulder. 'I don't know what I'm talking about, or why I'm crying,' she said. 'I just hate when he gets like that.'

Vivian patted Dot's back through the sheer, creamy fabric of her blouse. She could see the dark outline of her bra, the bulge at the middle of her back from the fastener. Turning her face toward Dot's ear, she felt the soft tickle of blond hair against her cheek and smelled the vanilla-clean scent of her shampoo. Vivian leaned in for some time, oblivious to the insistent ticking of the clock above the sink, its black hands pointing stiffly toward the gothic numbers and the rooster at its center arching its back and lifting one clenched claw, ready to scratch.

23

Vivian's birthday arrived on an overcast, muggy day. Dot had made reservations at an Italian restaurant in town. There would be six of them for dinner: Nowell and Vivian, Lonnie and Dot, Katherine and Max. Vivian's plans for a barbecue had never materialized, but they were all meeting at last.

The air was calm but ponderous with change as they left the house in Lonnie's jeep. Nowell shared the front with Lonnie while Dot and Vivian sat diagonally on the small back seat, their knees pointed toward each other and almost touching.

Leaning over the steering wheel, Lonnie squinted up at the gray sky. 'Feels like a storm,' he said.

Nowell stared impassively through the window. For the most part, the brothers had avoided each other for several days. Each morning Nowell started early in the study and at night, Lonnie often stayed out late, shooting darts at the local tavern with some of the road crew workers. Some days, he went fishing with them too.

Dot, likewise, ignored Lonnie's comment and stared at the passing scenery. The front of her hair was pulled back into a thick silver barrette, and the flowered sundress she wore was already wrinkling at her lap. She hadn't said anything about Lonnie's recent late-night habits, but Vivian sensed the tension between them.

Twice she heard them arguing quietly behind the door of their bedroom.

'Where did you say this place was, Vivian?' Lonnie directed his question to her, having given up on the other two.

'Down the street from the Post Office.'

'I saw that nightgown you got,' Dot said to Vivian. 'It's nice.'

'What nightgown?' Nowell twisted around in his seat. He seemed massive in the jeep, his knees pressing against the glove compartment and the top of his head just inches from the roof. Lonnie was equally cramped, having pushed up his seat a little to make more space for Vivian.

'From your mother,' Vivian told him. 'She sent me a silk gown and a robe.'

'Why didn't you show me?' he asked.

'They just came this afternoon.'

'She's going to show you later, that's why.' Lonnie nudged Nowell with his elbow.

Nowell rolled his eyes and pushed Lonnie's arm away. Taking this attention as a cue, Lonnie began telling him about the large carp he'd caught the day before with Jerry and his friends.

'Do you feel any older?' Dot asked Vivian.

'No, not really.'

'Twenty-eight, right?'

'Yeah.'

She leaned closer. 'I hope you don't mind that I made these plans. If you and Nowell wanted to do something alone…'

'No, I'm glad you did.'

'Katherine recommended the place. Supposedly, it's one of the best restaurants in town. Nowell said you like Italian.'

In the front seat, Lonnie described how Jerry had tripped over the ice chest while reeling in the fish.

'I love Italian,' Vivian said. 'Besides, we probably wouldn't have done anything if you hadn't planned it, so thanks. It's nice to dress up, isn't it?'

She nodded. 'We haven't gone out all together since we've been here.'

They listened for a while to Lonnie, who grew more animated as his story progressed. After a while, Lonnie slowed the jeep on a quiet street at the outskirts of town. 'Here we are, ladies,' he announced.

The restaurant was like a little house. The wooden shutters were painted white to match the lattice encircling a small front area landscaped with rosebushes and small trees. Strung through the branches and hanging from the awnings, tiny white lights dimly shone in the gray twilight. On the roof, green neon spelled Silvana's Ristorante in flowing, cursive letters.

'What a cute place,' Dot said. 'I never noticed it before.'

'Very nice,' Nowell agreed.

Inside, the place smelled of garlic and bread. The hostess, a fiftyish olive-skinned woman with vivid brown eyes, directed them to a table near a window. The streetlights outside cast a glow over the table and over Max and Katherine, who sat quietly talking.

'Hello there!' Katherine rose from her seat. She hugged Vivian and Dot and greeted the men.

Vivian introduced Max to everyone and Katherine complimented Dot on her dress.

They seemed to have an entire section of the restaurant to themselves. Only two other tables were occupied and both were at the far side of the restaurant, near the bar. At one, a lone man watched a baseball game on the television perched above the cash register and at the other, an elderly couple sipped at steaming mugs.

They sat down and Katherine handed Vivian a flat, square package. 'Happy birthday!'

'Oh, thank you. Thanks, Max. Should I open it now?' She looked over at Dot, who seemed to be in charge of the event.

'No,' Dot said. 'Wait until dessert. We've got something for you too.'

'They've got the game on over there,' Lonnie said. Dot shot him a warning glance.

Katherine said, 'The hostess is Josephina Riley. The restaurant was named after her mother, Silvana.'

'Sounds like an Italian name,' Vivian said.

'Yep,' Max said. 'Cecil Clement brought her over after the war.'

'She was a nice lady, real friendly,' Katherine said. 'Passed on now.'

A young man in a crisp white shirt brought them a loaf of bread, cut into thick slices. When he lifted the checkered cloth, sweet-smelling steam rose quickly.

'Cecil's parents disowned him for marrying Silvie,' Max added.

'Why?' Dot asked.

'His parents told him it was shameful to bring a wife home from a war, that he should have remembered why he was there,' Max said. 'But I think it was her being a foreigner too.'

'They were well off, heavy into society affairs,' Katherine said. 'What little society this town had to offer. They were the major funders of the history museum in the community center building, which is also called, by the way, "the cultural center".'

'There's a museum here?' Vivian asked.

'Shocking, isn't it? It's really a shrine to the Clement family. Original documents like land deeds, letters and building plans are stored there, artifacts like clothing and tools. All of it tells the story of the great William Clement and the building of his town.'

Max poured another glass of red wine. 'I've been there. I thought it was interesting.'

'Not a bad collection for a small town,' Katherine said. 'Depending on how you like your history told.'

'So Cecil's parents cut him off, just like that?' Lonnie asked.

'The only thing they left him was this house, which they'd given as a graduation present. He and Silvie lived in the back area for a while and set up the restaurant here in the front. The back is now the kitchen. They've added on quite a bit over the years.'

216

'Where does he live?' Dot asked.

Katherine set her glass down. 'Josephina's got him in the nursing home.'

The young-faced waiter returned and took their orders. The food arrived quickly and it was excellent, as good as anything Vivian had in the city. She loved Italian food, the subtle spices and the richness of it, but because she tried to keep her weight down, she didn't eat it often.

After they had finished their entrees and ordered a third bottle of wine, Dot pulled her purse onto her lap and retrieved a long, narrow box from its folds. She placed both presents in front of Vivian. Business had picked up in the restaurant; five tables were now full with recently arrived patrons. As Vivian scanned the room, her eyes fell on the hostess, Josephina. The plump, dark woman carried a brightly lit cake, followed by the waiter and another man. Vivian blushed as they reached the table and sang 'Happy Birthday to You' in uneven but enthusiastic voices.

She didn't bother to count the candles. She blew them out with two tries and began to pull them from the frosting.

The gift from Dot and Lonnie was a silver bracelet with star-shaped charms. She held it in front of the window, watching the stars reflect the streetlight in rapid flickers of white. 'I love it,' she said.

'It fit me, so it should fit you,' Dot said. She fastened the cool metal around Vivian's wrist.

Vivian twisted her arm so that the little stars bounced and sparkled. 'It's perfect.'

'Beautiful,' Katherine agreed.

She extended her arm across the table. 'Nowell gave me a set of perfume and body lotion. Here, smell.'

'Nice,' Katherine said.

'One more to open,' Dot said.

Vivian could tell Dot really enjoyed birthdays. While Lonnie and Nowell traded observations about the ball game and Max and

217

Katherine started on their cake, Dot watched Vivian open her gifts with bright eyes.

Running her finger carefully under the tape, Vivian slid a narrow book from the pink wrapping paper that looked like it was left over from a baby shower. On the cover of the book was a reproduction of 'The Birth of Venus', the red-haired beauty emerging from the luminescent grooved shell. Inside, the blank pages were lined in soft blue. 'A journal.' She held the book up for everyone to see. 'Thank you, it's great.'

'Look under the front cover,' Katherine instructed.

An envelope was taped to it. Inside was a newspaper clipping.

Dot leaned eagerly toward her. 'What is it?'

'That's just the ad for an introductory pottery class,' Katherine said. 'It's in a few weeks, all day on a Saturday. You said you liked the flowerpots I made and well, you can't do too much in one day, but I figured they'd have us make a vase or something, at least learn the basics. I hope you can go.'

'What a great gift,' Vivian said. 'Thank you! Are you sure you want to take the class again?'

'I could use a refresher. It's been a long time, and I still have that kiln wasting away in the garage. When you said you liked those pots, it made me remember what fun it was. I swear, I may be just like a beginner; I don't remember much.'

'Thank you, everyone.' Vivian caught Nowell's eye across the table. He looked as though he was a million miles away. Probably thinking about his book, she thought.

Katherine sliced the cake and distributed the thick pieces. It tasted faintly of coconut and reminded Vivian of a cookie recipe her mother brought back from Hawaii: coconut and vanilla wafers. Her mother made them almost every week for months. Baking had never been something she enjoyed. She had always orchestrated elaborate, multi-course dinners for the holidays, but she avoided the more mundane and regular forms of cooking.

Vivian loved to come home from school and find her mother sitting at the kitchen table with her book, waiting while the cookies baked. The house was warm and smelled of vanilla; traces of flour and sugar lingered in her mother's hair and eyebrows, sweet reminders of her weakness. Sometimes, she let Vivian sprinkle the transparent curls of coconut over the soft, steaming mounds of dough.

'Vivian gave us a copy of your book,' Max said to Nowell. '*Random Victim,* right? I'm waiting for Katherine to finish it.'

'It's great so far,' Katherine said. 'I'm at the part where the young man who's building the house is about to meet his girlfriend at the park. I have a feeling he's not going to make it.'

Nowell smiled. 'Are you asking me to tell you what happens?'

'No!' She laughed, her cheeks ruddy from the wine. 'I'd hate that.'

'I'm glad you're enjoying it.'

'Oh, I am. But I have a hard time reading it if Max isn't home. It's really creepy; the way that guy watches everybody. I wouldn't want to meet up with him in a dark alley!'

'I just started the book too,' Dot said. 'I've only read the first two parts, but I agree with you. I haven't wanted to read it at night either.' She glanced at Lonnie, whose eyes were on the television at the far end of the room.

'What makes you think of a character like that?' Max asked. 'Is it something you heard about, say, on the news? Or did you think of the idea yourself?'

Nowell took another drink of his wine and searched immediately for the bottle to refill it. 'It's hard to say.'

'The killer, for instance,' Katherine said. 'Is he based on someone you know? Not the part about him being a killer, but his personality?'

'Not really. Maybe he's an amalgam of many different people, things you pick up on the street.'

'On the street?' Max asked.

'In stores, on the news. People you run into and people you

know.' Nowell looked uncomfortable. He didn't like discussing his books in detail.

Max and Katherine leaned back in their chairs. 'What about the victims?' Max said. 'Why are they young men?'

Vivian grinned. 'I thought you hadn't read it yet.'

'I looked at the back cover. In books, usually it's young girls who get stalked like that. It's different, isn't it, having men as the victims?'

Nowell shifted in his seat.

'Not necessarily,' Katherine said.

Everyone, except for Max, could tell that Nowell didn't want to talk about it. Max turned to Lonnie. 'What do you think?'

Lonnie looked over. 'About what, who gets killed more by stalkers?'

'In books, yes.'

Nowell asked Vivian where the bathrooms were, and she motioned to a doorway beside the bar.

'I haven't read many books lately.' Lonnie plunged his fork into his second piece of cake. 'And I don't think Nowell wants me to read his.'

Nowell stood near his chair, having risen to go to the bathroom. 'What do you mean?'

'You never gave me a copy of your book. You gave one to Dot, but not to me.'

'Dot asked for one. I didn't think you wanted to read it.'

'Why wouldn't I?' Lonnie asked. 'I can read, you know.'

Nowell gave him a forced smile and left.

'Why are you always picking fights with him?' Dot's eyes were watery and only traces of her lipstick remained. They had all had a few glasses of wine.

They sat for a moment in awkward silence.

Dot asked Max about the store. He made a few remarks about business then changed the subject to baseball.

Vivian excused herself and went to the bathroom. It was a small room with peach-colored walls. Two black-and-white photographs of cathedrals were centered above the sink. When she came out of the only stall, she heard a jingling sound before Katherine walked into the room.

'Sorry about Max,' she said, raising her hand to smooth her hair. The bracelets on her arm jingled again.

Vivian was confused. 'What do you mean?'

'He's not the most insightful man. I swear, sometimes you have to hit him upside the head.'

'There's no reason to apologize,' Vivian said. The room seemed abnormally bright after the dimness of the restaurant. 'Nowell doesn't like to talk about his writing. Makes him nervous or something. I don't know why he acts like that.' She shook her head. 'He's mad if people don't show an interest and he's uneasy if they do. He never tells me anything about it. If I beg him, he might say something vague, but he'll never share the process with me. All this time, first with that book and now with this one, and it's like we're living separate lives. I don't know what's wrong with him, why he won't talk about it. I should be apologizing to you.'

'I shouldn't have said anything,' Katherine said. 'Calm down, now, really.'

Vivian realized how quickly and fervently she had been speaking. A single, hot tear slid down her cheek before she wiped it away.

Katherine pulled a chair from the corner. 'Sit here.'

'I don't need…'

'Sit.'

Vivian complied, setting her purse on her lap.

'Lean over.' Katherine pushed Vivian's hair aside and pressed a damp paper towel against the back of her neck. 'It's the wine,' she said, 'always sneaks up on me too.'

Vivian closed her eyes as the delicious coolness spread from her neck over her breasts and down her abdomen.

'Could it be something else?' Katherine asked.

Vivian heard a rustling as she pulled another paper towel from the dispenser. 'What do you mean?'

Katherine dried her neck. 'Now sit up, slowly. I don't know. You could be pregnant. I think that makes women emotional.'

Vivian exhaled loudly. 'No.'

'How do you know?'

'Because I do. I've been very careful to avoid it, despite all the pressure from Nowell.'

'He wants a baby?'

'Yeah.'

'And you don't?'

'Yes. No. Not right now, that's all. I don't understand why it's so important to him. What's so great about kids, I'd like to know? Look at you and Max. You've got a great life, your own house and business.'

Katherine turned and threw the crumpled paper towel into the trash slot. 'It's not by choice.'

'What?'

She faced Vivian. 'It's not by choice we don't have children.'

'Oh, Katherine. I'm sorry. You must think…' She put her face in her hands.

'Don't worry. People have different points of view about what they want out of life.'

'But it's so insensitive. I had no idea.'

'I know you didn't.' Katherine reached over and squeezed her shoulder. Her bracelets rang like a bell.

'Nowell's been acting strange for another reason,' Vivian said.

Katherine put on lipstick then blotted on a paper towel. 'You don't have to say anything.'

'It's something he found out.' She paused. 'What do you know about Nowell's grandfather's death? Did Mrs Gardiner ever talk about it?'

She sighed. 'That was a long time ago.'

'You know something,' Vivian said, her eyes widening.

'I know what most people know. It was a hunting accident.'

'But who was hunting with him?'

'I'm not sure. Friends, I guess.'

'Like Mr Stokes's father and grandfather?'

Katherine stopped rummaging through her purse. 'Yes, like those two.'

'So you know.'

'When something is an accident, what do particulars matter? I didn't want to influence your opinion of Mr Stokes.'

'But you told me about his love affair with Ronella Oates and about his strange habits.'

'This is a little different, don't you think?'

'Maybe.' Vivian stood up and looked at herself in the mirror. She retrieved her makeup from her purse. 'So what happened?'

'I really don't know anything,' Katherine said. 'They all went hunting and Jesper Stokes accidentally shot Russ, uh, Mr Gardiner. It's not hard to imagine something like that happening. Either he thought it was a deer or his gun misfired. I've always thought hunting was stupid, just men trying to show their superiority over nature. Sure, with a gun. Anyway, I'm sorry I didn't mention it, but like I said, I didn't want to make things uncomfortable for you.'

'His name was Russ?'

'Russell. Betty called him Russ.'

'How did Grandma Gardiner feel about living next to Mr Stokes and his father all those years, after what happened?'

'I know she didn't blame anybody. It was a horrible accident.'

'She believed that?'

'Listen, I think I know what you're hinting at, and I'm telling you, Betty didn't blame anybody.'

Dot pushed open the door. 'What's going on in here?'

'Just freshening up and gabbing a little,' Katherine said. 'We're on our way out.'

'Everyone's getting pretty anxious,' she said. 'Nowell has already paid the bill and taken your presents out to the car.'

'What's he in such a hurry about?' Vivian asked, and she gathered her things to leave.

24

The storm that blew in the night of Vivian's birthday was violent and short-lived. Lightning appeared like cracks in the surface of the glassy, blue-black sky; as the jeep rolled over the slick asphalt of the new main road, electric bolts branched in the distance and seemed to touch ground over the stirring fields. At the horizon, a strip of lighter blue divided land from ominous cloud, providing a glimpse beyond the storm. The rain came in sheets. Fighting bravely against the deluge, the windshield wipers cleared the glass for short moments of sight before the water rushed down, blurring things again.

Dot pulled a faded, fringed blanket from the back of the jeep and folded it over their laps. Vivian couldn't stop thinking about her conversation with Katherine. It had never occurred to her that she and Max might be unable to have children. She had assumed it was their choice, and she suddenly felt selfish for her own choice. What if I couldn't, she thought, and fear clenched her heart with its cold fingers. She did want children, but at the present she couldn't see where they'd fit into their lives. People should have a place for children.

The rain let up as abruptly as it had started; the oily smell of asphalt clung to the underbelly of the jeep. As Lonnie turned into the long driveway that led to the old, white house, Vivian noticed the small ponds that had formed here and there, the big drops still dripping from the porch awning. Above the house, the moon peeked now and then from the black and torrid sky.

It was the last rain they would see for almost two weeks. The short but intense downpour heralded a heat wave, cooled things off one last time before the sun baked the ground dry. In the 'Nation' section of *The Sentinel*, Vivian read about the fires raging through the southern parts of the country and in the confines of the house they faced their own battles with the heat. Grandma Gardiner had lived for sixty years without central air conditioning, and Vivian didn't understand how. Nowell still refused to open the windows in his study, which would have allowed a crosscurrent of air during the now infrequent afternoon breezes. The kitchen was the coolest room. As the sun dipped in the afternoons, the back rooms of the house were sweltering. At night, Vivian slept above the covers and they all kept their bedroom doors open, wishful for a gust of air.

But the night of the dinner for Vivian's twenty-eighth birthday was still cool and breezy after the storm. When they got home, the red light on the answering machine was blinking. Beverly had called to let her sons know her air conditioner was broken. What was the name of the man who fixed it before, she wanted to know, and did Nowell still have the phone number?

'I'd better call her,' Nowell said to no one in particular.

Lonnie put a bag of popcorn into the microwave and soon the kitchen reeked of its buttery odor.

Dot padded back into the kitchen, having changed into a long pink T-shirt and a striped pair of socks. The socks were thick and reached to mid-calf; one big toe poked through a hole. The shirt stretched to her knees, and the outline of her shorts was visible through the thin material. Vivian had the irritating thought that Dot looked good in anything she threw together. On herself, clothing often felt uncomfortable or ill-fitting, and there was always something to hide: a slightly bloated stomach, the flabby upper sections of her arms.

Lonnie dumped his popcorn into a large bowl, coated it with salt, then followed Dot into the living room. Vivian heard the faint buzzing of the old television as it warmed up.

Nowell had changed clothes too, into the shirt he'd been wearing for several days. He picked up the phone. 'Hi, Mom. No, we just got back from dinner. The four of us. Vivian's birthday, right. She's doing well, but she looks older.'

Vivian rolled her eyes at him then opened the freezer, looking for something to thaw for dinner the next day.

'Did you get any rain? Yes, only for a few minutes. I know, it really cooled off with the storm.'

From the living room, Vivian heard a woman's sharp screams. Lonnie loved horror movies; he thought they were funny.

'You're kidding, that warm? Do you think it's the filter again?'

A pool of blood had frozen in the freezer like a reddish-brown pond. Vivian found the steaks that had leaked through a narrow slit in the plastic wrap. She put them into the sink along with a second package.

'Mom, that was five years ago. Are you sure you don't have it in your file cabinet?'

In the living room, violins screeched a tense tempo. Dot said, 'Why would she go in there?'

Vivian dampened the kitchen sponge with warm water and took it to the freezer. The puddle brightened as it was moistened, its volume augmented by the water. The liquid seeped into corners and traveled fast over the plastic grooves.

'Isn't there a folder called Home Repairs? Yeah, I'll wait. Go ahead.'

Pushing the freezer contents away, Vivian soaked up the red mess. Then she took the darkened sponge to the sink and rinsed it out.

A piercing scream sounded from the living room and bounced off the hard surfaces of the kitchen.

'What are you doing?' Nowell asked.

She turned and saw that he was talking to her. 'Some blood spilled in the freezer.'

'Blood?'

'From the meat.'

'Yeah, Mom, I'm still here. You found it? That sounds familiar.'

Dot groaned in disgust while Lonnie laughed loudly, saying 'Look at that, look!'

Vivian finished wiping up the mess. When Nowell hung up the phone, she asked him: 'Were there any messages from earlier today?'

'No.'

She set the steaks on a plate in the refrigerator.

Nowell reached around her to grab the pitcher of water. 'Your mom's been out of town, you know that.'

'I wasn't expecting them to call,' she said.

He put his arm around her shoulders.

'I wasn't,' she said again.

'My mom said to wish you a happy birthday. She was already in bed. She has a bake sale in the morning.'

'That's all right. I already talked to her today when I called to thank her for the nightgown.'

His eyebrows shot up. 'Oh, yes, the new nightgown. Did you say it was silk?'

'Maybe I did, maybe I didn't.'

'Come on now, don't be coy.' Nowell nuzzled his face into her hair. 'Did you have a good birthday? If you don't like the perfume, you can exchange it.'

'I love the perfume. I loved everything. Thank you.'

'Listen, Viv, I know things have been different lately.' He turned her around. 'It's strange, being here. I feel so much pressure for this new book, not just with the deadlines but because the first one wasn't everything I thought it would be.'

She set the glass down. 'What do you mean? The book sold more than you expected.'

'That's not it.' He leaned against the refrigerator, crossing his arms over his chest. 'You start with an idea, maybe something incredibly simple. In the case of *Random Victim*, it was a single idea that sort of blossomed in my head to form networks of meaning. At first it all seems so clear in a confused, inexplicable kind of way. Then you try to write it down. Some parts turn out almost exactly as you imagined but some seem so lacking, and you don't know how to fix them.'

Vivian spoke carefully, as though the wrong word would break a spell and then he wouldn't talk to her anymore. 'If things change as you go along, that's not necessarily a bad thing, is it?'

'Ideas come along,' he said, 'and sometimes they are welcome additions, new avenues to explore.' He stared at the linoleum, concentrated on its simple pattern. 'But at some point it got away from me. I could feel it. It turned into something different from what I'd conceived.'

'Everyone says the book is good.'

'I'm proud of it, but it isn't the book I planned to write, not really. With this book, I want to stay in control, finish what I start. It's important to me that it turns out like I've planned it.'

'Is that possible?'

'What do you mean?'

She shrugged. 'The way you updated the first book as you went along, that's a more natural process, isn't it?'

'Maybe,' he said, his eyes growing distant. 'I'm going to work for a while.'

He's like a faucet, she thought. In one instant, he shuts down and shuts me out. These rare glimpses of Nowell – what his writing meant to him and what forces drove him – always left her feeling isolated rather than closer to him.

She went into the living room and watched the end of the horror movie with Dot and Lonnie and that night, she slept comfortably for the last time before the weather changed.

Two days later, she was gathering laundry when she found the birthday package from her parents under a pile of clothes in the bedroom. Nestled inside the packaging material were a sketchbook and pencils (although Vivian had never drawn) and an art book on Édouard Manet. Her mother had scribbled a quick note in her tilted, hurried handwriting:

Dear Vivian,
Just saw a new Manet exhibit and picked up this book for you. It was an unexpected trip. Please spend the money on something fun for yourself. Talk to you soon. I'll be home on Tuesday.
      Love, Mom & Dad.

She took the book to the kitchen.

'Where did you get that?' Lonnie asked.

'From my parents.'

He smelled of sweat and the grainy bitterness of beer. It was around noon and he'd been in town picking up a few groceries. He put down the bags and peered over her shoulder.

The cover of the book was a glossy reproduction of 'A Bar at the Folies-Bergère'. In the painting, the young barmaid stared sedately forward, her plaintive brown eyes revealing her despair, her empty spirit. She was the only clearly focused subject in the painting; the lace bodice of her dress and the sprig of flowers tucked inside, the gleam on her bronze bracelet – all were rendered with precise detail. In the background, the wide mirror shimmered back her surroundings, blurring the tables and patrons into patterns of muted color. The faces of the bar patrons were indistinct and in some cases, altogether blank. The mirror seemed to reflect her own perception, the vast, undulating plane of people she faced each night.

Lonnie asked: 'Isn't that the guy who painted that church a million times? I saw a documentary about him once.'

'I don't think so.'

'He had a pond and he couldn't stop painting those lily pads…'

'Oh, you're thinking of Monet. With an "o".'

'Who's this guy?'

'Manet. Contemporaries, actually. They're both Impressionists.'

'What's that? I've heard that before.'

'They painted their surroundings in a new way,' she said, 'not naturalistically like when you see a picture of a regular tree or a lake. They gathered impressions of things, and tried to paint how the scene felt to them. Their impressions.'

Lonnie nodded.

Vivian remembered when they discussed Monet's watercolors of Rouen Cathedral in Dr Lightfoot's Art History class. Flipping through several slides, Dr Lightfoot said that the forty pictures were evidence of a methodical and disciplined mind, perhaps even the work of a neurotic. To Vivian, Monet's effort seemed extraordinary but unmistakably scientific. She wondered how someone could feel inspired to paint the same scene so many times. One good thing about Monet, Dr Lightfoot joked, you can see his work just about anywhere.

Lonnie paused at the screen door. 'I want to look at that book later. Do you mind?'

'No,' she said. 'I'll leave it here.'

He started to whistle and went outside. Vivian brought the telephone to the table.

Her mother picked up on the second ring. 'Hello?' She sounded annoyed.

'Mom?'

'Vivian. How are you?'

'Fine, everything's fine. What are you doing?'

'I'm cleaning up around the house a little. Your dad's out back, pretending to cut down the weeds.'

'Pretending?'

'He does a poor job so I'll hire a gardener.'

'I thought you had a gardener.'

'Ricardo? He quit over a year ago. I've been trying to get your father to do it. I tell him it's to save money for retirement, but I really think it would be good for his health. He doesn't get any exercise.'

'I know,' Vivian said.

'He sneaks a book with him, tucks it under his shirt. He thinks I don't know.'

Vivian laughed. 'He probably knows that you know.' She twisted the phone cord around her index finger, tightening until the tip turned red. 'I called to thank you for the Manet book.'

'You like the Impressionists, don't you?'

'Very much. You saw an exhibit?'

'Yes. Sorry I didn't phone you, Vivian, before I left. It was all a big rush. I had to fly up to interview a woman for my book about the volcano eruption. An incredible old lady, just recovering from her second stroke. I wasn't sure how much longer she'd be around, so I decided to go up and get some preliminary work done.'

'How long were you there?'

'A week. The old woman, Mrs Pheola H. Roundtree if you can believe it, is eighty-six years old. The H is for Himalaya. Seems her mother was something of an eccentric; she gave each of her children a middle name after a mountain range: Sierra, Andes, Appalachia. Pheola has eight children of her own, all of whom were alive at the time of the volcano eruption. She was just thirty-five. Along with four of her neighbors, all mothers, she saved a group of school children.'

'Saved them? How?'

'The children attended school in an old church two miles from the volcano. When they heard the rumble, they all scurried up to the choir loft. At home, Pheola heard it too. She packed up her car with her four youngest children and a few neighborhood women and their young ones, and she drove straight toward the mountain to get her older children.'

'Wow,' Vivian said.

'Along the way, they convinced two farmers to bring their

tractors and a long, flat bed on wheels that they normally used for transporting fruit. When they reached the school, the lava was getting near and ash was falling like snowflakes. Pheola kept going back inside for children and in the end, they saved most of them. She suffered scorch burns on her arms and legs and she lost some sight in one eye. The other mothers pulled her away as the lava rolled down the hill. They could barely see through the black air. There were three children and the young teacher left inside; one was Pheola's oldest daughter.'

'How awful. They just left?'

'There wasn't anything they could do. The farmers convinced her that the building would stand. They promised to go back after the lava receded, but the town was evacuated that evening. The first eruption was minor compared to the second one the next day. Every building in their small town was leveled, every tree razed and every living thing killed.'

'Mom, that's a terrible story.'

Her mother inhaled sharply. 'But you should see this woman, Vivian. I felt so small in her presence. She was so matter-of-fact about what she did, almost embarrassed when I told her how impressive and inspiring her story was. Anyone would've done the same, she told me, and it still wasn't enough.'

'Where are the rest of her children now?' Vivian asked.

'Here and there, around the country. Most of them are doing well. She lost another daughter in an automobile accident, but the rest have lived long, full lives. She's got twenty-two grandchildren and six great-grandchildren.'

'What about her husband?'

'Mr Roundtree died about ten years ago. Heart attack. Pheola said they threw him a big party for his seventieth. One of her sons has a house out in the country, and most of the family gathered there. She showed me a picture, everyone lined up and her and Mr Roundtree in the center, sitting on chairs. Remarkable woman.'

'Sounds like it,' Vivian said.

'So that's where I've been. What have you been doing out there? How's the house coming along?'

'We're planning a yard sale. Dot and I have started organizing and labeling everything.' She realized immediately how mundane this sounded after her mother's story.

'Did you see anything I might want?'

Vivian laughed. 'I don't think so, unless your style of clothing has changed dramatically since I saw you.'

'No, still the same boring professor look.'

'We're hoping for a good turnout. There's a big reunion in town that weekend. Maybe some of those attending will drive out here.'

'What kind of reunion?'

'The family name is Clement. William Clement founded the town. His descendants have a lot of power around here. They own just about everything: the newspaper, the radio station, restaurants. In the town plaza, there's a big bronze statue of William Clement on a horse, like he was a war hero.'

'Was he?'

'What?'

'A war hero?' her mother asked.

'No. In fact, he moved here just about the time the Civil War was breaking out.'

'You're saying he avoided service?'

'I don't know. There's such a lack of objectivity about him that I find myself reading between the lines, looking for things to fault him with. They've been running historical pieces on the town and the Clement family in the newspaper, but it's all propaganda.'

'So how did he set about founding a town?'

Vivian shrugged. 'The usual way. He brought in engineers to design the downtown area and he financed several of the early buildings. He founded the first bank and helped people start farms and businesses. Most of the early real estate development projects have his stamp all over them. Even in recent years, Clements have built the town's hospital and started a historical museum.'

'That would make a good book,' her mother said. 'You have to admire people like that, Vivian.'

'People like the Clements?'

'I don't know about the whole family, but you have to admire William Clement for his vision and accomplishments. To pick up and move your family across the country and start a new life, to put your money and your hard work into something you believe in – it's rare.'

'You hardly know anything about him,' Vivian protested.

'Just what you told me, but it's enough. The man built an entire town. Do you know what that takes? People who act on their plans, people who make changes. Like Pheola. She's a hero because she acted, without anyone inciting her to do it. She changed her life. Many people talk a great deal about what they would have done, what they could do, what they might do. It's action that matters, that defines heroes.'

Vivian couldn't remember the last time she had had such a long conversation with her mother. But she felt an underlying intent to her mother's words and it made her uncomfortable.

'It's my one big regret, Vivie. I never did anything.'

'What do you mean? You've traveled all over, you've written all those books…'

'But I never did anything. Never fought for anything, never built anything, never made anything.'

'You made me.'

'Yes.' She paused. 'I know you may not always think so, but you're lucky.'

'Why?'

'We've always encouraged you to learn. I may not have done anything to make the world a better place, but I have really enjoyed my life of learning. My father didn't want me to go to college. He didn't think I needed to, because I was a girl.'

'I didn't know that.'

'I think he came to grips with me eventually. I venture to

think that he might have been proud, in his own way.'

'Mom?'

'Yes?'

'What would you have done?'

'What?'

Vivian pressed the phone into her ear. 'You said that you never did anything. If you could start again, what would you do?'

Silence clung heavy to the air, like thick paint on canvas.

'I don't know,' her mother finally said. 'I don't know.'

The fires in the south began the following day, or at least, that was the first day Vivian read about them in *The Sentinel*, which still was delivered only on Mondays, Fridays and Sundays. The heat was constant and unforgiving. Katherine knew a woman with a swimming pool, a fellow volunteer down at the grammar school, and a few times, she picked up Dot and Vivian and they went over and swam.

Lonnie had begun to prepare the outside of the house for painting, but none of them could bear the idea of beginning the work. It was too hot to work inside too. Twice, Vivian went to matinees in town with Lonnie and Dot. The old theater didn't have air conditioning either, but it was cool and dark inside. Lonnie talked them into seeing an action movie about the end of the world, and during the 'Tribute to Classics Week' in honor of the upcoming town festival, they watched a musical.

The heat wave continued for almost two weeks, right up until the week of the yard sale, the week that Clements began to arrive for the reunion.

25

Lonnie decided to cook a whole chicken in the ground. He purchased a huge clay pot, even bigger than the one he used for making his cobbler, and he simmered the bird in a concoction made up of a half-bottle of cheap white wine, the juice from two oranges, and a variety of herbs and spices the identity of which he would not divulge but which Vivian's nose recognized to be dominated by the distinctive aroma of cilantro.

Vivian helped Lonnie carry his supplies to the woods while Dot lingered in the shower, refreshing herself after another sticky, warm night. Nowell was in the study as usual. Vivian transported the chicken, still snug in its plastic wrap and sealed with small metal staples, and Lonnie carried his cooking utensils and the mysterious brown bag of ingredients.

'Feels like it's going to break,' he said as they rounded the house.

'The bag?' she asked.

'No, the weather.'

There were patches of dry, straw-colored grass that crackled loudly underfoot. Nowell still hadn't mowed the shorter sections and he hadn't done anything about the knee-high parts further back. On a couple of occasions, Lonnie had offered to take a look at the rusty old mower in the shed, but Vivian turned him down each time. It was a silent war she waged with Nowell, like the times she still opened the windows in the study. He promised to cut the grass and she'd hold him to it.

As Vivian clutched the chicken against her chest, a timid breeze tested the air. Lonnie was right: the morning was cooler than it had been for a while. They approached the thick line of trees, and she heard the soothing rustling of their leaves overhead. Once in the shade, the chicken felt cold against her body and she transferred its weight to both hands.

Set about fifty feet back and at an angle from the place where they had entered the woods, Lonnie's cooking spot consisted of two landmarks: an unimpressive shallow hole lined with ash-covered charcoal, and the roundish boulder on which he instructed her to set the chicken. He moved the used pieces of charcoal to the edges of the pit and filled the center with dark, shiny pieces.

Vivian looked through the trees in the direction of Mr Stokes's house. She hadn't been in the woods since the night she trespassed on his property, the night she entered his house. 'We should have been sleeping out here,' she told Lonnie. 'It's so much cooler.'

Leaning over the pit, he looked up at her, grinning. 'I did sleep out here, remember?'

'Just that once?'

'You said yourself, it's nice and cool.'

She shuddered. 'There are too many noises.'

'That damn rooster clock in the house just about ticks itself off the wall.'

'I'd rather be hot than eaten alive,' Vivian said.

'I think the weather is finally breaking,' he said again. 'Bring me the bird.'

Vivian lifted the chicken from the smooth rock and carried it to Lonnie. He raised it and bit into a section near its headless neck, ripping the plastic wrap with his teeth.

'Lonnie!'

'What?' He spit fragments onto the ground.

She watched him place the bird in the clay pot and pour the ingredients from a Tupperware bowl on top. The liquid was orange in color and filled with dark, floating bits.

'Is that cilantro?' she asked, whiffing at the air.

He looked surprised.

'Oh, come on,' she said. 'Enough with your secret recipes, already. Don't you want me to be able to cook for your brother?'

'No, I want him alive.'

'Very funny. I know that's cilantro.'

Lonnie put the lid on the dish and nestled it among the briquettes, which were smoldering. He walked to a nearby tree and pulled a branch down. The wood cracked as he pulled it from the tree; the branch left a greenish, gaping wound in the trunk. He laid it over the hole, secured the edges with two fist-sized rocks, then wiped his hands on his pants.

'Won't that catch fire?' she asked.

'Too green,' he said. 'Ready?' He put the wrapper into the brown bag.

'Why don't you do this closer to the house?' she asked.

'I like the idea of roughing it.'

When they reached the edge of the trees, Vivian paused. 'You're not afraid out here? I mean, after what happened?'

'What happened?'

'Chanelle Brodie. Don't you ever think about it?'

'No.' He pushed past the trees into the sunlight.

A vision of the young girl, her body splayed on the rock like a cloak thrown carelessly over a chair, flashed in Vivian's mind. She had imagined it so many times, the mud-caked sneakers lifeless on the ground, the fingers curled back, the weighty, smooth boulder, that she sometimes forgot that the detailed mental picture was the work of her imagination and not of her memory.

She followed Lonnie onto the grass and struggled to keep up with his long strides. 'It's strange to be out here,' she continued, 'so close to the place where someone died.'

Lonnie crumpled the bag in his large hands. 'I never think about it.'

'Do you think it was an accident?'

'That's what they say.'

'I know,' Vivian said, 'but they found her in a strange position.'

Lonnie stopped 'What do you mean?'

'Her arms were at her sides, like this.' She demonstrated.

'So?'

'If someone fell forward, they would try to break the fall, like this.' She held her hands up near her chest.

They had reached the trashcan beside the house. Lonnie asked: 'Who told you that?'

'Someone at the newspaper office. Don't you think that's strange?'

'I don't think anything about it. They have experts.' He opened the lid of the trashcan and pushed the wadded brown paper bag down on top of the garbage.

'In a small town like this, you think they have "experts"?' They stepped onto the front porch.

'I think it depends how fast you were going,' Lonnie said.

'What do you mean?'

He closed his eyes in a show of patience. 'If you were running very fast and you tripped, I think you'd find yourself on your face before there was time to do anything.' He lifted his arms and turned his palms upward. 'Besides, do you think your arms would do you any good? I mean, if the impact was so strong?'

'I guess you're right,' she said. 'People fly through windshields head first.'

'Exactly.'

She thought about what he had said and it seemed to make sense. If your momentum was so great that you had no time to react. 'What do you think of Mr Stokes?' she asked.

He lowered his voice. 'First you ask me if I think there was something fishy about that girl's death and now you ask me my opinion of Mr Stokes. Very subtle, Vivian.'

'Just forget it.'

'Tell me what you mean.' He watched her face.

She signaled him to the corner of the porch. 'Nobody in the town sees Mr Stokes for years. We move here and all of a sudden, he's everywhere. He showed up the evening that they found her, the Brodie girl. You had just left that day and I had just arrived. Then the day Mrs Brodie was here to see where they found her, here he comes again. And he followed me in the woods one time, scaring me to death. Then you run into him and he gets invited on your fishing trip, and he's here when we come home that night.'

'I didn't "run into" him, Vivian. I went over to his place because I wanted to ask him about his meat smoker.'

'But he was out there, lingering around.'

'On his own property!'

'Never mind,' she said. 'I just wanted to know what you thought of him.' She tried to walk toward the door, but Lonnie grabbed her arm lightly, just above the elbow. She jerked her arm away and when she saw the startled then humiliated look on his face, she immediately regretted it. They were both thinking of the night at Beverly's.

'If you must know,' he said in a low voice. 'I think he's pretty strange. He always seems to be sizing people up. That's his nature, I guess. Sometimes he looks suspicious. I don't mean he looks like he's done something; I mean he looks at others in a suspicious way. But that's just my point of view, which isn't good for two cents because I hardly know him and shouldn't be talking in the first place.'

'I was just curious,' she said weakly.

Lonnie leaned towards her. 'You've been watching too many crime shows, Vivian. The police think it was an accident, that's what they said. Hell, Sheriff Townsend is a good friend of the mother, and he's not nosing around.'

'Who's out there?' Dot called. A few seconds later, her face appeared at the screen door.

'Hi, honey,' Lonnie said.

'Where were you two?'

'Vivian helped me carry that chicken out to the cooking hole.'

'I'm afraid that was my job,' she said to Vivian, 'but I decided to sleep a little later. This hot weather is draining me, you know? I feel so tired all the time.' She opened the door for them and Vivian followed Lonnie into the kitchen.

'Are you sure that you know what you're doing with that chicken?' Dot asked.

'What do you mean?'

'What about salmonella or E. coli, which is it? I'm not sure that you can slow-cook chicken.'

'Do you really think I would poison you?'

'Not on purpose,' she said.

Vivian snickered from where she stood at the coffeepot.

'Your faith in me is unbelievable,' he said. 'Both of you.' He left the room, grumbling all the way down the hall.

Vivian walked across the kitchen and pulled back the curtain to the study. 'Nowell?'

He turned his head and smiled.

She walked over to the desk and squeezing herself onto his lap, pressed her face against his.

'What's all this for?' he asked.

'I don't need a reason, do I?' She glanced at the computer screen, which was filled with typing. One exclamation at the center of the page jumped out at her: *'What is it that you want?'* She couldn't imagine anyone shouting the phrase; it was so formal and awkward. 'How's it going?'

'Good,' he said. 'I'm about three-quarters through the first draft. I have to start thinking about tying up all the loose ends. Are you just about ready for the yard sale?'

'I think so. The ad actually starts in the newspaper today. They don't print on Tuesdays or Thursdays, so it'll run today and Friday, Saturday and Sunday. Tomorrow night we'll have to start setting up.'

'Sounds good. Do you need me to pick up anything in town?'

'Just those tables. Katherine said she'd meet you tomorrow at the grammar school at three-thirty.'

'How many am I supposed to get?'

'They're those long tables they use in the auditorium, so five should be plenty. We'll lay the rest of the stuff out on the grass. Yard sales aren't supposed to be high-class affairs.'

'Will Lonnie be around to help me with the tables?'

'I think so. You haven't talked to him since your argument?'

'Of course I've talked to him.'

'But you're still angry. You're cooped up in here like always, but now, even when you're around, you hardly speak to anyone. And Lonnie's been going out almost every night, sometimes after we're all in bed, I think.'

'What do you mean, "going out"?'

'He meets up with those guys. I guess they go down to the tavern. Dot seems pretty upset about it.'

'Don't start getting involved in their business, Viv.'

'I'm not, but it's affecting you so it affects me.'

'Lonnie going out has no effect on me whatsoever.'

She stood up. 'So there isn't a strain between you over that stupid shirt?'

'Maybe we've both been preoccupied.'

'With what?'

'I don't know if you've noticed, but I'm trying to write a book here. Dani's starting to set up stuff for the fall, maybe some book signings…'

'But you haven't finished,' Vivian said.

'We're going to promote *Random Victim* again before this one's released. I need to have the first draft done.'

'You never said…'

'Viv!' His voice was stern. 'I'm telling you now. Dani wants me to do a signing in the city at the end of September, then about five more in a tri-state tour. That's all she has planned for now, to start off locally. She thinks there'll be a regional interest we could capitalize on.'

Vivian got up and walked over to one of the tall bookshelves. It reached almost to the ceiling. Her eyes fell on a long line of encyclopedias, a shelf stacked with yellowed paperback westerns, and then a set of books entitled *Myths, Legends, and Phenomena.* Each book of this last set had a similar navy blue cover and a smaller title in jarring, neon letters. Vivian noticed one near the center on UFOs and wondered if Lonnie had seen it.

Nowell said, 'I've still got to go through those. I'll do it tonight.'

'I could take a look at them first,' she offered.

'No, that's all right. I'll take them down tonight and bring out the ones I don't want.'

She spun around. 'What am I supposed to do while you're running around with Dani?' The moment the words left her mouth, she was sorry. She wasn't jealous in that way. She was more upset with his secrecy and his tendency to be completely self-involved.

'I don't know, Viv. I hadn't thought about it. You see, I've been busy writing this goddamn book.'

'I didn't mean – look, it's just that we haven't been alone since Dot and Lonnie got here. I haven't said anything before, but you told me they were staying for two weeks.'

'You're jumping from one subject to another.'

'It's all related! We need time to work things out and it's next to impossible in this environment. You've been completely unavailable.'

'What do we need to work out?'

She shook her head. 'I think we both know there's something, we just haven't figured out what it is.'

'You're speaking so cryptically,' he said. 'I have no idea how to respond. As for Lonnie and Dot, I didn't know you wanted them to leave.'

'I never said…'

'I thought they were helping you with the house, which made me feel better because I haven't been. I also thought that you liked Dot and that they were keeping you company, something else I felt sorry about because I know I've been putting most of my energy into this book. The last time I talked to Lonnie about it, he told me they were having a great time. His new job starts soon, but if you want me to ask them to go earlier…'

'You're taking what I said out of context. The main point was that we haven't had any time together.'

He nodded. 'To work things out, you said. Other than the one issue we've been discussing, I didn't know there was anything else. I thought we both agreed, without saying so, to drop the issue of children for a while. Are there other problems I don't know about?'

'I'm not sure. Sometimes I feel like I don't know you anymore.'

'What?' Nowell was losing his patience.

'I think I'm a little depressed over my birthday,' Vivian said. 'I'm feeling restless, like I'm between acts.' She was losing her nerve. 'Don't worry, I'm just a little tired today. Maybe I'll take a nap later. Let me know when you're ready for lunch; I'll make you a sandwich.'

'You don't have to do that.'

'And you really should open a window. It's cooling down today, finally. There's a nice breeze and if we open this side of the house, the air can circulate.'

'You know it blows all my papers around.'

'Weigh them down with something.' She picked up the coffee cup that Dani had inscribed for him after his book was published. In black cursive letters it said Nowell S. Gardiner, Author. 'Use this.' She kissed him on the forehead and walked toward the kitchen.

After she let the curtain divider fall back into place, she turned and almost ran into Dot, who was hurrying past her into the hallway. 'Sorry,' Vivian said.

Dot's face was pale and her eyes darted around. Vivian could smell her vanilla scent and could see the faint line across the bridge of her nose where her sunglasses had blocked the sun. Dot smiled weakly and continued down the hall, softly closing her bedroom door behind her.

Did she hear our conversation, Vivian wondered. She may have misunderstood, thought that Vivian wanted them to leave. She didn't know if she should go after Dot or let it go. Part of her was getting tired of having so many people in the house, and part of her was afraid to be alone with Nowell, without diversions.

On the porch, leaves and debris danced in a circle, thankful and joyous in the cool breeze. Throwing her head back and feeling the muscles in her neck stretch and pull, Vivian let the first fingers of the wind reach her.

26

The next day, Vivian and Dot started hauling boxes out to the front yard for the sale. Lonnie tied a rope between two trees and they hung most of the clothing from it. The rest would be stacked on the tables, along with other items: small appliances, lamps, kitchen tools, pillows, linens and knickknacks. Furniture was placed on the porch, except for the pieces they were keeping until they moved out.

That morning, Katherine phoned to ask if Nowell could come down to the school earlier to pick up the tables. Because of all the incoming traffic for the reunion, the children were being sent home early. Vivian decided to make the trip herself. She wanted to hang flyers about the yard sale in the community center, in case many of the out-of-towners didn't pick up *The Sentinel*. She also wanted to get a glimpse of some of the Clements. The community center was being used as a meeting place for the reunion, along with the park across the street and for the evening events, the ballroom at the Best Western.

'Are you sure you don't want me to go with you?' Dot sat cross-legged in the center of the lawn, clothing fanned around her on the grass. On red stickers that they had purchased at the arts and crafts store, she wrote prices with a thick black marker, then affixed the stickers to the labels in the clothing or inside, along a hem. They hadn't been able to find a price gun like she'd wanted.

'No, thanks,' Vivian said. 'A couple of the teachers will help me load the tables, then I'll just stop by and post that sign.'

'I thought I'd make iced tea for customers, you know? Do you think we should put out some cookies?'

'Sure.'

Dot squinted through the amber-colored lenses of her sunglasses. Whitish cream was smeared on both of her shoulders, probably the citrus-smelling sunscreen that she used. Pale and prone to sunburn, she wore one of Lonnie's T-shirts over her bikini. It reached to her knees. Blond wisps had escaped from the plastic, shell-like thing that held her hair in a messy crescent, and she occasionally blew them off her face. 'Lonnie was asking about the lawn again,' she said.

'Tell him not to worry about it. That's Nowell's job.'

Dot nodded and went back to her work. Vivian wondered again if she had overheard her discussion with Nowell the day before. She didn't know what to say or do about it. She went into the house to get her purse and when she turned back toward the door, Dot was on the porch.

'Vivian, I wanted to talk to you.' Dot pushed her sunglasses back on her head and stepped into the kitchen. 'My mother called last night, after everyone had gone to bed. She's not doing very well, you know, and she asked if I would come and see her. Maybe one last time, she said, but I don't think it's that serious.' She twisted the corner of the long T-shirt in her hand. 'She can be difficult. Sometimes it's hard to see what's the truth and what isn't. I'd like to stay through the yard sale to help out, but I think it's best if I leave Sunday morning. Do you think you could handle the last day by yourself? You know, Lonnie and Nowell can help.'

'Of course, but...'

'Because if you really need me...' She looked down.

'No, you should go,' Vivian said. 'What's wrong with her?'

248

Dot looked up and sighed. 'She drinks, Vivian. Now there are other health problems, but it all starts with that.'

'Oh.' Vivian stepped toward her but stopped. 'Shouldn't Lonnie go? I mean, I don't want you to think he has to help me.'

'He wants to stay here. He hasn't met her, you know. The whole thing makes him uncomfortable. We'll wait until she's having an easier time.'

'Listen, Dot, I think maybe you heard me and Nowell yesterday.'

She shook her head. 'You don't have to say anything. I understand, really.'

'This has nothing to do with that? Because it's not really about you at all.'

'Oh, no. She called last night, really late. You were asleep.' Dot rubbed her arm with one hand as though she was cold, but even at mid-morning, it was already hot. 'To tell you the truth, Vivian, I think it's good I take a break for other reasons.'

Here it comes, Vivian thought. Why did I say that to Nowell?

'It's this fight between Nowell and Lonnie, you know? It's making Lonnie cranky and distant, and I feel like I should give him some space to work it out. Because it has nothing to do with me. All of it was there before I came on the scene. Does that make sense?'

Vivian nodded. 'Is there anything I can do? I mean, help you pack or talk to Nowell?'

'Thanks. Lonnie's going to take me to the airport. It's not too far?'

'No. It's a tiny place, just one rectangular building with check-in desks on one side and the gates on the other. You'll have a small plane like mine.'

'I'm not crazy about that,' Dot said. She opened the screen door, then turned back. 'Lonnie's afraid, you know? He feels like he's finally getting Nowell to open up about things.'

'What things?' Vivian asked.

'Family things.'

'Lonnie should worry more about his temper,' Vivian said.

Dot looked surprised but didn't say anything. 'I'm leaving Sunday morning and I bought a return ticket for the next Saturday. I hope that's okay. I'll miss the fireworks.'

Vivian nodded.

The screen door bounced back and forth on its spring, gradually closing.

Vivian took her purse outside and climbed into the truck. Lonnie was poking through the things laid out on the lawn. Both Vivian and Dot had asked him to look through the boxes for the sale, but neither he nor Nowell had taken the time. Now and again, Vivian asked Nowell about a specific item and she pointed out a few things to Dot for Lonnie. Beverly had told Vivian that Nowell's aunts had already been through the house to claim the things they wanted. So most of what remained would be sold; the men attached little or no sentiment to the belongings of a grandmother they hardly knew.

Vivian followed the now-familiar rolling road into town. When she pulled up to the school, Katherine and two male teachers were standing in front of the building and the tables were propped against a brick wall. She parked near the curb and hopped down. The men were already moving toward the truck bed with the first table.

'Right on time,' Katherine said. She introduced the two teachers. 'They're in a hurry to get home. The principal decided to close the place tomorrow too, so everybody got a nice break.'

'That's great,' Vivian said. 'They're having the big welcoming ball for the reunion, right?'

Katherine snickered. 'Yes, the glamorous formal affair is tomorrow evening. Not that any of us are invited.'

Vivian laughed. 'You're a cynic.'

Katherine put her arm around Vivian. 'As for me,' she said, 'I'll be attending the yard sale of my friend here. It promises to be a truly upscale affair.'

Vivian had two copies of the yard sale flyer to post. She thanked the men for their assistance and climbed back into the truck. Katherine waved. Vivian drove past the Best Western, where the billboard in front read: 'No Vacancy.' It also said: 'Welcome Clements, One and All.' When Vivian reached the narrow, tree-lined streets of the old, inner part of town, she parked the truck. Across the street, William Clement's bronze statue stood proudly in the plaza.

There was a marked difference in the town. Brightly clothed shoppers flowed down the central road; the bells of shop doors clanged as customers weaved in and out. Two street vendors had set up tables for business, both selling a variety of reunion souvenirs – T-shirts, books and postcards. The landscaped islands at each end of the street had been planted with bright pink and purple flowers, and a banner stretched overhead commemorating the date of the town's founding and that of the current year. The community center was two blocks from the plaza. Above the steps that led into the building, Vivian noticed a group of people surrounding a table. One was Deputy Bud Winchel, outfitted in his uniform just as he had been the other times she'd met him. To his right, a slender white-haired woman in a cream-colored suit hugged a black notebook against her chest. Next to her stood another woman, as expensively dressed but shabbier in appearance, in part because of her curly brown locks, which sprung and leaped from her head like an explosion.

Vivian began to climb the stairs and as she reached the top, the people behind the table came into view. Both were seated: a man with round, metal-rimmed glasses and a woman with long, dark hair.

'How many vendors are licensed for this area?' Bud asked.

The white-haired woman opened her notebook and pulled out a piece of paper.

'Two souvenir vendors, but also a table for materials from the museum inside and an information table for local businesses.'

251

'So four tables, plus Mr Delaney's here?'

The woman perused another sheet of paper. 'The information tables will have the position near the doors and the souvenir vendors should be away from the edge of the stairs.'

'I believe there's room up here for everybody,' Bud said.

The man at the table cleared his throat: 'We'd be happy to move over, if someone else has reserved this particular space.' His face was emotionless but pleasant, his eyebrows lifted slightly above his glasses. Next to him, the woman held a similar complacent expression. She gazed directly at the older women and at the deputy as each spoke. Her posture was rigid and her mane of black hair fell straight down her back like a cape.

'Mr Delaney,' the white-haired woman said tersely. 'You applied for a permit in order to sign and sell copies of your book.'

'And that's exactly what I'm doing.'

'If you had mentioned that your purposes were to distribute incendiary materials…'

Vivian tried not to stare at the scene as she passed. Deputy Winchel acknowledged her with an almost imperceptible nod. She opened one of the glass doors at the entrance of the building and stepped inside. As the door closed, she heard the deputy's voice: 'Now, Mrs Montrose, the man has a permit. I've seen it. It's perfectly legal.'

The voices were softer but still audible through the door.

'Excuse me, Deputy, but at the council meeting a few weeks ago, this woman was refused permission to attend this function.'

'That is untrue,' a feminine voice said. 'I was denied admission to the reunion ball and a permit to stage a peaceful demonstration.'

The man spoke. 'She's here as a friend to me, that's all. She agreed to man the table with me and help me with sales of my book. She brought a small informational brochure with her, which I am allowing her to set out on my table, in case anyone wants to pick one up. We won't be soliciting them in any way.'

252

'It was agreed at the meeting that this is not the proper place for this type of brochure,' the older woman said. 'We held a vote, Deputy, and I expect it to be enforced.'

'Now, Mrs Montrose, I know you've put a lot of work into this reunion, and I'd hate to see it start off on the wrong foot. I know your son still runs *The Sentinel*, but something like this could get out in other ways. It seems to me that these people intend to be peaceful and they've given their word that they won't be approaching or agitating anybody.'

'They're agitating me, Deputy Winchel. Come on, Frances. We need to take our complaint to a higher authority.'

'I'm sorry, Mrs Montrose, I just have no cause.'

'Don't worry, Deputy Winchel. I'm aware of your limitations.' The women's heels clicked sharply against the cement steps.

Vivian turned away from the door and immediately noticed a young man at a desk in the center of the room. His thin, sandy hair was pulled back into a short ponytail that hung limply against the back of his neck. He raised his eyebrows at her and smiled. 'Good conversation? I see one of the sheriff's lackeys out there.'

Vivian felt the heat in her face. 'Just being nosy, I guess.' She noticed he held a book. 'What's it about?'

'She's got a brochure that says she's a Clement too, but they don't believe it.'

'Oh,' Vivian said.

'Are you here to see the museum?'

'No,' she said, then reconsidered. 'Well, yes and no. First, I'd like to hang up two flyers. Is there somewhere I can do that?'

'Around this corner,' he pointed, 'there's a bulletin board that says "Public Action".'

'How much does it cost to enter the museum?'

'Normally it's free, but this weekend, it's two bucks. One dollar goes toward defraying the cost of the festival and one goes into a museum improvement fund. Contributions in excess of this fee are encouraged.'

Vivian handed him a five-dollar bill. 'Seems like a good cause.'

'Up the stairs and to your left, if you want to start in chronological order.'

'Thanks,' she said. 'I'm going to hang these first.'

She walked to the bulletin board and pinned a flyer at each end with bright-colored tacks, then scaled the steps to the exhibit.

At the top, a white placard directed visitors with a thick black arrow and the words 'Start of Exhibit'. She walked into the first room, which was subdivided into cubicles hung with an assortment of maps, documents and photographs. The building had the paper and ink smell of an old schoolhouse. Wood polished to dullness covered the floor and the doors were heavy and tall. The slapping of her sandals was loud and echoed because of the crude acoustics.

Vivian stopped at a big map that was supposedly the one used by William Clement when he set out on his cross-country journey. The paper was faded and torn at the edges; the state boundaries were clearly outdated but the general terrain was distinguishable by certain features. She wondered if the land turned out to be as William Clement had imagined it, those times that he had stared at the map and plotted the town.

Next to the map was a picture of the Clement family. Vivian leaned closer for a better look. In front of a modest, wood-framed house, Mrs Clement sat on a chair, nine children of varying ages surrounding her. The youngest was propped on her lap like a puppet, his plump legs straight out. In the back, William Clement towered over the brood, his shoulders thrust back and his hands on his hips. He looked rural and unsophisticated, nothing like the statue.

Other photographs on display included images of the construction sites of several buildings in town and the blurred, brownish scenes of town picnics and dances. In each, the people were dressed in modest style. The women wore long, simple dresses belted with calico aprons. Young girls wore shift dresses with white scallops around the collar and at the ends of the short sleeves. Young and older men dressed alike in plain, light-colored shirts and dark pants, the boys' reaching just above their knees.

Vivian found scant evidence of the Native Americans that Katherine had said populated the area at the time. Only in one picture, taken at the house of William Clement's son, Edward, did she spot one. In the photograph, the family was gathered under the shade of a wide willow tree. Edward and his wife, a wispy, pale-haired girl, had several young children. The wife held their small daughter and a young woman behind her held a baby. The woman had dark hair that was pulled into a large knot and was identified only as 'Maid' in the explanation below the photograph.

Another corner of the room was dedicated to a technical description of the farming that had been developed in the area. In this display, one sentence acknowledged the help of 'Indian labor' in the planting and harvesting of the fields.

Vivian walked slowly through the exhibit, which consisted of the first room then another filled with artifacts. There, she viewed garments of the type she'd seen in the photographs and a display of crude utensils and tools. When she glanced at her watch, she was startled to find that it was well after two o'clock. She still had to get the tables home and finish setting up for the sale.

She hurried down the stairs and passed the young man's desk, now unattended. When she pushed through the front door, the afternoon sun burned her eyes. The woman sat, unmoved, at the table. The man was gone. As Vivian approached, she noticed the title of the books set out on the table: *Another History: The Story of a Frontier Family*. She smiled at the woman and picked up a copy. On the back cover, it said that Mr Delaney had written an autobiography about his experiences as a member of a prominent family and about his discovery of another, hidden side of that family, the Native American side. She wondered how Mr Delaney had snuck past the reunion censors. 'How much does the book cost?' she asked.

'Fourteen ninety-five.' The woman's eyes were the brown of rich coffee, her lashes shiny and dark. 'But I'm afraid the author has stepped away for a soft drink, so you'll have to wait if you want it autographed.'

Vivian picked up on the brochures laid in front of the woman in neat stacks. The title on those was *An American Family* and there was one of the woman when she was a bit younger, next to a photo of William Clement. 'Are you a relative?' she asked.

'Yes,' she said, extending her hand. 'Delta Clement Burnside. You?'

'No,' Vivian answered. 'Vivian Gardiner.' She slipped the brochure into the book. 'I'll read this,' she said, then fumbled around in her purse until she found fifteen dollars. 'Maybe you could give him this for the book?'

The woman nodded serenely. There was something so self-assured about her, it was almost irritating. Vivian couldn't help but think she could be a little more forceful in presenting her case, but then she realized in thinking this, she was doing what those cranky old women were doing, expecting the woman to prove herself.

She remembered what her mother had said: Many people talk a great deal about what they would have done, what they could do, what they might do. It's action that matters. It hardly seemed fair that Delta Clement Burnside was forced into some type of action, when all she wanted was acknowledgment of a fact.

Vivian thanked her, walked to the truck and climbed up. From her elevated position, she left the town's now-bustling streets and headed back to the old white house.

27

At eight o'clock the following morning, two cars pulled into the driveway as Vivian was bringing out the last few items for the yard sale. Both cars were four-door, older sedans; one a white Oldsmobile and the other a light blue Chrysler. A woman stepped from each car; both were middle-aged and dressed in coordinating running suits and clean white sneakers. They seemed to know each other but went separate ways. Business-like and somber, they walked around the yard, pausing here to take a blouse from its hanger or there to pick up a glass and check for imperfections in the white morning sun.

Directly in front of the porch, Vivian had set up one of the tables and two chairs from the kitchen. She hadn't yet brought out the cookies, but she offered the women coffee.

Within minutes, they had scanned the contents of the yard. They met up again at the porch, where one of them asked if the rust-colored armchair could be brought into the sunlight. Vivian called for Lonnie, who was cooking his breakfast in the kitchen, and he easily lifted the chair and set it on the lawn.

The woman stood a few feet away, her forefinger pressed to her lips, then she circled the chair with long, slow strides. 'I'll take it,' she said.

Lonnie hoisted the chair into the expansive trunk of her car and tied the door down with the hooked, elastic cord she gave him.

The other woman bought the small end table from the living room, a wooden magazine stand and three cotton blouses.

Vivian and Lonnie waved as they got into their cars. The woman in the Oldsmobile almost backed into a car that was trying to turn into the driveway, and both cars paused at the entrance to the main road, waiting to see what the other would do. Finally, the Oldsmobile ambled onto the asphalt and the new car took its place in the driveway.

'This is a good start,' Vivian remarked.

'No kidding,' Lonnie replied. 'What time is it, anyway?'

'Just after eight.'

'These people aren't messing around.'

Vivian waved at the next customers, a young couple with a baby in a portable car seat.

The pace was bound to slacken and it did, shortly after nine o'clock. By that time, Lonnie had taken up a relaxed position on the fold-out lawn chair, with the previous day's copy of *The Sentinel* and a steaming mug of coffee. Two more cars had arrived after the young couple, but they'd been the last of the early morning sale hounds. The young couple bought some linens and a portable radio, and an elderly man looked at the couch for a while but eventually decided against it. Another woman spent almost five dollars on books. Mid-morning passed slowly; each time they heard a car noise, they perked their ears but only one more car stopped before eleven-thirty.

'Maybe a lot of people are working today,' Vivian said to Dot as they thumbed through magazines at the table.

'Have you seen any cars from out of state?' she asked. 'You know, people who might be here for the reunion?'

'No, not yet.'

'What was it like in town yesterday?' she asked Vivian.

258

'The parking lot at the Best Western was filling up,' she said, 'and there were people up and down the main street. I've never seen it so busy. Did I mention that I stopped by the museum in the community center?'

'No.'

'There was a woman there with a brochure. She claims to be a Clement but they're keeping her out of the reunion. She came with a friend who's a legitimate Clement.'

Dot shook her head. 'They should be ashamed, excluding her.'

'They have a museum on the second floor,' Vivian said. 'There's a special exhibit on the Clements. Maps, photographs, old clothing.'

'Did they have any old guns?' Lonnie piped up from his lawn chair.

'They had a couple of guns. Oh, and a big sword that was a keepsake from William Clement's grandfather or something. It had the old family crest engraved on the handle.'

'Really?' Lonnie said. 'I should go down there and check it out.'

'That's why I was late getting back.'

'Was it interesting?' Dot asked.

'Yes, but everything seems like propaganda. You don't know if you're getting more than one side of the story.'

'One side of a story is all people have,' Lonnie said.

'What if Nowell wrote a book about your family,' Vivian said, 'only he left you out completely or just mentioned you once or twice?'

He shrugged. 'Maybe that was the way he saw it. He might talk about things that were more important to him.'

Vivian sighed. 'It's not the greatest example. Writing fiction isn't the same as writing history or choosing items for a museum.'

After some time, Dot fixed sandwiches and sliced a watermelon for lunch. They ate outside in the shade. Vivian poured the seeds and the pale pink juice from her slice of watermelon onto the grass and wondered if watermelons would sprout there, by the bushes at the front of the porch. Lonnie cut a large wedge from the end and held it to his face, spitting the seeds onto the ground like tiny black bullets. When Nowell came out for his sandwich, he was surprised that they'd sold the armchair already and asked how much they took for it. Then he disappeared again into the shady house.

After one o'clock, people arrived in a light but steady stream. Katherine stopped on her way home from the dry-cleaning store. She asked Vivian to set aside a leather tool belt for Max and promised to come back the next day when they could look more.

Vivian was helping an elderly woman search for sweaters through the stacks of winter clothing when another set of tires pressed the dirt of the driveway. An old blue-gray truck ambled along, patches of rust at the tire wells and along its tall underbelly. Dust swirled behind the back tires like smoke. At that moment, a police car passed slowly on the main road. Vivian only glimpsed the driver – dark sunglasses and bulky shoulders – but was certain that it was Sheriff Townsend. The cruiser climbed the small hill to town as the door of the blue truck creaked open. A man stepped down from the cab and shut the door firmly. He ran his hand over his black-and-silver hair. When his angular body cleared the truck, Vivian recognized the familiar, uneven rhythm of his gait, the way his legs swung forward in a series of connected jolts. Mr Stokes.

She raised her hand silently and he nodded. When Dot rushed over to greet him, she felt a slight pang, anxiety about entering his house that night. She hadn't seen him for over two weeks, since the barbecue when he told her that he'd be away for a few days. He had dropped out of their lives as rapidly as he appeared, on that afternoon when he parted the trees and strode onto the undulating grass. Or was it something else she was feeling? She watched as Dot showed him the tools and outdoor equipment from the shed, leaning her head back and laughing, her teeth flashing in the sunlight like sparks.

The elderly woman found a white cardigan and a pale green

pullover amidst the multi-colored piles. They walked together to the front table, where Lonnie was guarding the shoebox full of money and listening to a baseball game on the radio. After she gave the woman her change, Vivian found a plastic bag in the kitchen and slipped the sweaters inside. Mr Stokes had parked behind the old woman's car; he went to move his truck so that she could pull out. Three people were poking around, and Vivian asked the most recently arrived if they needed help finding anything. When she looked over again, Mr Stokes had parked his truck along the main road and was making his way back up the long driveway. She met him halfway. 'Hello there,' she said. 'Haven't seen you around much.'

'It's been a while.'

She put her hand up to block the sunlight. 'How did you hear about the yard sale?'

'Saw your ad in the paper.' He squeezed his hands into the tight front pockets of his blue jeans, hunching his shoulders and letting his elbows extend to each side.

'Are you looking for anything in particular?'

'I thought I'd look at your tools,' he said. 'And I could use a new dresser.'

Vivian looked toward the porch, where some smaller furniture was lined up against the house. She suddenly remembered she had forgotten to have Nowell and Lonnie bring down the larger items from the attic. There was also the tall mahogany bureau, which she had considered keeping for themselves.

'I have one,' she said. 'Only I've forgotten to bring it out. It's a short, long dresser. Medium-colored wood. Pine or oak, I guess.'

'Reddish?'

'Yes.'

'Probably pine.'

'You can see it if you want,' she said. 'It's up in the attic.'

'I wouldn't mind taking a look at it. The one I've been using isn't good for much anymore. The other day, I opened a drawer

261

and the front panel came off in my hand. It's an old piece of furniture, but it isn't made well like some of those antiques are. My grandfather built it, and he wasn't the greatest craftsman. More of a hobby.'

'It's lasted this long,' Vivian said.

'That's true.'

They neared the front table, where Dot and Lonnie spoke in low tones.

'Hey,' Lonnie said to Mr Stokes. 'How's it going?

'Trying to stay cool. Some heat wave.'

'Sure is,' Lonnie agreed. 'Done any fishing lately?'

'Not around here. I was up north a couple of weeks ago, went fishing for walleye with some relatives.'

Vivian stepped onto the porch.

'Can I get you some iced tea, Abe?'

'No, thank you. I'll just take a look at that dresser.'

'Come on in.' She explained to Lonnie, 'I forgot to have you bring down the furniture from the attic.'

'Want me to do it now?'

'No, that's all right. I'll just show it to Mr Stokes and we'll interrupt Nowell in a little while to help you.'

Mr Stokes followed her into the dark kitchen.

'The stairs are pretty steep,' she said as she gripped the handrail. 'At the top, there's a trap door so you have to pull yourself up.' She looked down at him. 'Are you sure you want to come up?'

A lopsided grin stretched across his face, his lips whitish like a scar. 'Don't worry, Mrs Gardiner, I can make it.'

Encircling the rail with his large, calloused hand, Mr Stokes stepped onto the first step. Vivian stood over the opening and looked down as his head poked through like something bobbing to the surface of water. Easily, he pulled himself until he was sitting on the floor, then standing next to her in the attic.

A few assorted boxes, things they were keeping, were stacked in a pyramid against one wall, and the two pieces of furniture stood nearby. From another corner, the brass coat rack threw spindly shadows over the cleanly swept floor.

'Here it is,' she said. 'I was talking about the shorter one, here, but if you're interested in the bureau, we don't have any definite plans for it.'

Mr Stokes ran his fingers over the dusty top of the dresser, then knocked on the side, listening to the sharp sound. The drawers slid smoothly when he tried them. Vivian found a rag near the boxes and wiped the front of the purplish bureau.

They spoke at the same time.

'I found some of Sherman's things,' Vivian said, as he said, 'How much are you asking?'

'What things?' Mr Stokes asked after a moment.

'Clothing, mostly. A gun.'

Mr Stokes closed the bottom drawer and stood back a few feet, looking the dresser over.

Nowell is right downstairs, she reminded herself. You can hear everything from down there. 'Did you ever see Sherman Gardiner here?'

He leaned back on his heels. 'Sherman was the same age as my father. They went to school together.'

Vivian said: 'But you're older than Nowell,' and her face flushed for saying it.

'My father was just twenty when I was born,' he said.

'So your father knew Sherman?'

'Yes.'

She hesitated, watching his face. 'Nowell heard in town that your father, that he…'

He faced her, looked directly at her. 'Was the one who shot Russell Gardiner?'

She gave a small nod.

'That's the truth,' he said.

'But why didn't you say something?'

'I thought you knew.'

'No,' she said. 'Nowell didn't know.'

'But now he does.'

'Yes.'

'Maybe that explains why he was looking around my place,' he said.

Vivian's mouth dropped opened. 'What do you mean?'

He ran his rough hand over the top of the dresser. 'When he thought I wasn't home.'

'But, what…'

He turned away. 'I'll take the dresser, if it's still for sale.'

'Wait, Mr Stokes, uh, Abe. I don't mean to accuse you of anything.'

'You don't?'

'No, I don't. It was a shocking thing for Nowell to hear, after all this time. No one was at your place.'

'No one was?' he asked, one black-and-gray eyebrow raised. 'Someone was.'

Vivian didn't know what to say.

He crossed his arms, his lean muscles twisting like braided rope. 'I'll tell you what I know, Mrs Gardiner. Then, I hope we'll never have to talk about this again.' Mr Stokes looked out the triangle-shaped windows at the end of the attic. 'For a long time, my whole life just about, my father told me it was a terrible accident. He saw motion behind the blur of the trees and shot his rifle. That's all. He was just a kid then, only fourteen or fifteen. His father took him along on hunting trips, but he never cared for it much. Only did it to please the old man.' He leaned against the dresser. 'I've heard the rumors.'

'What rumors?' Vivian asked in a low voice.

'They say that Russell Gardiner was messing around with my grandmother. She was a looker, a real beauty queen, and he was a too-friendly neighbor. They say my father was just a kid but he knew about it. They say he shot Russell Gardiner on purpose, for messing with his mother. Is that close to what you heard?'

She nodded, embarrassed.

'For all those years, it made me angry that my father had to live with this, this accident. It just about ruined him.' The cords in his neck tightened. 'Betty Gardiner was a good woman. She made a point of telling my folks she didn't hold anybody responsible, but my father's guilt was something nobody could save him from.'

'It must have been very hard for him.'

'Yes.'

'And for you.'

Mr Stokes shrugged. 'Children have a way of teasing each other. I had my share of misunderstanding. The worst part was the way Sherman treated me. He was almost a grown man when I was born, but he looked down on me. He felt like I'd taken the life that was robbed from his father. I was born five years after the accident, but I think it helped him to blame me.'

'Did he do anything?' she asked.

'Tried to spook me, I think, in the woods. He and his friends used to shoot guns out there, get awful close to our place. Always gave me the evil eye in town. Before he moved away.'

'How often did he come back here?'

'Not much at first. I remember once he brought his two sons – they were just little tikes then – and one of them walked right up to my house. I guess now that it was Lonnie. Later, he came more often, especially in the last few years before I heard that he passed.'

Vivian lowered her voice. 'What did he do here?'

Mr Stokes shifted on his feet. 'I couldn't say.'

'Did he know Kitty Brodie?'

He met her gaze. 'You'd have to ask her about that.'

'You were a neighbor to both of them.'

His face spread into his lopsided grin. 'If it's one thing I learned from living with those stories about the hunting accident, it's don't open your mouth about your opinion of things.'

Vivian walked over to Mr Stokes. 'It was an accident,' she said.

He hesitated, then spoke again. 'My father had a long illness before he passed. He got weak and small before my eyes. That's a hard thing for a son. Sometimes he'd get delirious, from the pain or the medication, I don't know which. One time he said he was glad he shot Russell Gardiner.'

'He didn't mean it. He was dying, and...'

'He said that he waited until everybody was off somewhere. Russell veered to the left, to cover the wide plank, and he followed—'

'Enough!' Vivian said, covering her ears. 'We don't know if that's true.'

Mr Stokes gently pulled her arms down. His face was close; she could see the pores of his skin. 'It might be,' he said.

'You shouldn't repeat that story,' she whispered.

He released her arms. 'Don't you think I feel responsible? I remember those boys when they were young, you see, and I know what it's like, losing someone. They grew up without a grandfather, and I grew up without a father. He was never the same after the accident.'

Vivian stepped back, trying to process everything he had told her. He didn't believe his father had purposely pulled the trigger, but yet Jesper had confessed when he was dying. She was more confused than ever.

'The minute something happens,' Mr Stokes said, 'that moment is lost forever. There's no truth. Just stories. Just rumors. Isn't it the same? I know people talk about that accident, even now, just like I know they talk about Ronella Oates, and about Sherman and Kitty Brodie, and now, about Kitty's daughter.'

'What about Ronella Oates?' Vivian asked.

He shook his head. 'Ronella would sneak out and meet someone in the woods. She was staying at the house while my father was away. It gave her a kick, I think, to do it right under my nose. The man would park his truck along the main road, not far from the driveway over here, then meet her halfway back.' Mr Stokes stared through the triangle of windows at the rustling treetops. 'Everyone's got a heartbreak, Mrs Gardiner. It's nothing special to me. But there's something about the woods, haven't you felt it?'

She looked where he was looking, through the windows. 'No, I don't feel anything.' She turned back toward him. 'But how can I find out the whole story, I mean, about Sherman and Mrs Brodie?'

A crease spread across Mr Stokes's forehead. He wiped his palms against his hips. They made a dry, scratchy sound like paper. 'Haven't you been listening? The minute something happens, that moment is lost forever. So there is no story, not for sure, and even if there was, why would you want to know it?'

Vivian's gaze traveled from the swirling trees to a complex spider web she had missed in the far corner of the attic, finally coming back to rest on Mr Stokes's weathered face. 'You agreed to call me Vivian,' she reminded him.

In the twilight hours, business at the yard sale slowed again. The trees hung heavy with the day's heat and a faint buzz sounded through the fragrant air. Lonnie hovered near Dot as she reorganized the tables, shifting and condensing, and he pulled tables where she wanted them. Dot had an endearing vulnerability, which had nothing to do with her size or physical strength, but more with her assenting demeanor, the way she listened and let people make up their own minds. Vivian had felt it from the first moment, when she emerged from behind Lonnie then blushed charmingly when he forced them to embrace. She made people want to take care of her.

Vivian had taken up residence on the fold-out lawn chair. John Delaney's book, *Another History*, sat in her lap but she was distracted; her thoughts turned constantly to her conversation with Mr Stokes. As Nowell and Lonnie loaded the short dresser onto the back of Mr Stokes's truck, they waited on the porch with Dot. Mr Stokes asked if they were going to the festival the following weekend.

'I'll be gone for a few days,' Dot said. 'I'm going to visit my mother.'

'That's too bad,' Mr Stokes said. 'They're already setting up a carousel and some tents across from the park in that empty lot.'

'We'll be there,' Vivian said. 'Will they have a Ferris wheel?'

'I imagine they will.'

As Nowell pushed, Lonnie pulled the dresser up. His feet made dull thuds on the truck bed and when the end cleared the back, he jumped over the side, landing in a puff of dust. Nowell shut the tailgate, shaking it to make sure it locked.

They watched as Mr Stokes backed his truck out of the driveway. The early evening sky was motionless, a hazy, darkening blue. Here and there a wisp of a cloud, almost translucent, streaked across the sky like a brushstroke. The leaves in the trees shone with a light layer of wax.

'I'll be heading to town in a while,' Lonnie said to Nowell. 'You should come along. We'll probably just shoot some darts, maybe have a few beers.'

Dot walked down the steps to the lawn, where she busied herself moving around a stack of books.

'When are you going?' Nowell asked.

'As soon as I have something to eat. Maybe that leftover pizza.'

'I had the last of it for lunch.'

'There's some casserole left,' Vivian offered.

'Why don't we all have dinner in town?' Lonnie said. 'Let's go to that steak place.'

'We ate there before you were here,' Nowell told Vivian. 'It's in that mini-mall.'

'That's the one,' Lonnie said. 'Great burgers.'

'You men and your feedings,' Dot said.

'How late do you think people will come for the yard sale?' Nowell asked Vivian.

'Not too late.'

'I don't really want to leave them alone,' he said to Lonnie.

'Don't worry,' Vivian said. 'I don't think anyone will come after dark.'

'Why don't we all go?' Lonnie said again.

'Somebody should be here,' Vivian said. 'The three of you can go.'

'I'm staying,' Dot said.

'I'm tired,' Vivian said. 'Dot and I will put the smaller things away tonight, and tomorrow you can clean everything up. That's fair.' She thought it odd that Lonnie would go out, with Dot leaving in the morning, but it was none of her business.

After the men left, Dot went into the house to start packing for her trip, and Vivian leaned back on the porch swing. She watched the faded white planks as they swung, pendulum-like, over her head. But it's really me that's swinging, she thought. Maybe Mr Stokes is right. We'll never know the truth of what happened that day, the truth of what was in Jesper Stokes's heart, or any of them. What remains are the survivors, the stories, what people believe. But what if it's all a misunderstanding? Couldn't it be cleared up? Shouldn't it be? What about the time she got lost in the woods? Sometimes, in a dreamy state or her quietest moments, Vivian wasn't really sure what had happened. Did she wander off on purpose – it certainly seemed that she did – or did her guilt over the years lead her to believe that she had? Because it was terrible when her father came to get her, the way he clutched her and his coat buttons pressed against her side, the way his eyes glistened in the car and the way he lowered his head to her mother's accusations. Did it really matter what happened, or were they just left to deal with what remained?

'Oh, Vivian!' She felt a soft tug on her shoulder, a slight shaking. Groggily, she opened her eyes. She must have fallen asleep on the porch.

Dot stood over her, haloed by the porch light. 'I had no idea you were sleeping out here,' she said.

Vivian sat up, yawning. It was fairly dark already. 'What time is it?'

'Seven-thirty,' Dot said, chuckling. 'I fell asleep too.' She tilted her head toward the yard, where all of the yard sale items still sat out. 'I guess we're not used to having an actual job. Really tired me out. I slept for over two hours.'

The moon sat on the spread of treetops like a pale egg in a nest. It was a hazy moon, gray-white with blurred edges. In the city, Vivian had seldom noticed the moon's infinite variations and effects. The current moon held its surroundings in a pregnant lull; its soft light reflected from the old white paint and made everything glow. Other times, she had seen another moon, one with a texture like stucco that stood out boldly in stark relief against a cobalt sky. Its light was harsher, its range broader. But the light of this night's moon, the hazy, gentle moon, trod softly across the high grass and the short hills. Like candlelight, it flattered its subjects.

The moon could be painted over and over, Vivian thought, like Monet's water lilies. She felt at that moment her unique place in the world. She wondered how her impressions could ever be reproduced, because the distance between perception and idea was like the space between two skyscrapers. One had to leap across. If I were to measure and draw the scene according to proper linear perspective, the moon would seem smaller and further away than how it feels to me at this moment. Maybe everything doesn't fit into a pattern, she thought, maybe things are only as they appear in a single moment.

Crickets belted out their fractious melody underneath the house. One day soon they would leave this house, and Vivian would miss the openness and calm of the land, the way the trees stood guard like sentries, the moon like a changing spotlight on their lives. As the first night breeze collected somewhere in the distance and blew softly across her skin, she contemplated the changes to come.

270

28

The next day, Saturday, turned out to be the busiest of the three-day yard sale. People arrived early again, only this time, Vivian was ready with a thermos of coffee and a plate of warm cinnamon rolls.

Lonnie burst through the door and onto the porch. 'Vivian, tell Dot you don't want her to leave.'

Dot followed closely behind, carrying a handful of napkins to set with the rolls. 'Lonnie, please,' she said.

'We're going to miss you, that's all. Right, Vivian?'

'Yes,' she said.

'I have to go,' Dot said. 'Lonnie, you know it won't be a fun trip for me. Besides, I'll be back in a week.'

'If you run there every time she calls…'

Dot whirled around. 'What if she really needs me this time?'

He gave her a skeptical look.

She laid out the napkins, one over the other, in a half-circle. 'You'd do the same, if it was your mother.'

Vivian went back into the kitchen to pour herself a cup of coffee. In a few moments, Dot came inside. 'I need to pick up a few things for my trip,' she said. 'Do you mind if I leave for a couple of hours?'

'No, go ahead.'

'Lonnie is staying.'

'Thanks,' Vivian said. 'Nowell can be roused from his work too.'

'Okay.' Dot stood in the center of the kitchen, her hands on her hips. 'Okay,' she said again. 'Do you need anything from town?'

'No,' Vivian said. 'It may be pretty crazy down there today. They're having that parade at noon, then the big thing at the park.'

'You're right, it'll be crowded. I'll go now, while it's still early.'

'Good idea.'

'One more thing,' Dot said. 'Could I borrow the truck? Lonnie wants to do something to the jeep while I'm gone.'

'Do you think you can drive it?'

'Drives like other cars, doesn't it?'

'It's big, that's all. It took me a while to get used to it.'

She smiled. 'I'm a little taller than you and besides, you've got that pillow in there. I'll just sit on that, like you do.'

'The keys are hanging by the door.'

After she left, Vivian stared out the kitchen window. She could see the corner of the wooden shed and a distance from that, the gray stones of the musty-smelling well. Overhead, a brownish bird jumped from branch to branch, then buried his long beak behind his wings. From the study, Nowell's light taps on the computer keyboard were barely audible over the humming of the refrigerator, which had started up suddenly as she stood there. In the front yard, Lonnie called her name.

She walked outside and greeted a woman who had offered half-price for the brass coat rack. Vivian quickly agreed to her terms and asked Lonnie to load the item into her truck. 'I'm surprised anyone would buy that,' she said to him as the woman drove away. 'It's so tarnished.'

'You'd be amazed what you can do to old things like that,' Lonnie said. 'All you need is a good brass polish. Cleans right up, good as new. That was a nice dresser you sold to Mr Stokes, too. A coat of stain was all it needed.'

'Did you want it?' Vivian asked. 'I told you, if you see anything...'

'No, I didn't want it. I'm only pointing out that some things are worth saving. Like this jeep.' He patted the roof. 'It was rebuilt with junkyard materials. The engine is from a jeep that was totaled, and the body once caught on fire. It was a hobby with the guy who sold it to me, restoring things.' He walked around to the front and looked under the hood. 'Haven't had a single problem. It's got four good tires and a new battery. The seats were reupholstered after the fire. I guess they were pretty charred. We don't use the air conditioning much, but it works. I tested it the other day.'

'That reminds me,' Vivian said. 'Did your mother get her air conditioner at the house fixed?'

'I think so. You'd have to ask Nowell.'

She pushed her hair from her forehead. 'Your mom doesn't ask you for many favors, does she?'

Lonnie looked up, his forehead creasing into three long crevices. 'No, she usually asks Nowell. You know that.'

'Why is that?'

'Because Nowell is the one who'll come. He's trying to make it up to her.'

'For what?'

'For not being around earlier, for going off to college, for not taking over my dad's business.' He wiped the tip of a cable, the wire connection, with a red rag. 'Mostly, he's trying to make up for my dad. Only, I don't think he knows it.'

'What did your dad do?'

'He wasn't around either.'

Vivian felt a chill on her arm. 'Where was he?'

'Good question,' Lonnie peered at her sideways as he leaned over the open mouth of the jeep. 'Traveling for the business, trying to make sales.'

'He traveled a lot?'

'Not when we were real young, but later.'

'He didn't say where he was going?'

'Oh, sure. He could name towns. He talked about people he met and deals he made. At the time, I believed him.'

'But then you didn't?'

'Didn't what?'

'Believe he was going where he said he was going.'

Lonnie's eyes widened. 'I said that?'

Vivian sighed. 'Did you believe him?'

'What else was I supposed to think?' He walked around the edge of the jeep, turned a cap on something and yanked it off.

She smelled the dank rustiness of water and metal; she could taste it on her tongue. She was tired of dodging the subject. 'Did you know that your dad came out here a few times a year?'

Lonnie wiped the black rubber cap on the side of his shirt and tapped it back into position with his fist. 'He came more than that.'

She was shocked. Nobody else had confirmed what Katherine told her. 'How do you know?'

'I followed him one time, when I was sixteen or seventeen. I walked in as he was sitting in the kitchen there, having cake with my Grandma Gardiner like it was an everyday thing.'

'What did he say?'

'Nothing. I had been here a couple of times as a kid. After he pulled up to the house, I drove around for a while then came back. I didn't know if my grandma would recognize me after so much time, but she looked right up and called me by name. What a nice surprise, she said, that I came with him.'

'Why did he keep his visits secret?' Vivian asked. 'Why didn't he bring everybody – your mom, Nowell?'

'I don't know, maybe he didn't want to share. My grandma treated him like a king, and me too while I was here. Every morning she'd cook a big breakfast: homemade biscuits, sausage and gravy. I stayed for two nights then headed home. I think he stayed a couple more days that time.'

'And your mother never knew?'

'No.'

'You never wanted to tell her?'

'Sure I did.' Lonnie ran his hand through his dark hair, which had grown out a little since they arrived. 'I thought he would tell her. The business was really growing, and I think he was having some problems with Mr Ward, his partner. That's why he started traveling in the first place. I had no idea at the time how long it had been going on.'

'The visits?' she asked.

He blinked. 'Yeah, the visits. All those years, we quit doing things as a family. He'd say he didn't have time, he was trying to build the business for us. And here he was, coming out here while our own grandma was a stranger to us. He was selfish, that's all there is to it.' He wiped his forehead with his shirtsleeve, leaving a speck of oil. 'She remembered it, the time I followed him. Remember when I was laid up, after the motorcycle crash?'

Vivian nodded.

'When my grandma came, we talked about that visit. We watched a television show together while I was here, she said. Something about angels. I didn't remember that. I mostly thought about those big breakfasts.' Lonnie reached across the engine and adjusted something. 'It's a shame, my mom and my grandma both living alone. My mom was so lonely, especially after Nowell left. He always thinks that it was me, but she missed him a lot. She missed them both. Ever since I can remember, she's been lonely. That's why she spends so much time down at her clubs and at the church; that's why she volunteers to do all those things. I had to let myself off the hook. I couldn't do anything about what he did. I can't even regret keeping quiet about what I knew, because I don't think telling her would have made any difference.'

Vivian had been quiet, soaking in everything Lonnie said. 'Nowell never knew about your dad?'

'He doesn't want to know anything.'

'But you said he tries to make up for it.'

'And I said he doesn't know he's doing it. He'll never admit anything was ever wrong or that anything is wrong with her now.'

'You think something's wrong with your mom?'

'Ignoring something doesn't make it go away,' he said.

In all the time she'd been at the house, Vivian had felt that there was a mystery of sorts. But after what Mr Stokes had said, after she began to realize what role her own imagination had been playing, she wasn't sure. 'You said yourself,' she told Lonnie, 'it wouldn't do any good to tell her. Besides, he was just coming to visit his mother.'

Lonnie leaned against the door of the jeep, crossing his arms over his chest. Reddish-brown hairs poked over his green tank top, matching the whiskers that sprung from his jaw and chin. She had always thought that his beard was darker than Nowell's, but it was the same hue, exactly. 'It's about keeping secrets, Vivian. I've done the same as them, that's all. I had to pretend then and I still pretend now. Maybe I didn't do anything wrong, but I didn't open my mouth, either. I didn't force Nowell to come home and see what was happening, I didn't force my mom to stand up for herself. I stood by and let her fall. Dad was gone most of the time by then, just before he died. You know that argument I had with Nowell about the Father's Day shirt?'

She nodded.

'I think it stays in my mind because in a way, I was trying to get my dad to come back. It sounds crazy now. A tie or a shirt can't make someone do anything, but I thought it might. I wanted to pick something just right. I didn't have enough money, but I was willing to pay it back. I had just gotten a new job, a good one. I thought he'd be proud.' His eyes were glistening. 'That's why it made me so mad. It sounds stupid now, but sometimes I still think I could've done something. I just stayed there, just let her fall. I was as bad as Nowell, but at least he didn't know everything.'

Katherine's light green car turned slowly onto the driveway and pulled up next to the jeep.

'I worry about Dot,' Lonnie said. 'I wish she wouldn't do this alone, but she won't let me go with her.'

Vivian took a step toward Lonnie. 'What do you mean about Nowell not knowing everything?'

'And I've seen what can happen to women. They're defenseless sometimes.'

She didn't know who he was talking about – Dot, his mother, Dot's mother, or something else entirely. If Sherman had been visiting his mother without telling his wife, that was dishonest and maybe even childish, but Lonnie talked about his absences with such bitterness.

Katherine waved from the passenger seat and beside her, Max grinned behind the wheel.

Vivian turned back to Lonnie, but he had moved to the rear of the jeep and was pulling a red metal toolbox from behind the seats.

Katherine got out of the car first. 'Hello!'

'Is this the place I've been hearing about?' Max asked.

'Depends on what you've been hearing,' Vivian said.

'Great deals,' he said.

'Then this is the place.'

A station wagon stopped along the main road and two more customers walked onto the lawn. Vivian got the tool belt that Katherine had set aside for Max, and she answered a few questions for the other people. Lonnie was still tinkering around the jeep, ducking his head under the hood and pulling tools from his box. Vivian walked around with Katherine and Max as they inspected the items for sale.

'Have you been into town?' Katherine asked.

'Not for a few days,' Vivian said.

'It's packed down there. I've never seen it so crowded.'

'How are things going with the reunion?'

She picked up a ceramic flower vase. 'I think everything's running smoothly. We had the store open yesterday, so we saw all the people running around. Looks like a bunch of Clements to me.'

'You can't tell them apart from anyone else,' Max said.

'I'm just kidding. What do you think of this vase, Max?'

'For two bucks, it's a steal.'

Katherine tucked it under her arm; her bracelets clanked against its hard surface. 'They had an emergency city council meeting, over letting some woman hand out pamphlets during the celebrations.'

'I think I met her,' Vivian said. 'Delta Clement Burnside. I went to the community center and she was outside.'

Katherine leaned over. 'I guess hardly anyone bothered to show for the meeting. Seems everyone was pretty certain they'd keep that Fire – what was her name?'

'Burnside.'

'Right. Everyone was sure they'd keep her away. There were only twenty or so there, but here's the interesting thing. Guess who spoke up in favor of letting her attend?'

Vivian shrugged.

'Mr Stokes.'

'What does he have to do with any of that?'

'Got me,' Katherine said.

They watched as Max picked up an old wooden bat and practiced his swing.

'What did he say?' Vivian asked.

'Something about people's right to freedom. He said it wasn't fair to keep people away, that it was like putting animals in cages, keeping them from running. My friend remembered that, putting animals in cages. She thought it was a strange thing to say, but I guess he really made his point. Didn't matter, of course.'

'They denied her request,' Vivian said.

Katherine nodded.

A red hatchback pulled into the driveway behind Katherine's car. They watched as someone in a peacock blue outfit stepped from the car and walked towards them.

'It's Kitty Brodie,' Katherine said in a low voice.

'Good morning,' Vivian called.

Mrs Brodie's hair shone in the morning light. 'Hello, Mrs Gardiner.'

'Please, call me Vivian.'

She smiled. 'I drove by yesterday and saw all the things out here. I thought I'd come by and take a look.'

Max stepped forward and took her hand. 'How are you doing, Kitty?'

'I'm doing all right.' She looked back and forth between him and Katherine. 'Thanks for asking. How's business? I'm afraid I haven't been down to pick up that silk blouse yet. I've been absent-minded lately, can't seem to remember where I leave anything.'

'Don't worry about it,' he said. 'I've got things people have left since Christmas. Sometimes I think I should charge for storage.'

Mrs Brodie laughed. Her dark blond hair bounced on her shoulders.

Katherine stepped forward. 'Why don't you come out to the house for dinner sometime, Kitty?'

Releasing Max's hand, Mrs Brodie turned toward her. 'Thank you, Katherine. That'd be nice.'

Vivian was going to say something about the barbecue she'd been trying to organize, but she changed her mind.

Mrs Brodie walked around the yard, spending several minutes at the makeshift clothesline strung between the two trees.

Katherine and Max paid for the tool belt, the vase and a knife set. 'Wish we could help you more,' Max said.

Vivian shook her head. 'I'm just glad you found a few things you wanted.'

'I'd like to take that bookshelf and put it in the garage,' Katherine said, 'for all the pottery we'll be making.' She turned to Vivian. 'Let me know if it doesn't sell.'

As Katherine and Max walked to their car, Mrs Brodie approached the table. 'Excuse me, Mrs Gardiner?'

'Yes?'

Mrs Brodie looked tired. Her lips were two blurred stripes of red, like an equal sign. 'That afternoon I stopped by, you had the most beautiful blue suit in the kitchen there. I don't suppose it's for sale?'

Vivian walked around the table. 'It was out here somewhere.'

They looked for a few moments through the rack of clothing. Vivian stole glances at Mrs Brodie as they searched. Perspiration beaded at her temples and her jacket was wrinkled at the elbows. Vivian asked Lonnie if he recalled the suit, and he said he'd sold it the day before.

'Oh,' Mrs Brodie said. 'That's too bad. You see, I have a friend and the suit seemed like his size. I only saw it for a moment, but I thought of it when I saw that you were selling things.'

'I'm sorry it's gone, then,' Vivian said.

Lonnie stood nearby, his feet spread broadly on the grass. A steel socket wrench dangled from his hand.

'Maybe I'll look around some more,' Mrs Brodie said. 'That was a nice suit.'

'Would you like something to drink?' Vivian asked.

She laughed. 'You're just like her, like Betty Gardiner. Always offering something to drink on a hot day, something to snack on. I only met her a few times, of course, but that's what she did.'

'Katherine says the same thing about her.'

'Does she?'

They turned as Dot pulled the faded red truck into the crowded driveway, then backed up and parked alongside the mailbox. Vivian's reservations had been unwarranted: Dot maneuvered the truck like a pro, looking completely at home and in control in its tall, cavernous cab.

29

In the morning, Dot left as planned. Lonnie was lonely and withdrawn in the following days, and the house seemed quieter without his loud, jovial voice.

The yard sale had been a great success. Most of the larger items and a good deal of the appliances and smaller things had been sold. They moved everything else back into the attic. After some time, Vivian would go through the things again but she needed a break from the mound of someone else's belongings.

She spent most of the week preparing to paint. She hadn't planned on starting so soon, but it seemed like the next logical step. Throughout the house, she taped over doorframes and removed light fixtures. In the spare bedroom, she spread newspapers over the carpet and covered the windows. She would start in there.

At Clement's Hardware in town, she spent the better part of an afternoon purchasing supplies. The owner, Mr Garrison, took her through the entire painting process, helping her choose spackle, drop cloths, sandpaper, putty knives, brushes and rollers, and the ivory paint she planned to use on the interior walls. She had given up any fleeting thought of staying on at the house. She'd paint in neutral tones that a prospective buyer would appreciate. It would take time. They were still using most of the rooms in the house, but as soon as Lonnie and Dot left, she and Nowell could move into their bedroom while the master bedroom was painted. Then, she could transfer the remaining things from the living room into the spare room after it was painted. In this way, she could slowly get to every room.

The house was eerily sparse. All of the wall hangings had been taken down for the sale, and big gaps remained where furniture had been. She planned to have Nowell move the couch from the study into the living room after she painted, but for the time being, they brought in extra pillows and watched television from the floor.

Lonnie was gone much of the time that week. He slept in late, drove off shortly after lunch, and was usually still gone when they went to bed. One evening he brought videos from the rental store in town and the three of them sprawled on the floor, eating popcorn. All evening, Lonnie had a nervous energy and shifted frequently, first putting his feet straight out and propping himself up on his elbow, then sitting up, then lying back down again.

Vivian grew wary around him. His silences were intense and brooding, and she imagined him lurking around corners. Even in the afternoons when she was certain that he was gone, when she knew that he was sitting in a fishing boat or on a bar stool with his new friends, even then, she felt his nervous presence in the house, his raw incompleteness without Dot.

She couldn't stop thinking about the conversation they'd had about Sherman. Mr Stokes had practically confirmed that something had been going on between Sherman and Mrs Brodie, and Lonnie seemed to suspect his father of more than just clandestine meetings with Grandma Gardiner. During those two days at the house, when Lonnie had followed his father, perhaps he saw evidence of the relationship.

Vivian kept going back to something he said, something that had struck her quite differently at the time than when she thought of it later, remembering his tone: I didn't force my mom to stand up for herself. I stood by and let her fall. At the moments he spoke of Beverly and her self-deception, of her helplessness and the sense of hopelessness that left her weak and exposed, at those moments he sounded embittered, angry. His comments about Dot's past were similarly peculiar and disjointed. He expressed concern for her at the same time he seemed offended by her fragility.

And then Mrs Brodie came sniffing around the yard sale for Sherman's suit, and seemed so disappointed to hear that it had been sold. Vivian couldn't help but think that she wanted something of his as a memento.

They planned to go to the festival on Friday evening. There would be a live band, food from local restaurants, and fireworks after dark. The days were growing shorter; there was less time after dinner before the sun began its descent to orange behind the trees. Lonnie had been hesitant to go, but Nowell convinced him.

On Friday morning, Vivian was in the shower when Nowell called to her through the bathroom door. For some time, she'd been standing under the stream of water, letting its slippery tentacles slide down her body to the drain.

He opened the door and she felt a rush of cooler air. She had a phone call, he said. When he was working, he usually ignored the phone. She realized that Lonnie must have answered it and relayed the message to him. Whoever it was must have been waiting for several minutes already.

She wrapped a towel around her head and slid into her bathrobe. In the kitchen, the telephone receiver was perched on the counter. She picked it up. 'Hello?'

'Mrs Gardiner? Vivian?'

'Yes.'

'It's Kitty Brodie. Sorry to bother you. Your husband didn't wake you, did he?'

'Oh, no.' Water dripped from Vivian's temple onto her cheek. The telephone receiver stuck to her ear. She found a corner of the towel and dried her face.

'I have a favor to ask you,' Mrs Brodie said. 'I've been going through Chanelle's things. It's not a pleasant experience, as I'm sure you can imagine. I mean, after clearing out Betty's house.'

'If you need help…'

'No, no. That's not it at all.' She cleared her throat. 'I'm missing something of hers, something important. Chanelle's favorite necklace, gold with a little charm, a giraffe. She really loved it. She wore it all the time.' She paused. 'She collected giraffe things. She's got stuffed animals and books, and a little glass one with marbles for eyes.'

Vivian didn't know what to say.

'Giraffes got their long necks by reaching for leaves in the trees, did you know that? That's what Chanelle liked about them. She couldn't believe that something could change so much, just by trying.'

'So the necklace is missing?' she asked.

'I've looked everywhere. The police didn't find it. I've asked Sheriff Townsend to look again, but he says that they combed the area already. And he says you've been bothered enough.'

'Oh.'

'Maybe that's true, but I'd really like to look around one last time if you don't mind. I'm sure it has to be out there somewhere. I wanted to look for it the other day, but I was so out of sorts. I hoped that it would show up in her things. I've looked, but it's not here.'

'Mrs Brodie, that's fine. You can come over any time. It's no problem. In fact, I'll help you look, if you want.'

'What about today?'

Vivian glanced at the kitchen clock, at the lifted, curled claw of the rooster. 'Sure, whenever.'

'You've been so nice about all of this, really. I have an appointment, but I'd like to stop by about four-thirty.'

'Oh, we're going into town for the festival,' Vivian said. 'I think we're leaving around then. What about tomorrow? We should be here all day.'

'I was hoping to look today.' Mrs Brodie's voice faded.

Vivian pressed the receiver against her ear, listening to the silence. 'You can still come today,' she said after a moment. 'It's just that no one will be here. But if you want to come anyway, that's fine.'

'Are you sure? I'll only be a while. The sheriff showed me where they found her. I thought I'd just look around there.'

'No problem. Just park in the driveway behind our truck. We'll probably take the other car, the jeep, into town.'

'This is very nice of you, Vivian. You must think I'm a little strange.'

'No.' She shook her head at the incomprehensibility of Mrs Brodie's loss, which occurred to her again as a churning feeling of dropping, deep in her stomach. 'This necklace means a lot to you.'

'Yes, it really does.'

At the moment Vivian hung up the phone, Lonnie walked into the kitchen and Nowell pushed through the curtain. 'That was Mrs Brodie,' she said. 'She wants to stop by this afternoon while we're gone.'

Both stopped in their tracks. 'Why?' Lonnie asked.

'Her daughter had a necklace and she can't find it. She thinks it might be in the woods. I guess she wore it all the time.'

'Wouldn't the police have found it?' Nowell asked.

'I don't know. Probably. Maybe it'll make her feel better to look herself.'

Lonnie took the cup he was holding to the sink and turned the water on. It came out fast, splashing onto the counter. 'I don't know if that's a good idea,' he said.

'Why?'

'She's going to be poking around back there, when we're not here?' He dried his hands on the towel then tossed it carelessly toward the counter. It hit the edge and fell to the floor. 'Damn!' He seemed agitated.

285

'What time is she coming?' Nowell asked.

'Four-thirty,' she said. 'We're still leaving around four, right?'

'We could wait for her,' Lonnie said.

'Why?' she asked. 'It's not like she's going to rob us or something. She'll come out, look around for a while, then leave. What's with you, anyway?'

'Nothing.' Lonnie's voice was tense. 'She'll be on our property, that's all. What if something happens to her?'

'Like what?' Nowell took an apple from the bowl on the table.

'She could fall and break her leg,' Lonnie said.

'This is ridiculous,' Vivian said. 'I'm going to the festival at four o'clock. I feel sorry for her, but what can we do? I've been looking forward to tonight. It's probably the one and only event that will happen in this town for several years. The band is starting at five, and I want to be there. Now, is anybody going with me or do I have to go by myself?'

Nowell raised his eyebrows, looking first at Lonnie then back to Vivian.

'I never said I didn't want to go,' Lonnie said. 'Can't she come another day?'

'She wants to come today.'

'We'll just make sure we lock everything up,' Nowell said.

Lonnie seemed satisfied with this; he nodded his head and slowly walked back outside.

Vivian went back to the bathroom and stared at herself in the mirror. Her skin was smooth and unblemished and her eyebrows were perfectly symmetrical and full. Nice eyebrows. She turned her face from side to side, noticing the flat mole in the middle of her right cheek, the faint hair, like a small v in front of each ear. She had her father's eyes, brown and deep, and her mother's high forehead. She had been known for her attention to detail at her job at the water management agency. She showed up, she listened, she did her work on time. Extremely competent, her boss had written on her last performance review. There's potential, she thought. A chance. Something Chanelle Brodie would never get. She took a dry washcloth and in rapid movements, wiped the remaining steam from the corners of the mirror. Her arm clenched and unclenched as she scrubbed in a circular motion. Suddenly, she wanted to see everything.

30

Later that afternoon, Lonnie slowed the jeep when traffic grew thick on the main artery into town. Across from the recently assembled carnival area, a lot was partitioned into parking. The rest of the festival was five blocks away in the older, central part of town. Crowds circulated between the two locations and Nowell, Lonnie and Vivian fell quickly into the steady stream of people. Downtown, the streets were blocked off. In the plaza next to the statue of William Clement, a platform was raised and a band went through their warm-ups. A stocky man with a long, brown-gray ponytail thumped his fingers against a large microphone then pressed his mouth against it. 'Testing,' he said, 'testing.' Faces turned toward the stage in anticipation.

They walked down the main street. Near the plaza, food and beverage booths huddled together. Nowell suggested they walk to the end then come back and buy something for dinner. They saw booths with beaded jewelry, hand-woven baskets and preserves from a local orchard. An elderly couple operated an old-fashioned taffy-pulling machine; its silver limbs turned smoothly as the gooey pink candy stretched then fell between them. Local businesses had tables for distributing coupons and free samples and several people, mostly women, were roaming the street in nineteenth-century attire.

The band started their show with a slow-paced folk tune. Blankets and towels were spread around. People sat and reclined on them, some feasting from ice chests packed with food and cold drinks. Lonnie bought three large cups of beer. They didn't have anything to sit on, so Nowell found a spot of grass further back, across the street in front of the library. From there, they couldn't see much of the band through the crowd, but they could hear the music, which had picked up in tempo. The crowd merged and separated, veered and straightened before them.

Nearby, a group of teenagers sat in a circle. The two girls wore tight denim shorts and skimpy tank tops. Their abdomens were flat and hard; one had a silver hoop through a piercing in her belly button. With them were three boys, all with short, messy hair. Two wore oversized shorts and baggy T-shirts and the third was shirtless, reclining on the grass while the girl with the piercing held a cigarette to his mouth. Another boy leaned his white-blond head over and whispered something, and they all looked at someone in the crowd and laughed. Each had the glowing expectancy of youth, the chained energy of something about to happen. If Dot was right, inside each was the spark of some special talent. But as they sat on the grass, pushing and pawing each other not unlike a litter of kittens, they seemed to form a single, meaningful mass. Later, Vivian thought, they would drink too much and wander through the surrounding streets, which would be strangely lit and seem foreign for the night. She wondered if they were the same kids who cruised in their cars, the ones that Katherine said acted like they owned the place. Vivian remembered that feeling of control. These young people owned the approaching night and the invigorating feeling of being together, out on their own. She imagined Chanelle Brodie in their company.

From a vendor at the corner, Lonnie bought a pizza in a soggy box. The crowd grew larger as they ate. Vivian had two substantial pieces and finished her beer quickly. Lonnie went for refills and when he handed her the second, sloshing cup, which looked even bigger than the last, she silently admonished herself to drink more slowly.

Lonnie hadn't given himself the same warning. Within minutes, he was up again, asking if they wanted another. They both declined but Nowell was ready for a third when Lonnie went back for his fourth. When the band was on a break, Vivian headed to the bathrooms then came back.

The beer had relaxed Lonnie somewhat, loosened his tongue. He told Vivian he had beaten Nowell at darts the night before. Nowell ignored the bait; he stared at the crowd and picked at his food. And when Lonnie suggested they stand closer to the band, Vivian jumped up eagerly.

'Come on, Number One.' Lonnie extended his hand. 'The action's over there.'

Vivian's head swam as they maneuvered through the crowd. The second beer, which she had drunk slowly but nevertheless finished, had her head swimming. The band played an old favorite, a song about a woman leaving a man. Swaying to the music, Vivian and Lonnie sung the lyrics in wavering, unpolished voices. Colored streaks came out in the evening sky, like water that had soaked through paper. Nowell stood behind them, half-heartedly nodding his head to the rhythm and smiling unconvincingly whenever Vivian turned to check on him.

The band finished their show and announced the next band, which was slated to begin in half an hour.

'Want another beer?' Lonnie asked.

She nodded and Nowell waved him off. After he left, Nowell said, 'Somebody has to drive.'

'Would it kill you to have fun?'

'I am having fun.'

'Fooled me,' she said. 'But then, I probably don't remember what you look like, having fun.' She spotted Katherine and Max near a corn-on-the-cob booth. 'Look, there's Katherine.'

'Do you want to go talk to her?'

'Yeah, let's go.'

'I'll stay here and wait for Lonnie,' he said.

'All right.' She maneuvered her way through the crowd, and Max saw her first.

'Vivian, how are you?'

Katherine's chin was shiny with butter and in her fist she held a half-eaten corncob and a thick wad of napkins. She looked over Vivian's shoulder. 'Where's Nowell?'

'He's waiting for Lonnie to come back with beer.' She turned toward the beer stand and at the exact moment she picked Lonnie out of the crowd, she saw him fall backwards suddenly. He stumbled then lurched forward, gripping a red-faced man by the shirt. The crowd around them scattered like bugs as the men careened around in a tight hold.

Panicked, she tried to signal Nowell but couldn't find him in the broad canvas of indistinct faces. When she looked back, Lonnie was standing by himself, a trickle of blood running down his chin. A beige, wide-brimmed hat bobbed through the crowd toward the cleared area. It was Sheriff Townsend. On each side, people stepped back to let him through. Lonnie looked half-crazed, greedily scanning the crowd. Vivian had an urge to jump behind Max and hide.

Suddenly, Nowell emerged into the cleared circle like an actor beginning his scene. He put his hand on Lonnie's chest. Lonnie shrugged him off and walked rapidly in the opposite direction, and Nowell immediately followed. The whole episode lasted only moments.

Katherine saw the distressed look on Vivian's face. 'What's wrong?'

'I have to go.'

Before either of them had a chance to respond, Vivian pushed through the crowd in the direction the men had gone.

The sun was a mere amber sliver over the rooftops; a cool breeze swept down the streets. Vivian walked as quickly as she could

291

through the crowd, which seemed to get larger and denser as it slowly became night. They're coming for the fireworks, she thought. In a few minutes, she reached the Ferris wheel. She watched the tanned legs dangling from the top-most cars and the grinning faces as they swung around the bottom.

It occurred to her that Lonnie had probably gone to the jeep. Vivian hurried across the street to the parking area and quickly found the spot where they had parked. The jeep was gone. As she stared, counting again the rows from the street to make sure it was the right one, a gray minivan pulled into the space. Slowly, she walked back to the street. There was no sign of them. Nowell wouldn't leave without her, so Lonnie must have beaten him to the jeep and left. Nowell probably returned to the festival to look for her.

As she weaved through the cars, the twilight sun cast long, weird shadows. All at once, she knew where Lonnie was. He went to the house, she thought, after drinking too much and picking a fight with a stranger. He made such a fuss about Mrs Brodie coming over. All this time, she'd been suspicious of Mr Stokes, but he was trying to tell her something, something about Lonnie. More than once, Mr Stokes found Lonnie in the woods, and he warned her about his temper. Lonnie left the same day she arrived, the day they found Chanelle Brodie. She shook her head. She had known Lonnie for years; he was bearish at times but harmless. Wasn't he?

The sun at the horizon line was liquid orange like lava. In the parking area, the cars smelled of burning oil and dust. Vivian knew that Katherine and Max were waiting at the festival, concerned about the way she ran off. She stood at the edge of the road, her mind racing as the lights of the temporary amusement park glared down. A group of people walked toward her, laughing and talking. She recognized the teenagers who had sat next to them on the grass. It's action that matters, her mother had said. Vivian wondered what Pheola H. Roundtree would do, Pheola with the strength of a mountain range.

The bare-chested boy led the pack, swaggering and talking loudly. Vivian asked him where they were going, and he started to smirk until he registered the troubled look on her face. He named a bordering town. As she fumbled with her purse, Vivian explained where she needed to go and offered them money to take her.

The boy held out his hand, shaking his head. 'We don't need your money, lady. We'll take you.'

Over the vast fields and empty roads, and the areas that had been cleared for parking and amusement, the buzzing of night bugs blended in harmony with the telephone wires overhead. The two young girls exchanged amused looks.

'Thank you,' Vivian managed.

Their car was crowded with six and they drove mostly in silence. Vivian's mind raced and she felt queasy from the pizza and beer. She wondered if she should have found Nowell first. Rushing to the house suddenly seemed like a very foolish thing to do.

They dropped her off at the mouth of the driveway. Perched on its white wooden stake, the metal mailbox gleamed in the moonlight. The door was slightly open; white paper peeked through the slit. She had forgotten to retrieve the mail that day.

Behind the house, the moon was drawn on the navy canvas of the sky, a circle of chalk on a blackboard; it had gotten very dark since she left the festival. On the throne of the shallow incline, the house glowed from inside: yellow light seeped through its windows like a jack o' lantern.

Vivian walked past the jeep, which was parked halfway up the driveway. Underneath the hood, something whirred softly although the engine had stopped. In front of the jeep was Mrs Brodie's red hatchback.

31

Yellow light blared from the kitchen and the two windows in front twinkled like eyes over the big, gaping mouth of the porch. The door was open. As she got closer, Vivian saw that the whole house was ablaze with light; every window glowed except for the triangular panes at the peak.

Carefully, she pushed open the screen door, noticing where it had been bent at the edge, almost ripped off the hinges. The kitchen was loud with light and spent activity. Several drawers and cupboards were open, some of the contents spilled onto the floor.

Vivian walked toward Nowell's study, still dark, and her hand went to her mouth when she saw the scattering of paper and books. Through a crack in the curtain, a sliver of moonlight fell on the computer and over the center of the keyboard.

In the living room, the pillows they had left in the middle of the floor had been kicked against a wall and the light was left on. In the bedrooms, it was the same: drawers opened, closets explored. In the spare room, the newspaper she had arranged for painting had been trampled and torn, the bag of supplies emptied onto the floor. Their bedroom was dimmer than some of the other rooms. The light bulb in the overhead lamp had a low wattage

294

and they had sold the lighthouse lamps to Mr Stokes along with the dresser. He said they reminded him of a picture he saw on a greeting card once, a painting of a white-sailed boat perched on the back of a rolling, angry wave. He had kept the card tacked to one of his walls for years, he said.

Vivian became aware of a dull pain in her elbow, the familiar warning of impending bad weather. The curtain was open; normally, she closed it in the afternoon to keep out the heat from the setting sun. She had forgotten most of her regular routine that day. The mail, the curtains. Walking to the window, she stumbled over her jewelry box, a pale, velvet-lined one that played a lilting song. A present from her parents, her father really, on her thirteenth birthday. She picked it up and turned it over. The slight tear in the blue velvet lining was now a long slash and all of her jewelry was gone, except for a silver hoop earring that had gotten stuck on the frayed edge of the fabric. Suddenly, she noticed the shiny fragments, not gone but sprayed over the bed like mercury rain-drops. There was one of her dangling heart earrings, and here was the star bracelet from Dot.

Leaning her forehead against the cool window, she looked outside. A sharp mildew odor reminded her of the well outside, its brick lips open to the dark sky, and of the nights when her mother brought ice wrapped in a soft towel for her elbow, the times they sat in the quiet living room, listening to the thunder.

A glimmer appeared in the trees. Vivian's quick breaths clouded the glass. The light flickered, peeking out amidst the dense trunks, jumping haphazardly through the foliage. In a moment, it was gone.

She found the spare flashlight in the drawer of her nightstand. The bulb stayed lit for only a few seconds before it faded. She tossed it onto the bed and rushed down the hallway. In the kitchen, she wasn't surprised to find the other flashlight missing from the drawer near the pantry. Didn't they have another one somewhere else? She couldn't think straight. She called Lonnie's name. There was no answer, only the rooster clock ticking loudly in synchrony with the blood pulsing at her temples.

She picked up the telephone and listened to the dial tone. Sheriff Townsend was at the festival; he had seen Lonnie fighting. But this was Lonnie, big and childish but harmless, wasn't he? She hung up the receiver. Lonnie threw some sort of fit and went outside to cool off. He'd been spending lots of time in the woods. Maybe it soothed him. She just needed to find him. She would clean up the house, clean up Lonnie, before Sheriff Townsend came.

Vivian climbed the staircase so quickly she almost hit her head on the trap door. Throwing it back forcefully, she peered inside. The attic was dark but she could make out the silhouette of the purplish bureau, the several boxes along one side.

But Lonnie's had so much to drink, she thought, and he didn't want Mrs Brodie nosing around. He's so unpredictable. Maybe I don't know him, not really. And all this time, I've been thinking…

She flew down the stairs, ran outside and around the side of the house. The night air was falling in shelves of temperature. Now and then she hit a warm pocket as she leaped through the high grass. Her feet made quick cuts through the blades. She didn't know what was going on, but she sensed with every pore that it wasn't good.

Her eyes became accustomed to the moonlight. The woods were a very different place without the flashlight to guide her steps. She stumbled frequently, tripping over branches and stubbing her toes on small, jutting rocks. The way to Mr Stokes's house had become familiar to her in the confused, uncertain way that a recurring dream is familiar. The moon was a paper lantern peeking in and out of the tree limbs; its glow was muted and grayish.

The stories she had heard came alive as she ran through the woods: tales of love and loss, loneliness and death. The woods were the hiding place for Ronella and her lover and the secret route for Sherman to Kitty Brodie. They held the untimely graves of two people: Russell Gardiner and Chanelle Brodie. So many people had been influenced by this small piece of land, this chunk of wild kept safe from the asphalt road now winding its way into town. Betty Gardiner wouldn't abandon it, even when she was elderly and alone, Sherman returned to it again and again in his middle age, and Lonnie hesitated to leave now. Abe Stokes had spent a lifetime here, she thought. Even Nowell went into the woods, away from his veritable hermitage, his wife. Vivian was drawn as well.

The trees rushed by, formless and aloof, like they did the summer she separated from her father. That afternoon, she stayed calm for a long time, moving between the thick trunks, jumping over soft, leafy spots and pushing off stumps and fallen branches. She would stay calm now. Soon, the trees drew back and Mr Stokes's house appeared. Vivian felt a sense of relief and trusted it. Her suspicions about Mr Stokes were ungrounded. His house seemed warm and welcoming. Dark brown with darker trim, accented with reddish brick – the white marbling within just perceptible in the dark night – Mr Stokes's house pulsed, a dim light from what she knew to be the living room, its heartbeat.

Vivian passed the two stunted tree trunks in his work area, and the neatly trimmed bushes with their red blooms. The flowers had dulled and wilted; they hadn't survived the heat wave. She neared the house. The curtains were drawn over the dining room's wide window.

There's something about the woods, Mrs Gardiner, haven't you felt it?

The trees were still full and green but their leaves were dry, starting to fall. Vivian didn't know much about nature, only the little that she'd read and the things she'd been told by her father and later, Mr Stokes. Somewhere, there were animals already preparing for winter, but some plants hadn't yet flowered, late bloomers.

When she knocked on the door, the sound reverberated. She waited a moment and knocked again. Feet padded along the creaky old floors. Stepping back, she waited for the doorknob to turn, which it did, slowly, before it receded into the house.

A woman leaned into the opening, her long, black hair pulled over her shoulder like a shawl. She watched Vivian expectantly.

Vivian looked around the front of the house, as though maybe she'd come to the wrong place.

'Are you looking for Abe?'

'Y-yes,' she stammered. 'I'm looking for Mr Stokes.'

The woman's eyes narrowed, not unkindly, and Vivian inhaled sharply. 'You're Miss Burnside?' she asked.

She turned toward the interior of the house, as if she would call Mr Stokes, then turned back. 'Do I know you?'

'I bought a book from you last week, and took one of your brochures.'

She nodded. 'I remember now. Should I wake him?'

'No,' Vivian said. 'I'm his neighbor, that's all.' She motioned vaguely with her hand toward the white house.

'Is something wrong?' Miss Burnside glanced at her wrist watch.

'What? No. We've had a disturbance, but it's not his, he doesn't need to…' She thought about the two abandoned cars in the driveway, the disturbed state of the old, white house. I've had too much beer, she told herself. Maybe Mrs Brodie's car wouldn't start back up and she walked home. Lonnie threw his fit and ran off, like he always does.

'What kind of disturbance?' Miss Burnside gathered her night-gown around her neck and leaned slightly outside.

Vivian started to back away. He's got his own life, she told herself. It's not what you thought. This is our problem, our family. 'It's nothing, everything's fine.'

She looked over Vivian's shoulder and closed the door the slightest amount. 'I'll be sure to tell him you stopped by.'

Vivian began to cross the clearing, feeling foolish and strangely, hurt.

'Excuse me,' Miss Burnside called. The door was opened wide

again, and the light from the hallway passed through her sheer nightgown, tracing the outline of her long legs. 'What was your name, so I can tell Abe?'

'Vivian,' she said. 'Mrs Gardiner.'

In the doorway, someone came up behind her. Vivian instinctively stepped backwards. Miss Burnside turned toward the other person and their faces almost touched as they spoke. Mr Stokes, she thought. Suddenly, his dark form had eclipsed the white gown and he was out on the lawn. He wasn't what Vivian had thought he was, not at all. She imagined that he was lonely, suffering. She thought: his lopsided grin and the way he kept showing up to flirt with her. She didn't want his help anymore. Nobody was who she thought they were. She was blanketed amidst the tree trunks, camouflaged in darkness. She was sure he couldn't see her anymore. Picking up her pace, she plunged into the woods, determined to put an end to things.

32

The trees seemed taller now, the sky a dark, uncaring abyss. Vivian heard the crackling of leaves and twigs, and dirt crunching like asphalt under a roller. Branches reached out to scratch her arms and tiny rocks infiltrated her shoes, digging into the soft soles of her feet. She looked back once in the direction of Mr Stokes's house and saw only blackness. Kicking through small bushes and stumbling over dips and short rises, she moved faster. It was Lonnie, she thought. His temper. When he left town after helping Nowell, the same day they found Chanelle, it looked suspicious, so he came back. He's afraid. What's he doing out here tonight?

A branch snapped somewhere behind her, and she hurried to distance herself. What if Lonnie hears me and thinks I'm Mrs Brodie?

She ran as she had on the afternoon she hid from her father. That day, she was calm at first, plunging into the trees, an excited giggle stifled in her throat. When her father turned away for a moment to spread the blanket for their picnic, she slipped away noiselessly. Pressing her body against the cold bark of trees, she wrapped her arms around the wide trunks, letting herself blend in. At first he called out in the same calm tone he always used, but his voice gradually became louder, more frantic. She found more trees to hide behind, further away from him, deeper into the woods and just when she thought she'd had enough of the game, her body did something she hadn't expected. She ran.

'Vivie, Vivie.' Her father's voice echoed through the woods.

Fearless, she ran until fast breaths puffed from her chest. She was testing him. From her mother she had learned how to treat him, and more than anything else, even though she was only nine years old, Vivian wanted to respect him. She wanted him to come after her, to bring her back.

The minute something happens, that moment is lost forever.

'Vivie!'

She heard her father's voice again as she raced through these woods, nearly twenty years later and hundreds of miles from that first forest. He must have been frantic, she thought. How could I have done that?

Reaching a small clearing, Vivian scraped her shoulder on the rough bark of a tree. As she looked up from the scratch mark, a tall figure appeared in front of her. A large hand extended from the waist and closed around something shiny. She turned around and began to run back in the direction of Mr Stokes's house. The leaves were slippery underfoot, and her blood throbbed painfully in her ears. A low voice said: 'Wait.' Her left foot collided with a hard object. She tripped and was catapulted through the air for a dizzying, protracted moment before she crashed into a large, flat rock. Her wrists bent back from the force of the fall, her arms crumbling against her chest. Sharp pain shot up her arm to the elbow. Once she was stable, she rested her face against the back of her hand.

'Vivian,' someone said in the darkness. 'Viv.'

Gingerly, she pushed herself up. Her body was heavy. She turned as someone touched her arm and began to pull. A frightened cry escaped from her throat.

'Viv,' the voice said again.

She raised her head to its familiarity. Nowell. His eyes were wild and his features looked strange, unfamiliar as they had the

301

day he picked her up at the airport. She didn't remember the small dent in the soft tissue under his eyebrow, or the way his nose flared out at the sides. She had thought that his hair was lighter.

'Oh, God, Viv.' He kneeled on the dirt, laying his large head against her hip. 'Are you all right?'

She slid down the large boulder and he buried his face in her abdomen. Above her head, the turgid blackness pressed through the leaves, like the dark menacing cloud on the cover of his book. 'Nowell,' she said. 'What are you doing out here?' She awkwardly pulled herself to a sitting position.

Dirt fell from his knees as he stood up. 'Let's go back to the house,' he said.

'What are you doing?' she repeated. She saw the shiny object still gripped in his hand. Had he found the gun from the attic? Had he taken it out of the box? Was it loaded? She backed away from him on the rock. 'Is that a gun?' she asked.

'What?' He looked down. 'For chrissake, Viv. A gun?' He offered the item on his upturned palm. A flashlight. 'It burned out on me as soon as I hit the woods. Come on, let's go.'

'Nowell. What's going on?'

He turned his back to her. In the moonlight she could see the boomerang-shaped scar behind his left knee, where a nail in the bleachers at his high school had caught on his leg. It was delicate and luminous against the rest of his skin.

He walked back to the large rock and sat down. His body slumped next to her. 'Somebody broke into the house.'

'It was Lonnie,' she said.

Nowell shook his head. 'No. Mrs Brodie was looking for that necklace.' The dead look in his eyes scared her, and his lips were deep red as though he had bitten them.

'Why would she look in the house?'

'Because that's where it is.'

'What?'

'The necklace.'

Confused, she touched his arm. 'Why is the necklace at the house?'

'I put it there.'

'Nowell, please. What are you talking about?'

He looked at her then stared at some point on the horizon, past the trees. The clearing seemed smaller now, cramped. On each side, long, drooping branches leaned over, as though the trees were listening. 'I took the necklace. I found it out here and I hid it in a secret compartment in the antique secretary. It's been there ever since.'

'You found it?'

'Yes.'

Vivian propped her aching wrist with her other hand. She could barely feel the pain in her elbow over the throb of the injury. But it was there, muted. 'I don't understand,' she said. 'Did you know it was Chanelle Brodie's?'

Nowell shifted the flashlight from one hand to the other. 'She was hanging around the house. I saw her several times in the woods. The window at my desk looks right out at the trees.'

Vivian couldn't process what he was saying. 'Chanelle Brodie?' she asked. 'You saw her?'

Nowell took a deep breath. 'Well I didn't know who she was yet, but yes. At the time, I just knew someone was out there and nobody should have been. I went after her once. I didn't find her, but I found the necklace. I walked around for a while,' he continued. 'I went all the way to Mr Stokes's house. I didn't know him yet either, but I thought I saw him looking through the window with binoculars, which freaked me out.'

Vivian said, 'Why didn't you ask around, find out who she was and return the necklace?'

He shrugged. 'Shortly after that, she came to the house.' He looked askance at her. 'We talked a few times.'

Vivian stood up. 'You talked?'

'She was having trouble at school, she said. Her mother was

mean and wouldn't let her take a trip with her friends.' His nostrils flared. 'Kids at school said awful things to her, called her names.'

Vivian involuntarily chortled. 'Why didn't you tell me about this?' She couldn't believe what he was saying. What exactly was he saying?

Nowell scratched his temple with the end of the flashlight. 'Vivian, I had feelings—'

Nearby trees rustled and they both jumped. A large figure pushed through the branches.

'Who's there?' she asked loudly.

'Lonnie,' Nowell said.

'What the hell is going on?' Lonnie stepped toward them. 'How could you leave me there, Nowell? If I knew you were going to pull something like this, I wouldn't have given you Dot's keys. Why did you take the jeep?'

'Sorry,' Nowell said. 'I was worried about Vivian.' He turned to her. 'I saw you leave with those kids.'

Vivian realized she must have looked in the wrong spot for the jeep.

Someone stepped out from behind Nowell.

'Mrs Brodie?' Vivian asked.

There were no traces of her usual heavy makeup. Pale, small eyes flashed in the moonlight and her skin was ashen. She looked up when Vivian spoke to her, then looked at the ground, her blond hair falling in messy clumps, shielding her face.

Nowell stood up and Vivian stepped over to make room for Lonnie in the clearing.

Lonnie glanced at Mrs Brodie. 'We ran into each other,' he explained, his voice sharp.

'How did you get home?' Nowell asked Lonnie.

'Katherine and Max gave me a ride. They're up at the house.'

'I'm sorry,' Mrs Brodie said suddenly, putting her hands to her cheeks. 'About your house.'

'You did that?' Vivian asked.

She looked away, biting her lip.

'I found her sitting on a log,' Lonnie said. 'Then we heard your voices.' His voice rose. 'What the hell is going on?'

'I thought you all knew something,' Mrs Brodie said. 'You move into Betty Gardiner's house and the next thing I know, my daughter is found...' Her voice faltered.

Nowell shifted on his feet.

She went on in a musing tone, as though talking to herself. 'I've never trusted young men, not since I was young like Chanelle. They'll rip your heart out every time. They start telling you how to act, what you should look like, what to wear. Especially when they look like you.' She pointed her pale finger first at Nowell, then Lonnie. 'Dangerous. You've got that look about you, just like Chanelle's father.'

Lonnie was watching Mrs Brodie intently. His arms hung at his sides; he clenched and unclenched his fists. Vivian saw the knuckles pop up then recede, his fingers turning white then red at the tips. 'Who was her father?' he asked, his voice booming into the night.

The question startled everyone. It had never occurred to Vivian that Sherman might have been seeing Mrs Brodie for that long. But why not? Sherman had been dead for five years; Chanelle would have been about twelve at the time. Lonnie said that his father had made trips to the country for years.

Nowell's voice was faint. 'Dad was her father,' he said. 'She was our sister.'

'Seventeen years?' Lonnie said, shaking his head. 'It was going on that long?'

Nowell looked at his brother. 'You knew?'

Lonnie's eyes blazed. 'Yeah, I knew. Dad came out here all the time. What's really strange, Nowell, is that you didn't know. I knew something was going on, and it didn't take much detective work when I got here to find out who he was seeing.'

Mrs Brodie looked back and forth between them, her eyes squinted as though she could barely see through the darkness.

305

Nowell covered his eyes, squeezed the bridge of his nose, then looked at Lonnie. 'We had a sister, and you didn't tell me?'

'I knew about the relationship,' Lonnie said, 'not the kid.'

A bouncing light cast a beam into the clearing. Wordlessly, they waited.

Suddenly, Mrs Brodie stepped forward. 'Your father was a good man! I won't have any of you saying he wasn't.' Her bottom lip quivered.

A floating whiteness became the sheer nightgown of Delta Clement Burnside, scalloped by a dark blanket she had thrown over her shoulders. Next to her was Mr Stokes, one hand on her elbow and the other holding another flashlight.

'Evening, Gardiners,' Mr Stokes said. His presence was like a lightning rod. Everyone seemed to take a collective breath. 'What's going on?' He noticed Mrs Brodie. 'Well, the whole neighborhood's here.'

Mrs Brodie stepped into the pool of light. 'You've never liked me, Abe,' she said. 'I know that, heck, everyone knows that. You hold yourself to a higher standard, don't ya? You're just like anyone else, you know that?' She leaned towards him, her eyes gleaming. 'Surely you know that now?'

Delta Clement Burnside's eyes darted to Mr Stokes then back to Mrs Brodie.

'It's never been a matter of liking,' Mr Stokes said. 'I object to families being busted up and you're right, in that way, I'm mostly like everybody else.'

Mrs Brodie's pointed her finger at them. 'I won't have any of you talking bad about him! He doesn't deserve it.' She looked down at her crumpled and dirty shirt. 'I don't know what anybody deserves. Did I deserve this, did I? First that worthless man who left me, then losing Sherman, and my Chanelle?'

'Lonnie?' A voice traveled through the woods. 'Vivian?'

'It's Katherine,' Vivian said. She reached over and took the flashlight from Lonnie. She waved the light through the tree trunks. 'Over here!' she called.

Wide-eyed, Katherine and Max emerged from the woods. For once, Katherine was speechless. She clung to Max's arm and looked around at the circle of faces.

'I need to sit down,' Mrs Brodie said, and they all watched as she perched on the edge of the rock where her daughter had died. She didn't seem to remember the place. There was something unsteady about her, almost other-worldly. 'That's better,' she said. 'I'm so tired. Haven't been myself these days. I couldn't stop thinking about the necklace, that little giraffe.' She smiled. 'Chanelle wore it all the time.'

Katherine came to herself. 'Kitty, I think we should go back up to the house.'

Lonnie looked over. 'You're right. We should head back.'

'Wait,' Nowell said. They all watched as Mr Stokes took a step toward him. Vivian realized that Nowell was holding the flashlight like a weapon, gripped in his fist and raised up by his shoulder.

'Nowell!' Vivian said. 'Put that down.'

'What?' He saw what he was doing. 'Viv, it's a flashlight.'

And like the first day she met Mr Stokes, she felt like the men were exchanging glances about her foolishness.

Nowell turned toward Mrs Brodie. 'I have something to tell you.' He scanned the group of faces. 'Something to tell you all. I met Chanelle before she died.'

Mrs Brodie looked up at him; her shoulders slumped.

'She came to the house and we talked, that's all. Talked about school and the town. Talked about nothing.' Nowell cleared his throat. 'She was a nice girl, I want you to know.'

'I know that!' Mrs Brodie snapped.

'I've seen her in the woods too,' Mr Stokes said, then appeared ruffled by his admission. 'She must have enjoyed it, I guess, the trees, the fresh air.' He turned away.

Nowell stared at Mrs Brodie. 'The last time I saw her, she told me about you and my father. She told me she was my sister. Obviously, I was shocked and to be honest, I didn't believe her. I said some things—' He looked down. 'She ran off.'

Vivian's voice trembled. 'Did you follow her?'

Crickets echoed over the land, vast and endless now, not the small parcel they knew but a chasm of indiscretions and regrets. A stealthy wind gathered.

'Yes,' Nowell said. 'I followed her into the woods.'

Katherine stepped toward Mrs Brodie. 'But Kitty, Sherman Gardiner wasn't Chanelle's father, was he?'

Mrs Brodie sighed. 'I wish he'd been. Oh, you don't know how many times I wished that.' She looked at Nowell. 'Your father was a good man. He wouldn't have left me high and dry like her father did.' Suddenly, she smiled. 'He was a louse, Chanelle's father, but he was good-looking. Thick, black hair like a raven, tall and built solid. Like you boys. I didn't think I'd ever get over him, but I did. We have to keep living, right?' She gave a brief, dry laugh. 'We're all in this together.'

Mr Stokes stepped toward Nowell, his shoulders thrust back. One arm stayed back, motioning to Miss Burnside to stay put. 'What happened in the woods, Mr Gardiner?'

Nowell looked up, realizing he meant him. He looked instead at Mrs Brodie. 'Why would she say she was our sister if she wasn't?'

'Because I let her think it,' Mrs Brodie barked, saliva spraying from her mouth. 'You understand? It made her happy to believe it. Your father was good to her, always brought her a gift and took the time to talk with her. They had a trust between them.' She crossed her arms. 'I won't be ashamed of what I did. It was a gift I gave her, something better than history.'

'I guess that's why she started hanging around once the Gardiners came,' Mr Stokes said.

They all looked at him.

His eyes flashed. 'I already said I saw her out there sometimes.' In her long, white nightgown, Delta Clement Burnside stepped forward and stood next to him.

Vivian thought about the night she invaded his home, the illusions she'd had about him.

In the distance, a car engine whined and sputtered. All at once, the air smelled like rain.

Vivian turned toward Nowell. 'What happened in the woods?' she asked.

He took a deep breath. 'She ran and I followed her. I still didn't believe her but I shouldn't have yelled like that, shouldn't have lost my temper. I'd only been here for a short time. I didn't know my way around. I tripped a few times and I could barely see through the trees.'

'Did you see her fall?' Lonnie asked.

'Yes, no.' Nowell's hands went into his hair. 'I mean, I saw her drop out of sight, but I was still so far back. I thought I saw her after that. Her hair, through the trees. I thought she had gotten up. And some part of me realized if I kept chasing her, she might get hurt. I knew she lived back here. She was just headed home, I thought.'

'You should have made sure she got there safely,' Mrs Brodie said, her voice wavering.

Nowell's eyes widened. 'I didn't even know her!' He looked down. 'Sorry. Yes, I should have followed. But I thought I saw her again, after the fall. I could've sworn I saw her get up.'

'But what if she was alive,' Mrs Brodie cried. 'What if she suffered...'

'Mrs Brodie.' Mr Stokes's voice was steady. 'Sheriff Townsend said it was too fast, too much trauma. She didn't suffer, I'm sure of that.'

Katherine stepped forward, pulling Max with her. 'Let's go back to the house,' she said. 'We should call someone for Kitty.'

Lonnie walked past, smelling of sweat and liquor, and extended his large, rough hand to Mrs Brodie. She took it and stood up from the rock.

He led them out of the woods. Watching his broad shoulders

as he pushed through the trees, Vivian realized that all along, he must have known something about what happened with Nowell and Chanelle Brodie. Dot was wrong about Lonnie, she thought. He keeps things inside, just like everyone else.

Nowell brought up the rear of their somber line. Vivian lingered back. He caught up and supported her as they negotiated the uneven terrain. The pain in her elbow and wrist had dulled, leaving only a soft ache that stretched the length of her arm.

'You should have told me,' she whispered.

'I know,' he said.

'Why would you hide this? You didn't do anything wrong. Right?' She searched his face.

'Of course not,' he said, putting his arm around her shoulders. 'I just felt guilty, the way I had yelled at her, and when I found out what happened…' He paused. 'I didn't want to risk anything.'

She came out from under his arm and steadied herself. 'You've been so distant.'

'I'm sorry,' he said.

She thought about Nowell and Chanelle, sitting on the porch at the house, while she was working in the city. She pulled on his shirt to slow him down. 'There was something you said, something about your feelings.'

'Viv…'

'What feelings? You felt sorry for her?'

'She's a kid. I mean, she was a kid.' As they walked, the inconstant moonlight was filtered through the branches and segmented his face into shadows. His high cheekbones were highlighted in the silver glow; above them, his eyes gleamed. 'She had problems,' he added.

'Katherine said she was beautiful,' Vivian said, hating at once the pleading tone in her voice.

Nowell stopped walking, turned her body toward him. 'I think it's natural. I mean, we were apart for so long. It doesn't mean anything. I didn't *do* anything.'

She jerked her shoulders out of his grasp. 'What exactly are you saying?'

'I was attracted to her, I guess.'

'You guess?'

'No, I was.' He glanced ahead; the rest of their group had vanished into the dark, engulfed by the trees. 'I was all alone here.'

Her throat made an ugly, choking sound. 'So was I.'

'This is getting out of control,' he said. 'It was nothing. I don't even know why I mentioned it. Only, it was bothering me, because I thought she was my sister. And I wondered, why didn't I sense that?'

'It didn't bother you that you're married?'

His face darkened. 'Grow up, Viv. People have attractions.'

'And she wasn't your sister.'

'I know that now.'

She crossed her arms over her chest. 'What a relief that must be.'

Nowell placed his hands on her shoulders again and she felt the weight of them, the warmth. The burden and the comfort. Stubbornly, she turned her head away.

'Viv,' he said. 'The biggest relief I've ever felt was when you got up from that rock and I saw you were okay.'

She looked up: the soft flesh of his neck, the dark hair, smooth and cool to the touch, the crescent-shaped mark under his eyebrow. Nowell.

'I'm sorry,' he said again.

Vivian was still stunned by his revelation but already, the sting was fading. He wasn't the person she had thought, nobody really was. But he would never hurt anyone on purpose. She was sure of that.

'It's you and me,' he said. 'You know that.'

Reaching with her sore arm, she wrapped herself around his waist. His arms came down, enveloping her like a blanket.

'Are we okay?' he asked. His breath was warm on the crown of her head.

'I don't know,' she said. 'I really don't know.' She leaned back to see his face. 'It might take time.'

He nodded, pulling her close again.

Suddenly, it seemed that a page was turned, an intersection crossed. Her mind turned to the future. She needed to take more interest in his work, in him, and she needed to find work of her own. She remembered the pottery class she'd take with Katherine, the sketchbook her mother had sent, the worth she had felt from a day of honest work. Maybe she'd find another part of herself after all. Chanelle Brodie wouldn't get another chance.

'Number One!' Lonnie's voice broke through the quiet.

Nowell reached out and she took his hand. They continued on until they reached the others and silently, they proceeded as a group. As they broke through the trees, the path lightened; the glowing orb of the moon had cleared the woods as well. Shining brightly at a great height, it cast glimmers onto the tall blades of grass, which bent and crackled softly under their feet. After two weeks of stifling heat, the breeze was cool. Above their heads, swollen storm clouds assembled, a solemn tribunal.

Battered survivors, they made their way out of the woods. Brief connections, Vivian thought: greed, fear, happiness. Even if other systems of living exist, somewhere in the vast unknown, this, now, is our reality.

We're in this together.

Nowell stood in the tall, swaying grass. 'I need to mow the lawn,' he said.

Vivian remembered the first time she saw him in Geology class, the way he looked at her. Near his temples, the tips of his hair curled like a moist paintbrush, and he had the same dark eyes, deep as the well beside the house. She squeezed his hand and pressed her feet, one after the other, against the spinning earth. On the summit, Russell Gardiner's structure endured, a lighthouse on a sea of green, the brightness spilling from within making the unfamiliar familiar, and beckoning them home.

Thanking

I would like to express my sincere gratitude to:

The authonomy community, who offered encouragement, friendship and invaluable feedback.

Early editors and readers, especially Genevieve, for advice on the opening sections, and my local trio, Patty, Maria and Jenni, for not holding back.

My family, who tolerates my habits and loves me nonetheless.

Above all, Scott Pack and Rachel Faulkner at HarperCollins, for their support and expert guidance.

ABOUT THE AUTHOR

Mary Vensel White was born in Los Angeles and raised in Lancaster, California. She graduated from the University of Denver and lived for five years in Chicago, where she completed an MA in English at DePaul University. Her short fiction has appeared in *The Wisconsin Review* and *Foothills Literary Journal*. *The Qualities of Wood* is her first novel.

Vensel White currently lives in southern California with her husband and four children. She is working on another novel set in the Midwest, a place that flourishes in her imagination despite her sunny surroundings, and a collection of inter-related short stories.

ABOUT AUTHONOMY

Authonomy is an online community of authors, readers and publishers, conceived and developed by editors at HarperCollins. It was launched to provide unpublished authors with a platform to showcase their work. Authonomy is also dedicated to seeking out and publishing the very best new writing talent. To find other exciting new books or to join our brilliant community, visit www.authonomy.com